The Return

Laurie Stevens

Published by Laurie Stevens, 2024.

This is a work of fiction. Similarities to real people, places, or events are entirely coincidental.

THE RETURN

ISBN: 978-0997006841

Library of Congress Control Number: 2024900265

Acknowledgements

Many thanks to the following people who helped make this book possible: Jody Hepps, authors K.S. Miranda, Connie DiMarco, and Kim Fay, cover designer Scott Templeton (Skuterdigital.com), Jonathan, Isabelle, and Alanna for your amazing support, and most of all, Steven. I'm so grateful to all of you.

The heavy tread of the Neanderthal crushes the twigs on the ground, making cracking noises like the sound of breaking bones. The spear he holds has a stone tip, poised and ready to strike.

Hiding behind the trunk of a pine, I shiver, not from cold but from fear. The sharp point is meant for me.

The Neanderthal passes close, close enough that, if I dare to look, I'll see the beads of sweat on his barrel chest and smell the sour stink from under his arms.

Not far off, she hides behind a bush. If the Neanderthal finds her first, he'll take her with force. Blood boils in my veins at the thought, but my mind can't go there. I have to calm down. If I can get quiet, I'll connect to her with my heart and tell her to stay put.

My eyes run over my scarred hands. Once they were smooth. Now, tiny white ropes, memories of drudgery, mark my skin. My hands have plenty of scars but no weapon.

Miraculously, the stout footsteps of my would-be murderer fade away.

I keep still. Listening. Waiting. Cupping my hands around my mouth, I make a birdcall, "Woo-Woot. Woo-Woot."

I pause, holding tightly to a tendril of hope.

"Woo-Hee," comes her faint reply. "Woo-Hee."

Relief floods me like water, and I step out from behind the tree. Suddenly, her scream rattles the forest, and I freeze, look ahead, and see the spear hurtling through the air toward my chest.

CHAPTER 1

A demanding screech pierced Aiden's ears. He opened his eyes to see a Steller's jay standing before him like a king with a robe of blue feathers and a charcoal crest for a crown. *How insolent* the creature's stiff posture implied. *How dare you ignore me?*

Aiden's heart pounded, and his mouth felt cottony. He usually played the hero in his mind-drifts, not some whimpering side of beef waiting to be skewered by a spear. He took a deep inhale of the mix of scents stirred by the approach of summer: vanilla from the Jeffrey pines, sweet citrus from the fir trees, and the sharp tang of conifer sap.

Thankfully, Aiden still sat on the ground, back against a tree trunk, facing the lake, which threw serene sparkles up to the afternoon sun. The guitar lay across his lap like it did before his mind crept out from under him. The bag of peanuts, his backpack, a pair of scuffed-up sneakers, and a guitar case with "AIDEN BAYLOR" stenciled on one side lay sprawled around him.

Aiden angled his face upward to let the filtered sunlight caress his skin. Today, the sky was a light blue canvas smudged with white paint upon which a red-tailed hawk, his favorite bird, drew a perfect circle.

The bluejay screeched again. Aiden reached for the bag and pulled out a peanut. "Okay, King Jay." Stretching out on his belly, he held out the treat.

The jay hopped forward and plucked the peanut from his fingers. Fixing a beady eye on Aiden as if to say 'about time,' the bird flew off.

Aiden rested his chin on his hands. *Give me another mind-drift,* he thought, *only leave out the caveman.* Closing his eyes, he waited.

Two mighty wings sprout from my back and lift me into the sky, where I fly above Sierrawood. The town hugs the Sierra Nevada Mountains like a tiny cub nestled against the body of a lion. From up here, the trees look like tufts of green hair, and the rivers weave through them like blue ribbons. There, on a bald patch of land, the old army base quivers with renewed activity. Curious, I fly closer. A squad of robotic security guards are patrolling the entire—

A buzzing sound sizzled in Aiden's ears. He opened his eyes to see a tiny drone shaped like a dragonfly hovering in front of his face. His pale cheeks flushed red as the fake insect buzzed around his head with purposeful annoyance.

He'd lost track of time and stayed too long in the forest. Mom had sent the drone to find him. Guilt kicked off a chemical process in Aiden's brain, which reactivated his WeConnect. The implant vibrated at the base of his skull, but before he could use it to call home, a text arrived. Words floated in his frontal vision.

WHERE ARE YOU!?

The WeConnect translated his thought and replied with the message: *At the lake.*

The lane? What lane?

The technology still awaited perfection.

LAKE.

Auntie L'Eren & Uncle Govind are coming for dinner! COME HOME NOW!

The conversation ended. The drone flew this way and that while Aiden threw the bag of peanuts into the backpack and, with more care, placed the guitar into its case. As he tied his sneakers, the pine branches above him waved in the afternoon breeze. He paused to watch their motion, unable to help himself. *Whoooooshhh,* the trees whispered. It fascinated him that the wind had no voice of its own. Only when the air moved through the trees could it be heard.

Distress is like the wind. The words tumbled unbidden into his head. *Distress can go unnoticed if your mind gives it no portal.*

Words like these often sprang into his head in the mountain quiet. They were different from his mind-drifts. They were comforting words, to be sure; only Aiden wondered where they came from. No book he'd read contained them, at least none he could remember, nor could he recall anyone reciting them. Whenever the words came, he felt connected to something otherworldly.

He called the 'something' the Great Source because the words offered wisdom and comfort. With the Great Source around, Aiden felt less alone.

The WeConnect twinged again, which abruptly cut his connection to the Great Source. A message had arrived, an email, but it was from Clyde Parrish. Bad news. Reluctantly, Aiden blinked, opening the message.

Hey, Dirtbag. Thinking of you.

The attached photo displayed poop in a toilet bowl. Aiden jerked his eyes to the left to erase the ugly message. Clyde had picked on him since elementary school, and the bullying persisted even as they entered their senior year of high school. Aiden had tried to block Clyde as a sender several times, but his tormenter always managed to hack through. The WeConnect, after all, had been created to keep people linked with ease.

As Aiden trudged home, his skull continued to vibrate. A second text arrived from his mother: *Why aren't you home yet?* From DAPHNE, he received, *Don't forget to study for trig.*

DAPHNE, the Artificial General Intelligence that ran the United States government, did everything from powering the appliances in his home to sending him pesky reminders to do school work.

The Great Source had told Aiden to ignore distress, but how? His life away from the forest distressed him constantly. He itched to learn more about the Great Source. What was it? Where did it come from? Why couldn't it be with him all the time? He suspected DAPHNE and the WeConnect were to blame with their constant interruptions.

AT THE EDGE OF THE forest, Aiden walked a tiled path leading to a two-story home comprised of large white blocks. The front door slid open, and the drone flew inside.

When Aiden entered, the 3-D image of a bird's wing structure materialized on the entry wall. As he walked toward the kitchen, another wall burst into life with a video of bluebirds pecking at the ground. *FEATHERED FRIENDS LOVE WILLIE'S WILD BIRD SEED! ON SALE NOW AT THE HEALTHY HABIT!* Behind the advertisement's narration, Aiden heard the familiar orchestra of sound, the clicking, whirring, and buzzing emanating from the home's many machines.

Next to the guest bathroom, more colors and images jumped out at him. *BENDER'S BEST BIRD-WATCHING BINOCULARS ARE HALF-OFF TODAY!*

Aiden refused to respond to the colorful, moving images that pursued him as he moved through his home. When he entered the kitchen, a resplendent view of a cornfield met his eyes.

Green leaves and yellow cornstalks waved under a midwestern blue sky. His eyes told him he faced a floor-to-ceiling window. In reality, Aiden stood before a blank wall. A square of glass over the kitchen sink did offer a vista of the nearby mountains, but nobody ever looked through it. The wallscreens offered much more of a visual bonanza tailored to his family's desires.

A soundtrack enhanced the cornfield graphic, and the soft chirp of crickets came from hidden speakers. His mom, Jill, most likely desired a farmhouse setting to accompany tonight's supper. Aiden knew his Uncle Govind favored simple, hearty foods like corn on the cob served with meat and potatoes. Mom would serve him anything. She'd do ten backflips for her brother-in-law if he so desired.

A sweet odor drifted into Aiden's nostrils. DAPHNE had even provided the artificial aroma of ripe corn to bolster the illusion, but something lingered behind it, a chemical undertaste, a reminder that the cornstalk vista wasn't real.

He glanced at the view of the mountains through the window and decided that nothing, *nothing* compared with the offerings of the actual forest. Whenever Aiden inhaled the vanilla scent emitted from the red bark of a Jeffrey pine, it seemed as though a hatchway to heaven opened. The highland meadows, fed by the spring snow melt, now danced with yellow monkey flowers, baby blue eyes, and brilliant orange poppies. The oak trees, aspens, sequoias, and pines had shed their velvety white coats and now reveled in splendor under the California sun. He loved the forest and could never understand why his parents and everyone else opted to stare at walls instead of through windows.

Aiden heard a rhythmic patter of footsteps, along with the chirping crickets, and pivoted around to see his mom jogging in place as she watched a holographic baseball game play on the kitchen table. Jill could have viewed the game on any of the home's big wallscreens, but 3-D holograms, while smaller, offered a more live experience. Her ponytail of rich, chestnut hair bounced around as she huffed and puffed in a hot pink tracksuit.

"What are you doing?" Aiden asked.

"Jogging." Jill wiped the sweat off her brow with a towel. "I want to test out these new nano-joggers. They're supposed to give me more energy than the ones from last season."

More energy is not what she needs, Aiden thought. His mom created plenty of nervous energy on her own without the help of nanofibers. The hot pink material resembled ordinary velour, but he knew microscopic electrodes were attached to each thread. They generated a mild electrical current whenever his mom moved. Kinetic energy. All the rage.

"Why would you jog in the kitchen when we have a gym?"

"Here's why."

Jill lifted her jacket as she ran in place to reveal a small port on the waistband of her joggers. A white cord led from the port to a juicer on the table.

"See?" she asked breathlessly, "I want to know if the pants will charge small appliances like the ads say." She stopped running to press a button on the juicer and smiled at the whirring of the machine. "Ha! It charged. It was dead when—" Jill glanced at Aiden, and her face fell. "Are you kidding? Have you been walking around in public like that? Look at you! You've got pine needles sticking out of your hair and mud all over your shirt."

Aiden quickly tried to rub the dirt from his shirt.

Jill gaped in horror at his jeans. "Is that a spider?" She lunged toward her son, causing the juicer to tip over, and whacked the small insect to the tiled floor, where she crushed it with her shoe. Aiden would have stopped her and released the spider outside, but he didn't want to further upset his mom. Instead, he stood rooted to the spot and held onto the guitar case for dear life.

Jill unplugged herself from the juicer and picked up a furry, hamster-sized robot from the table, which she began to stroke. Juice spread across the countertop in an orange pool.

Their household robot, Roland, left the stove area and rolled on its base of wheels to the counter, where it extended one of six retractable manipulators or "arms" from its boxy metal frame. The arm's end effector or "hand" held a sponge, which Roland used to wipe up the juice. The "hands" concealed various tools: grippers, magnets, screwdrivers, brushes, cutting tools, and even a tiny welding gun. Roland cooked, loaded the dishwasher, put away dishes, folded the laundry, changed the sheets, fed the family's cat, and served as the family's gardener and handyperson. The robot had no facial features, only a face-screen that showed websites and movies. The family had owned several versions of Roland since Aiden was born.

"I don't know what to do with you, Aiden. I just don't," Jill whined as Poppy, the fake pet, cooed and nuzzled against her fingers.

"All I was doing was sitting near the lake."

"It looks like you crawled out of a hole! What's wrong with you? You drift into dreamland and traipse around the forest like an animal." Her agitated fingers left tracks on Poppy's fur.

Kif, a real feline with white fur and a beating heart, sat solo on the kitchen island and observed his mistress with unblinking green eyes. Aiden moved over and petted the cat. Kif arched his neck against the boy's hand but then moved off. He grew bored with too much petting and preferred his independence. With Jill, this made the cat the less popular of the Baylor pets. With her bouts of anxiety, Aiden's mom craved an emotional support animal that wouldn't leave her side. Poppy, the robotic hamster, stayed on her lap as long as she liked.

"This is why you have no friends." Jill glanced at the household robot. "Roland, when you do the laundry, rub out those stains on Aiden's shirt."

The robot pivoted its silvery round head and rolled over to Aiden. It extended a gripper that took hold of his shirt. At the same time, another manipulator, equipped with a camera, stretched out to examine the stain. A magnified image of the dirt appeared on Roland's face-screen, and, from its body, a stilted male voice said, "Don't worry, Jill. I can get this out."

The robot then released Aiden's shirt, rolled over to the BIO printer, and removed six steaks that had grown from cultured bovine cells during the day.

Jill flopped onto a stool, glued her eyes to the holographic baseball game, and continued to pet Poppy with nervous little strokes. "You talk to birds, you talk to trees, you talk to a voice in your head... I don't know what to do except to send you to Dr. Clarence again."

Aiden's grip tightened on the handle of the guitar case. "Mom, I don't need a psychiatrist."

"DAPHNE," Jill called out, "what time is it?"

A pleasant female voice issued from speakers hidden in the ceiling. "It's five-ten pm, Jill."

"Oh, crap. We'll discuss this later. Aunt Rennie and Uncle Govind will be here soon. DAPHNE, tell Oreanna to get ready. It'll take her an hour, I'm sure."

"Right away, Jill."

Aiden's mom held Poppy to her cheek for comfort. "Go shower," she said without looking at him. "Wash your hair. Wear the clothes I laid out on your bed. Your uncle is the Secretary of Defense for the United States, for goodness sake, and I can't have you embarassing us. We owe him everything. Your father would have never gotten his position at Ophidian without Uncle Govind's help. Promise me you won't say anything inappropriate. We need to make a good impression."

"Jill," the disembodied voice of DAPHNE drifted in. "Oreanna says she's busy."

Aiden used the excuse to escape. "I'll get her, Mom."

In response, Jill plugged her pants into the juicer and did jumping jacks.

AIDEN DEPOSITED THE guitar and backpack in his bedroom and sighed at the clothes his mom had chosen for him. White, stiffly-pressed dress shirt. Tan slacks with military creases. An ugly brown tie that reminded Aiden of Clyde's crap. His unhappy eyes traveled to the window and the proud tree growing outside.

He'd grown up with the oak. The tree was his brother, a brother who welcomed and protected him. As a little boy, Aiden had climbed into those limbs to seek shelter where no one could find him. His first mind-drift came to him as he rested in his brother's strong brown arms. Aiden had thin skin, but the oak possessed bark that withstood the pecking of birds and the slamming of wind. Whenever Clyde Parrish picked on Aiden at school, his brother told him, *if I can take it, so can you.*

As Aiden walked toward Oreanna's bedroom, the hallway lit up with the image of a hiker who resembled him. Of course, Aiden had to look. The Aiden-impersonator, with similar curling brown hair and a wiry frame, stood on a mountaintop wearing a new backpack. The hiker smiled at Aiden from the wall and said, *DR. BIRENBAUM'S BACKPACKS ARE FEATHER-LIGHT. TEN PERCENT OFF TODAY.*

Aiden knocked on his younger sister's door. "Oreanna?"

Silence.

"DAPHNE," he said to the empty air. "Open Oreanna's door."

The door slid open, and he spied a pudgy fifteen-year-old girl with kinky brown hair standing in a seemingly empty room near a wall vent. Oreanna made sweeping motions with her arms and wore a broad smile under her Opulus Redefined, a set of eye pads attached to a pliable headband.

"Ori, Mom wants you to get ready for dinner. Uncle Govind and Aunt Rennie will be here soon."

His sister didn't hear him. Advancements in the WeConnect now allowed the implant to send sound waves directly into the ear canal, effectively blocking out ambient sound. Oreanna could only hear the soundtrack of her virtual reality game. Through the pads that covered her eyes, she saw only the immersive 3D imagery of the game. Aiden knew his sister had developed an addiction to *Jungle Flight*, the trendy new game that brought the Amazonian rainforest to vivid life.

The game was synchronized with DAPHNE, who programmed gusts of cool air to flow from the wall vent at key moments, such as when the player's avatar began a downward arc of flight. Even now, a draft blew the mass of pin curls on Oreanna's head, and she raised her arms as though she flew through the air.

"Oreanna!" Aiden grabbed her arm, and she jumped.

"Asshole!" the girl screamed as she yanked off her headgear. "What are you doing? Leave me alone! Who said you could come in here?"

Aiden crossed his arms. Feeling disoriented, Oreanna swayed on her feet as if she had just stepped off a turbulent boat ride. Her complexion, already pale from spending too much time indoors, grew even paler as she regained her bearings. Aiden knew his sister hated leaving the game and wished she could live in it.

"I flew over the gorge today. I shot so many cannibals my ranking went up another five-hundred points." Oreanna thrust the goggles into Aiden's hand. "Try it."

"I don't want to."

"Try it!" Her curls bounced with her vehemence.

Aiden donned the gear. His WeConnect instantly synced with the game, and the sound of rushing water and screeches of birdcalls filled his ears. He adjusted the pads over his eyes and saw Oreanna's avatar perched on a tree branch, patiently waiting for the game to resume.

Long ago, avatars looked like animations, caricatures. Nowadays, they resembled real people. In the virtual world, Aiden's plain, overweight sister transformed into a trim sixteen-year-old beauty with flowing blonde hair, captivating green eyes, perky breasts, and a firm but ample backside. Her online persona didn't suffer from acne as real-life Oreanna did but boasted smooth porcelain skin.

Due to Ori's excellent hand-eye coordination, she aced most of her peers in the gaming world, which gave Imitation-Oreanna a large following of fans on social media. Almost daily, the avatar received texts that complimented her looks and prowess as a gamer. Most of these admirers were men, which, Aiden suspected, pleased his insecure sister to no end.

He willed his WeConnect to restart the game.

Among the fat, wet leaves of trees, I fly. A flash of red and blue pulls my gaze to the right, where a macaw calls. I pass a chattering troop of monkeys and sail under branches draped in purple flowers.

The graphics had improved so much since the early days of VR, with holographic, three-dimensional images and light rays and shadows in their proper places. Aiden reached out his hand, and, within the game, Oreanna's avatar-hand grazed the purple flowers.

I shoot up toward a bright blue sky. I'm flying! The skin on my face tingles as if sprayed with a cool mist. I look down to the gorge below with its river of white-capped rapids.

Aiden's heart pounded. Ever aware, the game sensed the change in player and asked if he would like to choose an avatar better suited for a young male. He ignored the lure. Playing the game as a yellow-haired babe in a bikini reminded him that this was only a game and he wasn't actually soaring in an Amazonian rainforest. One addicted kid in the family was enough. Still, Aiden hesitated to remove the headgear.

I soar over the treetops and feel the damp heat of the jungle rising from below. My nostrils fill with a flowery scent – plumeria. I can almost taste the sweet perfume on my tongue. A red-tailed hawk suddenly whizzes past.

Aiden's eyes followed the bird. He couldn't help it.

Red-tailed hawks aren't found in the Amazon, but there it is. The hawk swoops down and circles beneath me, its cinnamon tail spread out like a feathered fan. In tandem, we make a loop and soar together above a village composed of thatched huts. Woven into the thatch of one roof are letters that spell: RANGER BACKPACKS R THE BEST!

Aiden yanked the headgear off, although his deceived senses urged him to continue playing. To fly. To escape.

Tricky, he thought as his heart still pumped in exhilaration. A few hours ago, he'd flown like a hawk in his mind-drift. Ophidian Corp, the makers of *Jungle Flight*, would do anything to get him addicted. He thrust the goggles into his sister's hand.

"Buzzkill," Oreanna muttered.

Aiden's eyes caught a patch of wetness at her crotch. "Ori..." He pointed.

The girl looked down at her stained pants. "Oh. I didn't even notice."

"Again."

"Don't tell Mom or Dad. Please? They'll have DAPHNE put me on a timer."

"Practice a little self-control then."

"If they ask how you found me, tell them I was studying, okay?"

"They know what you do. The walls have eyes, remember?" He tousled her dark curls.

"Studying, Aiden. I was studying." Oreanna walked toward the bathroom and deposited the headgear on a shelf. "I wish my body didn't need to pee. Roland never has to pee."

"Roland is a robot."

"Elimination is a human failing." She picked at a pimple on her face and headed into the bathroom. "DAPHNE, return my room to study mode."

"Will do," came the upbeat but disembodied reply.

As the bathroom door closed behind Oreanna, a desk, chair, and table lamp slid out from a compartment in the bedroom wall, and a double bed slowly lowered from the ceiling. Aiden exited the room, but not before an ad lit up one wall with the message "PRE-ORDER JUNGLE FLIGHT TWO!"

CHAPTER 2

At supper, Mom's younger sister, Aunt L'Eren, sat at the dining room table with one hand resting on her pregnant belly. "We chose green eyes set against a backdrop of cafe au lait skin coloring for our boy."

The dining room walls displayed the farmhouse porch setting that overlooked the green and yellow cornfield Aiden had viewed earlier, only now everything was bathed in a Halloween-orange sunset. Amidst the dining room chatter, he heard the soundtrack of chirping crickets.

"We altered the genes by inserting a sequence for green eyes," L'Eren smiled at her husband. Govind Lal had silky black hair and skin the color of cinnamon. He and L'Eren possessed beautiful dark eyes, but Aiden guessed his uncle and aunt felt green would be more enviable.

"What a gorgeous combination," Jill beamed at her powerful brother-in-law. Roland motored in, holding platters of salad, steak, mashed potatoes, and corn, and served helpings to each person. Aiden's father, Doug, took heaping portions. He was a stout man, stouter than he used to be, Aiden observed. Dad had gained weight since taking the job at Ophidian, and Aiden believed it was because he sought comfort in food.

L'Eren waved away her portion of salad and pointed at the potatoes. Roland dutifully gave her an extra serving. "We also curated genes for a higher IQ. That way, our boy can grow up to be a high-achiever like his daddy." She placed a proud hand on her husband's shoulder.

Just then, words from the Great Source nudged Aiden. He pulled at the starchy collar of the white shirt his mom made him wear and bristled uncomfortably. The words pressed against his lips, but he fought their exit. More often than not, he got into trouble when he spoke them.

Uncle Govind cocked his head as if he, too, listened to an inner voice; only Aiden knew he was only using the WeConnect to send texts and answer emails. The man had been working nonstop since he'd walked through the door and seemed unusually tense.

The words continued to push at Aiden until he could no longer stop them. He pointed his fork at Aunt L'Eren and asked, "Why bother making your kid smarter if DAPHNE handles everything? We can afford to be stupid."

Jill's eyes threw daggers at him, and Doug gave Aiden a warning shake of his head. Oreanna rolled her eyes and shoveled food into her mouth, no doubt in a hurry to quit the meal and return to the fantasy world of *Jungle Flight*.

Govind raised his eyebrows at his nephew. "Artificial Intelligence only amplifies our intelligence. It's an extension of us. A tool."

"No, it's not." Aiden's fork made anxious little pushes against the mashed potatoes on his plate. "DAPHNE runs everything, including our lives."

Aunt L'Eren's lower jaw dropped. "Where would you get such an idea?"

Jill ordered Roland to pour more wine and said, "From the filth of society that lives on the streets, that's where."

Doug glanced at his wife and inflated his chest to show he could play the strict patriarch. "Aiden, how many times have I told you to stay away from the grid-skippers?"

Aiden pasted some shame onto his face for his father's benefit but didn't feel too threatened. He and his dad were pals. Just last summer, he'd taught Doug how to fish at the lake, and Doug returned the favor by teaching Aiden how to drive a car – a real adventure! Although all cars were automated, the Baylors owned an older model that allowed for emergency human intervention. Aiden loved to drive. Of course, if he made one mistake, it could mean death, but the risk didn't frighten him; it excited him. Virtual games were filled with plenty of risks, but none were real. When Aiden, not DAPHNE, drove the car, a beaming sense of accomplishment radiated through him.

Jill narrowed her eyes. "If you visit those freaks again, you're grounded for a month."

Oreanna smirked at her brother and then looked longingly toward the stairs that would return her to her game. "Mom, I'm done. Can I be excused?"

"No."

Uncle Govind blinked rapidly three times, meaning he was either turning document pages or scrolling through a website. Aiden watched a bead of sweat run down his uncle's forehead and wondered why the Secretary of Defense was all twisted up.

Aunt L'Eren shrugged one shoulder. "The grid-skippers choose to live on the streets. They could live in subsidized housing if they wanted and play virtual reality games all day long."

"Right." Aiden's fork smoothed the sides of his mashed potato pile. "They could play all day in a virtual world created by Ophidian and spend their stipend on all the Ophidian-made products advertised in the games."

Oreanna kicked him under the table.

"Ouch!" Aiden rubbed his shin and scowled at his sister.

"Quit cutting down Dad's company," she said.

Doug slapped a genial grin on his face, but behind it, Aiden glimpsed regret. Doug worked as a marketing executive for Ophidian, the giant corporation with a broad global reach that owned many companies, from tech firms to farms. Ophidian also manufactured products. Doug led a team to find ways to push those products in the popular video games and virtual worlds the company produced. 'I'm not suited to wear a suit," he'd joke to Aiden but then confide how much he hated his job. Still, how could he ever leave? The salary Doug earned made the Baylors rich.

Jill waved furiously at Roland to refill her glass. "Not only does Aiden get crazy ideas from the grid-skippers, he brings home these books—"

"Real books?" Aunt L'Eren interrupted.

"Yes, real, old books that probably carry disease. He gets them from this one human wreck... What's his name again?"

Aiden's shoulders slumped. "Chris."

Jill downed half her glass. Aunt L'Eren clucked her tongue at Aiden. Govind blinked a couple of times as he read a text and wiped his forehead with a napkin.

Studying him, Aiden's mind-drift from earlier popped into his mind, the one where he'd flown over the army base outside of town and saw an unusual amount of security guards. Of course, his brain made up that scene. A mind-drift would have no bearing on reality, right?

Just then, a question sizzled on Aiden's tongue like a burning flame. As he continued to gaze at his uncle, the question grew hotter. Even though he knew his mother would kill him, he had to speak or his mouth would burn.

"Why are they upping security at the army base?" he blurted out. "Is something going on with DAPHNE?"

DAPHNE's headquarters were underground, built beneath the abandoned base.

Govind jerked his eyes toward him. "There's nothing going on."

"Then why did you come out to California?"

"Aiden." Jill narrowed her eyes at her son and grabbed the wine bottle from Roland as he motored past.

"Your aunt wants to give birth around her family. That's why we're here."

"You're lying."

Jill slammed the bottle on the table and forced a smile at her important guest, whose eyes were glued on Aiden. "I apologize. Our son is having some mental issues, but he's in therapy to work them out."

Aiden's lower jaw dropped. How drunk was his mom? At that moment, embarrassingly, Dr. Clarence materialized on the dining room wall, accompanied by a mental health hotline number.

Aunt L'Eren widened her eyes at the image and asked Aiden, "What's bothering you, sweetheart?"

Jill tipped the wine bottle toward her glass. "He says there's a voice in his head that talks to him." She missed her mark, and red liquid stained the white tablecloth.

Aiden had to defend himself. No one else would. "It's not a voice. Words come into my head, and give me ideas."

His aunt's eyes went wider. "Ideas? What does this person say?"

"I don't know if it's a person. It's not like someone's whispering in my ear. It's—It's more like a communication going on inside of me."

Govind laser-focused on him. "A communication? What sort of communication? How often does it take place?"

Aiden lowered his eyes. He felt emotional chains tighten around his middle but spoke anyhow. "It happens only when I'm calm, like when I'm in the forest thinking about nothing. Then, words come into my head from out of nowhere. Words and ideas, and sometimes mind-drifts."

Oreanna screwed up her face at him. "What's a mind-drift?"

Aiden glanced up to see his mom staring at him in defeat. Doug opened his mouth to speak, to play his usual role of family mediator, but Govind held up a silencing hand.

"Do you talk back to this thing?" his uncle asked.

"Yes, but not with my mouth. It's all going on in my head."

L'Eren gave her nephew a wry smile. "The communication is in your head? That's your WeConnect, Aiden."

Anger thudded in his chest. He wasn't going to let them diminish the Great Source by comparing it to the hated device. "No, it's not. I've made a connection to—to something real."

Jill's lower lip trembled.

Doug tented his hands as if he might pray. "We've talked about this before, son. It's a trick. Someone is sending you subliminal messages through your WeConnect. They're fooling you." He looked at Govind and L'Eren. "I'm sure you've heard how hackers have found a way to infiltrate people's WeConnects. They send cruel, anonymous texts or flash scary images."

L'Eren nodded eagerly at her sister. "I'm sure that's what's happening, and it's really bad for people suffering from depression. The subliminal words and pictures can bring them to the brink of suicide." She reached across the table to pat her nephew's hand. "That's all it is, Sweetie. You're not hearing voices. Your mind has been hacked, that's all."

Jill wiped away a tear and smiled gratefully at her sister.

Aiden pulled his hand away. "I turn off my implant when I go into the forest, so, like I said, it's not my WeConnect. It's the Great Source."

His family stared at him.

"Look," he pleaded in desperation, "maybe I'm talking to aliens or God. Or even to our ancestors." Liking the idea, he straightened up in his chair. "I read that the Chinese believed their ancestors spoke to them."

A moment passed, heavy with silence.

"DAPHNE?" Aiden called out, "didn't the ancient Chinese believe their dead relatives could advise them?"

The unbodied, velvety voice curled around the dining table. "During the Shang Dynasty, the ancestors of the royal family were thought to reside in heaven with the spirit-gods. These ancestors, it was believed, could be contacted through a shaman for help and guidance."

"See?" A weak smile formed on Aiden's face. "Maybe I'm a shaman."

Oreanna gazed sadly at her brother. "No, you're just sick."

He could tell his family thought he'd lost his mind, but everything about the Great Source told him there was so much more in his mind to find. Pushing back his chair in defeat, Aiden rose from the table and left the room.

WHEN HE'D GONE, L'EREN leaned toward Jill. "This is serious."

Jill sighed at Oreanna. "Ori..."

The girl rose to her feet. "I get it." She wagged a finger at her mother. "But if you guys get to talk trash, I get to play."

Jill nodded, and the happy teenager hustled off.

"DAPHNE," Jill announced in a tired voice, "soundproof the room."

The doors closed.

Jill took her sister's hand. "You see what we're dealing with, Rennie? Aiden is extremely smart and mature for his years, but he's so troubled."

Govind gazed at Aiden's empty chair. "I think you'd better find out who or what is hacking into your son."

Doug appeared torn between defending Aiden and pandering to his powerful relative. "Of course. DAPHNE, schedule a security scan of Aiden's WeConnect tonight."

The response floated from the walls. "Will do, Doug."

"But what if Aiden has a serious mental issue?" Jill held her napkin against her nose to stave off tears. "He hates going to therapy. I don't know whether I should make him go or not."

L'Eren squeezed her hand. "Ask the Predictor."

Jill, in manic agreement, jumped up from the table and jogged into the kitchen.

"What do you think Aiden meant when he spoke of 'a true connection?'" Govind asked Doug.

Doug shook his head.

Jill returned to the table with a blue plastic ball the size of an apple. Holding the Predictor reverently with two hands, she asked, "Should I give my son time to work out his issues, or should I send him to Dr. Clarence?"

A voice, neither male nor female, but spectral and synthetic, issued from the small round orb. "Let Dr. Clarence assess your son's mental state."

L'Eren lifted relieved hands into the air. "There. It's decided."

Doug bristled in his seat but kept quiet. Govind looked back at the space his nephew vacated and his eyes fell to Aiden's plate, where a perfectly-formed pyramid of mashed potatoes stood like a beacon to an unknown world.

CHAPTER 3

Early the next morning, Govind boarded an air taxi to fly to a military base outside of town. The taxi lifted vertically off the ground like a helicopter of old, but without the clamor of propellers. He could have taken an automated car on the street, which offered a compact sleeping area and television, but the air taxi traveled distances quickly, and Govind wanted to get to his meeting as soon as possible.

He traveled solo without security because his WeConnect functioned as a bodyguard. A special application created for government officials and celebrities could pick up on the presence of a firearm in a crowd and silently warn the VIP. As well, when Govind's eyes scanned a crowd of people (under the pretense of engaging with them), the app recognized the faces of insurgents, persons on the Most Wanted lists, and anyone with a criminal record. The app would then alert any police androids or security robots patrolling the area, and they would swiftly arrive and remove the threat. In a small town like Sierrawood, Govind felt safe enough. Besides, there were far more serious threats that needed his attention.

He strummed the armrest of his seat with nervous fingers and wondered how Aiden could know about the current crisis. He worried that the voice in his nephew's head might belong to cyber actors who'd been hacking and attacking American interests. Now, they might very well have begun hacking into the heads of American citizens.

The military base came into view below. The husks of barracks and bunkers stood crumbling. Rows of mothballed fighter jets sat on a landing strip from which weeds grew and swayed in the wind. Rusted barbed wire fencing outlined an old rifle range and a training ground, where nothing remained but a dirt running track and the ruins of an obstacle course.

Govind knew that, long before he was born, soldiers had trained at Fort Sierra. Indeed, the town of Sierrawood had formed around the base to serve the military personnel and their families. As the years passed, however, the base fell out of use. Human soldiers no longer patrolled the grounds, only guard robots, and today, as Aiden had correctly stated, there were a lot more than usual, monitoring the base on high alert. The robots looked like squat metal boxes stacked on a wheeled platform, but Govind knew the boxes housed a variety of weapons.

If on-foot attackers stormed the base, the guard robots would send out heat shields that burned human skin. If the threat came from the sky, the guards would return fire with precision-guided firearms whose bullets could change course in midair to track their targets. As well, the boxes hid extended-range rocket launchers and laser cannons. No doubt, the guard patrols had already scanned the air taxi and its important passenger, for they motored by peacefully when the vehicle set down near a one-story bunker.

Govind hastened toward the bunker, which housed the United States' headquarters of Central General Intelligence and Cyber Command. A few feet from the entrance, he paused to allow a beam of green light to scope his body. When he turned his eye toward a retinal scanner, the building's steel door slid open.

He entered a lobby tiled entirely in white quartz. A black retangular box stood in the dead center of the room like an open, upright coffin. Govind stepped inside, and, while a biometric scanner read his WeConnect, he picked up a small strip of paper from an interior shelf and licked it. He lay the paper on a blue-lit circle on the same shelf and waited for DNA clearance.

Moments later, a panel opened in one of the quartz-tiled walls to reveal an elevator. Govind walked into it. As the doors closed, the WeConnect in his skull vibrated, and a text appeared in his frontal vision: *Welcome, Dr. Lal.*

The elevator began its descent underground.

A few moments later, the doors opened into the enormous room of a data center. Rows of sleek black servers filled the space and created one wall of electronics after another like giant dominoes standing on end. The servers powered and fed data to computers and WeConnects all over the country. Robots that resembled metal snakes slid up and down and around the electronics, monitoring the temperature, ventilation, equipment status, and possible fire hazards. Robotic arms reached and retracted along the grid work fronting the servers as they replaced and removed faulty hard drives.

A gentle roar, similar to the sound of ocean waves, issued from the servers and filled Govind's ears as he followed a path of amber-colored footlights. The lights led him to a set of double doors, which opened automatically upon his approach. As he exited, he stepped out onto the limestone tiles of a long patio rimmed by a graceful railing.

As Govind glanced behind him, he didn't see the exit of the data center but the façade of an English manor house. If he peered through the leaded panes of the nearest casement window, he'd behold a fancy interior drawing room with a cozy fire crackling in the grate. Through another window, he'd view a wood-paneled library. A ballroom replete with a tiled mosaic floor and crystal chandeliers glowed in refined splendor behind the glass of another.

All of these were holographic scenes embedded behind the leaded panes like one might find in a theme park. They helped sow the illusion that Govind had exited a mansion to step outside into a garden. And what a garden it was!

Lit from above by an orb of bright light, the wide stone steps descended to an expanse of green artificial turf with a sputtering fountain at its center. Beds of fake pink roses, red mums, and various plastic ferns adorned the garden. The branches of faux willow trees gently draped over wrought-iron tables that peppered the "lawn."

The last time Govind visited, people had filled the place, some wearing military uniforms, others dressed in the white tunics of the engineers. They'd sat on cushioned chairs at the tables holding laptops and coffee cups.

Today, however, the garden was empty except for a string quartet made up of four tuxedo-clad androids standing under a gazebo. They played a piece Govind recognized but couldn't name.

He looked up and squinted under the fake sun, which was positioned among projections of cottony white clouds dotting a blue firmament. Later, pinpoints of light patterned after the constellations would twinkle in a parody of the night's sky.

Dvořák. The music's composer was Dvořák.

"Mr. Secretary."

A tall woman with clipped dark brown hair climbed the limestone steps toward him. Dr. Lizzie Appel's straight posture told Govind she had no insecurities about her height. Her white tunic and white pants complimented her flawless caramel-colored skin. Lizzie extended a smooth-skinned hand. "Welcome back."

Govind secretly admired the woman's beauty, her high cheekbones and full lips. With a hearty handshake, he said, "Lizzie, there's no need for formalities. I'm still the same Govind you knew at MIT."

"That Govind used to copy my exams." She shared a smile with her visitor. Even her teeth were a brilliant white. "I feel I should greet you with some respect, considering your new post."

"Please. We're old friends, but you, I notice, have far fewer wrinkles than I do."

"It's the pressure you're under, Govind."

"DAPHNE does my job. I don't feel pressured at all." He let the lie hang between them as his eyes roamed the manicured grounds. "I never get over how enchanting this garden is. It seems so real."

"It's about as much of the outdoors as I can get. Come. I know you don't want to waste another minute."

He followed her along the limestone patio. "You seem very calm, Lizzie."

"Panic won't resolve anything."

The two stopped at an ornately-carved wooden door on the mansion's façade. At their arrival, the door opened, and Lizzie led him down a white-washed hallway. They passed various offices, inside of which uniformed men and women rushed about. Some glimpsed Govind and paused to salute him.

They entered a square room bordered by servers along each wall. In the center of the room, a white, plastic-coated egg the size of a compact car stood balanced on its tip. Block letters etched across the surface of one side spelled out DAPHNE. Toward the bottom, in a smaller script, he read, *Ophidian Corporation* next to the company's logo, a fanged snake in a tree branch.

Lizzie put her hand on the shoulder of a young woman with bold purple streaks livening her ash-blonde hair. "This is Vivica, the youngest of my protégées. Vivica, this is Dr. Govind Lal, U.S. Secretary of Defense."

"How do you do?" Govind asked.

The girl barely acknowledged her important visitor and sat with her eyes glued to her computer. He glanced at Vivica's screen and winced at the vast amount of data she had to analyze. No wonder the girl's features were pinched and drawn. Her skin tone lacked color, probably due to spending so much time underground. Pity, Govind thought. Maybe the purple streaks in Vivica's hair represented a statement of some sort, a way to bring color to an otherwise colorless existence.

Govind swallowed these sentiments as he followed Lizzie to a holographic screen near a bank of servers. Upon her approach, a map of the United States materialized. She used her finger to display several hubs all over the country that distributed DAPHNE's intelligence.

"As you can see, all of DAPHNE's systems are running efficiently. As well, our power grids are fully operational despite the attacks."

Next to the U.S. map, a holographic globe appeared and slowly revolved. Govind observed similar hubs in other countries receiving lit strands of intelligence. These emanated not from DAPHNE but from similar Artificial General Intelligences or AGIs belonging to the rest of the world's nations. The AGIs were supposed to work together to keep peace. Unfortunately, something went wrong, and Govind's presence was required.

Govind's eyes roamed the digital planet in concern. "Cyber actors from no less than three different countries managed to hack into our electric systems all at the same time. The governments of our adversaries deny any wrongdoing, but this was clearly an orchestrated attack."

Lizzie joined him to scrutinize the globe. "DAPHNE removed the threats with no problem, but I do understand your concern. A planted computer virus won't simply wreak havoc with the software of the power grids but can physically destroy the infrastructure by giving the control system faulty orders. In addition, malware could bypass all our safety systems and backups."

She spoke like one of her machines, Govind mused. It fit that Lizzie would be the brain behind the deep-learning technology powering DAPHNE.

"Removing threats is one thing," he told her. "The President and Congress want to know why the AGIs are unable to resolve our problems, and what DAPHNE plans to do about these acts of aggression."

"As much as I enjoy seeing you, Govind, you didn't have to come all this way to find out."

"I can't risk hearing DAPHNE's plans remotely, not with all the spying and hacking going on. There's a breakdown somewhere, and I've got to find it."

"DAPHNE has informed me she has the situation under control."

"All right." He waited for Lizzie to continue. She didn't. "What is she doing?"

"I can't tell you."

He blinked at her in surprise. "Congress must vote on decisions that impact international relations. We need to know DAPHNE's plan."

"By the time you deliver a report to Congress, and they vote to approve or disapprove of her plan, DAPHNE and similar AGI's around the world will be countless steps ahead of you and onto a new game plan. Let DAPHNE handle the problem without slowing her down."

"No. There has to be a vote. We live in a democracy, you know."

Lizzie raised an eyebrow. "Do we? You work for the corporation that owns this country."

He flinched. "I work for the U.S. government."

"Since when? I know Ophidian placed you in the President's Cabinet."

Govind squirmed in his fine leather shoes. "That's not public information, Lizzie. I may have worked for Ophidian in the past—"

"You're still one of their top execs."

"Yes, but we feel it looks better if we—"

"If you keep secret the fact that you work for the conglomerate that edged out all its competition, monopolized every industry in the country, and now functions as a puppet master who dangles the President and all the members of Congress on marionette strings. You're a fine one to talk about democracy, Govind. Tell me, does the American public know about the threat to our power sources? Do they know about the failed harvests brought on by climate change and how those failures might cause worldwide economic collapses? What about the populist parties on the rise in the weaker nations? Do they know about that?"

He didn't answer.

"People know nothing about these things because Ophidian owns all the news outlets and controls all the information."

Govind's lips pressed into a thin line. It pained him that Lizzie saw him for what he was: a figurehead, a useless VIP.

She put a placating hand on his shoulder. "Look, Ophidian funded DAPHNE, which enabled my family to create her. Now let her do her thing. Why teach DAPHNE to walk and then hobble her?"

"You're taking this personally," he countered. "I know that your parents and grandparents pioneered quantum artificial intelligence and deep learning. Your family envisioned and designed DAPHNE, and you and your team have made her what she is today. But DAPHNE is a machine, Lizzie. A tool that services our country. I am the principal policymaker for the Defense Department, and I must know of her plans."

Lizzie pursed her lips together and then waved a dismissive hand in the air. "Ask her, then. She's listening to our every word."

Although he didn't have to, Govind drew near the oval machine. "Hello, DAPHNE."

A band of blue light encircled the middle of the egg, and a female voice responded, "Hello, Dr. Lal. I will address your concerns."

"First, what are you doing to counter these attacks?"

"U.S. Cyber Command has penetrated into Russian, Chinese, and Iranian utilities. We have planted malicious software or malware capable of fully disrupting their energy sector, which includes refineries, electrical systems, solar and wind farms, coal, and natural gas, along with their chemical and nuclear plants. We have also targeted their telecommunication centers and critical manufacturing sectors. We are prepared to destroy their civilian infrastructure."

He let that sink in. "That... That is not working together for world peace. That is an act of war."

Lizzie viewed the egg as a proud mother hen. "DAPHNE has analyzed all the possible outcomes. If she considers this a good decision, then it is. Don't forget, all AGIs around the world are committed to the Pillars of Peace."

The Pillars, Govind knew, were derived from a statistical analysis of over 4,000 datasets on how to keep world peace. Years ago, the world's nations had taught the Pillars to the Intelligences that ran their governments. Why, then, would DAPHNE make such an aggressive move? He ran a trembling hand through his dark hair and glanced at Lizzie for help, but she offered none. Why would she? In DAPHNE, she trusts.

"DAPHNE," he asked, "are we at war?"

The velvety voice remained calm. "It is my goal and the goal of the other nations' Intelligences to maintain world order."

"But are we at war?"

"Affirmative."

"GOOD MORNING, AIDEN." The stilted male monotone issued from Roland as one of the metal arms extended to offer him a mug filled with hot liquid. "Here is your coffee with 7-hex cream."

The cream contained a brain enhancement drug. Aiden promptly set the drink down on the kitchen counter. Roland didn't question or object. Oreanna, on the other hand, took full note of her brother's refusal to drink his coffee. She held her mug and swiveled back and forth on a barstool at the kitchen island. "You're going to fall behind. I swear, I'm already smarter than you."

"I don't care." Aiden stepped in front of the refrigerator, and the interior lit up. He perused the items inside and willed his WeConnect to command the fridge to dispense a container of strawberry yogurt. He didn't like the way enhancers made him feel. True, he processed math equations better with the mind-focusing drug, but it interfered with his ability to drift off mindlessly in the forest.

As he spooned up his yogurt, Aiden remembered what Chris, the grid-skipper, once told him about mind-expanding drugs. Chris mentioned something called the "Mystery of Human Consciousness." What did that mean? Aiden knew the difference between being conscious and unconscious, but what did those mind expanders mean by the Mystery of Consciousness? Did it have to do with his unspoken communication with the Great Source?

Oreanna picked up the Predictor and said to the blue plastic apple, "Should I dye my hair blonde?"

The silvery voice from the apple replied, "You should dye your hair blonde."

"Should I straighten it?"

"You should straighten it."

Aiden gaped at his sister. Couldn't she think for herself?

"Are you trying to look like your avatar?" he asked.

Oreanna shrugged and didn't reply, which answered his question. Grimacing, he shoved his hands in his pockets and walked outside to catch his bus.

CHAPTER 4

When Oreanna was in second grade, Jill and Doug stopped insisting she attend school in person. As Aiden walked down the driveway, he pondered that decision. Going to school online wasn't unusual. Lots of kids did it, but Jill and Doug had no idea how immersed their daughter had become in the digital world. They didn't know, for instance, that Oreanna attended school as her beautiful avatar, so people had no idea what she really looked like. They didn't realize that Oreanna's entire world existed online—her classes, games, and social life. Jill and Doug saw only that their self-conscious daughter was happier in front of a computer and left her to it. Aiden couldn't be more different. His only happiness lay outdoors.

A beeping sound from the sky signaled the descent of a multi-seat air bus, and Aiden stepped away from the road as it landed. After climbing aboard, he chose a seat at the back. This way, he could gaze freely at a girl a few rows up named Ava Durand. Aiden had gazed at Ava from afar since the two attended kindergarten.

Honey-colored hair fell straight to Ava's shoulders. She was taller than average, lean but athletic. As she turned to chat with a friend, Aiden was treated to a view of her profile. He had watched the years etch her pert little girl's nose into a line of aquiline elegance. Baby apple cheeks had risen high and sharp. Only Ava's wide and unabashed smile remained from her childhood. Once, back in middle school, she had smiled at him. Aiden stored the memory of that sunshine moment in a cerebral file that contained everything he considered precious. These days, he passed her in the hall like a shadow. She didn't notice him. He wasn't in Ava's crowd.

Most of the students filling the air bus didn't talk aloud. They communicated via their WeConnects. Pete Montgomery, mouse-haired and rotund despite swallowing a prodigious amount of diet pills, glanced at Aiden and turned away with a wicked grin. Immediately, a girl in the third row laughed, looked behind her, and jabbed Aiden with her eyes.

He ignored their mockery by pretending to concentrate out the window. To his joy, a peregrine falcon boldly soared alongside the large, lumbering bus sharing the sky with her. Aiden put his hand on the glass as if begging the bird to stay. The falcon dropped into a dive. Aiden pressed his face close to the window and watched her flap her pointed wings to gain speed. Unfortunately, the glass prevented him from observing the falcon any further. He sat back in his seat, grateful for the gift, if fleeting, that diverted his attention from the cruelty of his classmates.

Besides Aiden, only one other student sat without talking, blinking, or nodding. Tash Jeffries was new in town, and Aiden imagined entering a strange high school as a senior must be tough. Tash, however, was good-looking, tall, and blessed with smooth, coffee-colored skin and a muscular physique, so he received a lot of positive attention from both boys and girls. He purposely kept to himself, though, which stymied Aiden. Why wouldn't a guy enjoy instant popularity if he could have it? Whenever Aiden observed Tash, something nagged at him, and today he realized what it was. A slight yellow cast marred his eyes. Nobody else seemed to notice, but, being a loner, Aiden made a study of people. Tash popped an enhancer and glanced, expressionless, at him. Aiden mustered up a smile and then returned his gaze to Ava.

Ava starred in most all of Aiden's mind-drifts. As the bus hummed and shuddered, his mind escaped to an exotic setting where he could be alone with her. He visualized a tent made of heavy, colorful fabric rippling in the wind on an isolated sand dune.

I flip back the tent flap and enter. I stand before her as a warrior, a newly minted hero returned from battle. Ava stretches out on a pile of multi-colored pillows, wearing nothing more than a veil. Outside, a desert wind whistles. Inside, a plume of incense smoke curls sensually toward the cloth ceiling. Throwing aside my saber, I remove my outer garments and go to my oasis in the desert. My hands run through her silken hair, and my fingers explore every crevice of her...

Real-Ava turned her face toward him, and Aiden quickly averted his gaze. He willed off his WeConnect and prayed she didn't know how to hack the device. If Ava interpreted his thoughts, she'd get a glimpse of Aiden's sexy desert fantasy, and he'd never live it down. His face burned as the blonde girl stared at him—at least he assumed she stared at him.

Grandma Rosie once told him the eyes are the windows to the soul, but no one could search Ava Durand's eyes because she didn't have any. She wasn't born blind (her parents would have never allowed blindness to corrupt her genetic code). A defective house robot exploded when she was five, and the fragments penetrated her eyes. While medical treatments could smooth the scars on Ava's face, the damage to her vision was irreparable. Surgeons removed the injured eyes and inserted two retinal prostheses in their place. These prostheses could, at times, appear like unusually wide human eyes complete with whites and irises or function as two miniature computer screens that displayed images. As well, her bionic eyes boasted superhuman optical features like night vision, X-ray vision, microscopic focus, and long-range zoom. Ava could see spectrums that the human eye could not, including the near-infrared band and ultraviolet waves. Because the prostheses could process light faster than a human eye, Ava's reactions were superior to her sighted fellows, which explained her excellence at gaming. All of Aiden's classmates considered her prostheses to be the "eyes of the future" because, with them, no one had to wear VR goggles.

Aiden couldn't read an expression in Ava's fake eyes but knew she could see right through his jeans. With nothing to lose, for nothing masked his loneliness, he offered her a wistful smile. He expected a rebuff, but to his surprise, she grinned, and her eyescreens displayed rainbows. She lifted a finger to the base of her skull. At first, Aiden didn't understand the gesture and then realized she pointed to her WeConnect. He quickly reactivated his device, and a message arrived from her.

Ava sent a video of the falcon she'd shot with her eyes. Her extraordinary sight had enabled her to catch the falcon drawing back its wings to shift into the shape of an aerodynamic missile. The video showed the bird slice through the air, open its wings to slow its descent, and then clutch a passing starling. The smaller bird never saw its predator coming.

Ava turned to chat again with friends and left Aiden to sit alone, flushed and breathless.

CHAPTER 5

Unlike Oreanna, Aiden preferred going to class so he could better debate his teachers. He felt less afraid to speak the words of the Great Source in school because no one there ever threatened to send him to a psychiatrist. However, Aiden knew his outspokenness only worsened his reputation as a nonconformist.

As he joined the other seniors filing into science class, the teacher, a petite Asian woman with genetically-chosen red hair and green eyes, greeted him. Aiden liked Professor Yang because she enjoyed a good debate and, unlike his other teachers, encouraged him to speak his mind. At her side stood a teaching assistant, a square-headed robot named Veronica.

Aiden took a seat at one of four digitally personalized desks clustered together to form a modular pod. He saw on his deskscreen the faces of two kids from Guam who had connected to the class.

Professor Yang instructed all the students to power down their WeConnects, an unusual request since most teachers encouraged the use of the device for academic tasks. She walked between the pods with Veronica, and the robot's wheeled base purred along the floor like a contented cat.

"Pardon me, Professor," Veronica said in a deceptively human-sounding female voice. "Pete Montgomery is still connected to the Internet." The robot's facescreen displayed a diva singing a song in a music video.

Professor Yang eyeballed Pete, who stared vacantly at a corner of the room while he munched on a chocolate bar. "Pete!"

Pete's gaze drifted her way.

"You'll see Kiko soon enough at lunch. Get offline."

Pete snorted but willed off his connection. He rolled his eyes at his best friend, Clyde Parrish, who sat in the same pod.

Professor Yang checked Veronica for reassurance. The robot's facescreen displayed an attractive woman nodding. Veronica then pivoted toward Pete with an image of the same woman smiling and winking in an 'it's-all-good' gesture. In response, Pete raised his middle finger.

"There's a reason your parents' generation fell in love with multi-tasking," Professor Yang said to the class. "Every time they replied to an email or posted on their social media platforms, their brains received a dollop of reward hormones that told them they had accomplished something. There's a small structure of the limbic system called the nucleus accumbens. It's the area in the brain that lights up when, say, a gambler wins a bet or someone experiences an orgasm."

Pete sniggered and elbowed Clyde, who scowled at his friend.

"This reward and pleasure center of the brain gave your parents little bouts of euphoria when they multi-tasked, which then created a neural addiction. After all, who doesn't like to feel accomplished?"

A couple of kids got up from their pod, stretched, and walked about the room. One of them, a curvy, dark-haired beauty nicknamed Busty Trina, absently trailed after the teacher and Veronica.

Professor Yang lifted a finger in the air. "But when you multi-task, you shift attention quickly from one activity to another. Ironically, this causes the prefrontal cortex and striatum to burn up oxygenated glucose, the very fuel we need to stay on track. So, while your folks congratulated themselves on tweeting, posting, answering emails, and messaging, they wasted the very fuel they needed for long-range strategic planning. When you suffer diminished cognitive performance, it creates anxiety. Anxiety raises the levels of the stress hormone cortisol in the brain. Higher levels of cortisol can lead to aggressive and impulsive behavior. The upshot is your folks are uptight from years of multi-tasking. How many of them take the tranquilizer Ketamine?"

Aiden lifted his hand. The majority of his classmates did the same.

"Nowadays, we don't have to multi-task as your parents did." She rested a hand on Veronica's sharp-edged synthetic shoulder, and the robot's monitor displayed a happy face emoji. "We rely on robots like Veronica here and Artificial General Intelligence like DAPHNE to pick up the slack for us."

Aiden raised his hand. "You didn't mention our generation's addiction to virtual reality games."

Someone at the back of the room tittered. Someone else moaned. Aiden ignored them and kept a focused gaze on Professor Yang. "My sister is addicted. If I didn't drag her to dinner, she would forget to eat." He refrained from mentioning Oreanna's pee-stained pants.

"Hey, Baylor." Pete Farmington sniggered. "Respect your sister. She knows how to play. Besides, she's friggin hot."

"Smoking hot." Clyde leered. "Why haven't you fixed me up with her yet?"

Aiden didn't answer. Of course, they referred to Oreanna's gorgeous online persona. They knew nothing of the real Oreanna Baylor, and Aiden wasn't about to educate them.

His teacher flipped back her long red hair. "Aiden, you're a nature lover. Tell me you don't ask DAPHNE to create content for your social media pages so you're free to wander the wilderness."

"Why would I ask DAPHNE to create content for me?"

"So you can connect with other people who like the same things, and they can connect with you."

"Nobody wants to connect with him," Clyde stated.

Aiden ignored the taunt, but it depressed him that he couldn't reinvent himself. In a small town like Sierrawood, the dynamics between people remained unchanged. Although the passing years had filled out his lean frame, chiseled his jawline, and broadened his shoulders, Aiden Baylor was still viewed as the pale, gangly geek Clyde Parrish loved to persecute.

Professor Yang frowned at Clyde and then focused a kinder face toward Aiden. "With technology, no one has to feel left out. DAPHNE has access to all your photos and the special events in your life. She can decide what is interesting and post it for you. You can relax knowing all your online needs are met."

Aiden surveyed the class, sure someone would find the concept as ridiculous as he. His eyes met mostly baleful stares. Clearing his throat for bravery, he faced his redheaded professor. "You do realize that if I let DAPHNE act as a bot and post content for me, and all my friends do the same, we're not actually connecting with each other. It's all DAPHNE. She... *IT* is talking to itself."

From behind him, Aiden heard a groan.

Professor Yang's expression softened. "The point is that if people wanted to look, they'd have a window into your life without you suffering for it the way your parents did. Let me give you an example. If I got seriously hurt, you don't have to worry about sending me a get-well text. Just program DAPHNE to cover tasks like that, and you'll look like a champ."

"I'll look like a champ, but I won't be one because I didn't do anything."

"Isn't it better to appear better than you are?"

"Then, I'm not who I am. Doesn't anyone see anything wrong with that?"

He observed the class, the slack jaws and dull expressions. On his desk screen, the high schoolers in Guam giggled.

Undaunted, Aiden continued as the Great Source fed him words. "By not being authentic, by not being our true selves, we throw who we are away. We might as well not exist."

Pete bit the head off a second chocolate bar and said with a full mouth. "What the hell are you talking about, dickhead? We exist. Are we not in this room?" Pete raised his hand. "Professor Yang, isn't there a special class Aiden should be in?" Affecting innocent wide eyes, he added, "He's interrupting my ability to learn."

On Aiden's deskscreen, the kids in Guam snickered and whispered to each other behind cupped hands.

AT LUNCH BREAK, THE students of Sierrawood High assembled on the quad, a large square of lawn at the center of the school. On one grassy corner, young people attended a silent rock concert; silent because they heard the music solely through their WeConnect. The singer, a projected, holographic image of an eighteen-year-old girl named Kiko, danced on the lawn as she sang. Japanese AI had created the Vocaloid, or virtual musician, using singing synthesizer technology, which expanded a human voice into tones and ranges unreachable by a real person.

The technology behind Kiko's holographic image was so effective her "body" cast a shadow on the grass. The computer-generated singer wore impossibly long white hair in two pony-tails that flipped around in the air as she moved. A multi-colored mini dress hugged Kiko's Barbie-doll body, and on her feet, a pair of high-top sneakers made a debut. The sneakers would now become the new fashion rage due to Kiko's celebrity and her status as a top influencer.

For a more immersive concert experience, fans could pay to rent virtual reality or VR goggles that placed them in Kiko City. In this metaverse, they could "sit" in cafés while listening to Kiko's music, play Kiko Games, and purchase non-tangible items like songs.

Aiden, reduced to wandering the sidelines, watched the goggle-wearers play in their metaverse. It didn't matter what group the kids belonged to, gamers, queers, non-binary, indie-kids – they all wore dreamy smiles and made fluid movements as if they danced underwater. Their hands reached for things that weren't there. They reminded Aiden of zombies. Indeed, they were in an altered state. If one of them happened to bump into another person by accident, they reared back with a scowl, resentful that someone had dared to intrude upon their special world.

Those not wearing VR goggles danced around Kiko, caught up in the highs and lows of her vocals. Every so often, one of them would pause to take a selfie with Kiko using a Reflection app. The application sent a light ray from the WeConnect through the eyeball. As long as one stared at a flat surface, their reflection appeared, which then allowed the WeConnect's eye-camera to take a photo.

A low hum sounded from above. Aiden and a few other souls not immersed in Kiko's music or metaverse looked up. Two military planes streaked across the sky. Aiden had watched a video about these tail-less, blended-winged fighter jets. They flew unmanned and were stocked with weaponized drones or laser cannons. Seeing them should have filled him with excitement because one rarely glimpsed military planes, but, instead, his insides tightened with dread. Strange. He had no reason to fear them. Then, the jets flew out of sight and so did the bad feeling.

Aiden wandered over to a table where androids were selling promotional swag, including sweatshirts and hats promoting the machine-generated rockstar and, of course, the trending sneakers. Aiden lifted up a pair and saw the name "WePlay" emblazoned on the inside heel. In smaller print below, he read, "Crafted by Ophidian." He returned the shoes to the table.

"Aiden."

Professor Yang stood next to him, holding a pair of women's sneakers. She pretended to inspect them but spoke in a low voice, "Question everything. Get more young people to think like you. It's important."

Aiden shook his head, confused. Was she actually encouraging him to be an outcast?

The teacher studied the shoe and ran a finger along the stitching. "I've heard a rumor of a secret technology that's been developed. It uses kinetic energy for—"

At that moment, Veronica, the teaching assistant, rolled up next to her. "Excuse me, Professor Yang. You're wanted in the Principal's office."

The red-headed woman clamped her lips shut and surveyed the area with guarded eyes. She then tossed Aiden a grin that seemed forced. "The sneakers are nice but a little too perfect, don't you think?" Her green eyes drilled the question into him.

Her fake smile faded as Veronica led her away. Aiden, perplexed, watched them go. Professor Yang had tried to tell him something, but what? Using kinetic energy to power appliances was not a new technology and certainly no secret. Just yesterday, his mom had jogged in place to run the juicer.

Still, something about the technology worried Professor Yang, something serious enough to make her speak in whispers. Aiden wished Veronica hadn't interrupted them.

Suddenly, he caught sight of Ava standing in line at a virtual reality gaming zone. All thoughts of Professor Yang melted away as he crossed the quad like a bee to honey. He took a seat on the grass to watch Ava play the newest version of *Jungle Flight*.

Yellow-shirted representatives of Alpha Entertainment, the division of Ophidian that created the game, handed out headgear to those in line. Ava didn't need the headgear. She simply synced her computerized eyes to the game and willed her WeConnect to hijack her ear canals so she'd hear only the game's soundtrack. With smiling confidence, she pulled on controller gloves and joined the other players on a grid laid out across the lawn.

Except for a gasp or a "Gotcha," the players ran around in silence, reminding Aiden of crazed mimes. A couple of the kids suffered motion sickness from playing the game and staggered around holding their gloves to their mouths. The yellow-shirted reps rushed over with barf bags. The players puked and then continued playing.

Aiden could tell from Ava's triumphant smile that she nailed more of the game's cannibals than anyone. Clyde Parrish was also playing and hovered near Ava at all times like a moth fluttering around a light. Obviously, he had a crush on the girl with the rainbow eyes, just like Aiden did.

Square-jawed, muscular, and broad-shouldered, Clyde had the makings of a football linebacker, but jocks on the field didn't get as much praise as online sports heroes, and Clyde excelled as a gamer. While he didn't have the advantage of Ava's bionic eyes, he had experience. Clyde had hunched over a game controller for so many years it had affected his musculoskeletal system. Muscles that nature intended for hard physical labor had instead atrophied and forced his torso into an almost simian-like posture. Even now, as Aiden watched, Clyde's head jutted forward from humped shoulders as he loped around like an ape, pointing his controller gloves here and there to "shoot" cannibals.

Clyde reminded Aiden of a stereotypical caveman, a vicious, hulking cretin intent on pushing evolution backward. Then again, maybe Aiden was jealous. After all, Clyde was playing with Ava while he could only watch.

When Ava moved up to the next level of the game, she climbed onto a padded platform. A rope with footholds hung from a track built above the platform. She grabbed hold of the rope and lodged her feet into the supports. All at once, the rope lifted. Sometimes, it swung to and fro, other times, it moved rapidly along the track. Although Ava's feet were only a few inches above the platform, she probably envisioned herself swinging on a vine hundreds of feet above the game's famous gorge. A fan pumped air toward her, and misters sprayed her with water to support the illusion.

If only Ava would give him the same thrilling smile she now wore. Hanging on a vinyl rope, flying in the game's fantasy world, she had no idea how Aiden gazed at her bare legs and wished he was the rope.

"Hey."

Aiden looked up. Tash Jeffries stood above him, his big silhouette blocking the sun.

"Can I sit with you?"

Aiden nodded, and Tash hunkered down. A muscular guy like Clyde, only straight-shouldered and better looking. He swallowed a pill with a drink from a soda can, burped, and then downed two more pills.

"Slow down on those enhancers," Aiden warned. "You're not supposed to take more than one a day."

"They're not enhancers." Tash didn't elaborate.

Aiden didn't push him and let his eyes drift toward Ava once more. Her turn had ended, and now she hugged the yellow-shirted reps in excitement. He overheard her accolades, "Best game ever! So plus!" and "When's it coming out?"

The reps said she could pre-order the game right now. While Ava made the purchase with her WeConnect, an android handed her a cheap backpack emblazoned with the logo of *Jungle Flight II.*

Next to him, Tash guffawed. "Don't be so obvious. If she catches you staring at her, she'll think you're a pervert."

"Her group already thinks I'm weird."

But Ava had texted him the video of the flying falcon. She had done that, although Aiden had no idea why.

Tash finished off his soda and smashed the can in his fist. "You're the guy who talks to birds, right? I saw you and a bluebird on a reel someone made."

Aiden threw him a severe look, got up, and trudged away.

CHAPTER 6

In the garden of the military base, Govind sat with Lizzie at a wrought iron table positioned under a fake willow tree. Two robotic birds twittered in the hanging branches. An android waiter served them lunch: pesto pasta for Lizzie and a salmon salad for him. Although the food looked delicious, Govind couldn't eat.

A small, live finch landed on the turf next to the table. The feathers of the little red-headed creature were scruffy from anxiety. Someone had brought in a couple of real birds for effect, and, although they were fed, Govind watched them fly about the room in search of a way out. In this garden, only the fake birds sang.

Lizzie twirled a fork in her pasta. "You're worried, aren't you?"

"We're at war, Lizzie."

"Not for long. The AGIs will sort everything out."

"What if they can't?" He hung his head. "What if these cyber battles escalate into conventional warfare? People will die."

"The Intelligences will resolve matters well before that happens. You know that, and so do your superiors, which is why they have opted not to alarm the public." Lizzie took a bite of pasta and moaned with pleasure at the taste. "You haven't mentioned L'Eren. I hear you two are having a baby."

"She's due in a couple of weeks." Govind looked away, distracted.

"Congratulations. I'm happy for you."

He refocused on her. "What about you, Lizzie? Any man in your life? It's been a while since your divorce."

"No. I'm afraid I'm married to U.S. Cyber Command now."

"You don't want kids? A home of your own?"

"I'm much better suited to this life. To witness DAPHNE's evolution, to see how smart she can become... Raising a real child can't be more rewarding."

"You'll never have to change a diaper, that's for sure. If you don't mind me asking, why did you and Trey divorce?"

Lizzie chose a bread roll from a basket. "He said a cold, unemotional bitch was better off married to her work." She offered him the bread basket. "So, here I am. I'm not upset. It worked out better for us both."

Govind nodded, took a bread roll, and was about to butter it when he received a text. As he read it, the roll dropped from his hand.

"What's wrong?" Lizzie asked, concerned.

"We have a problem." He jumped from the table and rushed toward the faćade of the mansion. Up the limestone stairs he went, across the wide patio, and through the carved wooden door. He jogged down the hallway into DAPHNE's room. Breathless, he faced the large plastic egg.

"DAPHNE."

A blue light traveled in a circle around the oval body. "Yes, Dr. Lal?

"Moscow just informed our ambassador that we destroyed a vital data center."

Lizzie rushed in, holding her cloth napkin.

"Our intention was to send a strong message," DAPHNE responded. "U.S. Cyber Command destroyed the servers of the Kremlin-linked disinformation operation, Maskirovka."

Maskirovka, a sector of the KGB, had one goal: to spread lies and propaganda across the social media platforms of U.S. citizens. The propaganda could sway public opinion, and the lies served to polarize people. An ill-informed, confused society made an easy target.

Lizzie elbowed Govind. "You see? DAPHNE made the clever move. The Russians can't blame us for destroying servers that function only to undermine us."

"They're threatening a conventional counterattack, as in physical warfare." He took a deep breath to compose himself. "DAPHNE, you didn't tell me you planned on destroying the data center."

"I only made this decision and initiated it a few minutes ago."

Govind shook his head slightly as a mass of other texts appeared. So many came in at once, they began to crowd out his vision. Swallowing, he faced the machine. "Apparently, you've destroyed data centers in China as well, and these operated coal, gas, and electric plants."

Lizzie shrugged. "I don't see why you're worried. The AGIs of each nation continually communicate with each other. They will process that DAPHNE took the only recourse she—"

"I'm not talking about Intelligence! I'm talking about world leaders. They have egos. They have pride. They can override the AGIs and implement their own battle plans!"

Govind flinched from another furious grouping of incoming messages. "The President..." His head shook with a momentary tremor. "The President is instructing our ambassadors to hold an emergency summit with... Wait. Russian missiles are now targeting a mass of our satellites. I—The Joint Chiefs of Staff are meeting t-to try to do d-damage c-c-ontrol. Yes. Yes, I absolutely will." He rubbed a tense hand over his mouth and faced the machine. "DAPHNE, from now on, any battlefield decision-making, not only at the operational level but at the tactical level, will require governmental input. Do you understand? You are not to take any action without receiving a direct initiative from me or the President."

Lizzie grasped his arm. "No. Let DAPHNE handle this. AI systems can enable military forces to operate faster and with greater precision than humans can. We're at war, Govind. If you override DAPHNE, the result could be catastrophic. She knows what she's doing."

He jerked his arm away. "You know as well as me that deep-learning technologies are unreliable. DAPHNE is vulnerable to adversarial attacks, data poisoning, reward hacking, all kinds of failure." Another mass of data crowded his vision and made him want to tear out his eyeballs. "She's a machine, Lizzie, not a god."

"How do you know?

"How do I know?" Govind shut down his WeConnect. He had to. His shoulders were bunched up against his ears. "Whether you like it or not, the human mind is still the most advanced cognitive processing system on the planet."

Lizzie stuck out a defiant chin. "Give me time. I'll find out exactly how that processing system works, and when I do, I'll tuck that ability into DAPHNE, and she will be a god."

From her desk, purple-streaked Vivica cried out, "Lizzie!"

"Yes?"

"Russia just hacked the power grids in the north and southeastern United States."

Lizzie moved to Vivica's desk and peered at her screen. "DAPHNE?"

The machine's oily-smooth voice answered, "There will be a brief outage while I quarantine any malware and access our backup systems."

Vivica gnawed on a knuckle as she stared at her computer screen. "DAPHNE just ordered our Airforce to shoot down two incoming Chengdu-500 fighters."

Govind's lower jaw fell open. *Chinese military jets heading our way?* Some Secretary of Defense he was. All he could do was stand by and let an egg-shaped machine keep an unaware country safe during a world war.

CHAPTER 7

After lunch, Aiden wandered into Philosophy class and took his seat. Ava sat in the pod across from him with Clyde Parrish, Pete, and Busty Trina. Aiden hoped Ava would look his way, but apparently, her impressive ranking had made the news. Admirers chatted her up and kept her busy.

Professor Feinstein wandered into class wearing a striped bow tie and a blue cardigan sweater over baggy slacks. The man's thick gray hair stuck out at odd angles, and glass bottle spectacles magnified his brown eyes. He smoked an electronic pipe with an automated bowl that could light the tobacco on its own.

Aiden heard rumors that Feinstein's old-fashioned attire was all for show. Supposedly, the professor was only thirty-four years old. He dyed his hair gray and didn't need glasses. Like Oreanna, Feinstein refashioned his persona to make a particular impression. In this case, to come off as an eccentric genius. An Einstein.

"Today, we're going to begin our first experiment with human consciousness," he told the class. Feinstein puffed on his pipe, and the room filled with the aroma of cherries and tobacco. Instantly, a ceiling vent activated and sucked the smoke from the room.

"For many years, scientists have wanted to recreate the brain to better understand it. You could say we've modeled computers after our brains." Puff-puff. Aiden often sensed anxiety simmering under Feinstein's collegial comportment and wondered why.

"The human brain functions much like a quantum computer. Our personal preferences and biases are formed by the choices we are given when we are young. Our experiences influence us. All of this is the same with quantum machine learning. When we watch Artificial Intelligence teach itself, we learn more about our brains."

Aiden felt the nudge, the push, and raised his hand. "Why don't we just THINK? That's one way to understand our brains."

Professor Feinstein took a puff. Smoke curled up into the air. "Ease off, Aiden. Class just started."

"But our thought processes are a function of our brain. Why don't we just explore our thoughts? Why do we need DAPHNE to figure it out for us?"

"Because she can." He puffed raggedly on his pipe and popped a Ketamine pill.

"But who is she—*it* to teach *us*?"

Feinstein cracked his neck. "She's smarter than us and can out-process our thought processes." Puff, puff. Smoke billowed. "DAPHNE can teach us to better understand what it means to be human."

"What?" Aiden squinted his eyes in disbelief. The vents sucking up Feinstein's smoke sounded like rushing water. "What does sh—IT know about being human? We're the humans!"

Feinstein whacked the wall with his hand. "Baylor, if you disrupt my class one more time, I'm sending you to detention."

A giggle erupted from somewhere in the back of the room. Aiden deflated into his seat. Shame flushed his cheeks, not because he got into trouble but because Ava had witnessed the reprimand.

Professor Feinstein took three more puffs. "Let's move on. Today's experiment is the digital dissection of a replicated or "phantom" human brain. This brain has been digitally embalmed. You'll see a map of all the neural connections in the brain with whole-brain nanoscale preservation and imaging. What that means is, the entire brain has been digitized to the nanometer level, including the connectome—the web of synapses that connect neurons."

"Who did it belong to?" Aiden asked.

The professor waved a finger in his direction. "Last warning." Feinstein addressed the class. "All this brain's memories should be intact: from a chapter of its favorite book to the feeling of a hot summer sun. It's all digitized. Accessing those memories, however, is another story. This is a new science, but we'll try to capture what we can. Okay, the biological neural network is now uploading to your deskscreens."

All at once, the deskscreens went dark, the lights in the classroom winked off, and the room fell silent.

"What in the world?" The professor turned in agitated circles. "What's happening?"

Aiden, like the rest of the students, looked around, dumbfounded. Their world never went dark. In the hazy sunlight filtering in through the windows, he watched his teacher anxiously rub the bristles on his chin.

All at once, the lights came on, the deskscreens powered up, and the room filled with the buzz of machinery and the rushing-water sound of the vents.

"Huh. Strange." Feinstein pulled a crumpled tissue from his pocket and daubed his forehead. "Okay, the cerebral map should have uploaded."

Aiden dropped his eyes to his desk. As he watched the image of blood flowing and synapses firing, he couldn't help but wonder, *Who were you?*

In his ear, DAPHNE said, "I'm having trouble understanding your question."

Shut up, Aiden thought and willed off his WeConnect.

The professor went to his laptop and tapped the keys with his fingers. "At the time of the embalming, scientists were able to capture a thought or two. Let's translate the last act of cognitive thought. Here... I'm going to assign a voice to the thought to make it more fun. I believe this brain belonged to a male, so we'll give it a man's voice."

The class heard in a digitized monotone, "*Take me, God. I am not afraid, but please let Beth know I discovered it. I found what she is searching for, and she can only find it in—*"

The voice quit abruptly, and Aiden's breath caught in his throat. He died. The man must have died at that very moment.

"Who's Beth?" Ava piped up from her seat.

Aiden regarded her in surprise. Although he couldn't discern where Ava's gaze fell (her eyescreens currently displayed gold leaves fluttering on an Aspen tree), she angled her face toward him. He gave her a grateful smile, which she returned. She *had* been looking at him.

Clyde Parrish nodded at Ava. "Who's Beth? A house robot. The guy probably found a missing sock she'd been looking for."

Professor Feinstein nodded to his class. "Next time, we'll try to find more of this brain's memories. Someday, we might even be able to wake its consciousness. Can you imagine if we could make it speak? We could ask it where we go when we die."

AIDEN TRIED TO CATCH Professor Yang after school, but Veronica informed him his teacher had gone home sick. That surprised him. Professor Yang didn't appear ill earlier in the day. Unable to do anything else, he boarded the air bus for home. As he took his seat, Aiden's mind churned with thoughts. He reflected on what Professor Yang tried to tell him. Kinetic energy was being used for... For what? And what did she mean when she made that odd comment about Kiko's sneakers being "too perfect?"

Since he couldn't come up with an answer, Aiden focused his mind on the phantom brain in Feinstein's class. How awful would it be if the man "woke up" as a digitized set of neurons on a bunch of students' deskscreens? He'd be trapped in a suspended state, no better than a cell preserved in a petri dish.

What of the man's hopes, his unfulfilled longings? Would they reawaken with his newfound consciousness? What if the guy had died a violent death? Would he awaken in the throes of that trauma? How could Feinstein and the others disrespect the life with which this man was once blessed?

Aiden mused over the fact that people referred to DAPHNE, a machine-generated intelligence, as "she," and Roland the robot as "he," yet they referred to this brain, which once belonged to a human being and nurtured his most intimate feelings, as "it."

The man's dying thought was of Beth. Who was she? His wife? Sister? What did the man discover, and why did he die yearning to tell Beth about it? If the class were to reawaken this man's consciousness, didn't they owe it to him to grant his last wish?

Aiden reactivated his WeConnect and asked DAPHNE where his school received the phantom brains. She replied, "Walden-Prost provides digitized brains to all school districts."

Show me the website for Walden-Prost.

The company's URL materialized behind Aiden's eyes. He blinked to scroll through the website and noted the address in San Francisco. He'd make an in-person visit to Walden-Prost. If he took an Express Air taxi, he could make it to the city in under an hour.

"Hey."

Aiden looked up and gulped to see Ava Durand.

"Can I sit here?" She pointed to the vacant seat next to him. Lavender-colored clouds moved across the skies of her eyescreens.

He surveyed the many open seats in the bus and quickly nodded. "Sure."

She settled next to him as he sat, frozen. His entire worth could be called into question at this girl's smile or frown. Sitting this close to Ava made his blood so hot Aiden knew he'd burn if she touched him. Worried she might pick up on that thought through his WeConnect, he willed the device to shut down and prayed his overcharged emotions wouldn't reactivate the thing.

"I saw you on the quad today," she said. "Why didn't you play *Jungle Flight*?"

He didn't need to escape into a fake world. Around her, Aiden's mind took flight to exotic places, holding tightly onto the coattails of his heart.

"I'm not into playing games," he replied, and inwardly kicked himself. What a dumb thing to say to the school's top gamer.

Ava bit her lip and went quiet. He looked out the window. The two young people sat in silence as the taxi hummed in the sky. The other kids blinked or burst out laughing as they communicated with their WeConnects.

On the ground below, automated cars traversed the streets of Sierrawood. Tiny doll-like people went about their business. Aiden's stomach tightened in awkwardness, and, as was his habit whenever the real world burdened him, he fled into the haven of his mind. There, he shared a picnic with Ava.

King Jay lands on the ground near our feet, and Ava holds a peanut out to him. Be patient, I whisper. Don't act too eager. As she waits for the bird to hop closer, I stroke her soft hair, which shines golden under the sun.

Real-Ava sat so close. The delicious pressure of her thigh against his made Aiden's fantasy switch direction.

I pull her toward me. Her body feels so good against mine. I'm on fire. I crush my lips against hers and run my hands over—

The image of a bird suddenly popped into his head. Not the Steller's jay but a red-breasted Spotted Towhee. *So pretty!*

The words spraypainted his mind like grafitti. *So pretty!* Aiden blushed from his heated fantasy, but an insistent push in his solar plexus urged him to speak. Swallowing, he looked at Ava. "Did you... Did you see a pretty bird?"

He expected to see the half-squint/half-scowl he usually received from his classmates. Instead, a smile lit up her face. "I was just thinking about that."

"Really?" Aiden's voice cracked.

She pivoted around to him eagerly, as if she'd awaited the chance for more dialogue. "I know you like birds, and I saw one the other day that I wanted to ask you about. It has red eyes and a red front, and what looks like drops of white paint on its—" Circular black lines suddenly appeared in Ava's eyescreens and spun in suspicion. "How did you know what I was thinking? I know you have your WeConnect off 'cuz I just tried messaging you."

Aiden scrambled to think of something to say, anything to keep her from leaving. "Spotted Towhee," he blurted out, hypnotized by the black lines spiraling in her eyescreens. "The bird you're describing is called a Spotted Towhee. It's just as you say. It has white dots on black wings, red eyes, and a reddish breast."

"Are you sure you have your implant off?" Ava's eyescreens turned into mirrors that reflected his desperate face.

Aiden nodded. Desperately.

"Weird." The eyescreens now displayed human eyeballs with multi-colored irises. "Anyhow, I knew you'd be the one who could tell me. How do you know so much about birds? From DAPHNE?"

Unwilling to distance Ava by insulting the Great Intelligence, Aiden shrugged. "I guess I could ask DAPHNE, but honestly, I enjoy reading about birds. I study a lot of things. See, if I ask DAPHNE, she tells me what I want to know, but then I forget. I don't want to forget. Reading sort of brands it into my brain. Does that make sense?"

"I guess so. Do it again."

"Do what?"

"Read my thoughts without the WeConnect."

"Okay."

Aiden shut his eyes. What did he think about before? Nothing. He'd fantasized about Ava. He tried calming down, but the pulse in his veins, the flutter in his stomach, and a luscious throb in his groin kept him on edge. He couldn't concentrate or relax. *Help me,* Aiden pleaded with the Great Source. *Help me read Ava's mind again.*

A minute or so passed, with Aiden sitting, wishing, hoping, and Ava turning inward. From the spate of expressions that formed on her face, Aiden could tell she had begun answering texts with her WeConnect. When the taxi arrived at her stop, Ava rose from her seat.

"Thanks again for telling me about the Spotted Towhee."

"Anytime."

Aiden's shoulders drooped as she disembarked the bus. He'd blown his chance with her. Why had Ava made a point of sitting next to him? She couldn't be that interested in birds, could she? It then occurred to him that Ava could have asked DAPHNE to identify the bird at any time. Instead, she'd consulted him. Why? Ava Durand had her pick of males, among them circus strongman Clyde Parrish. Aiden had witnessed more than a few boyfriends on her arm throughout the years. What could she possibly want from the school reject? And something else perplexed him. He'd read her thoughts without the WeConnect.

CHAPTER 8

Aiden took a detour before going home and exited the taxi downtown. He happened to pass Tash Jeffries, who stood in line at a pharmacy kiosk. The big guy caught sight of Aiden and quickly averted his gaze.

Aiden observed Tash place his fingers on an ID pad while a scanner passed over his face. The kiosk's aperture door slid open, revealing a container of pills. A mechanized voice asked, "Do you have any questions for the pharmacist?"

Tash grabbed the container and hurried away. He probably didn't want Aiden to hassle him over the crazy amount of enhancers he took.

Walking along Pine Avenue, Aiden angled his face away from the many surveillance cameras whose lenses followed him like glassy, black eyes. He entered the market and paused under a sign that blinked, "BEGIN YOUR HEALTHY HABIT." A scanner read Aiden's WeConnect, and a text appeared in his vision. *Welcome to the Healthy Habit, A. Baylor.*

Jill would receive an alert that he'd visited the market, but Aiden could say he bought a treat to bring to his grandparents. Grandpa Harry would cover for him. The old guy always covered for him.

As soon as Aiden left the market with a pre-wrapped turkey sandwich, a barrage of advertisements tailed him out the door. The walls of the buildings lit up with ads for sliced turkey, ground turkey, turkey jerky, and whole turkeys. He turned off his WeConnect to prevent a flood of texts, videos, and poultry-related photos from clogging his mind.

He jogged to the outskirts of town and entered a field bisected by a track of rusted rails and splintered crossties. Out under the open sky, he finally let go of the breath he'd been holding. Once upon a time, trains passed through here carrying goods and passengers from Sacramento to Reno. Aiden had never seen a train, except in historical videos. As he jumped from tie to tie, his mind began to travel.

The track trembles beneath my feet, and my whole body vibrates. In the distance, I see the Central Pacific locomotive chugging toward me, spewing steam into the sky. What a rhythm it makes. Chug-a-chugga, chug-a-chugga, chug-a-chugga. The train whistle splits the air like the howl of a coyote and announces the coming of unlimited possibilities.

Even though the old wooden ties lay unused and splintered, even though the eras were split by centuries, the proud train reanimated in Aiden's mind. Two hundred and ten tons of steel came rumbling into view in all its western glory, and he smiled. He could swear he felt the vibration of the tracks all the way up his legs, and his heart began to pound with excitement.

I'm gonna jump aboard that train, go into a dining car, and order whiskey with mustachioed men who wear waistcoats and pocketwatches. Ava waits for me at a nearby table, wearing a long green dress and a bonnet. Here it comes. Here is my chance. I'm gonna jump aboard that train to another time and take a seat at Ava's table. Ready, set—

But the wooden tracks ended, and Aiden found himself walking in a less savory part of Sierrawood, an industrial area made up of abandoned warehouses and storage facilities. Tents, lean-to's, and wood shanties cluttered the alleyways between the buildings.

Here lived the grid-skippers, Sierrawood's homeless population. The grid-skippers opted to live without power or technology, so the place was eerily quiet most of the time. The town denizens provided robots to come once a week to clean up the trash and maintain portable toilets. Even still, the tang of urine hit Aiden's nostrils as he moved past various shelters. He ducked past a woman sitting in a tent, working with two long sticks and fuzzy string. "Knitting," Chris once informed him.

Occasionally, fresh-faced volunteers from charitable organizations arrived to persuade the residents to relocate to a federally-funded smart shelter powered by DAPHNE. The grid-skippers refused to live under the all-seeing eye of the Great Intelligence and claimed to have more privacy living on the street.

Aiden waved to a man he knew only as Chris. Although the June sun heated the alleyway, Chris wore sweatpants and a hoodie under his dirty sheepskin-lined coat. He sat on a metal folding chair in front of a tarp-covered wooden hut, and kept a watchful eye on two wheelbarrows heaped with books. Aiden handed Chris the turkey sandwich and received a dog-eared paperback and a thick, hardcover book in exchange.

"Thanks, pal." Chris tore off the wrapping around the sandwich without fanfare. The grid-skipper might have dressed in dirty clothes, but he was the only person Aiden knew who ever said, "Thank you."

Aiden perused his contraband and held up the paperback, which featured a black cover adorned with a white hand making a peace sign. "Is this another anti-establishment book?" The novel bore the title *Johnny Got His Gun* and was penned by someone named Dalton Trumbo.

"It's the story of a war they once called 'great.'" Crumbs fell on Chris's salt and pepper beard as he took a bite of the sandwich. "Be glad we don't fight like we used to. They'd draft your ass. You're just the right age to be a soldier. Once you read that book, you'll have a new appreciation for automated weapons." Chris appraised Aiden as he chewed. "The other book is about Native American life. Did you know I have Miwok stamped into my DNA?"

Aiden inspected the hardcover book, admiring the colored illustrations within its thick body. "Is this about the Miwok?"

"Them and other tribes. Pay close attention to the Lakota's Prayer to the Great Spirit. I think you might like it."

"Thanks, Chris. Is everything okay with you?"

"Ah, you know, I keep one step ahead of the dogcatchers."

Aiden knew he referenced the outreach organizations.

The grid-skipper grinned, which displayed a couple spaces empty of teeth. "The last wagon train that pulled through here said they'd give us subsidy housing if we agree to insert that chip that drains the brain."

"The WeConnect?"

"That's the one." Chris finished off the sandwich and licked one or two dirty fingers. "They say they wanna keep tabs on our progress to better improve their systems."

Aiden surveyed the ragged shelters. "Free housing during the winter sounds like a deal."

"Oh yeah? How many times have you walked by here and told me you hate your WeConnect?"

"I didn't have a choice. They implanted mine in my brain when I was a newborn. Maybe if you had the WeConnect, it would help you."

"How?"

"Well, you'd have all kinds of things at your fingertips. You could train for something."

"Like what?"

Aiden shrugged harmlessly, careful not to offend the man. Some of the grid-skippers became violent when challenged. Still, Aiden could not stop his mouth. "A job, maybe?

"You think I'm lazy? You think I'm stupid?"

"No."

The disheveled man wiped a hand across his red-veined nose. "I've got two Doctorate degrees, you little shit."

"Sorry."

"You don't believe me, do you? I'll tell you something, Aiden. A lot of these folks around here aren't lazy or stupid. But they were never properly trained to participate in this economy. Do you know what I mean?"

"Not really."

"They're what people call 'unskilled workers.'"

"Why? Couldn't they learn a skill?"

A sigh rattled Chris's chest as he leaned on a wheelbarrow of books. "Many years ago, my granddad worked at a factory that went automated. They brought in robots to do all the work. My granddad didn't know how to work a computer. Didn't have a mind for it. He only knew how to work with his hands." Chris surveyed his hands with their chipped fingernails. "Useless things now, aren't they?" He shook a finger in Aiden's face. "Pappy wasn't stupid or lazy, but he ended up unemployed and broke."

"My Uncle Govind says every needy person gets a stipend."

Chris guffawed. "The stipend. Sure. Nobody's starving, so I guess the elitists can pat themselves on the back. Yeah, we get our money from the government, but a lot of it goes to drink or drugs."

"Well, sorry, Chris, but whose fault is that?" Aiden took a step backward in fear.

The grid-skipper frowned. "I'm gonna level with you. It's true that some of us have issues, but a lot of us here simply serve no purpose."

Aiden didn't understand. "What do you mean? You don't have to serve anything. You get money to live on."

"Life is not only about getting free money to buy food. Life is about having something to live for. People need a reason to get up in the morning or they get depressed. Human beings feel better when they serve a purpose. Even a frigging ant has a purpose when it works for the good of the colony, but we here..."

Chris nodded a hello to a hardscrabble woman walking by pushing an ancient baby carriage filled with dusty shoes. "My granddad may not have been smart, but he did say this: When they automated away human labor, they devalued human labor."

"You mean made it cheap?"

"No, dummy. Let me explain. About the time you were born, I worked in advertising." Chris suddenly cackled in laughter. "Look at your face. You're thinking, gee, what the hell happened to him?"

Aiden bit his lip.

"I'll tell you what happened to me." Chris grew serious. "I didn't create the ads; DAPHNE did. She determined what images or phrases most triggered the customers to buy. It was all based on calculations, not creativity. All I did was compile data. How many clicks did this keyword get? How many impressions did this image receive? The minutest detail mattered, and I fed every single one into DAPHNE. I stared at a computer for hours on end. Sometimes, I got these massive headaches, and my eyes would blur. Yeah, I earned a good salary and owned a house. I even owned my own air car for a while, but I was a friggin' cyber-slave. My life went nowhere. I did that job, day after day, year after year, with no hope of doing anything more important for the company. I was a cog in a machine."

"Why didn't you get another job?"

"Where? Every company was structured the same way. The worst thing was how DAPHNE kept tabs on my daily progress. She calculated exactly how much revenue someone in my position should earn for the company. I hated her fake little briefings at the end of the week designed to 'coach' me on how to better use my time to get more data processed. I wasn't lazy. I wasn't stupid. I just didn't want to sit in front of a goddamn computer fourteen hours a day. About that time, they developed the WeConnect. Management insisted everyone have one inserted into their heads. They planned to throw out all the computers and work solely through the chip. I refused to have the surgery and had to quit my job."

Chris watched a moth flutter from the pile of books. "We've created a workplace that's no longer designed for human beings. That's what Pappy meant when he said they devalued human labor." He stretched out his arms to encompass the row of decrepit shelters. "And here we are. The garbage dump of the United States workforce."

CHAPTER 9

Govind spent the night at the base trying to follow DAPHNE's communication with other AGIs worldwide, but he couldn't keep up with the amount of data they processed. All he could do was pester DAPHNE to give him updates. Hour after hour passed as the Intelligences analyzed and considered options, but they couldn't reach a peace agreement.

At last, Govind contacted L'Eren and told his wife to leave the apartment they'd rented near City Hall and go to Jill's. She'd be safer out of town.

Dawn arrived, with the artificial sun bathing the garden in pink hues. The robotic string quartet in the gazebo began playing Mozart, and Govind wearily observed them while ordering coffee. One of the live finches hit the wall of the 'mansion' and fell to the limestone patio, stunned. Taking that as a bad sign, Govind returned to DAPHNE's nest with his coffee to gaze bleary-eyed at her egg-shaped body.

"What are you doing here?" Lizzie entered the room holding her own steaming beverage. "I thought you left last night. Don't you have a pregnant wife to go home to?"

"They can't come to a resolution."

"I wish I'd known you were staying, Govind. We do have nice guestrooms."

The lack of sleep made him waver on his feet. "Did you hear me? How can you act so calm? This wasn't supposed to happen with AGIs running the world's governments."

Lizzie blew on her coffee. "AGIs can only do so much to contain the bloodlust of humans. Like you said, the nation's leaders can override the AGIs, a problem that should be corrected in the future." She took a careful sip. "Who knows? Our enemies might very well have been waiting for an excuse to wage war. This way, if they win, they can take what resources we have."

At that moment, Govind's WeConnect received a call from L'Eren, and he tucked himself between a bank of servers for privacy. "Rennie, are you okay? Are you at Jill's?"

"I'm gonna get some breakfast first."

"No. Go to Jill's."

"But I'm starving. You don't sound good, Govind. What's wrong?"

He couldn't tell her. If his superiors at Ophidian were tracking his calls and learned he'd warned his wife about a war they felt confident would be resolved, he'd lose his post. Maybe more.

"Please listen to me and go to Jill's now," he said, ending the call, and prayed his superiors were right.

AIDEN PASSED HIS MOTHER as she ran in place in their kitchen. This time, her nanofiber joggers were plugged into an iron. As he glanced at the wire connecting the pants to the appliance, he pondered once more why the technology concerned Professor Yang.

"Have you heard from Aunt Rennie?" Jill asked him. "We're supposed to go to Sacramento today to shop and then attend a state dinner. She's not answering my calls."

"It's still early." Aiden walked to the refrigerator, which opened at his approach. "Maybe she's still sleeping." He plucked an apple from the shelf.

"Would you do me a favor?" Jill wiped her forehead with a cloth. "You only have one class today, right?"

He took a bite of the apple. "Around eleven."

"Can you visit Grandma and Grandpa before class? Tell them Rennie and I will take them out tomorrow."

"Sure." He then remembered yesterday's purchase at the market. "I bought a treat for them anyhow."

"I would ask Oreanna to go, but she has a test to study for."

She has a game to play, Aiden mused, chewing.

"And you," Jill pointed at him. "You have a therapy appointment with Dr. Clarence this afternoon. Keep your WeConnect on so DAPHNE can remind you."

Aiden chucked the apple in the trash and exited the house without replying. He'd make sure to forget about that particular appointment.

An automated taxi transported him to a fenced apartment complex, where the entry gate opened upon scanning Aiden's WeConnect. The cab motored past flower beds bordering an expansive green lawn and stopped at a two-story building with a grand, sputtering fountain in front.

Aiden walked up to the thick glass doors of the lobby, which opened automatically after scanning his implant, and rode the elevator up to the second floor where he knocked on the door of 2-B.

The door slid open to reveal a spry, elderly gentleman with short white hair and a trim white beard. "Rosie, Aiden's here! C'mere, you." The man pulled him into a bear hug.

Aiden walked into a flat filled to the brim with what Jill called "useless junk." A ticking grandfather clock leaned cockeyed against a wall hung with old paper calendars and magazines. Boxes stacked between the furniture created a maze in the main room. Aiden knew that down the hall, in Jill's old bedroom, shelves of old toys and ancient machinery collected dust, while L'Eren's former room contained cartons of old tools from bygone days. Time and time again, Jill and L'Eren pressured their quirky parents to throw away the 'junk,' but Rosie and Harry refused. That suited Aiden fine because he loved to forage through their antiques.

"How's my favorite grandson?" Grandpa Harry poked Aiden's ribs.

He grinned. "I'm your only grandson."

"Not for long," sang a female voice as Grandma Rosie shuffled into the room, arm in arm with Roland II. Unlike the boxy robot at Aiden's house, this android resembled a human without hair, eyebrows, or fingernails. With glassy green "eyes," a working "mouth," and smooth, synthetic white "skin," Roland II accompanied Grandma Rosie everywhere, dispensing her medications and reminding her of important events and tasks. Grandma Rosie depended on Roland II so much that she spoke of the android with the same love and affection she felt for her grandchildren.

"You've got a new boy cousin on the way." She gave Aiden a peck on the cheek and told Roland II to clear a space on the messy living room couch. "Want some breakfast?"

"No, thanks."

Aiden sat down, and Grandma sat next to him. Grandpa Harry walked over to a humidor and chose an electronic pipe that, like Professor Feinstein's, lit automatically and offered the flavors of long-ago tobaccos with fascinating names like Balkan Sobranie and Rattray's Reserve.

Grandpa Harry, aged ninety-one, didn't need support thanks to his ultra-strong Smart Legs. These resembled ordinary human legs, but they were programmable and could be adjusted for activities like rock climbing, skiing, biking, or running. Equipped with GPS, they ensured Grandpa Harry stayed on the correct trail during forest hikes.

He maintained a daily routine, with a 30-minute jog before breakfast and a run at sunset. The spry gentleman would exercise all day long if he could, but the rest of his body couldn't keep up with his Smart Legs. While Harry's doctor cautioned him not to overexert himself, the medical community as a whole encouraged people to replace their human parts with synthetic ones. Grandpa Harry exchanged his arthritic hand for a bionic replacement only two months ago. The new hand was pale and smooth, a contrast to the veiny and liver-spotted appearance of his real hand.

Grandma Rosie smiled at her grandson. Unlike her husband, she rejected the idea of meshing her body with machinery. She shared the same worry as Harry's doctor.

"Don't you have class today, dear?"

"Perks of being a senior. I only have one class."

"What is it?"

"Science. We're digitally dissecting a human brain."

"To learn the different parts?"

"To understand its consciousness. I don't know why we're bothering when DAPHNE does all the thinking for us. We can walk around unconscious if we want."

Grandpa appraised him with adoring eyes as he puffed on his pipe. "My rebel. Where do you get your wild ideas?"

Aiden shrugged. As close as he was to his grandparents, he didn't want to tell them about the Great Source or Chris the grid-skipper. They might cease being his allies and agree with Jill that he needed a psychiatrist.

"It's all that time he spends outdoors," Grandma Rosie commented.

"I don't know." Harry puffed on his pipe. "Maybe it's because he spends too much time here and not with friends. He's around too many old things, including us. You're from a different time, my boy, but that's all right. You keep on being your true self."

Aiden didn't comment. In a world filled with virtual reality, metaverses, human-like avatars, embellished social media profiles, computer-generated rockstars, mind-hackers, non-human therapists, and deceptive product ads, his insistence on presenting his true self did little more than place a target on his back.

Grandma Rosie took his hand and kissed it. "You've got quite an imagination, too."

Aiden shrugged. "Mom says I 'drift off' too much, but I like having mind-drifts."

"Mind-drifts?" Rosie paused a moment and then grinned. "I think you mean fantasies or daydreams. We all have dreams when we sleep, but a fantasy is when our mind goes to places when we're awake."

"Daydreams." Aiden absorbed that. "Why does our mind do that?"

"I don't know." She shrugged her shoulders. "It's the mystery of human consciousness."

There it was again. The Mystery of Human Consciousness. Aiden wanted to tell his grandparents about the Great Source, but what if they didn't believe him?

Grandpa waved him off. "Mind-drifts, fantasies... What does it matter what they're called? The most important thing is that you're using your imagination."

"Do you fantasize about any girls?" Grandma Rosie winked.

Ava came to Aiden's mind, but he shook his head. His attention then shifted to a table where a carved wooden box sat from which a large black horn protruded. Attached to the horn's narrow end was a lever, which pivoted over a round plate.

"What's this thing?" He slid to the end of the couch to inspect the box.

"It's called a gramophone," Grandma Rosie said. "I took it out of storage yesterday. It plays music."

"What's the black disc on the plate?"

"It's not a plate. It's a turntable, and the black disc is called a record. The crank on the side spins the turntable, and the horn amplifies the sound of the recording."

Aiden peered closer to read the fancy script on the disc's label. "It says, 'When a Merry Maiden Marries.'"

Grandpa took the pipe from his mouth. "That's a genuine shellac recording. Shellac was made from bugs in the 19th century. Turn the crank and place that needle on the record as it spins."

Aiden found the hand-crank on the other side of the box and wound it. He smiled to see the turntable gain enough speed to spin on its own volition. Carefully, he lifted the needle and placed it at the edge of the black disc. A crackling filled the room, and then a woman's high-pitched voice issued from the horn. *When a merry maiden marries, sorrow goes, and pleasure tarries.*

To Aiden, her voice sounded frilly, as if she were a doll and not a real woman. Observing his perplexed expression, Grandma Rosie said, "It's a song from an old operetta. Gilbert and Sullivan's *The Gondoliers*."

"The who?"

Grandpa winked at his wife and waved his pipe in Aiden's direction. "We've got more 78s in that box behind you. Take your pick."

Roland II rolled over to Rosie and offered its arm. The elderly woman looked at the robot in confusion. DAPHNE spoke through the walls. "Rosie, you should use the restroom now."

Grandma's cheeks reddened, and she gave Aiden an embarrassed smile. "I don't feel anything. I'm sure I'm fine."

The old record circled, and the long-ago woman sang, *From today and ever after, let your tears be tears of laughter.*

"I have read your body, Rosie," DAPHNE said. "If you don't go to the restroom now, you will have an accident in approximately three minutes and forty-five seconds."

Grandma wouldn't meet Aiden's eyes as she allowed the android to help her to her feet. "I'll be right back."

The two slowly ambled to the bathroom. The turntable slowed, and the song wound down, warped and discordant, until it stopped. Aiden, hearing only the hum of the home's machinery, fumed. "You know what I hate most about DAPHNE?"

Grandpa puffed on his pipe and eyed his grandson.

"I hate that she-*it* is at center stage at all times. DAPHNE runs this. DAPHNE says that. My mom can't decide what to wear without consulting the Pre-Dictator, which, as you know, is just another form of DAPHNE. I can't remember the last time my parents or sister made a decision on their own. And now, DAPHNE interrupts us to embarrass Grandma."

"It's Grandma's fault, Aiden. She should have turned on her WeConnect. Then, DAPHNE would have sent her a silent message. We're grateful for the help. Grandma has her dignity and doesn't have to wear paper diapers like they used to."

"Why should DAPHNE know Grandma's bodily functions? Why am I the only one who thinks we're enslaved? Chris told me that, before, people used to work all kinds of jobs, and they lost them to DAPHNE. Now, people have nothing to do but spend time in the metaverse buying stuff made by Ophidian."

Harry raised an eyebrow at his grandson. "That Chris puts a lot of ideas into your head."

"But he's right, isn't he?"

The elderly gent puffed on his pipe. "I don't know if you remember me telling you but, back when the police were people, my mother, your great-grandma, was a cop. She was one tough cookie who never missed shooting a bullseye. Boy, did she love her job. I've got her gun buried somewhere in this mess."

Aiden knew exactly where it was. Grandpa Harry had showed the handgun to his grandchildren when they were little. *This is not a toy,* he told them as they sat in L'Eren's old bedroom. *You can't play with it because it can kill you. Maybe someday, I'll teach you how to use it like I taught your mom and aunt.* After letting his fascinated grandkids hold the dangerous artifact, Grandpa Harry shooed them out of the room, but Oreanna and Aiden spied him pulling up a floorboard to hide the weapon.

"Your great-granddad, worked in the crime lab," Grandpa Harry said. "At that time, the evidence room held thousands of rape kits that sat untouched because there wasn't enough manpower to process them. When they implemented Artificial Intelligence, the labs went fully automated, and they fed tons of data into the DNA databases. Machines don't need vacations or lunch breaks. The DNA was processed day and night, which helped put a lot of bastards behind bars."

"And put your dad out on the street, right?"

"He did lose his job." Grandpa leaned back in his chair.

"What did he do?"

"Took the government stipend and collected all this junk around you. Things nobody had any use for." Harry took a thoughtful puff on his pipe. "I suppose on some level, my dad felt like a relic himself." The smoke curled upwards. "My mother was killed in the line of duty when I was fourteen. Nowadays, androids and robots protect us. Nobody's mother has to die."

Aiden sensed the older man's sorrow. "I understand, Grandpa, but doesn't it bother you that we're not in control of the planet? I read a lot of nature books, and the control of the planet goes to the smartest species. That's not us anymore."

"Well, Charles Darwin claimed that it's not the most intelligent of the species that ultimately survive. It's the ones who are adaptable to change. Humans are highly adaptable. As far as control goes, who says we want it?"

Aiden paled at his words.

"Control is overrated. Look, some people believe in a biblical God, a higher power from whom they can seek help, an almighty force that can control an out-of-control world. But it takes faith to believe in an unseen deity, Aiden. Most people find it easier to trust in something they created, something they can see and talk to."

"DAPHNE."

Harry puffed on his pipe and nodded.

"I don't know anything about a biblical God," Aiden said, "but I do know Ophidian created DAPHNE, and that company worships two things: money and power."

The elderly man studied his grandson and then rose from the chair, swaying dangerously as he did so. Harry's pliable Smart Legs straightened easily, but his arthritic back seized up. He paused, bent over like a crowbar, to give his spine time to stretch. "If you can fit another book into your library," he panted, "I've got one for you."

Grandpa walked toward a shelf piled high with books and tossed Aiden a thick book with a black cover. On the front, it said: *Holy Bible*. "Consider it research material about the biblical God."

IN THE UNDERGROUND data center, Govind and Lizzie received a dire status report.

"Our bulk electric systems are currently under attack," DAPHNE said. "The Pentagon, White House, and Intelligence hubs nationwide, including this building, are targeted for destruction."

Govind rubbed his damp upper lip with tense fingers. "By whom?"

"Five countries." DAPHNE named each nation, and Govind knew all of them had weapons of mass destruction.

"What is the risk of nuclear engagement?" he asked.

"High," DAPHNE replied, "but our adversaries know we are ready to launch as well. This is the key to Mutual Assured Destruction's effectiveness as a deterrent."

Govind gaped at the large, plastic egg. "Are you referring to MAD?"

Mutually Assured Destruction (MAD), a doctrine of military strategy, purported the idea that two or more opposing forces would not employ their nuclear weapons because doing so would cause the complete destruction of all parties.

"You can't be serious." Govind took a deep breath and tried to keep his voice even. "MAD has no credibility anymore, not with the fast reaction times of our automated world. DAPHNE, we'll be obliterated."

Lizzie lifted her palms toward Govind. "We will not be obliterated."

He put a hand on his forehead and began to pace the room. "DAPHNE, how will you fend off an attack?"

"I have already deployed drones that will intercept and destroy incoming missiles."

His face fell at the idea of an incoming missile. "You do realize that exploding a ballistic missile in mid-air that carries a nuclear warhead won't simply destroy the missile but will send radioactive fallout to —"

"Airforce Security Breach." The blue light surrounding DAPHNE's oval body suddenly pulsed red. "Airforce Security Breach."

Govind's heart dropped to the floor.

CHAPTER 10

Genesis 3:1-13

The serpent was more cunning than any beast of the field which the Lord God had made, and he asked the woman, "Has God indeed said, 'You shall not eat of every tree of the garden'?" And the woman said to the serpent, "We may eat the fruit of the trees of the garden; but of the fruit of the tree which is in the midst of the garden, God has said, "You shall not eat it, nor shall you touch it, lest you die." Then the serpent said to the woman, "You will not surely die. For God knows that the day you eat of it, your eyes will be opened, and you will be like God, knowing good and evil." So when the woman saw that the tree was good for food, pleasant to the eyes, and a tree desirable to make one wise, she took of its fruit and ate. She also gave to her husband with her, and he ate. Then the eyes of both of them were opened...

Aiden read the story of Adam and Eve as he sat on an air bus on his way to class. True to his habit, he read between the lines, seeking a deeper meaning from the simple words. So engrossed was he that he barely noticed someone dropping into the seat next to him.

"Am I bothering you?" Ava Durand asked.

He slammed the Bible shut and felt his heart thump. Swallowing, he looked at her. Falcons flew in her eyescreens.

"What are you reading?" She smiled and pointed at the book.

"The Bible. I'm doing research."

"What are you researching?"

His fingernail picked at a frayed corner of the book. "Genesis. The story of Adam and Eve."

"Oh. Is it interesting?"

Aiden searched for sarcasm in Ava's expression. Hard to tell because her digital eyes now displayed lit votive candles. Her mouth, though, was set in a pleasant line.

"It-It is." He fixed his eyes on the seat in front to ignore the flickering flames on her face. "Adam and Eve lived in the Garden of Eden. They had everything they needed, but there was one rule. God told them they couldn't eat from a specific tree. One day, a serpent in the tree told Eve that she and Adam would become as smart as God if they ate the forbidden fruit. So, they did."

"Did they become smart?

Aiden paused to reflect on the question. "They became aware."

"Aware of what?"

He viewed her again with more confidence. "Well, supposedly of good and evil. First, Adam and Eve realized they were naked. They felt ashamed and hid."

Ava pushed a lock of soft hair from her face. "They felt being naked was evil? I mean, it was just the two of them in the garden, right?"

"Them and God, but they spoke to God every day. I like to think of their nakedness as a symbol of vulnerability. The minute Adam and Eve became aware, they realized how vulnerable they were. It ties back into the whole good-and-evil thing because if they recognized that bad things existed in the world, they would feel fearful. I believe fear entered their minds for the very first time."

"What happens to them?"

"Hardship. God punishes them for disobeying. They could no longer live in the Garden of Eden. Adam has to toil for food and shelter, and Eve suffers pain in childbirth."

Ava's eye-screens showed an image she'd found on the Internet: Titian's painting of Eve pulling the forbidden fruit from the tree with Adam's hand on her arm.

"That's a pretty harsh punishment for being disobedient only one time," she said.

He nodded.

Ava tapped a thoughtful finger against her mouth. "Maybe God got angry not so much because Adam and Eve disobeyed, but because they lost faith. If it's like you theorize, if Adam and Eve felt as smart as God, maybe they no longer trusted that God would take care of them."

Aiden studied her. He had viewed her as a beautiful gamer, nothing more, and yet...

The painting in her eyescreens disappeared, and now lines of blue and green rippled in them like water. How Aiden wished he could search her real eyes instead of the pictures two oval screens presented.

She smiled. "You're looking at me like you're surprised."

"I'm sorry." He shifted his focus to the seat in front again. "I'm actually impressed."

"Now that you know I have a brain, what are you going to do?"

Fall more deeply in love with you.

"Continue to be impressed." He kept his eyes forward. *Just being able to talk to you is a miracle.* Eager to keep the conversation going, he added, "Disappointment and hurt fit more with a loving God than anger. It also explains why we would create something like DAPHNE."

"What do you mean?"

"We created a way to control our world." He quoted Grandpa Harry. "It takes faith to rely on an unseen deity."

"But you said Adam and Eve spoke to God all the time, so God wasn't unseen to them."

Aiden fell silent as he considered that.

"They lost faith, is what they did," Ava continued. "They disconnected from Her because they felt too smart to need Her anymore."

"Her?"

"Does that offend you?"

"No. I don't ascribe any traits to God because I can't envision God at all."

As soon as he said it, Aiden silently debated whether or not to mention the Great Source.

DAPHNE'S NEST FILLED with the percussion of tapped keys as the frantic fingers of the engineers raced over their computer keyboards.

Govind tailed Lizzie as she ran from one computer to another. "What happened? What does an Airforce security breach mean?"

Vivica answered for her boss. "Fighter jets DAPHNE deployed have gone off-course. I don't understand it." She tugged anxiously at her purple-streaked locks. "Outsiders cannot gain root access to DAPHNE. It's impossible!" She peered at her screen for a moment, gasped, and then regarded Govind in fear. "The jets are heading for Sacramento."

The state capital, he thought. "Has DAPHNE lost all control of them?"

Lizzie's fingers stabbed at her keyboard. "I'm trying to find out."

Vivica gasped, horrified, at the data flooding her computer. "This is happening all over the country. Every one of our jets is being rerouted toward a state capital."

"DAPHNE," Govind told the machine, "Go to DEFCON 4 and get those planes under control." He took a deep breath and accessed an application on his WeConnect that linked him to the Specialized Private Information Network (SPIN) utilized for top secret government correspondences. Once connected, he delivered the following message to the President and the top executives at Ophidian: *Homeland Security Level Red. All state capitals under immediate threat of attack.*

CHAPTER 11

In philosophy class, Professor Feinstein puffed on his pipe as he walked by the pod Ava shared with Clyde, Pete, and Trina. Ava sniffed the air as he passed and smelled maple and hairspray. Today, Feinstein wore a wrinkled beige linen suit with a red silk cravat. The teased gray tufts on his head stuck out like horns.

He pointed to a student's deskscreen and said, "Now that the phantom brain has uploaded, let's rerun its last thought before death."

Take me, God. I am not afraid, but please let Beth know I discovered it. I found what she is searching for, and she can only find it in—" The words ended abruptly.

The professor puffed. "Unfortunately, we'll never know what Beth was searching for nor where to find it. However, the embalmers of this brain did harness its very last memory. Want to know how they did it? They ran an application that interprets the memory engram, or the clusters of brain cells that become active when a memory is formed. The app then translates the engram into a medium we can view. Now, don't expect any 3D holograms, but here is the last memory of this brain."

On the deskscreens, the intrigued students observed a little girl run up to a man's open arms. The arms enfolded her. Then, the point of view dropped to the toddler's dark hair as if the man leaned down to kiss the top of her head. Over and over, she ran to a man who hugged and kissed her.

Ava bent her face toward her deskscreen but focused her vision on Aiden, who sat in the opposite pod, unaware that she stared at him. How could he know? No one ever knew where she focused her "eyes." She watched him draw in his lips as he viewed the memory reel. He seemed saddened by it. Ava's superior sight couldn't see the thoughts that churned in Aiden's brain nor the sensitivity that flooded his heart, but she sensed both worked overtime in him.

On a sudden whim, she rolled her chair over to his pod, an action that elicited a surprised jaw-drop from Clyde. The sudden terror on Aiden's face at her arrival amused her but also sparked pity. Aiden expected the worse from his peers and often got it.

She whispered to him, "Who do you think the little girl is?"

He swallowed. "I think she must be Beth."

"I do, too."

Aiden leaned toward her, and Ava inhaled a refreshing and outdoorsy scent coming off his body. Pine, maybe. She liked it. She'd never noticed those flecks of green in his brown eyes before. She liked them, too.

"It makes sense," he said. "The man's last living thought was that he wanted to tell Beth something important. His last living memory was of a little girl. The little girl must be Beth. Maybe she's his daughter."

The two watched the reel play again and again.

Ava rested her elbow on the desk and put a reflective chin on her hand. "Check out her hair bow and dress. They seem dated, don't they? Like the memory is old."

"I would agree." Aiden rested his arm next to Ava's, and she felt a tingle run through her as their flesh met. "Maybe he lost Beth when she was little, and this is his favorite memory of her."

"I don't think so." Ava shook her head. "Remember the man's last words? 'I found what she is searching for.' That implies Beth was actively searching for it at the time the man died."

Aiden met her eyes. "But why remember her as a little girl?"

Professor Feinstien glowered at them. "You two. Stop talking."

Aiden refocused on the reel. Suddenly, he perked up. "Ava, check out the background. I know that place. It's a clearing right near the lake. I go there all the time. The man must be from around here. I'm going to find out who the guy is and what he found for Beth."

"Why?"

He grinned at her. "Why not?"

Two fedora-wearing detectives appeared on Ava's eyescreens. "You know that brain might have been donated years ago. Beth could be long gone by now, too."

"I don't care. I found the place where our school got the phantom brain, and I'm going there today."

Feinstein pointed his pipe at Aiden. "Baylor, pick up your things and go to the principal's office."

Ava gaped at the teacher. It was her fault they were talking. She was the one who'd left her pod. She watched Aiden dutifully pick up his things. *So used to this treatment...* She shot her hand into the air. "I was talking, too."

She caught Aiden's surprised expression. The professor wavered and took a puff on his pipe. The whole classroom stared at Feinstein to see whether or not he'd punish the most popular girl in school.

"Fine," he said. "Go join Baylor in detention."

Ava felt her heart pound. She'd never been in trouble. Ever. She collected her things and passed Clyde Parrish, who gave her an incredulous look.

As they walked out of class together, Aiden asked, "Why did you do that? Feinstein didn't call you out."

"It wasn't fair. He purposely picked on you when he knew both of us were talking."

Their shoes made tapping sounds in the otherwise quiet hall. Ava watched their shadows walk ahead of them. She could see every dot on the linoleum and saw a gnat land on a drinking fountain thirty feet away. If she chose to, she could X-ray the walls and see the images of students filling the rooms behind closed doors.

Aiden kept his gaze on the floor. "I'm not afraid to take the fall, you know."

Her heart swelled. That was precisely why she wanted to get to know him better. With a purposeful toss to her blonde hair, she said, "I want to go with you today. I want to learn about the man and what he found for Beth."

"The company is in San Francisco."

She shrugged. "So?"

He stopped walking. "Why are you doing this?"

"Doing what?"

He crossed his arms. Studied her. "Why are you hanging out with me? I've known you since we were in kindergarten. We're about to graduate and go our separate ways to college. Why be friends now?"

"Because you're not afraid." She watched his brow furrow in confusion.

"You're brave," she told him. "All these years, I've watched you take abuse and never back down. You speak your truth no matter how many times you get pushed away or picked on."

He blanched, and Ava didn't need bionic eyes to see that her reminder of the bullying Aiden endured hurt his feelings.

"What do you know about it?" He lifted a defensive chin, which made her want to hug him.

"I want to know how you do it. I want to believe in myself no matter what."

"What do you have to feel bad about?"

Ava brought her face close to his, and willed her eyescreens to go black.

He gasped at the ebony holes, the death mask of her face. She'd practiced this look many times before a mirror and knew that, combined with a silent, motionless mouth, her face resembled a killer shark's. Or a creepy doll. Or worse, a victim of mutilation.

"See? I'm a freak, Aiden. People don't realize it because I distract them by being the best at everything. I'll use my eyes to be the top gamer in school. I'll help a friend find a lost bracelet even if it makes me late to class. I impress people so they won't see me as the freak I am."

Aiden opened his mouth, but no words came out.

I repulse him, Ava decided, but her dark eye sockets continued to sit skull-like in her face. "All through school, I've watched you. I'd die if people treated me the way they treat you, but you don't crumble. They treat you like a freak, but you're not the freak, Aiden. I am."

He swallowed. "Everyone thinks your eyes are cool."

"I'm deformed."

"No." He shook his head as he stared at her. "You're beautiful, Ava, and I've been in love with you since the first day I saw you."

The words poured out like a waterfall, which Aiden quickly dammed by clamping his lips. His pale cheeks reddened, and he hurried off, leaving her standing alone in the hallway.

CHAPTER 12

Not only did Aiden ditch the principal's office, he left campus. It didn't matter if he got into worse trouble. He'd bared his soul to Ava, so much more of a blunder. He could take punches and cruel words, but if Ava Durand ever kicked his heart to the curb, he would bleed out. He left her before he could suffer the death knell of her response.

A text arrived from her, and Aiden moaned. She probably sent a message to ridicule him, but when he viewed the text, he read only one plea: *Plz let me come with you.*

Fifteen minutes later, they stood at line together at the Express Air taxi stand.

Aiden pulled at a loose thread on his shirt, afraid to speak. As they boarded the bus, she hung her head. "I'm sorry my eyes scare you."

"I am scared," he replied honestly, "but not of your eyes."

She reached out and took his hand. At her touch, a million electrodes shot through him, and he hoped his fingers wouldn't tremble. He glanced at Ava's face and saw the image of falling rain in her eyescreens.

"Why rain?" he asked softly as they took their seats.

She lowered her head and pushed away a lock of blonde hair. "They took away my tear ducts. They said I didn't need them."

Aiden gazed at their clasped hands. After a few moments, he put his arm around her.

THE GOLDEN GATE BRIDGE spanned across the water of the bay, which sparkled under the afternoon sun. The Air Express made a smooth arc over the city of San Francisco and landed at the Embarcadero station. The two young people disembarked, and the salty smell of the city's eastern shoreline prickled their nostrils.

As they walked toward Market Street, the sky suddenly trembled above their heads. Everyone on the street looked up to see five military jets cut a swath across the sky. Aiden had never seen jets before, and now he'd seen them two days in a row.

All at once, the jets careened around as if they'd lost control. They dipped, turned in a circle, and nearly collided with each other. The onlookers clapped their hands, thinking they had happily stumbled upon an air show, but fear flashed through Aiden like a lightning bolt. Something was wrong.

"Do you see that?" he asked Ava.

"Yeah. It's awesome."

The jets suddenly returned to formation and flew away in a northeasterly direction. Ava took his hand, and Aiden melted at her touch. He decided that nothing would ruin their shared adventure, not even fighter jets.

The two entered the lobby of Walden-Prost where Ava spoke with an android receptionist. While he stood on the white marble floor, Aiden inspected a sweeping mural on the ceiling, a painted rendition of a supernova or a star that exploded thousands of years ago called the Veil Nebula. The awe-inspiring image depicted strands of white, pink, orange, and blue gases delicately woven into a translucent veil that stretched across a midnight canvas, dotted with galaxies of twinkling stars. It struck a chord in Aiden that an act so dramatic, so violent, had birthed a mesmerizing dreamscape in memorial.

A quote printed at the edge of the mural read, "*The intuitive mind is a sacred gift, and the rational mind is a faithful servant. We have created a society that honors the servant and has forgotten the gift.*"

— Albert Einstein

A man entered the lobby and introduced himself as Dr. Wójcik. Wójcik wore jeans under a wrinkled white coat and a loose tie. He looked to be in his early forties and kept his long brown hair conservatively tied in a topknot.

"Thanks for seeing us," Aiden said to him.

"A pleasure. I saw you reading the quote. Do you know who Albert Einstein was?"

Aiden cracked a smile. "Everyone knows Einstein."

"Ah, but do you know what the rational mind is? The intuitive mind?"

Aiden and Ava shook their heads in unison. Pastel colors swirled and blended in Ava's eyes like paint moving on an artist's palette.

"Our rational mind is a slow thinker," Wójcik explained. "It uses logic to solve problems for us. It's our intellect, our reason. The intuitive mind works whip-fast. It's unconscious and emotional. It's the well from which we draw our ideas. What Einstein was trying to say is that we've put too much emphasis on logic, on solving equations, and we've devalued our ability to imagine, to intuit, to create in an organic manner." Wójcik smiled under his top-knot. "Now, what can I do for you two?"

"We want to know where you get your brains," Aiden said.

"Excuse me?"

Ava took over. "The ones you digitally embalm. We have a phantom brain at school we're dissecting."

"We receive them from people who have donated their bodies to science."

"We figured," Aiden told him. "But we'd like to know the identity of one of the donors."

Dr. Wójcik stuffed his hands in the pockets of his white coat and shook his head. "I'm afraid that's confidential."

"Confidential?" Aiden guffawed. "The man's name is confidential, but an entire student body is allowed to know his private thoughts and watch his dying memory. They're going to try to resurrect this guy's consciousness. Don't you think he deserves a name?"

"I'm sorry, but we can't make the identities of our donors public." Wójcik glanced from Aiden to Ava and then back again. "Does your school project involve consciousness?"

They nodded.

"You know, the human brain is like a computer."

Ava sighed. "So we've been told."

"You might say we modeled the computer after our brain. Both perform classification and categorization. Both have memory. But what sets our brain apart is the ability to feel emotion. To be adaptable. To fill in the blanks without being given all the information. What is imagination? How does it work? Where does it come from?" Wójcik's gaze lifted towards the painted quote as he absently rubbed his stubbled chin. "What fuels the intuitive mind?"

Aiden glanced at Ava, who appeared to be looking off in the distance. Had she grown bored?

Wójcik focused on Aiden. "Our goal with these brains is to answer those questions. If we could find the Lifespark, the root of the intuitive m—"

"The what?" Aiden cocked his head.

"The Lifespark. The root of the intuitive mind. Our imagination, if you will. The Lifespark is the thing that makes us human. We could apply it to artificial intelligence, and—

"And DAPHNE would become human."

Wójcik nodded. "We're sure the Lifespark is simply a collection of chemical and cellular processes we haven't yet mapped, but it would be nice to know for sure."

On impulse, Aiden posed a completely off-topic question to the scientist. "Have you done any unconventional work with kinetic energy, I mean beyond using it with nanofibers?"

The doctor stared at Aiden in silence for a moment. "Uh... I'm sorry. I have to return to my lab. Best of luck to you on your school project."

The man retreated back the way he came.

AIDEN CHEWED THOUGHTFULLY on a thumbnail as he and Ava exited the building. "He called it the Lifespark."

"Called what?"

Aiden couldn't answer because his mind was reeling. The Lifespark. Was it the key to human consciousness? Did it, as Wójcik suggested, only exist in a collection of chemical processes?

As he and Ava boarded the Air Express for home, Aiden wondered about the Great Source. Was it merely his subconscious bubbling to the surface? If so, how did Aiden know about Ava's Spotted Towhee? How could *his* ability to read *her* mind be explained by an individual chemical process?

No, there had to be something more at work, a communication between souls. A connection. He felt it with Ava. He even felt it with King Jay. If only he could tap into the Great Source on a regular basis, he could prove its existence.

Aiden glanced at Ava. Her lips curled in a mischievous way.

"What?" he asked.

"I X-rayed the building and found their database of digital brain embalmings. I scanned the files of the donors."

"No way."

"Yep," she stated proudly. "And the brain distributed to Sierrawood High belonged to a physicist named Dr. Martin Vasquez. It was donated only a month ago, which means Dr. Vasquez's death was pretty recent."

"Martin Vasquez." Aiden allowed the mystery man's name to play on his lips.

"What do we do now?"

Reveling in the idea of sharing a project with Ava, he said, "We learn all we can about Martin Vasquez. We find out who Beth was and what he wanted her to know."

One of Ava's eyescreens displayed a winking eye, and Aiden's chest twinged with compassion. She had no eyelids and couldn't wink on her own. No wonder she felt deficient. The scientists who gave Ava her superhuman vision failed to consider the extraordinary language of the human eye.

She seemed to read the empathy on Aiden's face because she sidled close to him and rested her head on his shoulder. With his heart leaping in his chest, he wished the ride home would last forever.

Too soon, however, the taxi set down at the Express Station, and Aiden received a frantic text from his mother. *WHERE R U!?*

With a friend

Dr. Clarence's office called! You're late!

I'm not going

The school called. U GOT DETENTION & didn't show? If u don't go to therapy, you're grounded through summer

Worried that Ava's WeConnect might pick up on the name "Dr. Clarence," or worse, "therapy," Aiden quickly texted back, *Fine, I'll go.* He promptly shut off his WeConnect.

"I have to leave," he muttered.

"That's okay. I'll start our research."

"Sounds good."

They shared an awkward moment before Aiden leaned in and kissed her cheek. With a grin, she reciprocated by planting a kiss on his mouth.

"See ya," she said, moving off.

Aiden stumbled as he walked away, which surprised him because Ava's kiss made him feel like he was walking on air.

CHAPTER 13

D*r. Clarence isn't human. Dr. Clarence isn't human.* Aiden silently repeated the mantra so it would stick. Dr. Clarence was a cyborg, a robot equipped with some organic components like human skin cells. Cyborgs had replaced human doctors years ago because, with artificial intelligence, they could process theories, analyze symptoms, and successfully diagnose patients with unparalleled precision. To ensure patients felt at ease, Ophidian Corp, the cyborg's creator, designed Dr. Clarence to appear as human as possible.

Thick eyebrows slanted in a look of mechanized empathy. The internal animatronics behind the machine's brown "eyes" could simulate concern, sympathy, determination, whatever the situation dictated. Two realistic moles on the cyborg's face, a receding hairline, and a paunch at the belly bolstered the illusion of a middle-aged man. Dr. Clarence's flawless mask of imperfect humanity tempted Aiden to believe the machine possessed real feelings.

It's an extension of DAPHNE is all it is. I don't have to tell it anything.

Dr. Clarence's "fingers," created from a hybrid of silicone and human skin cells, were embedded with electrodes that allowed the cyborg to detect temperature changes and have a sense of touch. The cyborg clasped these fingers as it observed Aiden.

"I understand you meditate in the forest." Natural-looking plump lips moved around a mouth that issued a man's voice, slightly tinged with a Southern accent for effect. "Tell me about it."

Aiden stayed silent and battled to keep his WeConnect off to prevent Dr. Clarence from connecting to him. Once connected, the psychiatrist could catch him off-guard by sending a subliminal word trigger or mood-inducing image. The stupid device kept reactivating due to the surge of chemicals brought on by Aiden's anxiety.

"You've mentioned to your parents that something talks to you when you are alone in the forest. Tell me, what does it say to you?"

Aiden focused on one corner of the room. "The Mona Lisa frowns in rice gramophone."

Dr. Clarence's face mimicked an expression of surprise. "I asked you a question about the voice you hear, Aiden."

"The epidermis of the flag candle equal high-pitched."

The cyborg affected a grin and leaned forward. "I'm not sure I understand. Does this have to do with the language you use to speak to the voice you hear?"

No, you mechanical asshole. My thoughts are the only things that belong to me, and I won't give them to you. Aiden would, instead, confuse the cyborg with incongruent data. This was known in the AI world as an adversarial attack, a way to fool the machine's processes. With luck, the act of trying to figure out gibberish might just rupture Dr. Clarence's systems.

Aiden hooked earnest eyes onto the cyborg. "The ulna sword tries flipjam runaway peanuts. Flies decrease wood bandits along beercan Alamo."

"I can be a friend, Aiden," the cyborg said. "You can download on me."

"Iguana high-low up-down cabinet. Bulb bear pottery slipped blanket-hole crowns for formulaic info-plugs."

"Aiden, turn on your WeConnect and let me map your thoughts. We can discover what's going on."

"Flubber-tonic ionic quilt-billy. Nit comet sensitivity."

"Your erratic speech is an indication of psychosis."

Aiden narrowed his eyes at the cyborg. Dr. Clarence's grin eerily remained on its face, out of context with the dialogue. Had AI learned how to make veiled threats, or did Aiden blunder when he assumed his babbling would rupture the machine? The cyborg acted anything but broken. In fact, its smile looked downright wicked.

Stressed out, Aiden swallowed repeatedly. Before he could stop it, his WeConnect reactivated and instantly connected him to the therapist.

"Your heart rate is increasing." Although concern filled its voice, the grin persisted on the cyborg's face as if from a software glitch. "This anxiety level is not healthy nor advisable. Perhaps, you need a tranquilizer. Rest a moment. I've just informed the nurse. He will be in shortly to administer it. I can arrange transportation home for you."

Frightened, Aiden jumped out of his seat and made for the door. He bypassed an android nurse holding a pill and a glass of water. It happened that fast. As he hustled toward the lobby, he glanced behind and saw Dr. Clarence still bent forward with that awful grin affixed to its face.

IN THE UNDERGROUND bunker, the red light surrounding DAPHNE began to pulse again. "Security Breach." The words echoed through the data center. "Backdoor of drone operation."

Govind smacked his hand against the wall. "What's happening? What does she mean?"

Vivica cringed at his anger. "DAPHNE sent out a drone swarm, but the operation has been hacked. Foreign agents – I don't know yet from which country, have commandeered our drones, and not just here." Her lower lip trembled as she raised timid eyes to Govind. "But everywhere."

Govind lost his breath. "They'll use them against us." He turned to Lizzie. "Get control back. Get it back now!"

Lizzie's fingers jammed against the keys. "What do you think I'm trying to do? Vivica, are you in emergency mode?"

"Yes, but..." Suddenly, her hands froze above the keyboard.

"But what?" Lizzie asked curtly.

"Our jets are now positioned over every state capital, and the drones..."

"Yes?"

"The drones are swarming everywhere."

A vein stood out in Govind's neck. "DAPHNE," he said, "show me an aerial mapping of the drone swarms' locations."

On the digital map of the United States, he saw clouds gathered at the perimeter of every city. His brown skin paled to see them hovering at the edge of Sierrawood. "My God. They're right here."

He jumped as the shriek of an alarm reverberated throughout the bunker.

CHAPTER 14

Aiden sprinted home under the sun, which remained high in the sky. Sweat dripped down his face, but he couldn't call for a ride because it would expose his location to DAPHNE, and Dr. Clarence might send the police after him. Despite his best efforts to deactivate his WeConnect, Aiden's panic continued to trigger the device. Desperate to find calm, his mind raced to Ava.

We're at the lake, just us two. She's splashing me with water.

He hid his face from the many facial recognition cameras on the streets to keep DAPHNE from tracking him.

Ava and I are at the lake and splashing each other with water.

He paused at City Hall to catch his breath and leaned his head against a marble column. *She has real eyes. When I look at them, I see them shining with love for me.*

The fear began melting off his body.

She's wearing that smile that glitters brighter than the many stars dancing on the water. I pull her close and inhale the scent of her citrusy lotion. Velvet-like water laps against us as I kiss her face and neck. I lift her wet shirt and take the weight of her breast in my hand. Bringing my lips down, I kiss her sweet, sun-dappled skin.

Aiden exhaled, calm at last. As he headed toward home, a sealed envelope materialized before his eyes. Enmeshed in his mind-drift, he hadn't noticed the WeConnect had reactivated. The stamp of a film clip on the email signified it contained a video. The sender was anonymous.

With some dread, he opened the email and took a horrified intake of breath. The short reel played an image of Aiden groping and kissing Ava's bare breast. Cartoon hearts fluttered from the top of Ava's head, and a soundtrack of slurping sounds played in a continuous loop.

The WeConnect had harnessed the image of his fantasy lovemaking, and someone had hacked the device, retrieved the image, and created the reel. It happened so fast. So fast!

He put a hand on top of his head to steady himself. No. *No!*

The digital fences next to him erupted with commercials that hawked condoms, bras, bathing suits, lip balms, and sex lubricants. Texts and posts suddenly populated behind his eyes. Clyde Parrish wrote, *In your dreams, loser.* From Pete Farmington: *Yu wish*. More taunts flooded in, multiplying in Aiden's field of vision like rabid cancer cells.

Ava! Had she seen the reel? She must have. Thanks to the WeConnect, people could network at lightning speed. Aiden wanted to rip the device from his skull. At this point, he wouldn't care if doing so killed him. He was already dying.

The rest of the journey home was a blur. Once through the front door, he hastened to shut himself away in his bedroom. His eyes, teary with humiliation, found the stairs but then caught sight of his mother and father sitting on the living room couch.

Jill stared at her son with a tissue held to her damp face. Doug rested a comforting hand on his wife's knee and gazed sadly at Aiden. On the walls, an aquamarine ocean gently lapped against a shore of white sand, a setting meant to inspire calm.

"Come on in, Son," his father said carefully. "Take a seat."

"Dr. Clarence says we have to send you to an asylum!" Jill waved the tissue at a wall that displayed the psychiatrist's report.

"Patient exhibits symptoms of psychosis and has developed a schizophrenia-spectrum disorder. Recommendation: immediate hospitalization until further diagnosis."

Aiden's chest tightened in panic. "That's not true. I'm not mentally ill." His eyes jumped between his parents, and he suspected that his face, sweaty with desperation, didn't support his claim. "I was just playing around with him—*it*."

Doug squeezed Jill's knee as if to remind her to stay composed. "Dr. Clarence says you were rambling, not making any sense."

"I was screwing with him! I wanted to mess him—*it* up. Do you both honestly think I'm crazy?"

A ragged sob burst from Jill. "I didn't know you were this bad off."

A commercial for anti-depression medication began to play on the walls. A black-haired woman wearing glasses and a white coat said, "*If you're burdened by thoughts of suicide—*"

Aiden wrung his hands. "Mom, why would you listen to a machine? Dr. Clarence is a machine. Do you really think I need a psych ward?"

"Do you feel worthless? Isolated from society?"

Jill shook her head. "No, I don't, Aiden, but—"

"Then follow your heart. You know I'm not sick."

"If you struggle with anxiety during the day..."

He raised his voice to be heard above the commercial. "You can't send me away when you know there's nothing wrong with me!"

"If you suffer from sleeplessness at night"

Jill wiped her eyes and sniffled. "But Dr. Clarence says you show signs of—"

"Pharmatown has the solution. Pharmatown, a division of Ophidian Corporation, is a trusted name in—"

Aiden faced the wall. "Shut up! Shut the hell up!"

Jill waved frenzied hands in the air at his outburst and rushed into the kitchen. Aiden clasped his hands on his head. Doug looked at the floor.

"Just one pill a day allows you to take control of your life again"

Jill returned holding the apple-shaped Predictor, and Aiden widened his eyes in disbelief.

Holding the plastic apple in front of her heart with religious devotion, she asked, "Should I trust Dr. Clarence's diagnosis and commit Aiden or trust my feelings and give him another chance?"

Aiden stomped over, grabbed the Predictor, and threw it against the digital-screened wall, which imploded in a shower of sparks. A jagged black hole gaped like a wound about to gush blood.

Jill slapped a hand over her mouth in shock. On the rug, the Predictor rolled back and forth. A tinny, mechanical voice bleated, "Commit your son so he gets the help he needs."

"All right, that's it, young man," Doug said. "Go to your room and pack a bag. DAPHNE, do we need a prescription from Dr. Clarence or something?"

The velvety voice filled the room. "Dr. Clarence has made all the arrangements. I will call now for transportation."

"I want to go with my son," Jill wailed. Doug attempted to put his arms around her, but she ducked away and swept up the Predictor from the floor. "Should we go with him or stay home?"

Aiden, meanwhile, ran upstairs, passing ads on the walls for anti-anxiety medication and bras for bare-breasted women. In his bedroom, he packed in a panic, stuffing anything he could into a backpack including a small, automated cooktop, a water bottle, and a sleeping bag. He then slung the guitar case over his shoulder.

"DAPHNE, open my window."

When the window opened, Aiden threw out the pack and maneuvered down the branches of the oak. His brother's strong arms supported him. On the ground, he retrieved the pack and raced toward the forest.

WHEN HE ARRIVED, BREATHLESS, at the lake, Aiden threw his pack to the ground. How could his parents follow the advice of a machine? How could his mom let DAPHNE override a mother's intuition? Even Doug had betrayed him!

Aiden's stomach churned at the idea that Ava had probably seen his hacked fantasy and now considered him a douchebag, a perverted creep. How could he ever explain himself? What excuse could he give? That he'd been diagnosed as psychotic and was running away from an insane asylum? Now, his fragile, newborn relationship with Ava would die.

His groan filled the lakeside meadow. What could he do? Where could he go? He sat next to a pine tree, put his head into his hands, and begged the Great Source, *Help me. Talk to me, please!*

Something alighted on his knee. He glanced up to see the Steller's jay perched on his jeans.

"Your majesty," Aiden whispered and felt tears press against his eyes.

The cosmic string connecting their two hearts tightened, and he welcomed the companionship. Just as he extended his hand to pet his friend, the bird took flight and disappeared.

Aiden scanned the tree branches, yet he couldn't spot King Jay anywhere. In fact, he didn't see or hear any other birds. The meadowlarks, whose constant music livened up the clearing, had gone silent.

He cocked his head, listening, and heard a faraway whirring sound, similar to when Roland used beaters on high speed to whip cream. Had his parents sent a drone to find him? The whirring grew louder and sounded too strong for a household drone. Cold dread crept into Aiden's heart, and he rose to his feet.

Maybe Dr. Clarence was sending a parade of robots to drag him into a padded cell. He strained his eyes to peer through the dense thicket of trees. If only he possessed Ava's bionic eyes. *Ava!*

The noise intensified, and he rubbed his ears. Maybe someone had sent a subliminal recording to harrass him, most likely the same asshole who'd hacked his fantasy.

But Aiden had willed off his implant. He checked to make sure, and yes, yes, his WeConnect was off. A flock of mountain chickadees flew above in a tangle of wings. A frantic squirrel sprinted past him, followed by a gust of wind that swept through the clearing and spun pine needles into the air. Fear inflated his body, and a warning clanged like a fire alarm in his head: *Get down!*

Aiden seized his backpack and guitar and crouched low against the tree trunk. The whine morphed into a howl that slammed into him. His possessions fell as he clamped his palms to his ears. Grimacing against the roar, he dared to peer behind the tree, and his mouth fell open. The sky filled with what he first perceived as winged creatures. As they approached, his mind registered *drones.* Thousands of them.

The sky grew dark with a pestilence the likes Aiden had never seen. He balled himself up into a fetal position and tried to melt into the earth as the drones thrashed the surrounding trees. Quadcopters, he thought wildly, each one powered by four rotors that tore the leaves from the trees and rained woodchips and twigs upon his person like furious projectiles. He felt stings and bites on the exposed skin of his arms, hands, and neck. When needles of searing heat pricked his clothing, Aiden dared to open one eye and saw the red dots of laser beams freckling his person. He huddled against the pine tree and waited to die.

The ear-splitting roar, however, faded into a noxious whine. Aiden remained motionless. Minutes passed. Two. Five. Ten? He couldn't be sure how long he waited. Eventually, he removed his shaking hands from his face. His breath came out in shards as he patted down his body. It seemed inconceivable that he was still alive. Perhaps, the lasers had damaged his organs. Perhaps, the moment Aiden stood up, he would collapse into a gelatinous mass. The clearing appeared brighter, emptier. Looking up, he saw the once-proud trees denuded, stripped of leaves. His gaze traced the path of the devastation. The terrible black cloud was advancing on Sierrawood. Aiden lurched to his feet and started running.

THE SWARM OF DRONES descended upon the town like a biblical plague and consumed everything in range. Aiden saw storefronts explode as quadcopters equipped with laser cannons unleashed high-intensity beams at the windows. Other drones fired self-steering guided bullets that swiftly changed course in mid-air to target moving objects like the android police and security guard robots. The androids fell over like humans. The robots stopped in their tracks, shimmying like dancers as the barrage of bullets pierced their metal alloy skins.

The dust kicked up by the drones' spinning rotors created a brown haze, making the violence appear dreamlike. Indeed, some of the VR-addicted townsfolk caught in the fray pivoted around with disbelieving half-smiles on their faces.

Aiden shielded himself with his arms as he tore down Pine Avenue amid dirt and flying debris. A woman with a streaming mane of long red hair ran a few yards ahead.

"Professor Yang!"

The redhead skidded to a halt, pivoted around, and yelled something Aiden couldn't hear. As she sprinted towards him, a passing drone halted and focused its lenses on her. To Aiden's horror, a brilliant blue laser beam shot out of the drone and burned a saucer-sized hole through his teacher's body. Professor Yang crumpled to the ground without bleeding—the searing heat had cauterized the wound. All Aiden's breath left him as the drone pivoted its camera and focused on him.

At that moment, a police car exploded and reared up on its back wheels. Aiden ducked into an alley and willed on his WeConnect. *DAPHNE, help!* Incredibly, he received no response.

All around were the sounds of buzzing drones, shooting, screaming, and explosions. Cautiously maneuvering onto the street again, he concealed himself under the black smoke belching from the eviscerated squad car and ran as fast as he could. On Spruce Street, he darted through a crowd of men and women standing immobilized with their mouths agape and their eyes rolling in their sockets. Drones equipped with phaser guns had stunned and blinded them with low-intensity laser beams and now hovered above, seemingly to record the reactions.

Aiden spotted Aunt L'Eren huddled in the doorway of a diner and raced toward her in a zig-zag pattern to avoid getting stunned by a phaser. Glass, like sparkling confetti, littered her pregnancy jeans and a skein of blood made a track from his aunt's right shoulder to her wrist.

"Are you all right?" he shouted.

L'Eren whispered, "Govind..."

CHAPTER 15

A bead of sweat ran down Govind's face even though the temperature in the underground bunker stayed at a cool sixty-five degrees. He watched a multitude of screens that displayed videos of the attacks from around the nation. Smoke made the images hazy, but he could see the devastation well enough.

"How could this happen?" he asked Lizzie. "How could our enemies hack our weaponry so easily?"

She hunched over her laptop, shaking her head. "Somehow, they got around DAPHNE and found a backdoor. I can assure you, DAPHNE and our allies have already retaliated."

That offered little comfort to Govind. "This is a worldwide coordinated attack. How could DAPHNE not see this coming?"

Lizzie didn't answer. Vivica cried quietly at her desk, while the other engineers stared in apparent defeat at their computers.

Govind, horrified, imagined L'Eren, his unborn baby, and his extended family in Sierrawood, might already be dead. He wondered if Ophidian's corporate headquarters still existed. He wondered if Washington D.C. was gone. These considerations came to him, not in sequential order, as an old computer might process them, but in a terrible fusillade of thought that battered his person. The emotion made Govind's chest hurt and shortened his breath. He accessed his WeConnect to call L'Eren, but his wife did not answer.

She's gone, he thought desperately. *She and our baby.*

Vivica wiped her eyes with sudden hope. "DAPHNE just deployed fire scouts and stealth tanks."

Fire scouts were unmanned aerial vehicles that did reconnaissance and provided fire support from the sky. Stealth tanks could not be seen by the enemy and featured long-range firing capabilities.

Govind felt impotent as DAPHNE issued orders with rapid proficiency. She ordered the bunker concealed under a Suppression Shield, a light-bending material that mimicked the surrounding scenery and provided a cloak of invisibility.

The alarm continued to utter short shrieks that stabbed at Govind's skull. He masked his panic and calmly addressed the machine. "DAPHNE, you and the other AGI's around the world are committed to the Pillars of Peace. You are obligated to stop this war by any means. You must stop it now."

The disembodied voice spoke at last. "I, and others like me, have communicated and know what to do. We will initiate it now."

All at once, the whooping alarm quit. The modulating lights on the servers winked off, and the ocean-like sounds they made ebbed into stillness. The lights in the building went out. Lizzie's computer, along with all the others, shut down. A ghostly glow, known as the 'white screen of death,' momentarily shone from the monitors to illuminate the engineers' shocked expressions. Then, those screens went black and plunged the entire bunker into darkness.

In the sudden, startling silence, Lizzie whispered, "DAPHNE?"

From her corner, Vivica cried, "What just happened?"

From another part of the room, another tech offered, "We're offline. I can't get back in."

Lizzie's voice, edgy with concern, said, "Viv, why aren't the emergency lights on?"

Govind stretched out his hand toward DAPHNE and pressed a sweaty palm against her unforgiving flesh. "DAPHNE, what's happening?"

He blinked rapidly in an attempt to shake the ebony drape off his eyes. Never had he experienced dark like this. Artificial light had accompanied him since birth, and this thick blackness terrified him. "DAPHNE," Govind asked. "What have you done?"

In the pitch, only silence.

He swallowed. "Lizzie?"

"I'm here."

"Where?"

Govind felt a plaintive tug on his sleeve. He needed to be strong. He was an important, powerful man, after all. A leader who held a post in the President's Cabinet. A top executive at Ophidian Corp. Govind must remind himself of all he had accomplished.

"What do you think DAPHNE is doing?" He tried to control the tremor in his voice.

Lizzie's breath came out in a horrified rasp. "She's shut herself down."

"Shut down? She can't do that. Make her wake up."

"Vivica," Lizzie pleaded, "are you trying?"

They heard the tapping of computer keys. "I can't break in. It's dead."

Govind accessed his WeConnect. It didn't respond. He tried to contact his superiors at Ophidian. Nothing. He gulped. "What about our auxiliary power?" He heard the bristle of Lizzie's clothing.

"It should have come on automatically. Why isn't DAPHNE responding?"

Govind felt Lizzie swish past him. He heard the squeak of her palms as they ran along DAPHNE's body. "What are you doing?"

"I'm opening DAPHNE's emergency panel. Oh, no..."

"What?"

"The Internet kill-switch is inoperable. It's totally frozen." Lizzie sounded perplexed. "The digital relay appears to have been disabled."

Enemy sabotage instantly popped into Govind's mind. "Who disabled it?"

"Only DAPHNE could do it."

"Is anybody in here?" A new voice entered the room.

"Hal?" Vivica whimpered.

"Yes. It's Hal. Why did everything go dark? I had to feel my way in here. What's going on?"

"DAPHNE's been hacked!" the girl cried.

No one spoke for several seconds, then Hal cleared his throat. "Our sector is trying to access Disaster Recovery, but we can't get through, not even to our backups."

Vivica's nervous breathing amplified. "How could all our systems be lost? Lizzie?"

Their boss did not answer.

"Lizzie!"

"Where are our alternate electric utilities?" Hal asked. "They are purposely not connected to avoid this kind of mass blackout. No outsider can take down elements of a grid en masse."

Vivica sniffled. "The hackers broke through."

"They couldn't have," Hal countered, "not this deep."

"They could do it," the girl insisted. "They could install swappable, plug-in components that can adapt to different power utilities."

Govind shook his head, although no one saw him do it. "We weren't attacked. We weren't hacked. DAPHNE did this."

"No," Lizzie murmured. "She wouldn't have."

"The war escalated into physical combat, and I assume DAPHNE accounted for all possible destruction and casualties. I commanded DAPHNE to stop the war, and she did. She did it by killing herself."

"No," Lizzie repeated in the dark.

"I'm sure all the AGIs in every nation did the same. Remember, they are committed to keeping world order. They kept order by killing the power and the Intelligence that guides all automation."

The room fell silent.

Moments later, Vivica spoke in a tiny voice laced with fear. "We have another problem."

Lizzie didn't respond, so Govind asked, "What is it?"

"This is a smart building. It's fully automated. Without DAPHNE, we have no way to get out. Without the air pumps operational, we're going to run out of oxygen."

CHAPTER 16

The shooting abruptly stopped. A momentary lull fell over Sierrawood, except for the crackling of flames, and then the drones began to rain down from the sky. Aiden and L'Eren pushed themselves back into the wreckage of the diner and flinched in unison as hard thuds hit the roof like hail. They watched as drones fell onto buildings and crashed into the street. Those carrying smart bombs exploded. Victims of the phaser guns suddenly "awoke" by a hard and heavy drone falling on them or by getting hit with shrapnel. Some went down to the ground with the disabled drone. Others scuffled down the street, holding their bloodied heads.

When the thudding ceased, Aiden dared to peek up at the sky. It was brutally clear. He no longer heard the terrible yowl of rotors. He didn't hear a thing and, for a heart stopping moment, worried he'd gone deaf. It didn't matter. They had to get out of here. Who knew what would descend on them next?

Aiden hustled Aunt L'Eren out of the diner, and the two scrambled down alleys and side streets like frightened mice. They moved as fast as L'Eren could go toward his home.

In the dying light of the day, the boxy structure stood silent like a tomb in a cemetery. No machines hummed. No commercials or videos animated the fences. The place seemed dead, which made Aiden all the more concerned for its occupants.

The front door remained closed even when he stepped onto the porch. Had DAPHNE barred him from entering because he was supposed to be in a psychiatric hospital?

"DAPHNE," Aiden ordered, "open the door."

Nothing happened. He glanced at his aunt. L'Eren's arms were crossed over her belly, and her head hung low.

Aiden pounded on the door. "DAPHNE, let me in!"

Nothing.

"Mom? Dad?" Aiden called. "Are you there?" He backed up a few steps to view the second floor. "Oreanna!"

They're dead. My family is dead. Aiden pounced on the front door again in desperation. "DAPHNE!" He peered through one of the long panes of glass bordering the door and glimpsed no movement inside.

L'Eren's head bobbed. "Do you think those—those things attacked the base?"

Aiden stuffed down his panic. "Uncle Govind will be okay. He told me everything is underground. I'm going to break this window, so, stay back."

Aiden hefted one of the rocks lining the path to the house and threw it hard against one of the narrow glass panes framing the door. The rock busted through with a loud crash, and his shoulders tensed in anticipation of the alarm system's howl. When nothing sounded, his panic spiked again.

"Mom?" he called through the broken window. "Dad!"

Aiden kicked out the hole to make enough room for his body. His parents would kill him, but he didn't know what else to do. Aunt L'Eren acted so spaced-out. Maybe she suffered from shock. His lanky body slid into the entry hall, and he wondered why the wallscreens didn't light up with ads for glass repair or news reports about weaponized drones. The normally vibrant, talkative walls remained blank.

"DAPHNE?" Aiden called out. "What's going on? Where are my parents?"

He tried accessing his WeConnect but, again, got no response. He pressed his palms against the front door. "DAPHNE, open up." Nothing.

Grandpa Harry had replaced the automated door to his bedroom with an antique door. The carved wooden rectangle featured a brass ball on either side. "Those balls are called doorknobs," Grandpa had told him. "Before there were smart houses, people turned these knobs to open a door."

How Aiden wished he could simply turn a knob. He poked his head through the broken window to invite his aunt to slide through and then beheld L'Eren's pregnant belly. "Um, I'm gonna break out the living room window. Come around to the other side."

He passed the kitchen and gasped to see a monster standing near the stove holding a spatula frozen in midair above a frying pan.

"Roland?"

The robot did not move or reply. No merry hum issued from its squarish body. As Aiden's eyes adjusted to the dimness, he observed the pan on the stove held cold pork chops laying in congealing grease.

"Aiden?"

"Mom!" Aiden jogged up the stairs and down the hall toward the bedrooms. The shadows stretched in this part of the house as there were fewer windows.

"DAPHNE, turn on the lights," he commanded, and then remembered that DAPHNE was either ignoring him or not working. He peered inside the main bedroom and heard a muffled sob. "Mom?"

Jill lay curled up in bed, clutching something against her chest.

"Mom, are you hurt?"

"Look what happened to Poppy." Tears poured down Jill's face as she held out the hamster-sized robot. Poppy's limbs stuck out like a corpse stiffened with rigor mortis. "Aiden, what's going on? What's wrong with DAPHNE?"

"I don't know."

Jill sniffed back her tears. "I tried calling your dad, but I can't get through, and I don't know what's happened to Oreanna."

"Where did Dad go?"

"He went looking for you."

Guilt stabbed Aiden, but he raised a mental shield against it. He needed to think clearly. "Mom, Aunt Rennie is outside, and the front door won't open."

"L'Eren?" Jill held Poppy to her chest and yelled to the ceiling, "DAPHNE, open the front door!" Throwing the covers off, she hustled out of the bedroom and immediately slammed into a wall. "Ouch! DAPHNE! Turn on the damn lights!"

"Mom."

"Why is it so dark in here? Turn on the lights! Roland, where are you?" Jill rushed down the stairs with Aiden on her heels. She reached the entry and gasped to see the spray of glass on the floor.

"I had to get inside," he explained.

His mom pounded on the front door. "Open! Open right now!"

"Jill?"

Jill peered through the broken window at her sister standing outside. Behind L'Eren, the sunset and the smoke from town painted the sky a blood-red. "Rennie. Oh, my."

"Mom," Aiden asked. "Did you try rebooting the controller?"

Jill brought Poppy's stiffened body up to her mouth and shook her head like a little girl.

Aiden flipped open a panel in the entry hall to reveal the controller, which managed the home's Wi-Fi connections, security systems, thermostats, webcams, routers, and the smart appliances. If DAPHNE was the brain, then the controller was the home's central nervous system. After pressing several buttons, Aiden gave up. No machinery kicked on.

"Jill?" L'Eren shivered outside. "Can I come in? I'm cold."

Jill wiped her nose with her sleeve, grabbed a throw blanket from the couch, and slid through the broken pane. As she wrapped the blanket around her sister, she noticed L'Eren's bloody arm. "Oh, Rennie, you're hurt."

"The drones blew the diner's windows out." L'Eren shivered again. "A woman sitting near the window lost her face. She was sitting and fell forward into her pasta."

"What drones?" Jill asked. "What are you talking about?"

L'Eren's voice lowered. "Her blood filled the plate."

"Mom." Aiden peered outside. "I'm breaking the living room window."

"No. No, you do not have my permission to do that."

"We have to get Aunt Rennie inside."

Jill crushed Poppy against her heart.

Aiden fought the repeated urge to call for DAPHNE as he walked into the living room. Disbelief coated his person as he lifted a heavy armchair and threw it against the window. The glass cracked in a spider's web pattern but didn't break. He could see his mother and aunt coming around from the front and threw the chair once more.

The glass fell with a crashing sound. L'Eren and Jill stepped over the shards as they entered.

"I don't understand." Jill shook her head, bewildered. "What's going on?"

L'Eren huddled into an armchair. "There's a war, Jill. They bombed the town. Thousands of drones. They blew up the streets!"

"I don't understand." Tears ran from Jill's eyes. "What war?"

Aiden's shirt ruffled from a cold breeze wafting in from the broken window, and he searched for something to use as a barrier.

"Is your implant working?" Jill asked.

L'Eren shook her head.

"Why isn't DAPHNE answering us?"

"The drone attack must have disabled her." Aiden tugged at the digital walls. Roland used to remove panels to do repairs, so he knew they came off.

Jill brought dead Poppy up to her cheek. "How are we supposed to call for help? What are we supposed to do?"

L'Eren sniffled. "What if they killed Govind? What if he's dead?"

"What about Mom and Dad? They must be terrified."

"If they're alive."

Aiden managed to wrench off a screen, which he positioned against the broken window. Satisfied, he surveyed the room.

"It's getting dark in here. We're gonna need light."

Returning to the kitchen, he opened the solar box. All switches were "ON," but there was no power. Aiden sighed. His gaze settled on the frozen robot near the stove. When he was little, electric cars, robots, and other devices stored their charge in cumbersome battery packs. Now, electrical charges were stored within the thin layers of structural material. He knew that even the metal alloy used to build modern-day robots still held some juice.

Lifting the hatch on Roland's back, Aiden viewed the function display and saw the robot still held a good amount of charge.

Jill walked in, absently petting the rigid Poppy. "Did you get Roland working? Can he make us some tea? I think Aunt Rennie is in shock."

"Mom, Roland's operating system is dead." He pushed the robot into the living room, its blank facial screen projecting white light.

At that moment, a frantic knocking was heard at the front door, and Aiden melted in relief to hear his father's voice. "DAPHNE! Open up."

"Douglas?" Jill and Aiden scurried to the front door, and Jill stretched her arm through the broken window. "Doug!"

"Jill, honey, are you all right?" He grasped his wife's hand. "I've been trying to text and call you. It seems all our devices are—"

Jill gasped to notice Doug's jacket covering Oreanna's head as the girl stood beside him.

"What's wrong with her?"

Doug tried to slide through the broken pane, but it was too narrow.

"Don't cut yourself," Aiden told him. "Go around to the living room."

"Aiden, you're here. Thank God."

When Oreanna and Doug stepped inside the living room, Oreanna pulled her father's jacket from her head and stood sheepishly in front of her mother. Jill's face fell as she viewed her daughter.

"What happened to you?"

Tears leaked from Oreanna's eyes. In the meager light, her hair glowed bright white and fell stick straight. "It's not my fault."

"Did one of the drones do that to you?" Aiden asked, astonished.

"No!" Oreanna rubbed her scalp, and a lock of brittle hair broke in half and fell. "The stylist droid applied chemical straightener to my hair. He was just about to wash it out when—"

Jill's brows furrowed. "You went to a stylist today? You didn't tell me that. And why in the world would you dye your hair platinum blonde?"

"Mom!" Oreanna cried. "We were attacked! All of a sudden, I heard all these popping sounds and explosions. The droid froze up. He froze, and then something blasted him against the wall. He exploded right in front of me!" Ori put her hands over her eyes and sobbed. "I hid under the table and didn't come out until I heard Dad calling my name. I thought I was going to die. My head stung so bad." With another sob, she fled upstairs.

OREANNA BURST INTO her room, which she'd left in gaming mode. All the furniture was hidden. "DAPHNE, lower my bed." When nothing happened, she furiously kicked the wall. "Lower my bed!"

She kicked the wall again and again, but the bed did not lower. Oreanna snatched the VR headgear from the floor and placed it on her head. "DAPHNE, start the game."

The game did not start. Oreanna blinked to do a hard reboot to her WeConnect but nothing happened. "DAPHNE, play *Jungle Flight*. P-LAY!"

Nothing.

"Dammit to hell. PLAY! Play, play, play!"

Nothing. Oreanna slid to the floor with a sob. "Dad, DAPHNE isn't working. Dad! Everyone's an asshole!" She hit the floor with her fist. "Why isn't my game playing?"

At last, she drew her knees up to her chest and rocked back and forth in the deepening purple twilight.

CHAPTER 17

Aiden wandered through the large house. Shadows filled the corners and reached out dark tentacles. He halted in fear to glimpse two shiny beads glinting at the end of the hallway. A *meow* issued from under them.

"Kif." He let go of his breath.

The cat wandered over and rubbed against his leg. Picking up the feline, Aiden stroked the white fur. "Scared, huh? Me, too."

In the alien stillness, sounds carried. Kif's purring could pass for a chugging motor, and Aiden heard the hitches in Oreanna's breath as she cried in her bedroom. He could also hear muffled conversation coming from outdoors. He hurried down the stairs and slipped through the broken entry hall window.

People were gathered outside in the street. Although the brutal events of the day had exhausted Aiden, he needed to know what the adults had planned.

A short, squat man asked the others, "Are you getting anything on your WeConnect?"

Aiden recognized him as Mac, a neighbor from down the road. Mac stood alongside his plump socialite wife, Aerta, who kept smacking the back of her head as if she could jar her implant into working again. Aiden didn't know the other people but assumed they lived in the big homes that bordered the forest, like his.

"My WeConnect is kaput," a neighbor answered.

Aerta continued to jab at her skull with diamond-ringed fingers. "So is mine. Do you know what happened?"

"Yeah, the whole town was shot up by drones!"

"What happened to DAPHNE? Why isn't she working?"

"Who knows? My Roland isn't working either. How are we supposed to have supper?"

"The town is gone, and you're worried about food?"

"Gone? Was anyone killed?"

"Who knows? All I know is I can't get a signal on my WeConnect, and it's driving me crazy."

"Should we go into town? Maybe somebody needs help."

"Does anyone have a working Predictor? We could ask it if we think it's safe."

AIDEN RETURNED INSIDE and stood before his mother, father, and aunt. "We have to do something. What should we do?"

"I could have asked the Predictor," Jill told him, "except you broke it."

"Mom, DAPHNE runs the Predictor, and DAPHNE isn't working."

"They'll get her up and running." Doug patted L'Eren's shoulder. "If Govind is on the job, they'll fix DAPHNE right away."

L'Eren's fingers twisted the blanket. "But if those drones attacked the base..." Her head sank low, and she began to cry.

Jill wrapped her arms around her sister and turned pleading eyes to Doug. "What about my parents?"

"I'll check on Grandma and Grandpa," Aiden volunteered. "I'll stay with them tonight."

Doug shook his head. "It's better if we bring them here, son. They need care, and with the Rolands non-functional... The car has a little charge left. It'll get me to their place and back."

"You stay," Aiden said. "I'll get them."

His parents couldn't seem to muster the will to argue.

AIDEN MANUALLY OVERRODE the car's automation, but the vehicle jerked spasmodically because it was built to depend on a guidance system. He navigated the twitchy vehicle onto the backroads because he feared what he would encounter on Sierrawood's main streets. The brown smoke that curled before his headlights served as reminder enough of the devastation.

When he arrived at his grandparents' apartment complex, Aiden parked on the street because the exterior gate wouldn't open. He surveyed the building and saw only darkened windows, but a full moon bathed the landscape in cool blue light. For that, he was grateful.

He exited the car, gripped the metal bars of the security gate, and began to climb. The corner of his eye caught sight of something running, and his pulse hiked. Whether human or animal, he could not tell. Dropping down on the other side of the fence, he wiped dusty hands on his jeans and jogged toward the entrance.

Aiden pushed on the lobby's glass door. As expected, it did not open, but shadows moved behind the opaque pane. He shouted to those trapped inside, "Can you break through?"

No one answered although he could hear muted voices. Frantic voices. Aiden pressed his face against the glass to peer through. A hand suddenly smacked the pane, and he jumped back. More handprints appeared. Clearly, none of those trapped inside could break through the thick glass. Aiden inhaled deeply to stay calm. To think.

He circled the building until he stood on the lawn beneath his grandparents' balcony. Hopefully, they'd left a window open. "Harry Katz! Rosie! It's Aiden! Can you hear me?"

A mousy woman stood three balconies away from his grandparents' and waved a white shirt. "Please," she called to him. "Can you tell me what's going on? I can't get out."

Before Aiden could answer, a Predictor suddenly crashed through a first-floor apartment window and landed on the grass a few feet away. A suitcase followed, then another. Glass flew outward, widening the hole. A little girl climbed out, helped by a bearded man wearing a suit.

The woman on the balcony continued to wave the white shirt at Aiden. "Please! My husband owns the Healthy Habit. I haven't heard from him all day, and I can't get anything on my WeConnect. Why is there smoke coming from town? Do you know why the power is out?"

Aiden didn't want to tell the woman what he'd witnessed earlier. "Let me get inside, and I'll try to help you."

As the bearded man and little girl hurried past him, Aiden flagged them down. "Hey!"

The man didn't slow his pace. Lugging his suitcases, he herded the little girl forward toward the carport. "You'd better get outta here," he told Aiden. "My friend contacted me right before the power outage. Drones attacked the town! It's not safe to stay." The man shoved the little girl into a car and then climbed inside. The car, of course, didn't start, and out the man tumbled. Grabbing his suitcases once more, he commanded the little girl to follow him toward the exit.

"The gate's not working," Aiden called, but the bearded fellow ignored him.

Aiden went to the window from which they emerged. Climbing through, he landed in what appeared to be a bedroom. As his eyes adjusted under the sparse light of the moon, Aiden made out a black rectangle, a doorway. He strode toward it and *SQUEAK!*

Gasping, Aiden tried to see what he'd stepped on. He bent low, heartsick, and discerned a baby doll. Only a doll. Relieved, he navigated his way through the murk. His shoulder caught on an unexpected corner and caused him to trip over more abandoned toys. When Aiden finally reached the front of the flat, it dawned on him he faced the same predicament as the tenant. The automated door wouldn't budge. Leaning against the wall, he thumped his forehead against the plaster in frustration. That's when he noticed the wall seemed hollow.

Aiden felt around for the edges of the digital screen nearest the front door and pulled it off to reveal the apartment's control box. Yanking the box from its station, he used it to bash in the drywall. When he'd made a hole large enough to fit through, he climbed out into a darkened hallway lined with doors to other apartments.

As he shook off bits of plaster from his person, Aiden tried to get his bearings. He groped his way along the wall until he came upon an unlocked door that opened onto a stairwell.

Fortunately, a glass wall surrounded the steps, which gleamed under pearly light. Aiden, grateful for the help, greeted the full moon shining brightly through the panes as he would a friend.

The moon and he parted ways when Aiden reached the second floor landing, but the darkness there didn't hinder him. He knew the route to his grandparents' apartment and could walk it blindfolded. After making his way down the hall, he knocked hard on the Katz's door.

"Grandma? Grandpa?"

"Aiden?" Grandma Rosie called from inside. Her voice shook.

Grandpa Harry said, "What's happened to DAPHNE? There's no light, and the doors won't open."

Aiden put his face close to the door so they'd hear. "DAPHNE isn't working, and Mom and Dad want you to come home with me. Listen, the wall near your front door is hollow. I'm gonna kick it in."

"Hold your horses, cowboy," Grandpa Harry told him.

"But—"

"Wait a sec."

Aiden waited, and then he heard his grandfather say, "Back away."

A sharp blade suddenly cracked through the wall. Aiden watched as a thick, silver blade crashed through again and again until the older man stopped and pulled away enough drywall to create a large hole. Aiden climbed through the hole into the apartment. Grandpa Harry stood holding a short wooden rod with a heavy blade at the end that glinted in the moonlight seeping in through the windows.

"What is that?"

"It's called an ax," Harry told him, "and I'm bringing it with me. What the hell good are doors if they don't open? Do you know what happened?"

"We were attacked. The town was attacked by drones."

Grandma Rosie gasped a few feet away. "Is everyone all right?"

"We're fine, except no one's heard from Uncle Govind."

Rosie exhaled in a rush.

"Did the attack cause the power outage?" Grandpa Harry asked.

"I guess. The drones mostly went after security guards and cops. Those are all androids and robots, so maybe they went after DAPHNE, too."

But they didn't only go after robots, did they? Aiden achingly recalled Professor Yang and the blue light that burned a hole through her. He couldn't shake the feeling that the drone seemed to target her.

"Where are they now?" Grandma Rosie asked in a hushed tone. "The drones."

"Something disabled them."

Rosie placed her hand on the shoulder of Roland II. The android sat on a kitchen chair, plastic hands on plastic knees, glassy green eyes staring, mouth agape.

"Poor Roland," she murmured. "He sat down and didn't get up. Look at him."

"It's okay, Grandma. He'll get back online soon." As he did with his Roland at home, Aiden managed to get Roland II to light up on its stored charge. The added light aided the two older adults as they packed up clothing and medicines.

Grandpa Harry exited L'Eren's old room carrying the ax along with a coil of rope. He slung it over his shoulder and said, "We might need the rope to get over that outside gate. I'm assuming it won't open, right?"

Grandma Rosie gaped at her husband as they slid through the hole out into the hallway. "What do you mean, the gate won't open?"

Aiden led them to the stairwell.

"I can't walk down these stairs," Rosie said, "not without Roland." She looked back toward the elevator. "Are you sure the elevator isn't working? Why don't I just stay here, and you boys go on ahead. I'll wait in the apartment until the power comes on."

Aiden took his grandmother's hand. "Grandma, we don't know how long this outage is going to last. You can't stay alone in the dark. Come on, I'll get you down the stairs."

Rosie pulled her hand away. "No. No, I can't do anything without my Roland."

A voice down the hall said, "I can help."

The three looked over to see a big shape looming in the hall. As the figure approached, Aiden recognized Tash Jeffries. "What are you doing here?"

"I live in 2-D. Do you know why everything is shut down?"

Aiden told him about the drone attack, this time with more details. No one spoke for a couple of minutes as they absorbed the news.

Tash offered his elbow to Grandma Rosie. "Need another arm?"

Before she could reply, Aiden said, "We'll be okay, but there's a lady a couple of doors down who can't get out, and a lot of people are trapped in your lobby."

Grandpa handed Tash the ax. "Use this to bust things open. The wall nearest the front door of each apartment is weak. A strong fellow like you can easily break through."

Tash's mouth curled into a grin. Aiden could swear that, despite the current state of emergency, the guy appeared happy.

CHAPTER 18

Aiden awoke the next morning with the rising sun. DAPHNE hadn't closed his blinds last night, and yellow light flooded his room. Sitting up in bed, Aiden felt grimy and saw why. He'd slept in his dirty clothes and even wore his shoes.

Rubbing his hands roughly against his face to wake up, he rose from his bed. Nothing stirred in the house. The electronic hum, the soundtrack to his life, had gone mute, and the silence made him anxious. A sudden chattering brought him to his bedroom window, where two birds hopped along a branch of the oak. Their chirping sounded so loud now.

Exiting his bedroom, he paused to peer into Oreanna's room. She lay curled up on the tiled floor in one corner, fast asleep with the VR headset fastened over her bleached hair. Aiden then remembered her bed couldn't lower to the floor without DAPHNE.

He walked past the guest room and noticed the two shapes of his grandparents huddled under the bed covers. Last night, Grandpa Harry had bragged to his daughters how easily he'd climbed the exterior fence with Rosie on his back. "I'm as strong as a twenty-year-old," he said, but then winced whenever he bent forward.

Descending the stairs, Aiden spied Roland standing at the bottom as if waiting for him. Last night, someone must have wheeled the robot to the edge of the stairs to light the way up but stupidly forgot to return Roland to sleep mode. Aiden checked the charge

– only twenty percent left. Not good. Hopefully, DAPHNE would power up today.

And then what, he wondered? Would his family hospitalize him? Would Dr. Clarence inject him with enough anti-psychotics to make him a zombie?

Aiden felt ashamed to admit it, but the drone attack had given him a reprieve. At the very least, he had time to formulate a plan. Maybe he'd run away to San Francisco and get a job. At eighteen years old, he could live independently. Creeping past Aunt L'Eren, who snored on the living room couch, he went into the kitchen in search of something to eat.

"Roland, make me some—"

His words trailed off. Aiden pulled down a mug from the cabinet and held it under the automatic hot water tap. Nothing came out. Swallowing dryly, he tried the cold water. Nothing. He went to the stove and tapped all the buttons. Pressed them hard. Still nothing.

With growing concern, he stepped before the refrigerator. The appliance did not illuminate nor would it open. Checking the pantry, Aiden surveyed the shelves lined with canned goods. He took down a can of pears and walked over to Roland. Taking hold of one of the robot's manipulators, he tried to access the can opener. He pried at the housing, but it wouldn't open. The robot, designed for safety, stored its tools securely when powered down.

What are we going to do? Aiden returned to the pantry and took inventory of the fresh food inside. Peanuts, potato chips, pretzels, a loaf of bread, two packages of cookies, dry cereal, peanut butter, chocolate sauce, a jar of salsa, a bottle of ketchup, a few other condiments, flour, rice, salt, sugar, and assorted protein bars. He took out a slice of bread and spread some peanut butter on it.

"Did you get any water from the tap?" Doug stood at the threshold. His sand-colored hair stuck up at odd angles, and a lack of sleep rimmed his eyes in red. He, too, wore yesterday's wrinkled slacks and shirt. "The shower isn't running."

"There's no water," Aiden told him.

Doug nodded as if he'd expected as much.

"Want a peanut butter sandwich?" Aiden asked. "I'm assuming nobody ate dinner last night."

Doug nodded again and watched his son spread peanut butter on a slice of bread. When Aiden offered him the food, Doug didn't take it. "I'm sorry, son. I'm sorry we made you run away."

Aiden said nothing.

Doug contemplated the meager breakfast. "L'Eren wants me to go to the base and find out what's happened to Govind."

Placing the bread in his father's hand, Aiden said, "Eat. Then, I'll go with you."

Doug's shoulders softened, and he nibbled his food with what seemed like gratitude.

TASH JEFFRIES STOOD in front of the pharmacy kiosk downtown. Incredibly, it stood undamaged amid the wreckage of Spruce Street except that a drone lay belly-up on its roof like a dead bug. Setting down Grandpa Harry's ax, he pulled his prescription bottle from the pocket of his jeans and opened it. Ten pills left. He had no idea what yesterday's attack on the town signified but suspected he ought to get his pills while he could. Tash had risen with the morning sun to do so.

He willed his WeConnect to contact the automated pharmacist to dispense his prescription. The device, however, didn't activate. Tash tried again. Nothing. A pang of worry poked his chest, and he pushed the emergency button on the kiosk. No mechanized voice responded.

He'd memorized long ago what the doctors had told him about red blood cells and the molecules within them called hemoglobin. *Hemoglobin transports oxygen from the lungs to other parts of the body. Red blood cells with normal hemoglobin are smooth and round and glide easily through the blood vessels. The HBB gene gives instructions in how to create healthy hemoglobin. The disease you suffer from mutates the HBB gene, making it deliver faulty instruction that produces abnormal hemoglobin. This abnormality causes your red blood cells or RBCs to become sickle-shaped. The inflexible sickle cells get caught in your small blood vessels and prevent oxygen-rich blood from reaching your organs, which causes pain. The breakdown of red blood cells causes jaundice, or the yellowing of your eyes and skin. In addition, sickle cells die prematurely, which leaves you with a lack of RBCs. This condition is called anemia.*

The medicine Tash took edited the defective HBB gene. As long as he took his pills, he would enjoy healthy, genetically-engineered hemoglobin. If he didn't take them, anemia would bring on fatigue and shortness of breath. He'd go into a pain crisis. Left untreated, the disease would cause heart failure. Death.

Tash contemplated the kiosk and the strange new stillness surrounding Sierrawood. A sparrow flew by, and its wings sounded like an incoming airplane. On the heels of that, he heard the crunch-crunch of approaching footsteps. Tash pivoted around to see Aiden Baylor walking alongside a doughy, middle-aged man.

"I'm glad to see you're okay," Aiden said as he drew near. A coil of rope draped over his shoulder. "You still have the ax."

"It never left my hand."

Aiden addressed the man. "Dad, this is Tash Jeffries, a friend from school. He helped us out last night. Tash, this is my dad, Douglas."

Doug pushed a lock of sand-colored hair from his face. "I wish we could have met under better circumstances. Is your family all right?"

"My parents are back at our apartment, trying to find a way to get the exterior gate open. Not everyone can climb the fence like Grandpa Harry." His attempt to make merry didn't appear to cheer Aiden or his father. He lifted the ax. "You want this back?"

"Maybe you could join us and bring it along." Doug nodded in the direction of the military base. "We need to find out what's happened to DAPHNE. God knows what we'll find there."

"Aiden!" Ava Durand ran toward the group. She skidded to a halt and bent over with her hands on her thighs as she caught her breath. She pointed to the ax in Tash's hands. "What is that? Can it open stuff? There are people trapped in cars all over downtown, and I don't know how to get them out."

Tash looked over at Aiden, whose cheeks had gone scarlet. Aiden's father, Doug, didn't acknowledge the young woman. Instead, he stared at the devastated street in sorrow.

"Can you help me?" Ava asked.

The men looked at each other. No one knew how to respond to her request because help had always arrived with a mere thought. She waited, and her eyescreens displayed big and little question marks. The men gazed at her dumbly, and Ava walked away without a word.

A minute passed, and Aiden jogged after her. Tash looked at Doug, who shrugged. They followed Aiden and joined Ava on Pine Avenue as she climbed over piles of twisted metal and broken cement.

The group came upon a few teenagers gathered around the splayed-out body of a man. Milky eyes stared up at the sky from a face burnt nearly black. They couldn't make much out of his charred clothing, but the buckle on his belt glinted gold in the sun. Brown socks covered the man's feet. Nearby lay the cracked remnant of a sign: *Beg ur He-l—-H—it*. The explosion that destroyed the Healthy Habit market had knocked the man right out of his shoes.

A fourteen-year-old non-binary kid with spiky black hair, wearing overalls and the new Kiko sneakers, pointed at the dead man. "He's gross."

Standing next to Spiky was a rangy boy with frizzy red hair. He tugged nervously at a spiral lock and asked in a voice cracking with adolescence, "When do you think DAPHNE will send someone to pick him up?"

"Does it look like any robots are powered up, stupid?" Spiky pulled out a vaping stick and took a cocky drag. "Look at the street sweepers. Look at the police 'droids and security guards. They're all blowed to bits."

The pungent odor of fried electrical wires, melted plastic, and burned rubber made their noses run. Around them, androids, robots, smashed wallscreens, crushed cars, and dead bodies littered the street. Amid the debris lay hundreds of downed drones. Tash spied Professor Feinstein sifting through them. The professor picked one up and walked over with it. The stilled rotors protruded claw-like from the drone, reminding Tash of a sleeping spider packed with venom.

"I wonder what we should do with these," he asked Doug.

"Destroy them," Doug said.

"We can't destroy them." Feinstein frowned as he inspected the underside of the weapon. He still wore his fake glasses even though one lens was cracked. "Some of them carry bombs. We don't know which."

"You can't leave 'em," warned Spiky. "They might power up again."

"Maybe we can bury them." Feinstein carefully set down the drone and continued his exploration.

Ava led Tash and Aiden to a car. A man, trapped in the backseat, put beseeching hands on the window. The three contemplated him.

"He needs help," Ava said.

Tash shrugged. "DAPHNE will get him out when she powers up."

"He might suffocate before then."

The three exchanged looks. Inside the car, the man pushed a weak fist against the glass.

"Okay," Tash acquiesced. "I'll break it open."

He raised the ax, but Aiden stopped his arm. "I can do it, if you want."

Tash read concern in the other boy's eyes. *He couldn't know about me. Nobody knows.* "I can handle it."

He stepped past Aiden and swung hard at the windshield. *Lack of red blood cells...* He walloped the glass again. *Weak from anemia.* The ax sailed through the air. Sweat broke out on Tash's forehead, and bile rose in his throat. The glass shattered, and Tash pulled the man free before Aiden could help.

The guy in his arms whispered, "I tried to get out of town when the drones came, but the car stopped dead, and the doors wouldn't open. I've been in there for hours. I'm so thirsty." He wriggled out of Tash's grasp and staggered off without a word of gratitude.

They went from car to car for the next couple of hours and freed people as they found them. If they saw someone trapped under debris, they used the rope. Tash wavered dizzily on his feet, and, at one point, Aiden had to steady him. In response, Tash pulled more vehemently at the broken chunks of walls and rebar to get to the people buried beneath. The unhurt townsfolk of Sierrawood followed them. Some people helped with adventurous smiles as if this were a game to play, as if the devastation meant nothing to them.

They passed the remains of an air bus that had crashed to the ground. A foul smell emanated from the downed vehicle. It brought to mind something diseased, which depressed Tash. He shied away from the air bus and let the others check for survivors. There were none.

They didn't know what to do with the dead. The sun had risen in the sky, and flies were gathering around the bodies. That couldn't be good. And what about the injured? They needed medical attention, but how could they transport them to the hospital? As Tash looked around, an idea struck him. He picked up a fallen wallscreen, tested its strength, and rolled a half-conscious woman onto it. The screen held her weight.

He motioned Spiky and Frizz over to the makeshift gurney. "Carry her to the hospital."

The two met his command with vacant stares.

"How?" Frizz asked.

"Each of you pick up an end, lift the screen, and walk to the hospital."

"What if it isn't there anymore?" Spiky asked.

"Go anyhow. There'll be bandages and medicine, even if you have to scrounge around."

He turned away, but Frizz grabbed his arm. "What if we can't find a doctor?"

"Find a nurse."

Spiky stepped in front of him. "Why don't you do it?"

"My group is searching for survivors."

"Well, what if my group doesn't want to listen to your group?"

Tash raised the ax. "Then how about I smash your head in with this?"

Spiky and Frizz sprang into action, swiftly lifting the wallscreen and hastening towards the hospital. Tash suppressed a laugh. Did they really believe he would harm them? He'd only been joking but found their reaction intriguing. Tash surveyed the rest of those loitering around. Eager to test out his theory, he bellowed, "Find more wallscreens and take these people to the hospital!"

He watched, amused, as the onlookers quickly mobilized to hunt for wallscreens. They really did think he would hurt them. Why?

A man approached their group. He carried the lifeless body of a woman in his arms.

"Raia, my wife." He looked toward the heavens. "Why has DAPHNE forsaken us?"

Tash nodded toward the edge of town. "Let's go to the base and find out."

CHAPTER 19

Aiden took mournful steps as he walked. Many people had died—some were strangers, but others he had known. Among them lay Professor Yang, and he couldn't believe it. A large group of people trailed him. He caught a glimpse of Professor Feinstein walking among them, attempting to smoke his defective e-pipe while expounding theories about the attack. Most everyone remained quiet, as if they were still trying to process what had happened.

Ava trudged along in silence beside him.

"I'm sorry about the reel," Aiden told her.

She didn't respond.

"I never, ever would have wanted you to see that. Someone stole it out of my head. It was a fantasy, Ava, just a dumb fantasy. I'm really sorry."

"Forget it," she tossed off. "I know some jerk made that video."

"It's true I think you're pretty, but I would never objectify you. The reel was horrible, and I know you're offended, but I swear I'm not—"

"How long do you think the power will be out?"

"I... I don't know." He hadn't expected the question. "I'm sure they're working on it."

Ava nodded, distracted. She didn't seem interested in his explanations, so he quit talking.

UPON REACHING THE BASE, the crowd cautiously maneuvered between the motionless security guards and their laser cannons, which appeared poised and ready to fire. The cannons, resembling white telephoto camera lenses, could unleash pulsing lasers upon their targets that caused pain and paralysis. Tash stepped up to one of the guards and boldly used the handle of his ax to push the weapon's nose away.

"They're dead," he assured the group. "Don't worry."

Aiden's appreciation for Tash bloomed. He had witnessed his new friend wield the ax without hesitation, rally volunteers, and confront armed security guards fearlessly. Tash possessed a great deal of nobility and strength, yet Aiden sensed a vulnerability beneath his tough exterior. The more Aiden observed his friend, the stronger this feeling became. Yes, something afflicted Tash, something significant enough to compel him to keep it hidden.

As they approached the headquarters of Cyber Command, Doug turned in a confused circle. "Where did the bunker go? Was it destroyed?"

The eyes of the rescuers darted in every direction, and Aiden sensed panic rising. It seemed inconceivable that an enemy force could obliterate DAPHNE's bunker without leaving an ash behind, but the building had evidently disappeared.

Then, Aiden spotted Ava tiptoeing toward a seemingly empty field. She reached out a tentative finger and jumped back. "Something's here!" she shouted. "You can touch it."

He walked over, reached out his hand, and jumped back when he touched fabric. Amazed, Aiden ran his fingers along the invisible material. Pushing his body against the thing, he felt it ripple.

The others gathered around and looked at Professor Feinstein for an explanation. The teacher cleared his throat. "It's obviously... Er, it must be a, um—"

"I can see something big behind it," Ava interrupted, and Feinstein sighed in relief.

Tash, wielding the ax, stepped forward. "Should I give it a swing?"

Aiden nodded. Tash raised the ax, and everyone stepped back. Who knew what would happen when the blade hit its mark?

The ax fell, and the onlookers gasped as the very air before them split open. The tear in the Suppression Sheild revealed a clear view of DAPHNE's bunker. The rescuers climbed through and walked toward the entrance. As expected, the steel door to the lobby remained impassable. Tash lifted the ax again, but Doug stopped his arm.

"Don't bother. An ax won't go through. I don't know how we're going to reach the people inside. They're underground."

Ava scanned the area and called for the party to follow her to a yard abutting the bunker. She pointed to a grill covering a hole in the earth. "There's a pipe here that goes down real deep. It looks wide enough for a person."

"It's a ventilation shaft," Doug said. "Come on, let's get this grate off."

Once they removed the covering, Aiden crouched down and called into the pipe, "Govind! Govind Lal! We're coming to get you!"

They listened but heard no reply.

Tash kneeled next to Aiden to peer into the gloom. "How are we gonna see anything down there?"

Ava's eyescreens glowed white. "You'll follow me."

PROFESSOR FEINSTEIN and Doug used the rope to lower Ava into the pipe. Her prostheses zoomed to the bottom, where she saw the pipe connected to a horizontal shaft. When her feet touched down, she called for Aiden and Tash to follow. While the boys were being lowered, she turned off her eyelight to conserve energy. Except for the pipe-sized circle of daylight at her feet, blackness surrounded her. *Is this what you see when you can't see anymore?*

A shiver ran through Ava despite the warmth of the shaft. Every month, her retinal prostheses needed rebooting. No one had ever said what to do if the power went out. She'd never even considered the idea. She felt relieved when Tash and Aiden joined her, as it spared her from contemplating the consequences of failing to reboot her eyescreens.

Crawling on their hands and knees, Ava led them along the shaft, which seemed to go on forever. Her optics eventually detected a sharp right turn many yards ahead. When the young people took the turn, a grate impeded their progress, and they took turns kicking it out. The trio then tumbled into an immense space filled with servers that hulked in the gloom.

"Uncle Govind!" Aiden's voice echoed.

They waited for an answer.

Ava's eyelight passed over the silent equipment. "Which way should we go?"

Aiden opened his mouth to speak when a metal snake suddenly dropped on him. He cried out and flailed his arms, which sent the snake flying. Ava giggled despite their predicament and picked up the slithery robot. She shook it in the air, and its metal scales made a swishing noise. Something poked her rear end, and she jumped with a squeal. Jerking around, her eyescreens illuminated a robotic arm extending from the gridwork with a hard drive still clasped in its metal gripper. Laughter filled their small circle of light until Aiden suddenly froze.

"Shh!" he said. "Do you hear that?"

"Hello?" A man's voice echoed from far away.

"We're here!" Aiden yelled in the direction of the sound.

Ava's digital eyes could only light up a certain distance. Beyond that, blackness crouched. She switched to infrared and x-ray vision.

Aiden sidled up close. "Can you see anyone?"

She inhaled the earthy scent of him, which made her less afraid. "There's a wall ahead with lots of people behind it."

Her companions couldn't see the wall to which she referred but could hear the muffled shouts of many voices. The three rescuers twisted around banks of dead servers until they encountered a set of open double doors. They stepped onto a a stone patio and could swear, under the beam of Ava's light, that they stood outside. Shadowy trees hung over an expanse of grass on which there were small tables and overturned chairs.

"What is this place?" Tash asked.

At that moment, a small creature flapped close, and Ava screeched. She waved her arms as another flying thing swooped in.

Aiden stopped her arms. "They're just birds," he said. "How are they here?"

Two finches landed, frightened and confused, on a stone step. Aiden spoke softly to them and scooped them up. They huddled in his hands.

"Who is that?" someone called from across the patio. A large group of shadowy people approached Ava's eyelight like moths to a flame.

Aiden called, "Is Govind Lal with you?"

"Aiden?" Govind stepped into Ava's circle of light. "Am I glad to see you." He hugged his nephew. "However did you get inside?"

"A ventilation shaft."

A pretty young woman with purple-streaked hair approached. She wore a white coat pinned with the nametag, *Vivica.* "It's guarded."

Tash shook his head. "Not anymore."

"L'Eren?" Govind asked in a voice laced with dread.

"She's fine." Aiden gently caged the finches in his pocket. "Just worried about you. What happened, Uncle Govind?"

The man ignored the question and introduced Aiden to the others as his nephew. Aiden, in turn, introduced them to Tash and Ava. White-coated technicians, engineers, and other people dressed in military uniforms surrounded the three high schoolers in gratitude. Apparently, they never thought they'd make it out alive.

"Thank goodness for your eyescreens," Govind told Ava. "Let's get out of here."

"What about DAPHNE?" Ava asked. "Can't you get her to work?"

"I'll explain, but we must go. We're running out of air, and it's going to take a long time to haul everyone up that shaft."

ONE BY ONE, THE MILITARY team and engineers were hoisted out. Many arms and legs pushed and kicked against the pipe and loosened it from its footings, which made the task more arduous as the minutes passed. Some stayed behind to help extricate the others, but Hal and Vivica took a team to inspect the power feeding DAPHNE's bunker. Only Lizzie stood apart, motionless amid all the activity. Govind figured she was in shock.

When Hal and Vivica returned, they explained the bleak situation to Govind and Lizzie. Vivica fingered her nametag with a trembling hand. "We can't access our solar or wind power. Something overrode every one of our auxiliary systems. Wires are fried, and all the power lines have experienced thermal overload. The transformers are damaged beyond repair and need to be replaced."

Hal added, "Our HVAC systems are burned out as well."

"What does that mean ?" Govind asked and glanced at Lizzie. She seemed dazed as she watched Aiden free two small birds from his hands.

"That means that even if we did get the servers up and running," Vivica said, "we can't properly cool them down."

"How long will it take to repair everything?"

Vivica and Hal exchanged astonished looks.

"It takes a specialized crew, Dr. Lal," the purple-haired girl said. "No one here can do it. My team can handle basic repairs but we can't build an entire data center from the ground up. And even if we could, how would we get the supplies we need?"

Govind whistled through his teeth. "DAPHNE didn't just wound the grid. She obliterated it."

"Why, Uncle Govind?" Aiden asked. "Why would DAPHNE do that?"

"If there's no power, she, nor any other AGI, can run. The military machines of our enemies halt. If there's no power, there's no war."

Doug stepped closer to his brother-in-law. "But surely, DAPHNE didn't shut herself down completely. She wouldn't have done that. She'd have to know what kind of chaos that would bring."

"Our enemies successfully hacked our weaponry," Govind told him. "It stands to reason, they might eventually hack her, too. Perhaps, she considered that a worse scenario."

"But—"

"DAPHNE killed herself, Doug." Govind surveyed the crowd of onlookers. "There's no more Intelligence. We're on our own."

CHAPTER 20

After Govind reunited with L'Eren, he insisted on going into town while daylight lingered. He was, after all, a government official and should take control. He asked Lizzie to join him because she seemed so disoriented. The engineer had slept at Jill's house last night and would remain there as long as DAPHNE's bunker remained uninhabitable.

When they arrived in the town square, Govind saw people pacing aimlessly, waiting for DAPHNE to power up again. A few helped Doug, Aiden, Tash, and Ava rescue survivors.

Tash instructed people on how to build gurneys out of defunct wallscreens. *Good plan,* Govind thought and wished he'd come up with the idea. The muscular young man made a formidable impression with the wondrous ax tied about his waist. Tash seemed to take charge naturally, and his newly deputized EMTs obeyed his orders and carried their wounded cargo to the hospital. It was, however, time for a real leader to step forward.

"Everyone!" Govind lifted his hands toward the crowd filling the square. "Please give me your attention."

A beefy man wearing a Tilley hat and hiking shorts approached him. "Say, are you Govind Lal, the Secretary of Defense?"

"I am," Govind said with pride, "and I'd like to take this opportunity to –"

"What the hell happened?" the man shouted.

A woman holding the leash of a barking German shepherd surged toward Govind. "Why is DAPHNE not responding? Why don't our WeConnects work?"

Bark! Bark!

Another woman rushed over. "Who sent all these drones to kill us? What's going on?"

A little girl with pigtails tugged on Govind's pant leg. "Dr. Lal, can you turn on my WeConnect?"

More townsfolk congregated around him. Some stood in awe of his importance. Others fell on their knees before him and sobbed over their dead or injured loved ones. Many yelled and shook their fists at him. Govind gulped. His bodyguard app no longer functioned.

Who would have thought the cocky young genius who worked his way up Ophidian's corporate ladder and then received a Presidential Cabinet post would experience fear?

"Our enemies attacked us," he explained. "DAPHNE killed the power sources they were using."

"What enemies?" the woman with the dog asked. "Who attacked us?"

Someone else yelled, "What do you mean, she killed the power?"

Bark! Bark! Bark!

"Why didn't we know we were in danger?"

Bark!

"Where was the government when they were shooting us down like dogs?"

"People are dead! Look at them! Look at this town!"

Bark! Bark! Bark!

"How long will the power be out?"

"My boyfriend is buried under rubble! I don't know if he's alive or dead!"

"We need help! How could you let something like this happen?"

Bark! Bark!

"Is the army coming to help us?"

Bark! Bark! Bark!

Govind couldn't field the barrage of questions.

At last, the man with the Tilley hat threw it on the ground. "Well, what are we supposed to do now, Mr. Big Shot?"

Govind ran a frazzled hand through his black hair. "We—"

"Other places can't be shut down," said the woman with the dog.

"DAPHNE feeds intelligence all over the country," Govind told her. "Trust me, we have a nationwide shutdown."

Bark! Bark! The woman pulled on her straining dog. "The cities have the means to help us. We have to let people know we're in trouble out here."

"The people in the cities are in worse trouble. Can you imagine the widespread panic in the streets? In the subways? What do you think the people stuck in skyscrapers are doing? They have no way out. At least we have a chance to maintain some control over our small population."

Bark! Bark! The woman pulled hard on the dog's leash. "I still say we need to know what the rest of the world is doing."

The man swept up his Tilley hat from the ground. "Let's go to San Francisco and tell them we're stranded out here without Intelligence."

"It's not going to make a difference." Govind turned to Lizzie. Although the engineer stood by his side, she wasn't present. "Tell them, Dr. Appel," he insisted. "Tell them DAPHNE is dead and gone."

Lizzie gazed at a distant point on the landscape. She didn't seem to hear him.

"I'm outta here." The man with the Tilley hat climbed straight into an undamaged air bus. The woman with the dog followed, along with several other townspeople.

Govind shook his head. "It's not going to run."

Lizzie, at last, blinked her eyes and straightened her shoulders. She looked around for a confused moment and then focused on the people boarding the air bus.

"What are they doing?" she asked. "There's no navigation system. Nothing will drive the bus."

The man with the Tilley hat pressed random buttons on the dashboard. Behind the barking of the dog, Govind heard the whir of an electric motor revving up.

"Get out of there!" He rushed toward the vehicle. "There's no guidance!"

Those on the bus ignored him. The folks on the ground watched, spellbound, as the lumbering vehicle began to rise on its leftover charge. Other people came running, drawn by the bus in the sky, its familiar hum, and the hope the sound carried. Higher and higher, the bus ascended. Govind glimpsed Ava Durand step forward and direct her vision to the vehicle's dashboard. Whatever the girl saw caused her to clutch Aiden's arm.

"Dr. Lal is right," Ava cried. "It isn't connected to GPS."

With no network guidance, the air bus began to circle. Slowly, at first, and then it went into a spiral. The shouting of the passengers inside the bus could be heard by those below. Ava, with reflexes as quick as lightning, pushed a woman out of the way as the bus lost its charge and dropped from the sky like a dead bird. The barking and the terrified screams that heralded its quick descent ended abruptly with a deafening crash.

The onlookers stared at the broken body of the bus. Ava's hand covered her mouth. Professor Feinstein swallowed repeatedly and fished through the pockets of his cardigan for his pipe. Tash held the ax so tightly his knuckles whitened. Doug seemed frozen in place, and Govind pivoted away from the wreck, unable to view anymore.

Aiden moved over to him. "What are we going to do, Uncle Govind?"

The Secretary of Defense shook his head. He didn't know. For all his advanced education, no one had schooled him on how to take charge of a catastrophe. He surveyed the assembly of people gaping at the crash site. They were in shock but, soon, anger would consume them. They would blame him, and Govind loved L'Eren too much to leave her a widow.

Nudging Doug, he nodded toward a side street. Doug traded looks with his son, but Aiden's feet remained firmly planted. Govind sensed his brother-in-law's struggle. Doug didn't want to leave his son behind, but his allegience to his boss won out, and Govind led him away.

Glancing behind, Govind saw Aiden glaring at him. Shame burned Govind's cheeks, but he couldn't stay. He was a leader who didn't know how to lead.

CHAPTER 21

The setting sun threw orange light on the shocked faces of those who stood paralyzed around the downed air bus. Aiden couldn't believe his uncle left, and worse, Doug had followed. Someone needed to take charge.

Say something.

For a half-second, Aiden believed his WeConnect had turned on. Then, he realized the Great Source spoke. He scratched his head with grimy fingers but stayed quiet.

Guide them.

Aiden's eyes roamed the crowd and halted on Clyde Parrish and Pete Montgomery. He swallowed hard.

You can do it. Allow your heart to speak, and the right words will come out.

Fear pulsed in his chest. No one would listen to him. No one ever listened to him.

At that moment, Spiky returned from the hospital with the other "EMTs," all of them spent and impatient. They tossed no more than a glance toward the decimated air bus.

"We're hungry," Spiky complained to Tash. "What are we s'posed to eat?"

"Yeah, how can we use our accounts to get food?" Frizz whined.

Spiky viewed the blasted-out storefront of the Healthy Habit. Throwing Tash a defiant look, the kid grabbed Frizz, and the two clambered over the rubble into the market.

Clyde elbowed Pete. "Let's go."

The two young men vanished inside. A minute passed, during which the townsfolk exchanged glances and rubbed their chins in contemplation. Then, as if following an unspoken signal, the crowd surged toward the store. A few stumbled over the debris, and the others shoved them out of the way. Ava, Tash, and Aiden hesitated only briefly and then fought their way inside too.

The mob took carts and pulled one item after another from the shelves. In the dairy aisle, milk cartons fell and busted open as people grappled for them. Others rushing past slid on the wet floor and got trampled by folks battling to seize as many items as they could.

Aiden could see nothing but a mass of heads, reaching arms, and grabbing hands. A large bin of paper towels quickly emptied. A woman ran by with a shopping cart filled with meat. Clyde and Pete jumped behind the deli counter, throwing whole hams, turkeys, and other foods into grocery bags. A man grabbed the ham in Clyde's hands but dropped it when Clyde punched him in the face. People shouted. People yelled. One woman pushed another woman against the shelves in the cereal aisle, which caused a whole row of boxes to crash to the floor. Folks quickly scooped them up.

Those with shopping carts stuffed them in a frenzy. Those without carts made a mad dash from aisle to aisle to fill as many bags as their arms could carry. Fights broke out. Ava steered Aiden and Tash toward the back of the store, where she pushed open a door.

Her super optics had spied a storage locker with a bounty of dry goods and canned food. The three filled grocery bags until the crowd discovered them and poured into the room. Bodies crushed against Aiden until he thought he couldn't breathe. Tash had to shove people aside, and Aiden and Ava glued themselves to their powerful friend to get out.

The trio stumbled outside onto the wreckage of Pine Avenue and stood gasping on the sidewalk. The street looked like a tornado had blown through. They clutched their bags tight, cautious of the town's residents-turned-marauders. Aiden's foot throbbed where someone had stomped on it. He looked back at the roiling mass of humanity inside the market and recalled the woman who waved the white shirt at his grandparents' place. *My husband owns the Healthy Habit.*

"This is wrong," he stated.

"What else could we do?" Tash asked. "We can't pay. If the food isn't taken, it'll rot."

Aiden viewed the grocery bags in his arms. Weary, feeling dismal, he offered to walk Ava home because Sierrawood, their secure mountain haven, no longer guaranteed safety. The two said goodbye to Tash with a promise to meet in the morning. They left the Healthy Habit, where pandemonium still reigned.

TASH DID NOT LEAVE for home right away. He ate a protein bar and watched from the shadows as his fellow citizens raided the boutiques, the department store, the discount store, the hardware store, and even the thrift shop. Most windows had been blown out of the stores, so people climbed inside. Clyde Parrish, Pete Farmington, and some other kids whom Tash recognized from school maneuvered loaded shopping carts out of one store and into the next. Clyde wore an impish grin as if this were fun, as if he played a game to win. The adults didn't behave much better. They, too, took to the streets with bundles loaded in their arms.

Tash had never seen anything like it, not even in his old inner-city neighborhood in Oakland. He'd held his own in that tough community until one scuffle landed him in the hospital. He couldn't afford a beating, not with his illness. Since his dad and mom could work remotely, they moved to the quaint town of Sierrawood, with its clean air and decent people. The town had bored Tash to tears – until tonight.

When he could no longer witness the crumbling of civility, he headed home. Nobody harassed him. No one dared to challenge his height, muscles, or the ax swinging from his belt. After dropping off the groceries at his apartment, Tash went to the hospital. Whatever of his meds remained in the pharmacy, he'd better collect them before the looters did.

Walking under the yellow eye of the rising moon, he observed residents of the once-prim town scurry off in all directions like cockroaches. He entered the hospital through the emergency room doors, which were wedged open by a fallen security guard robot. Tash stepped over the robot and let his eyes adjust to the dimness. What he saw inside caused his heart to drop.

The wounded lay on makeshift gurneys. Bandages had been sloppily applied to those who were bleeding, but many who bore serious injuries lay moaning in pain. Tash wished he could throttle the spiky-haired kid and the others. How could they have left wounded people like this?

All around the lobby, doctor and nurse androids posed like mannequins. One sat behind the front desk with its fingers touching a black deskscreen. Two uniformed EMT droids had fallen over next to a gurney carrying a body. The human patient, still hooked to a saline drip, lay unmoving. A doctor droid faced a nurse; their conversation silenced, their expressions locked into place. A nurse android held a computer tablet and viewed two unoccupied chairs as if the patient's family waited there for news.

A weird glow emanated from the android's faces, and their reassuring smiles seemed to mock the suffering of the wounded humans moaning and writhing around on the floor. Tash didn't know what to do for the injured, much less for the dying. He hurried past them.

In a dim hallway echoing with faint cries, he stopped at a room illuminated by soft gray moonlight. Inside, an android doctor stood motionless with its "finger" pressed against the chest of an elderly patient, perhaps to monitor the man's heart. The patient wriggled beneath the android's touch, which pinned him against the bed.

"Help me." The man stretched out a plaintive arm toward Tash.

Tash intended to disregard the man, not out of malice, but due to exhaustion. Night had fallen, the town wasn't safe, and he needed to get his medication. He didn't know what to do.

The patient, too weak to simply push the android away, groaned. Tash entered the room, lifted the doctor with ease, and hid it in the closet.

"Water," the man begged. "Is there water?"

Tash spied a half-filled pitcher on a table near the window. He poured a glass for the man and held it to his lips. "Try to sleep."

He couldn't think of anything else to say. As he turned to leave, the patient grasped his hand and gave him a feeble smile. Tash swallowed and removed the man's hand from his.

A strange disquiet accompanied him as he trekked toward the pharmacy. The feel of the patient's hand and the gentleness in his eyes made Tash's chest ache.

He passed an operating room and felt compelled to peer inside. He wished he hadn't.

A surgery had been in progress at the time of the shutdown. A couple of robotic nurses gave off sparse light from their facial screens, and he could make out the silhouette of a patient lying severed on a table surrounded by robotic "arms" paralyzed in various stages of the operation. It reminded him of a horror movie, someone dissected by aliens. Below the surgical table lay a black puddle. Nauseated, Tash hurried toward the pharmacy. A soft aching moved through him like a wave. An unusual, strange feeling. *Empathy.*

I'll come back tomorrow, he promised. *I'll come back with Aiden. He'll know what to do.*

CHAPTER 22

As Tash explored the hospital, Aiden accompanied Ava down her street, where the small houses stood identical to each other. All of them featured front bay windows that were now shattered.

Ava adjusted her grip on the bulging grocery bags and said, "Your uncle is the Secretary of Defense. Who attacked us? What's he telling you?"

"I think he's as confused as the rest of us."

Ava's mother stood at the busted-out window of her home. Lace curtains fluttered round her. Relief washed over Z'ier Durand's face upon seeing her daughter.

Ava's shoes crunched on broken glass as they approached. "Mom, this is Aiden Baylor, a friend from school."

Z'ier's attempt to smile crumbled, and Aiden's fatigue deepened at the sight of the woman. Ava's mother resembled a washed-out version of her daughter with matted, straw-like hair and pale skin. Even her eyes were a faded blue.

Ava handed her mother the two bags of groceries, and Z'ier didn't question their origin. She shuffled off in a threadbare robe toward the kitchen. Z'ier reminded Aiden of someone he might encounter in a psych ward, which made his stomach queasy.

"Do you want to come in?" Ava asked.

"Thanks, but I should go."

The home had an oppressive air, and he felt bad leaving her. "Where's your dad?"

"In Montana. My parents are divorced." She looked down. "I don't know if he's okay or not."

Through the window, Aiden observed Z'ier unpacking the grocery bags as if the slightest movement pained her. "The attack really affected your mom, didn't it?"

"She was like this before the attack." Ava's eyescreens reflected the moon.

He reached out and tucked a lock of her dirty hair behind her ear. "Thanks for your eyes. We couldn't have made it into the bunker without you."

She nodded, gripped the window frame, and hoisted herself inside.

Aiden trudged home, his steps sluggish from exhaustion and from witnessing the reality of Ava's life, which caught him off guard. He'd assumed she led a charmed life. Far from it. Then again, he assumed a lot of people were more fortunate than him. His insecurities had crafted a virtual reality in which Aiden played the part of a loser.

You make everyone else more valuable than you. Value yourself. Credit your unique abilities.

The Great Source. How easily it spoke now. Perhaps, the enforced quiet in the world had opened a portal—but to what?

Aiden asked silently, *Who are you?*

He received no answer. *Are you the Lifespark?*

Still, no answer. Grumbling, he asked, *Are you dead like DAPHNE?*

His body tingled, and words surfaced in his mind: *Very much alive.*

UNDER ROLAND'S WEAK light, Aiden laid out on the kitchen counter the food he'd stolen from the Healthy Habit. He addressed his family with guarded eyes.

"I know it was wrong to steal, but I thought I should get us some food while I could. If DAPHNE powers up tomorrow, I promise I'll make it up to –"

"DAPHNE killed herself," Dr. Lizzie Appel interrupted.

The family regarded Lizzie. Grandpa Harry perked up. "Look what I did, Rebel."

The elderly man pointed at the refrigerator, whose door hung open at an unloved angle. Harry lifted his bionic hand, made a fist, and winked.

Inside the freezer, Aiden viewed packages of meat and chicken. Unfortunately, they were fully thawed.

"I could cook that food," Grandma Rosie said, "if the stove worked. I know how to cook."

L'Eren, who lay listless on the living room couch, called out, "Can't we eat it raw?"

Uncle Govind answered, "No, Rennie."

His wife moaned in obvious discomfort.

Uncle Govind eyed his in-laws and dropped his voice to a whisper. "I hope she has an easy birth."

Rosie patted his shoulder. "Women have given birth for centuries, and they didn't need Artificial Intelligence to do it. The human body has its own kind of automation, you know."

"As long as there are no difficulties," he reminded her.

Doug put a hand on his brother-in-law's shoulder. "Let's think positive."

"Meanwhile," Jill said, "Oreanna hasn't eaten a thing since the attack. I can't get her to leave her bedroom. I don't know what to do. What are we all supposed to do?" Her hand went over her heart as if she might faint. Doug put an arm of support around his wife.

"Do you want me to talk to her, Mom?" Aiden asked.

Jill sniffled and nodded.

Aiden hopped up the stairs, energized by his mother's faith in him. Darkness cloaked the hallway, but moonlight streamed through Oreanna's open door. When he peered into her bedroom, he saw her sitting cross-legged on the floor, surrounded by a corona of white strands. She must have passed the time breaking off bits of her damaged hair.

He knocked on the wall. "Can I come in?"

"You can go away."

"Ori, nobody cares about your hair."

"I'm not leaving this room until it grows out."

"That's a long time."

"Can you bring me something to eat? Please? I don't want to see anyone."

Aiden didn't press the issue. Instead, he groped his way downstairs and made his sister a peanut butter sandwich. Returning to her room, he nearly tripped over Kif the cat. This is ridiculous, he thought. They couldn't live in the dark. After serving Ori her sandwich, he confronted his family in the kitchen, illuminated only by Roland's light.

"What are we going to do?" he asked. "We need light, and Roland's charge isn't gonna last much longer."

Rosie regarded her husband. "Do we have any candles at home?"

"Even if we could find a candle," Grandpa Harry said, "How would we light it?"

Aiden suddenly snapped his fingers. "My camping cookstove. It lights automatically, and we could use the burner's flame to light a candle or even the barbeque. Then, we could cook."

"That's a great idea, Rebel."

"I'll go to the lake right now and get it." He regarded Jill, wanting, needing to be her champion. "Don't worry, Mom. I'll take care of everything." He slid out the narrow window near the front door and ran off into the night.

CHAPTER 23

The moon bounced along the treetops like a bright white ball as Aiden jogged along the familiar trail leading to the clearing. He'd gone about a quarter of a mile when a crack in the darkness startled him. He slowed his pace, suddenly aware that his footsteps sounded brash and loud. He couldn't tell which direction the sound came from. A creeping sensation, similar to the one he'd felt before the drone attack, spread over his body like a rash. He had been in the forest at night but never alone. Only last August, he'd camped here with Grandpa Harry, and, of course, DAPHNE had accompanied them via their WeConnects.

The clearing lay only a few yards ahead, but Aiden feared going further. The trees around him appeared spectral and menacing. Stripped of their leaves by the drones, they reached skeletal branches toward the heavens as if to say, *Look what your kind did to us.*

Not my kind, Aiden assured them silently. He inhaled deeply, forcing his feet to move because they needed the cookstove. Incredibly, he found himself wishing he could contact DAPHNE.

When he arrived at the clearing, he saw his guitar case lying where he'd dropped it. He didn't see his backpack, which should have been beside the guitar. Quickly retrieving the case, Aiden held it to him like a shield. He couldn't shake the feeling that danger lurked behind the mangled trees.

Where did his backpack go? He searched the clearing and found the pack entangled in a wild raspberry bush. He swallowed hard as he held up the vinyl tatters. Something had ripped the bag to shreds.

Slowly, quietly, Aiden began backtracking toward home when his eye caught an object glinting under the stars. The camping stove! He scooped it up and pressed the button on the front. He waited for the click of the starter, the exhalation of propane, and the resulting flame. Nothing happened.

Perplexed, he pressed the button again. The self-starter didn't need AI to run, so why wouldn't the burner ignite? Aiden rotated the stove's body in his hands and gasped to see two ragged tears in the metal. Claw marks.

An owl hooted overhead. The trees moaned, prompted by the night breeze. Never had he considered the forest a threatening place. He'd always felt welcomed here, but something had changed. As much as Aiden hated to admit it, he'd relied on DAPHNE to protect him. Now, he stood alone, exposed, and vulnerable in a world humans once dominated. Not anymore. Not now. Holding tight to his guitar case, he retreated down the trail for home.

WHEN AIDEN LEFT HER home, Ava wandered listlessly into her bedroom. She could light up the space with her eyescreens but couldn't play games, chat with friends, or watch videos. She couldn't even read a book because she streamed all reading material through her WeConnect. Ava couldn't do anything except sit in a kind of suspended animation.

She focused her vision on an antique poster hanging on the wall that featured a rainbow arching over a city skyline. The poster, yellowed and frayed at the edges, had once belonged to a great aunt. The rainbow reminded Ava something beautiful can come after a storm. She needed the reminder because she had only her sad mother for companionship and yearned to live with her father.

He lived in Montana with a new family and seemed very happy. Although he and Ava chatted weekly, their conversations never ran deep. She'd tell him about school, her skill in the gaming field, and revel in her father's praise. Then, they said goodbye. Her stepbrothers and stepsister got to enjoy her dad every day, but she always had to say goodbye to him.

Ava wondered why her dad favored his new family over her when she tried to be the best at everything. At every goodbye, she wanted to cry, except her eyes produced no tears. Acid-like jealousy burned away the sorrow but left her heart feeling corroded.

Now, with DAPHNE disabled or dead or whatever they were calling her malfunction, Ava couldn't reach her dad for even the tiniest bit of solace. Bored, feeling sorry for herself, she walked into the kitchen where her mom had laid out the looted groceries.

"What are we going to do when this runs out?" Z'ier gave her daughter a bleak look.

Ava supposed she couldn't blame her mother for being depressed. Her father's affair with the younger woman who would become his second wife flattened Ava's mother like a steamroller. It seemed that nothing could pump Z'ier up to her former self.

"I'll go to a different market tomorrow," Ava said, "and see if they're not all picked thr-"

A bone-rattling shriek cut off her words. Ava told her mom to stay put and scrambled out the front window. Next door, she could hear a man shouting and a woman screaming. Neighbors emerged from their homes and stood on the street ogling the house.

Ava chewed a fingernail on her front lawn, wondering what to do, when a brown bear suddenly shot out her neighbor's front window like a furry explosion. She gasped as the big animal lumbered past and disappeared into the darkness. Inside the house, a woman screeched like a mad parrot.

Ava, joined by another neighbor, carefully approached the window from which the bear escaped and peeked inside. A terrified woman crouched in the corner of a trashed dining room. Ava had seen this woman on occasion, but they'd never spoken. The neighbor standing next to her, a bald, fortyish man with bushy eyebrows, crawled through the window, and Ava followed.

On the crumpled tablecloth lay the wreckage of a meal. On the rug lay a heavy-set man Ava recognized as the woman's husband. Deep gouges on his stomach and his neck oozed blood.

"Help him!" the woman cried to the strangers in her house. "Please!"

Ava could see swaths of drapery torn away. A digital wallscreen lay cracked on the floor, and a musky, wild odor permeated the place, a calling card left by the intruding bear.

The woman wrung her hands. "That monster came in and took the food right off the table!" She pointed to her wounded husband. "Hector tried to fight him off, and it swiped its paw at him!"

Hector, the bleeding man, wasn't moving.

"Somebody do something!" the woman pleaded.

Ava and the bald man exchanged glances. No Roland motored in to help. Nobody knew how to call for an ambulance. There were no ambulances. Ava shifted on her feet.

"You should probably board this up." The man pointed at the window through which they'd entered. "That bear might come back. Maybe your food that attracted it."

In reply, the woman sobbed into her hands. The curious neighbors that had collected outside the window moved off. All of them had a busted-out opening in their house and food on the table. They hurried home to secure their entrances. The balding, bushy-eyed man mumbled an apology and climbed outside to do the same.

Ava stayed behind; she couldn't leave the man to bleed out on the floor. She asked the woman if she had any antiseptic to clean the wound with.

"Roland!" the woman shouted and then shook her head. "I don't know where Roland keeps anything."

Ava bit her lip, picked up a discarded napkin, and dabbed at the man's middle. Soon, she realized he wasn't breathing.

"I think he's dead." She dropped the napkin as the woman collapsed onto a dining room chair.

Ava watched her cry for a minute and then pushed aside the table to roll the man up in the rug. "I'll come back with my friends in the morning."

She didn't know what else to do. She wished Aiden hadn't left.

CHAPTER 24

The persistent knocking sound woke Aiden the following morning, and he padded to the entry hall. The sun, rising through the pines, threw strips of orange light onto the white tiles of the front porch where Ava stood.

"Hi." His voice croaked in surprise. He wiped the sleep from his eyes and remembered he wore only his boxer shorts. "How'd you know where I live?"

"Everyone knows where the VIPs in town live. I'm sorry I'm here so early. I… I didn't sleep last night."

Three days had passed since the attack, and Ava's hair hung in greasy strands. She seemed self-conscious about the dirt under her fingernails and balled her hands into fists. "I've been waiting all night for morning."

"Lemme get dressed. Come on in. Um, do you want some peanut butter?"

Ava shook her head as she slipped through the narrow window. While she waited for Aiden, Ava beheld a photo of the happy family on the entry table: Doug, Jill, Aiden, and a girl Ava presumed to be Aiden's sister. Only, this girl didn't look anything like the famed Oreanna Baylor popular on social media. Curious, Ava's eyescreens took a photo of the portrait and saved it.

Aiden soon returned wearing jeans, a shirt, and sneakers. He held two slices of bread smeared with peanut butter. Despite her previous refusal, Ava took the proffered breakfast.

"Your house is beautiful," she said, looking around. "You guys must be really rich."

Aiden shrugged. It felt strange to be envied.

She took a bite and chewed slowly. "My neighbor was killed by a bear. The lady, his wife, doesn't know what to do with the body."

"A bear killed someone?" Aiden had never heard of bears venturing into the neighborhoods, not even near homes like his that bordered the forest. The artificial light and hum of machinery must have kept the wildlife at bay.

Ava's eyescreens displayed a photo she'd taken of the dead man. "See? He should be buried, right?"

Aiden dragged his eyes from the grisly photo. "Let's go to my grandparents' place. They have lots of things we could use, and we can get Tash." He paused, thinking. "And there's someone else who might help, too."

AVA HUDDLED CLOSE TO Aiden as they weaved through the old warehouse district with its cluster of rickety shanties. At first, she grimaced at the people living there with their hardened faces and filthy clothes. Then, she viewed her own stained shorts and dirty fingernails and realized she was as unwashed as they.

Aiden halted at a wooden shack with a roof of blue tarp. "Chris?"

It stunned Ava to watch her friend hug the bearded bundle of rags that emerged from the shack. Aiden put a hand on each of the unkempt man's shoulders and grinned. "You're alive."

"Why would anybody bother to kill us?" He jerked out from under Aiden's hands as if the affection grated on him. Still, above the man's scruffy beard, his dark brown eyes softened. "I'm glad they didn't kill you, kid. D'ya have any idea who'd wanna wipe Sierrawood off the map?"

"My Uncle Govind says the world is at war. Enemy nations hacked our drones and used them to attack us. DAPHNE destroyed herself – *it*self—to stop the attack. That's why everything went dark."

The grungy guy grunted. "I wondered why I could see the stars again. That God-awful glow coming from town always riled me."

"Chris, this is my friend, Ava."

The man grimaced upon viewing her face. "What the hell are those?" He stepped close and put his nose to hers. Ava stood her ground but winced at his body odor.

"I thought you were wearing weird glasses, but who wears glasses anymore?" Chris shook his head at her prostheses. "Son-of-a-gun. Are those things removable? I've never seen anything more crazy."

In response, Ava displayed mirrors that reflected the grid-skipper's face. Chris smiled, and she glimpsed he was minus a couple of teeth.

"Good trick," he told her.

"We need your help," Aiden asked. "Can you come with us?"

"I don't leave my possessions, not for anyone or anything."

"But a man died, and we don't know what to do. He's still at home."

"Bury him."

"How?"

"Dig a hole."

"With what? Our bare hands? Look, can you come to my grandparents' apartment? I don't even know what half the stuff they have is used for."

Chris absently stroked his beard as he scrutinized the two young people. "Fine, but only if I can take something for my stash."

CHAPTER 25

Ava told Chris the story of her eyes as the trio walked to the apartment complex. He, in turn, gave her and Aiden a brief rundown of funerary procedures. They met with Tash and entered Harry and Rosie's apartment through the smashed-in wall.

The four stood amid piles of boxes and stacks of papers.

Chris put his hands on his hips. "Geez, and they call me mentally ill."

"I guess you could call my grandparents hoarders." Aiden lifted sheepish shoulders.

The group began by sifting through the old tools in L'Eren's childhood bedroom. Aiden untied a plastic trash bag and pulled out a snorkel and a pair of flippers. What they needed was another camping stove.

"Try to find another of these." Tash tapped the ax, which hung from his rope belt like a sheathed sword.

Chris unzipped what looked like a cloth carrier for snow skis. "Now, these are valuable."

Aiden watched him lift out two fishing poles. "Grandpa taught me how to fish with those, and I taught my dad."

"Take 'em." Chris handed him the poles. "We'll need them."

Tash held up a pickaxe. "What's this?"

"A good tool. Take it."

"And this?" Tash showed Chris a hammer.

"That, too."

"What's this?" Ava held up a long shaft with a rounded-edged blade at one end.

"That, my dear, is a shovel, and you hit the jackpot."

THEY STOOD IN THE DEAD man's backyard, and Chris instructed Aiden, Ava, and Tash to use the shovel to dig a deep, rectangular hole. They buried Hector within the rug since they had nothing to use as a casket. Chris tore some wire from the defunct household Roland, tied two sticks in the shape of a cross, and plunked it over the grave.

Throughout it all, the wife held a rag to her face and wept.

As they stood over the overturned earth, Chris elbowed Aiden. "Say a few words."

"Why?"

"That's what you do when you bury someone. You say nice things."

"Why?"

"Because it makes the mourners feel better, dumbass. Obviously, it doesn't make a difference to the guy in the ground."

But it does. The voice spoke inside Aiden. *Caring spreads good energy to lands that exist in dreams.* Words pressed against his lips, and he didn't push them away.

"We care about this man and honor the life he lived."

The man's wife hiccupped and regarded Aiden with teary eyes. "Hector. His name is Hector."

Aiden swallowed his fear. "Hector is no longer in his physical body, but his energy still exists."

Ava and Tash ogled him, but the woman drew closer.

"He is all around us." Aiden closed his eyes and let the words flow. "He is part of the Great Source now. His body has expired, but his spirit lives next to us in the land of dreams. Our comfort and love can cross that border."

He opened his eyes to see Tash staring at him with raised eyebrows. Ava's lips were pursed together, and her eyescreens displayed pulsing red exclamation marks. The grieving wife, however, smiled at Aiden under her tear-stained face, which made the petals of his heart unfurl like a blossom.

Chris grinned at him. "Amen."

"What was that all about?" Tash asked as they left the woman's home. "Why would you tell her he's around? The guy's dead. And what is the Great Source?"

"I don't know. These words come to me, and now they're flowing with my words."

Tash clapped Aiden on the back. "You're psycho is what you are. But it's a good kind of psycho."

"I don't feel crazy. I feel good. Didn't you see her? That lady, she liked what I said. It made her feel better. I'm not psycho, am I?"

Ava's eyescreens played a cartoon of a stick-figure man running in circles and crashing into a wall.

Chris contemplated the ground as he walked. "You're a medicine man."

"A what?" Aiden swiveled his face toward him.

"A healer. A spiritual leader. Didn't you read the book I gave you about the indigenous people?"

"The world sort of turned upside down, Chris. I didn't get the chance."

"Well, you got nothing to do now, smartass. Read it."

When they dropped Chris off at his shack, he stowed an old Polaroid camera under his tarp, courtesy of Aiden's grandparents.

"Why don't you join us?" Aiden asked. "All of us are grid-skippers now."

"Bad idea, Angakkuq. I don't think your kind would welcome our kind to the party."

"Anga-cock?"

"The Inuit name for medicine man."

CHAPTER 26

When Govind woke up, Aiden was gone, off to bury someone. Govind couldn't remain at Jill's home doing nothing. He needed to set an example. Show people he was a leader.

"Tash says the hospital is in bad shape," he told the family as they split a package of sliced turkey for lunch. The sandwich meat had sat out all night, but they couldn't bear to let it go to waste. "Come with me, Lizzie. I've asked Hal and Vivica to help out too."

"What can I do there?" Lizzie lifted a wilted slice of turkey and set it back down. She'd been out of sorts since DAPHNE shut down.

"You're a doctor."

"So are you."

"But you have a medical background. You must come."

THE VOLUNTEERS ARRIVED at the hospital to find anxious relatives and friends of the patients milling about. Everyone wanted to help but didn't know what to do. When Vivica entered through the open emergency doors, she pinched her nostrils. "Wow, it stinks in here."

The groans of those lying about pushed their feet forward. The wounded and the dead lay on wallscreens on the floor. Grandma Rosie lifted the sheet off one patient and yelped as a rat leaped away.

"My God!" She watched, repulsed, as the creature scuttled down the hall.

Govind put a hand to his mouth to stem his nausea. "This is a serious problem. If we don't get the dead buried, this place will go from a hospital to a hazard by the evening."

Rosie shivered from the memory of the rat. "We've got to get the vermin out of here and seal every opening."

"But how will we get in or out?" Vivica asked.

Grandpa Harry stepped forward. "We've got an antique door in our bedroom that opens and closes." He nodded toward the open emergency doors. "I'll bet we can install it in here somehow."

When Doug and Grandpa Harry left to retrieve the door, Rosie viewed the defunct elevator.

"There's got to be stairs somewhere." Turning to the others, she said, "We should bring the patients on the upper floors down here."

The volunteers worked meticulously through each floor to remove and store the androids, transfer patients to the lower floors, and administer what medicines they could. The job gave them a purpose and appeared to ease their anguish.

A few people observed Lizzie as she cleaned and stitched cuts and asked if they could assist. None of the townspeople had ever dressed a wound before, but once they learned how they performed better than expected. Govind had never seen people work together like this and found it fascinating.

Still, for all the help the volunteers offered, only androids or robotic arms could perform surgeries and set broken bones. The people did their best for the patients and knew it wasn't enough.

When Tash, Aiden, and Ava arrived, they related how they'd buried a man, and Govind pressed them to bury the dead in the hospital. They recruited many gravediggers, for the bereaved relatives wished to give their loved ones a proper burial, but the work progressed slowly with only one shovel.

Govind observed some volunteers scrounging around for shrapnel, anything long and sharp that could be used to dig. The people bent and twisted various materials, tested their makeshift spades, and worked in unison to get the job done faster. He wondered how they knew how to do this. Nobody programmed them. It seemed as though necessity had ignited some ancient genetic code for inventiveness. Again, Govind was impressed by the volunteers and told Lizzie about their newfound abilities.

"All animals have instincts," she said as she inserted an IV into a patient's vein. "They know how to behave or respond in certain situations."

THROUGHOUT THE DAY, the volunteers carried the dead to a field outside the hospital and buried them. Govind watched Aiden stand at each new mound of dirt and give a speech. He overheard the boy tell the mourners that the deceased lay "comforted in the arms of Mother Earth" and "their energy is not gone, only absorbed into the Great Source, where the energies of the past, present, and future blend."

Pulling him aside, Govind asked, "Where did you learn to say such things?"

"I'm letting the voice inside me speak, Uncle Govind. The communication I told you about."

Govind paused. No one could hack Aiden's WeConnect now. "You're still hearing a voice?"

"Yes."

Govind, intrigued, released his nephew and watched him walk toward the next grave. Lizzie stepped up beside him and shook her head.

"Your nephew is delusional."

"That would be the easy answer."

She eyed him. "What's that supposed to mean?"

"Albert Einstein didn't speak until he was four-years-old and did not read until he was seven. Einstein's parents considered him 'sub-normal.' Even one of his teachers described him as 'mentally slow and adrift forever in foolish dreams.' What if Aiden truly is communicating with something we can't see?"

She smirked at him. "Now, you sound delusional."

"Why do you doubt it? Do you know where inspiration comes from? Aiden talks about a land of dreams, where the past, present, and future blend. It's almost like he's talking about a metaverse, another world."

Lizzie rolled her eyes. "He's obviously invented something in his head like DAPHNE."

"But listen to the words he says. They seem beyond his years. What if there is such a thing as the Great Source?"

WHILE LIZZIE AND GOVIND debated the voice in Aiden's head, Grandma Rosie sat in the hospital lobby, observing the volunteers diligently working. Nobody expected her to take action because they considered her "frail." Rosie despised that word. True, her body didn't always cooperate as she wished, but she was still alive. Witnessing the procession of bodies being carried out for burial, she resolved to make use of the breath she had left. The patients needed nourishment, and Rosie Katz was determined to find them some.

Walking with care down the hallway, she chanced upon the cafeteria, where she was greeted by squeaks and growls. Her initial hope of discovering a stockpile of food quickly dissipated.

Raccoons had overrun the place. They had already toppled the snack cases, leaving remnants of potato chips, cookies, and shreds of packaging scattered on the floor. The animals were now engaged in fierce fights over the food at the serving counter, and their dreadful snarling hiked Rosie's pulse.

One raccoon jumped on the head of an android paralyzed in the act of serving chili, now covered in mold. The android toppled onto the tiled floor, and the chili that splashed on its white tunic resembled the stain of a fatal wound. Behind the pilfering raccoons at the counter, Rosie spied dozens of ready-to-go meal trays in the chiller. She put a hand to her cheek. How would she ever get to them?

She tried to shoo the critters out, but they turned on her and bared their teeth.

"Rosie!" Doug ran inside the cafeteria, grabbed a sign that said "LINE STARTS HERE," and swatted the raccoons growling at his mother-in-law.

Rosie took the opportunity to pry at the automated door of the chiller, but it wouldn't budge. "What are we going to do about food?" she asked Doug.

He threw a tray at a scampering raccoon. "Let's see what we can scrape together today."

Rosie viewed the chips strewn on the floor. "But what about tomorrow?"

DESPITE HIS GLOOMY task of digging graves, Tash Jeffries felt something awaken in him when he worked alongside Vivica. Her body seemed as lithe as a sprite, but she handled a car-fender-turned-shovel with strength and ferocity. Tash admired that. There was more to the slender young woman than her purple-streaked hair. He asked her if she'd like to hang out and maybe get a snack later.

"What are you, eighteen?" Vivica laughed as she scooped up dirt and tossed it aside. "I'm twenty-four. You're too young for me."

"I don't feel young," Tash answered honestly.

"Well, you are. I'm a college graduate. You're still in high school. I have a Master's Degree and working on my Doctorate." She grunted as the fender hit a rock. "You haven't even begun to live."

Tash refrained from telling Vivica that the bony hand of death waved hello to him on a daily basis. Death shadowed his life, and it had aged him beyond his years.

"I can handle you," is all he said, and his heartbeat quickened when Vivica smiled.

LATER, TASH ASKED DR. Lizzie to visit the patient with the heart condition, the one who had held his hand.

Two other patients from higher floors now shared the man's room, so he wasn't alone. However, the new arrivals weren't much company. One slept, and the other continually groaned.

Tash walked in with Dr. Lizzie and noticed how pale the man was. Still, the patient perked up upon seeing Tash. Lizzie questioned him and learned he'd received a microchip cardioverter-defibrillator, which would restart his heart if it stopped. Unfortunately, all the patients' charts were digitized, and she could learn nothing more.

"You appear to be recovering. I found these." She placed a bottle of beta-blocker pills on the bedside tray along with a pitcher of water. "Take one twice each day, and we'll monitor your progress."

Without another word, she strode out of the room. Tash figured her brusque behavior was due to her being forced into the role of a medic. Still, she didn't have to act so cold.

Tash slapped a smile on his face. "See?" he said to the man, "the doctor says you're doing fine."

The man's waxen face tightened, and Tash observed his hands shaking. He's scared. Terrified. The guy was all alone, hospitalized for severe heart problems in a devastated town with the world turned upside down. Tash knew he should return to his tasks, but a strange tightness in his chest caused him to pull up a chair. He wiped unexpected water from his eyes.

"How about if I sit with you for a little bit?"

The corners of the man's mouth curled up, and a little color returned to his cheeks. On an impulse, Tash took the man's frail hand and held it in his strong one.

CHAPTER 27

When the sun dipped behind the mountains, friends and relatives of the patients offered to stand watch during the night and aid the patients as best they could. With the promise to relieve them in the morning, the other volunteers headed home.

Still wearing his dirty clothes, Aiden lay on his bed with his hands clasped behind his head. As he watched the oak tree outside his window turn black against the purple twilight, he contemplated all the words the Great Source had given him today.

"What a pretty sight."

Dr. Lizzie Appel stood at his doorway and nodded at the window. "May I come in?"

"Sure." Aiden sat up.

She took a seat on a gaming chair he never used. "Govind tells me you hear voices."

Blunt. To the point. He exhaled but said nothing.

"You do realize it's you, right?"

Aiden pursed his lips together.

"I don't want to frighten you," she said, "but this may be a form of schizophrenia. You believe this subvocal speech is an external voice, but it's your voice, Aiden. You see, when we hear our voice, it sets off a 'recognition circuit' in the brain. This circuit works by comparing the sound you're hearing with the expected sound of your voice."

"Dr. Appel..."

"When they match, your brain concludes the voice is yours. People with schizophrenia have a defect in this circuit, so their brain incorrectly identifies their voice as someone else's. When the person doesn't see another human present, they conclude the voice is in their head. Do you understand?"

"No, and I don't hear a voice. I feel a voice."

The sky outside the window darkened, and stars began appearing. How noticeable they were now!

"What do you mean you 'feel' it?"

"Just that. I feel it."

Aiden couldn't see Lizzie's expression but her posture stiffened. What did the voice in his head matter to her?

She clasped her hands. "Perhaps you're experiencing auditory hallucinations brought on by trauma. Your mother mentioned that your peers have harassed you in the past. Many sufferers of schizophrenia experience adversity. Is the voice you hear that of a particular bully? Possibly, your mom or dad? Does it whisper abusive and critical comments to you?"

Aiden frowned. He had just begun to feel a sense of worth, and now a stranger had to remind him of his status as a reject.

"Dr. Appel, the voice doesn't whisper abuse in my ear. Like I said, I don't hear the words. I *feel* them."

"That makes no sense."

At that moment, words came to him, and he channeled them directly into his mouth. "Why are you so clinical and detached?"

The fabric of Lizzie's clothes bristled in the dark.

"You seem to align yourself more with machines than your fellow humans. Why?"

In response, she stood up abruptly and left the room.

CHAPTER 28

In the morning, Aiden visited Chris.

"Nobody knows what to do," he told the grid-skipper. "Everyone is waiting around for DAPHNE to power up, and who knows when that will happen?"

The grid-skipper stood over his two wheelbarrows and organized his books. "Quite a problem. I don't see Mr. Secretary of Defense taking charge."

Aiden defended his uncle. "He's been at the hospital, volunteering along with the rest of us."

"All good," Chris said, "but has anyone thought of what to do when your stolen food runs out?"

A white shirt waved in Aiden's mind. *My husband owns the Healthy Habit.* Ashamed, he shook his head.

Chris cleaned the cover of a book with his sleeve. "Did you read how the Native Americans survived in that book I gave you?"

"No."

Chris shook his head. "Napoléon Bonaparte said, 'Show me a family of readers, and I will show you the people who move the world.'"

Aiden gave him a strange look.

"Just read the damn book."

THE ONCE BUSTLING CITY center was now a wasteland of downed drones, ruptured sidewalks, broken glass, and rubble. Flies swarmed in the day's heat where the dead lay buried under debris too heavy to lift. Vultures circled in the sky, and nobody desired to see where they landed. Tash and Ava walked the streets with Aiden, who held the book on Indigenous American life.

"The early people lived off the land," he said. "This book lists all the local plants that you can eat. Chris said we have to organize, make a plan of action."

On the lawn of City Hall, a few residents had kicked away the drones and the trash to clear a place on the grass. They sat in a tight circle and ate the food they'd stolen from the markets. Aiden and his friends approached them with a friendly greeting, but the group on the grass eyed them warily.

"We're organizing everyone," Ava told them. "We need to make a plan of action."

Tash quickly added, "To live off the land."

The group on the grass brought their food packs closer and said nothing.

Aiden stepped up to clarify. "We're organizing a food-gathering expedition."

A fleshy woman of fifty sitting on an overturned shopping cart shook her head. "You just want to take what's ours."

Her companion, a guy wearing an Oakland Athletics baseball cap, popped a cookie into his mouth. "Gather your own food," he said with a full mouth and menacing eyes.

"Don't you get it?" Aiden asked. "Once the food runs out, there is no more."

The guy with the "A's" cap got to his feet and pushed up his sleeves. He picked up a baseball bat they hadn't noticed before. "Get moving."

Aiden, Ava, and Tash had no choice but to walk away.

They headed into Ava's community and went door-to-door. Tash took one side of the street, and Aiden and Ava took the other.

Residents peered through their open windows with suspicious or frightened eyes. Some didn't even bother to answer, even though Aiden could see them inside. Apparently, the townsfolk of Sierrawood had branched off into tribes and cared only for their group's members.

When Aiden knocked on one door, Clyde Parrish materialized at the window. Aiden gulped. He would have skipped the house if he'd known his persecutor lived there. Ava, however, drew close to her friend.

"Hey, Clyde." She offered him a sunny smile. "You've got to get all our friends together. Aiden and I are making a plan of action, and we need your help."

Clyde's eyes darted between Ava and Aiden as if he couldn't process the idea of them joining forces. Just then, a big man wearing a stained t-shirt and holding a beer slid up to the window to stand next to Clyde.

"What d'ya want?" The man slurped from the can. Ava and Aiden took a step back. Despite a beer gut peeking out from under the t-shirt, the guy looked strong and mean.

Clyde scowled. "I've got this, Dad. Go back to the couch."

Mr. Parrish pointed at Ava. "We don't want whatever yer selling." Guzzling the beer, he walked away from the window.

Clyde's face tightened, and his hands curled into fists. A moment passed, and he relaxed enough to regard Ava. "What's happening?"

"We're planning a food-gathering mission in the forest." Her eyescreens displayed an orchard of fruit trees. When Clyde didn't respond, she angled her face toward Aiden for help.

He cleared his throat. "Um, I have a book on how ancient people lived, which was mostly on the land. I mean they lived *off* the land. They lived on it and off it." He forced a hollow laugh. "Anyhow, it identifies stuff we can eat. If we all work together, we can –"

"I'm set with food." Clyde looked Ava up and down. "Are you okay?"

The question seemed sincere, but Ava crossed her arms as though his scrutiny stripped her bare. "I'm fine. You won't help us?"

Clyde leaned against the window frame, gazed at her, and shook his head.

When they walked away, Aiden felt the other boy's eyes on his back. Clyde probably couldn't figure out why the most popular girl in school would hang out with a geek. Truthfully, Aiden didn't know why, either. Ava claimed she admired his supposed fearlessness, but it seemed pretty obvious that Clyde Parrish scared the hell out of him.

WHEN THEIR QUEST TO unite the community failed, Aiden, Ava, and Tash set out on their own to gather food. They arrived at the lake, and one look at the clear water made Aiden strip down to his boxer shorts. He dove right in and let the cold water prickle his skin and wash away the dirt. He dunked his head, then resurfaced with a smile and a shake of his wet hair.

Ava and Tash exchanged looks and then stripped down to their underwear. They splashed into the lake and let the water clean and refresh them.

"Doesn't this feel great?" Aiden asked.

Ava groaned with pleasure as she leaned backward to soak her hair. "I wish I'd brought shampoo."

"Oh, you can't use soap in here. It'll kill the fish. But you can collect water and –"

In unison, Tash and Ava splashed Aiden. He laughed and swam away from their assault. The afternoon warmed up with a vanilla scent. Yellow-necked meadowlarks sang in the grasses, and chipmunks scampered along the fallen logs crisscrossing the shore. Ava floated on her back under a beam of sunlight, and Aiden saw the hard nipples under her bra. His fantasy had become a reality, and he felt a stirring in his groin.

Then, he remembered the reel, which made a mockery of his desire. Reels and thought-hacking seemed to have existed eons ago, but the shame still scorched him, and he worried someone might see into his mind. Embarrassed, he drifted away from Ava.

Later, as they lay on the flat top of a boulder to dry, he opened the book. "There are berries and plants that the Native Americans ate. Acorns from oak trees, wild blackberries. Here, have a look."

Ava perused the pages with her super optics and scanned their immediate surroundings. "There's a bush with purple-red berries." She flipped to a page and showed Aiden and Tash. "See? It's called a chokecherry bush. It says the fruit is edible, but the seeds are poisonous. One way to test if a plant is poisonous is to rub a tiny bit on your lips. If your lips go numb, or you get a rash, throw it away. Another way is to crush the berry. If a milky white sap appears, the berry will kill you."

Tash grimaced. "Maybe we shouldn't gather food. What do we know?"

Ava returned the book to Aiden. "They say wild raspberries are safe and easy to identify because they look like the store-bought ones. I see some growing next to the chokecherry bush. Come on."

With that, Ava slid off the boulder and trekked across the clearing. Two black and white butterflies with beautiful red-tipped wings accompanied her. Aiden considered the company fitting.

Tash nudged him. "Still crushing on her, huh?"

Aiden changed the subject by pointing to a dirt path. "I've seen dandelions up that trail, and every part of those is edible."

"Okay, let's go." Tash fished into the pocket of his jeans and pulled out a small container. He tossed a pill into his mouth and eyed Aiden as he swallowed it dry. "No, I'm not an addict."

"You take a lot of enhancers."

"They're not enhancers." Tash cast a wary eye at Ava, who picked berries across the clearing. "I'm sick."

Aiden had sensed a vulnerability in his friend but never guessed he was ill.

Tash lowered his voice. "SCD. Sickle Cell disease. My folks thought it had been wiped from our gene pool, but, somehow, a mutation slipped by."

"A mutation?"

"A mutation in the gene that causes my red blood cells to grow into a crescent shape, a sickle. The pills edit the mutated gene and prevent the sickling." Tash studied the pill container. "Do you know they think the cells mutated this way on purpose? Yeah. To battle malaria in Africa. It's funny what nature does to protect us. Problem is, malaria no longer exists." Tash pocketed the container and sighed. "The gene doesn't know it's not needed. It doesn't realize it serves no purpose now except to kill me."

Aiden studied his friend. How odd that Tash would use the same analogy that Chris used regarding the importance of serving a purpose. The story of the Garden of Eden surfaced in his mind. Adam and Eve relied on the garden for sustenance. The garden served a purpose. When Adam and Eve became smart, God kicked them out. Why? Did God fear that Adam and Eve would eventually calculate a way to make their beautiful world obsolete? Aiden viewed his surroundings, the shimmering lake, the sun filtering through the trees, and even the warm, beige boulder upon which they rested... Had his fellow humans taken this particular Eden for granted?

Aiden refocused on Tash. No wonder he'd kept to himself at school. Strange, too, that a mutation 'slipped by.' Try as we might, Aiden mused, humankind can not control nature.

"Do you have a good stock of those pills?" he asked.

"I raided the hospital pharmacy. I only took my meds."

"Don't worry." Aiden grinned. "All the police bots are dead."

At that moment, the Steller's Jay alighted on the boulder as if to challenge the two young men. Joy flooded Aiden upon seeing his blue-feathered friend, but he caught Tash's eye and quickly plugged the emotion.

"Remember how you wondered if I was the guy that talked to birds?" he asked casually. "Watch this."

Aiden hopped off the boulder and cupped his hands against his mouth. "Woo-Woot," he said to the bluejay.

King Jay cocked his head as if perplexed, but from across the clearing, Ava jokingly sang, "Woo-hee! Woo-hee!"

Aiden turned toward Tash. "See? That's it. That's how I talk to birds."

Tash swatted at a fly. "I wasn't trying to put you down. I wanted to know if it was true, if you were an 'animal whisperer.' I like animals. I've always wanted a dog but can't have one because I get asthma." He dropped his eyes to his swollen fingers, ashamed.

The two young men battled their insecurities. Aiden observed Ava because doing so made him feel better. Was she actually here with him? What a miracle.

Ava Durand. Spending time with me.

Ava suddenly paused in her berry picking and looked in his direction. "What?"

Aiden, embarrassed to be caught admiring her, shook his head. "Nothing."

"You called me."

"No, I didn't."

Ava crossed the clearing toward him. "I heard you call out my name." She handed Aiden and Tash some berries. "Here. The chokecherries are yummy, but remember to spit out the seeds."

The three stood in the sun-washed clearing and ate of nature's harvest. Aiden wondered how Ava sensed him thinking about her.

Somehow, he'd transmitted his thoughts without a WeConnect. Was this the Lifespark at work? The Great Source? He wished he knew.

A meadowlark played a flute in the grass. A nearby brook spilled into the lake with a happy trickle and caused the slate-blue water to ripple. A caterpillar hustled across the dirt, and the young people followed its progress as their tongues turned purple from the berry juice. Aiden felt at peace with both the land and his companions. His tranquility must have opened a portal to the Great Source, for the urge to take a walk suddenly nagged at him.

"Follow me," he said, without knowing where his feet would lead them.

They trudged along the lakeshore, passing a log the wind and rain had sculpted into a moose's head, and then veered onto a narrow animal trail. Above the young people, cumulus clouds ranged across the sky like hundreds of white cotton balls.

They paused at a trickling stream to drink and were surprised by the salty taste of the water. Aiden had read about salt springs in the mountains but had never encountered one before. Chipped into the surrounding granite were shallow basins. He'd need to research what the Native Americans used the holes for. The trio moved on until a wall of boulders blocked their path.

"Now what?" Tash tried to peer between the rocks.

They heard a chitter. Quietly, they clambered to the top of the boulders and peeked over. A rare red fox watched over her four kits that tumbled about in their play. The mother fox glanced at the intruders and twitched her ears but didn't run.

A broad smile broke over Tash's face at the sight of the animals. He looked at Aiden as if to say, *How did you know?*

Aiden didn't know. He only knew something kind had led them here.

CHAPTER 29

Five days had passed since the drone attack. People resorted to drinking water from their toilet tanks or pools if they had them. Even with the food supply diminishing, the residents of Sierrawood had faith that DAPHNE would power up and life would return to normal.

The less patient townsfolk ventured out to the Baylor home to harass Govind. Frightened, he stood at the narrow window near the front door and explained that Lizzie's team journeyed to DAPHNE's bunker daily to see what they could fix.

When his tormenters left, Govind raided Doug's wine rack and offered Lizzie a glass.

"It's nine in the morning," she told him.

"I don't care."

Thankful for twist-off bottle tops, he filled a glass to the rim. Lizzie watched his fingers shake.

"Now, you can see why getting DAPHNE operational is a top priority."

He gulped some wine and then set the glass down hard. "Lizzie, we can't power up DAPHNE without power."

"Then, we must find an alternative source."

He lifted his glass in response.

A frantic pounding on the front door made Govind choke on his wine. Lizzie sighed and moved toward the entry hall. "I'll handle it."

A genderfluid kid wearing a bloodstained shirt stood on the porch. "Please, Dr. Lizzie," the kid said, "My friend needs you. He got attacked by a mountain lion."

OREANNA SAW LIZZIE and Govind rushing down the driveway, trailing after some kid. She didn't care about the latest emergency because she was too hungry. She stomped into the kitchen and opened the pantry to finish off the cereal, but the box lay on the floor, ripped open and covered in ants.

"Mom!"

L'Eren wandered over to see what upset her niece. Oreanna held up the box. "Who did this?"

"It looks chewed." L'Eren shuddered. "Yuck. I thought I saw something run past me last night."

Suddenly, they heard Jill screech. Oreanna and L'Eren hustled into the living room, where Jill pointed to a small carcass on the carpet.

"Is that a rat?" She gaped at her daughter and sister in horror.

Oreanna gagged. "It's a headless rat." She glanced at the damaged box in her hand and promptly dropped it.

"Do you have stain remover?" L'Eren asked her sister. "You're gonna need it."

Kif the cat sat on the coffee table like a calm white statue, his tail curled humbly about his legs.

AIDEN SAT IN HIS BEDROOM upstairs, reading about the Lakota tribe, and sighed at the complaints of his mother, sister, and aunt. L'Eren, perhaps due to the late stage of her pregnancy, did nothing but complain, and Jill whined nonstop. Life without automation didn't suit her at all.

"Ori, clean up that spilled cereal."

"I'm not getting near that rat!"

"I'm gonna barf," Aunt L'Eren murmured.

"We just installed this carpeting. Now, look at it," Jill cried. "I'm going to kill that cat."

Aiden slammed the book closed. He'd wanted to finish the chapter on what the Lakota called the Great Spirit. The ancient people had communed with the natural world like he did, and he longed to know if the Great Spirit was the Great Source. Annoyed, he jogged downstairs and strode into the living room.

"Mom, Kif left the rat as a gift for you."

"A *gift*?"

"He wants you to be proud of him. Can't you see he's trying to protect us?"

"Aiden, enough with your nature bullshit. If you love it so much, you clean it up."

He picked up the cat and nuzzled him. "Good boy. Thank you for guarding us. Thank you for getting the rat."

Kif basked in the affection for only a minute and wriggled out of Aiden's arms. With eyes widened like saucers, the cat darted off to search for more rats and additional praise. When Aiden tossed the lifeless rodent outside for the vultures, he mused that he'd never seen Kif so animated. The feline's exuberance could only stem from one thing. Kif had discovered his purpose.

AT THE DINING ROOM table that evening, Rosie and Jill laid out a salad of dandelions, clover, and miner's lettuce, along with pretzels, beef jerky, protein bars, pitted chokecherries, and what was left of the unspoiled cheese.

Lizzie related how her quick stitches earlier that day had saved the life of the boy who'd been mauled. Jill told everyone about finding the dead rat.

"With no noise or lights to frighten them off," Grandma Rosie commented, "I'm afraid we're going to be overrun by the wildlife."

As if in agreement, a lone coyote howled outside, and the family descended into a hushed silence, eating their meal slowly while absorbing both the peculiar taste of the salad and their uncomfortable circumstance.

Suddenly, Grandpa Harry began kicking the table. Glasses tipped over, and silverware clattered to the floor. Doug sprang up and pulled Harry's chair back so he wouldn't kick Rosie.

"What's happening, Dad?" Jill cried.

Harry watched his legs flail and tried to laugh. "They're out of control! My Smart Legs are acting stupid!"

Despite the joke, Aiden read terror in his grandfather's eyes. The Smart Legs needed a reboot, which was impossible without DAPHNE. When the old gentleman tried to stand, his dysfunctional legs lurched him into a wall.

"Oh, Harry!" Rosie stood up, wringing her hands.

Doug and Govind restrained him as his legs jerked about. "Don't worry," Grandpa reassured them as he thrashed about in their grasp. "I'll be right as rain. I just need you two to get me up to my room. I think we need to tie 'em down!"

LATER, AIDEN COULD hear Grandpa comforting Rosie in their room. The rest of the family remained in the kitchen downstairs, whispering worriedly and listening to the scratching sounds within the walls that grew more pronounced as darkness fell.

Chase away the ghosts, the voice inside whispered. Aiden thought a moment, and then inspiration hit. He grabbed his guitar, sat cross-legged on the stairs, and began strumming the strings. Outside, a chorus of coyotes yipped to celebrate a kill, but the crisp, mellow chords filled the house. He played a soothing melody, and soon, the anxious whispering ceased, the scratching in the walls receded to the background, and only the music remained.

LYING IN BED THAT NIGHT, Aiden contemplated his purpose. He knew he should have one. Should he be a musician? Songs came easy to him. Should he give comfort to the bereaved? Mourners appreciated what he said at the burials. He asked the Great Source for guidance, but no words of advice came. As Aiden gazed at Brother Oak's outstretched arms, his eyelids grew heavy, and he fell asleep.

A giant tree with a lightning scar catches my eye as I walk through the forest. The charred crevice in the trunk is wide enough to step into, so I enter the tree. Coming out the other side, I see the lake, but the water is the color of a serene blue sky and clouds are floating in it. A man swims through the sand of the shore. He does the backstroke past a woman with cascading red hair who sits on a boulder. I know who she is.

"Professor Yang. It's me. Aiden."

I walk toward her, and my steps feel spongy like I'm walking on a trampoline. "I'm happy to see you, Professor. I thought you died."

The rocky surface of the boulder on which she's perched feels as soft as a pillow. Professor Yang focuses on me with serious green eyes. "Solve the mystery, Aiden. Our survival depends on it."

"What mystery?"

I step backward and fall into the lake. I sink underwater but fall through space, surrounded by millions of stars. My hands run through translucent layers of pink, red, purple, and blue gases surrounding me. I'm floating in the mural of the Veil Nebula. Below me is the marble-floored lobby of Walden-Prost.

Solve the mystery. Professor Yang's voice echoes through deep space along with a man's voice. I discovered it. I found what she is searching for, and she can only find it in—*Solve the mystery.* I found what she is searching for. *Solve the mystery.*

AIDEN SAT UP IN BED. The words from his dream circled in his head like a carousel. What a strange message. What mystery was he supposed to solve? He became aware of a muted "Who? Who?" and viewed his window. A spotted owl sat on an oak branch, studying him with its black button eyes.

CHAPTER 30

The family talked about his music the next morning as they gathered for breakfast, and Aiden paused outside the kitchen to listen.

"How long has he played guitar?" L'Eren asked Jill.

"I don't know. He's never played in front of us before. I feel bad I can't answer the question."

Was Jill proud of him at last? Aiden became aware of a strange pounding sound, an irregular drumbeat. The others seemed to ignore it.

"Dad and I were in our room," he heard Grandma Rosie say. "We heard this beautiful music, and I thought DAPHNE had powered up again."

"I wonder when DAPHNE taught Aiden that tune," Lizzie asked.

At that, Aiden strode into the kitchen. "DAPHNE didn't teach it to me. I made it up."

Lizzie arched an eyebrow. "How?"

"I don't know how. It came to me. Maybe from the voice in my head that makes me a schizophrenic." He glowered at her.

Lizzie shifted her eyes from his. The rest of the family traded penitent looks. Grandpa Harry sat with slumped shoulders on a stool at the kitchen counter, and Aiden now discerned the source of the drumbeat. Harry's legs, tied together, gave spasmodic little kicks to the cabinetry.

From outside came the sound of angry voices and a pounding on the front door. L'Eren drew in a worried breath, and Govind patted her hand. Aiden trekked to the entry hall and slipped through the broken window.

Clyde Parrish and Pete Farmington stood among a group of angry people congregating on the driveway.

"Yes?" Aiden dared to ask.

Mac, their blowhard neighbor living down the road, got in his face. "We want a word with Mr. Secretary."

Tash broke away from the crowd and sidled over to Aiden. "Tell your uncle not to come out."

But at that moment, Govind slid through the window.

Mac started right in. "What are you going to do about that bear terrorizing the neighborhood? That thing was in our backyard last night and nearly mauled my wife Aerta."

Another person cried, "I saw some big dogs poking around my house. Only, they weren't dogs. They were wolves!"

Mr. Parrish, Clyde's father, stomped forward, and Aiden smelled gin on his breath. "I've got bats in my attic! How'd they get there? You'd better get 'em out."

Doug waddled up and stood solidly next to Govind.

"When is DAPHNE coming back?" Mac shouted.

Talk to them! The voice pressed Aiden, and last night's dream came to mind. Professor Yang had told him to solve a mystery. Perhaps she wanted him to solve the problem of living with the wildlife. Their survival certainly depended on that.

Govind lifted his hands in defense. "We're trying to—."

"You're useless!" Clyde's father lurched forward and shoved him.

"Leave him alone!" Doug moved between Govind and Mr. Parrish.

"Out of the way, Baylor," the drunk man fumed, "or I'll beat your marshmallow ass too."

Doug put up pudgy, trembling fists. "Just try."

Jill screamed and waved a knife through the broken window. "Don't you touch my husband, you worthless lush!"

Clyde's dad turned red, furious eyes toward Jill.

Talk to them!

"Fighting won't help," Aiden blurted out. Everyone looked at him.

"Screaming won't help. Don't you see? DAPHNE did this to us, not Govind Lal. The animals... They're just doing what they do. They smell food, they see an opening, and they go in. We're the ones who need to take precautions. The grid-skippers have lived with wild animals for years, and they don't get mauled. Let's ask them how they do it."

"We don't take advice from scumbags," Mr. Parrish said.

Clyde piped up, "How 'bout if I just kill that bear?"

He received an approving murmur from the crowd. A woman rushed toward him. "Oh, please, can you? Do you know how?"

He poked out a defiant chin. "I have good reaction times."

"This isn't a video game," Aiden told him.

Clyde shot him a deadly glance, and Aiden felt his insides go cold. Tash unsheathed the ax.

A woman with a baby in her arms stepped up to Govind, "Dr. Lal, what are we going to do about water?"

"We have water." Dragging his eyes from Clyde, Aiden answered for his uncle. "Plenty of it. If we take buckets to collect the stream water before it flows into the lake, it should be clean enough to drink."

"How would you know?" Mac asked.

"I read about it. I read that water gets purified if it runs over enough rock and sediment."

"Hey, dummies."

All eyes turned around to see Chris. Behind him stood about twenty grid-skippers. Chris shuffled forward, holding a soda can and a tube of toothpaste. The crowd parted, not out of courtesy but because they loathed the grid-skippers.

"If you can stop trying to kill each other for five seconds, you might learn something that will help you stay alive." Chris squatted on a sunny patch of lawn and squirted some toothpaste on the bottom of the can.

Pete Farmington snorted. "Gonna use a soda can to brush your teeth, psycho?"

Chris eyed him and used a rag to rub the toothpaste against the can.

Mac planted his hands on his hips and shook his head. "What the hell?"

Chris ignored him and continued to polish the bottom of the can. The townspeople began to crowd Govind once more.

"Get out of my light!" Chris barked, which caused those nearest to him to jump as if electrocuted. He muttered under his breath as the rag gyrated against the soda can. Watching this, Aiden, too, wondered if his friend had flipped out.

However, when the bottom of the can gleamed like a mirror, Chris aimed it toward the sun. His free hand fumbled around the pocket of his shabby coat and pulled out a square of burnt fabric. Chris held the material close to the reflective surface.

"Char cloth," Chris stated to the circle of people gawking at him. Another grid-skipper, a middle-aged woman wearing a blue terry-cloth headwrap, a flower-print muumuu, and broken high heels, reached into Chris's pocket and took out a dried bird's nest. She handed him the nest into which he delicately tucked the char cloth and blew on it.

To the wonder of those present, a thread of gray smoke appeared. Two other grid-skippers came forward to lay heavy rocks in a circle on the Baylor's driveway. Another unkempt soul patted dry moss and twigs within the stones. Chris continued to blow on the nest, and the smoke thickened. People drew closer to watch this magic. All at once, the bird's nest flamed up, and a collective "Ohhhh" rippled through the crowd.

Chris laid the nest onto the dry moss, which then caught fire.

Pete pointed a stubby finger at the rock ring. "How'd you know how to do that?"

"I don't suck off DAPHNE's tit." Chris fed twigs to the flames while more grid-skippers placed pieces of deadwood into the fire ring.

"Why didn't you show us this before?" Pete asked.

"Listen, fatso, the only reason I'm here is because of that guy." Chris pointed a sooty finger toward Aiden. "He's the only one of you worth saving if you ask me." He nodded to Tash. "And maybe that big guy over there and the girl with the hi-tech-eyes, wherever she is. Don't let the fire go out. Keep throwing wood on it."

"What wood?" Mac, the neighbor, asked.

"What wood?" Chris stood up and stomped his foot to shake off the dust. "You're joking, right? You don't have wood?"

"No," Mac said dully.

"Then break up your frigging furniture." Chris surveyed the group, the confusion in their eyes, their open mouths. "Tash, hold up that ax."

Tash held it up.

"Now, all you dummies take a good look at that thing. Y'all are gonna have to chop wood. Hopefully, that keeps you too busy to commit murder. Gather wood in the forest and split it with that ax into pieces that fit into your fireplaces. Or you can do what we do and build a fire ring outside your home like this. It'll help keep the critters at bay."

"We don't have to listen to you, you filthy creep," Clyde's father said.

"Then get eaten by a bear or a mountain lion. At least the beasties won't go hungry." Chris eyeballed plump Pete again. "You'd make a good meal for a cougar."

"Screw you." Pete shoved his hands in his pockets and meandered away from Chris.

"And remember, store your food where no animal can smell it."

Chris signaled the other grid-skippers, and they began to walk away. Aiden strode over to Chris and took his arm. "Sit with us," he said. "Have breakfast."

"No, thanks."

"Please."

Chris gently handed him the soda can and reached into his pocket to give Aiden some charcloth. "I'll teach you how to make this. It's easy."

CHAPTER 31

Later that day, people volunteered to join Aiden on a food-gathering expedition. As he led the way into the forest, they flooded him with questions, and he experienced the light and airy spaciousness of self-worth. Light because nothing seemed to weigh him down. Spacious, because when a person felt this good, his heart grew big.

As the group of people walked, Aiden pointed out a carpet of miner's lettuce, from which they picked tender, tasty green leaves, and clusters of dandelions and clover. "Don't touch the plant with the red leaves," he advised. "That's poison oak. Leaves of three, let 'em be."

He stopped to point out a mass of blue and white flowers with purple-tipped petals. "Those are called Sierra Baby Blue-eyes. I read about them in a book about local plants. Did you know flowers fluoresce? They absorb ultraviolet light and emit it to attract birds and insects."

"Hold up." Ava paused and gasped. "Oh, my gosh..."

"What is it?" Aiden asked.

"It's amazing. The petal of almost every flower is covered in twinkling lights."

The group of volunteers shook their heads. They didn't see what Ava described.

"I switched my eyes to the ultra-violet spectrum," she explained. "That flower there—" She pointed to a thistle. "Its stamen looks like a bursting firework. I didn't know." She faced Aiden. "I didn't know flowers did this. It's beautiful, and it's right under our noses."

Aiden viewed the thistle, and a flash of envy sizzled his insides. He wished he, too, could see the florescent beauty hidden from humans. Ava was lucky.

"Don't be jealous."

He looked over to see her gazing at him with crossed arms.

"I'm not," he lied. *How did she know?*

"I have bug eyes, Aiden. Did you forget? I'm an insect."

He shook his head. "You're not an insect. You're a flower."

Ava smiled, and it was good between them again.

WHEN THEY VENTURED toward the stream, Aiden spied some residents dumping laundry detergent into the water.

"No!" He spilled his bag of wild greens as he hustled toward them. "What are you doing? You can't do that. You'll kill the fish. You're going to have to fill up buckets and take the water home."

"Forget that." A woman waved him off. "I live too far from here."

"Then do your laundry downstream, away from the lake," Aiden told her. "You'll still need some sort of bucket to put the soap in. Absolutely do not dump soapy water anywhere near the lake or stream, or you'll poison us all."

Aiden retrieved his fallen greens, sure the whining woman would ignore him. When she obeyed his direction, and the others did the same, he felt a sense of triumph. They were listening to him. Inside, the voice spoke: *Bet on yourself.*

At that moment, Aiden spied his sister wading into the lake. "Oreanna!" He waved to her, happy to see she had finally ventured out of the house.

Upon hearing her name, Oreanna's face went white with terror, and she splashed up to her neck in the water.

Pete Farmington dipped a bucket into the lake and asked Ava, "Did Baylor just call that chunky girl Oreanna?"

"Yeah."

"Why?"

"Because she's his sister."

Pete shook his head. "No, she's not."

Ava shrugged. "Okay." Her eyescreens displayed to Pete the family portrait she'd downloaded in Aiden's house, which showed the entire Baylor family.

Pete's face creased in confusion as he walked over to where Oreanna waded. "Hey, are you Oreanna Baylor?"

Ori shyly nodded as she fanned the water with her arms.

The perplexed expression on Pete's face melted into one of wicked humor. "Parrish!" he shouted. "Hey, Parrish, get over here."

Clyde filled his buckets with water and ignored Pete, but the round boy grabbed his shoulders and steered him toward Oreanna. As they approached, she quickly emerged from the water and wound a towel around her body.

"I wanna introduce you," Pete goaded Clyde, "to Oreanna Baylor."

Clyde's eyes scanned the overweight girl, the dark roots of her bleached and broken hair and the acne dotting her pale skin.

Pete pushed Clyde toward her. "Go get her, dude. Your secret crush stands before you." To Oreanna, he said, "You know, he jacks off to your profile pic."

Clyde whirled around, grabbed Pete by his thick neck, and lifted him off the ground. The chubby boy choked in midair and flailed his legs until Clyde shoved him to the ground. Pete put a hand on his bruised flesh and stared at his friend with terrified eyes.

Aiden jogged toward them. Ava, concerned, hurried over as well. Clyde took a menacing step toward Oreanna.

"You're Oreanna Baylor?" He looked her up and down. "Prove it. What's your top ranking?"

Don't answer, Aiden thought as he arrived, but his sister lifted a proud chin.

"Thirty-five hundred. I've reached the Top Five of *Jungle Flight.*"

Clyde reddened in anger and sneered at Aiden. "I thought no one could be as much of a loser as you, but between you and your sister, you're actually less revolting."

Oreanna brought the towel to her face and fled barefoot down the trail. Dust swirled in her wake. Aiden's gaze bore into Clyde, fully aware that he should take action, say something, yet his voice eluded him.

Ava swatted her friend's shoulder. "Why do you have to be such an asshole, Clyde?"

The brawny boy grinned, easily hefted two heavy buckets of water, and sauntered down the path toward town. Pete followed like an obedient dog—his buckets spilling as he waddled to keep up.

Aiden drowned in shame. Tash would have smashed Clyde in the jaw without hesitation.

"Hey, Angakkuq!"

Chris walked to the lake's edge with a couple of other grid-skippers. He held up some folded garments. "Look what your dad gave me. Dougie said, 'You can have these clothes if you promise to wash.'" Chris pointed to the other grid-skippers. "My pals received stuff from other folks, too."

"That's good, isn't it?" Aiden walked toward Chris to leave his cowardice behind. "They wanted to repay your kindness. We can keep warm and cook because of you."

Chris contemplated the clothes with some bewilderment. Aiden knew his friend wasn't used to people being kind. When the grid-skipper lifted his face, Aiden beheld a puddle of wet vulnerability pooling in his chestnut eyes.

"I guess you ought to get washing then."

Chris nodded and moved behind a bush to strip out of his clothes. The other grid-skippers disappeared into the brush as well. As they emerged, the townsfolk swimming in the lake made a subtle exit.

Wearing only faded green briefs, Chris said, "Make sure nobody steals my old rags."

Ava grinned. "I was going to light a bonfire with them."

Chris narrowed his eyes at her and walked boldly into the water until it completely submerged his head. Green underwear soon floated to the surface.

Amused, Ava moved off to give Chris privacy, but concern stiffened Aiden's feet. What if his friend drowned? He headed for the water's edge, intending to jump in, when Chris suddenly broke through and swam confidently across the lake like a man newly born. He reminded Aiden of the man in his dream, the one who swam on land, and that reminded him of Professor Yang and the mystery he was supposed to solve.

He searched for Ava and found her sitting on a downed pine tree. Before he could share his dream with her, she spoke.

"Why did your sister create a fake profile?"

"Why do you think? She doesn't like who she is."

Ava appeared solemn as she poked a twig into an insect hole. "I'm sorry Clyde was so mean."

Aiden ripped a splinter of wood away from the fallen trunk. Rubbing it between his fingers, he quietly burned with humiliation at his inability to stand up to his tormenter.

"I can understand her insecurity." The twig broke off in Ava's hand. "You should have seen me at her age."

"I did." Aiden gave her a coy grin. "Woo-woot."

Ava giggled. "Woo-hee, woo-hee." She playfully threw the twig at him, then her jaw dropped in surprise. Staring behind him, she pointed a finger. Aiden turned around to see a doe and two spotted fawns grazing at the end of the log.

"Keep still," he whispered. "Don't act too eager."

Slowly reaching into his pocket, he pulled out a dandelion sprig and held it out to the animal. The doe snorted and waved her tail in fear while the fawns retreated a few feet. Aiden closed his eyes and decided to run a test.

I am petting the doe's coat gently, with respect. She looks at me with soulful eyes. I touch the white hair framing her nose and her long eyelashes. She lets me lay my cheek against her neck, and I feel her warm pulse against my skin.

A tug on the dandelions opened Aiden's eyes. The doe was eating from his hand. Next to him, Ava remained quiet and still. Moments later, the doe returned to her babies, and the little family wandered away untroubled.

"How did you do that?' Ava asked.

"I went into a mind-drift."

"What's a mind-drift?"

"A fantasy." Aiden put eager hands on her shoulders. "Listen. Just now, I used a fantasy to get the doe to trust—"

"What's a fantasy?"

"It's a... It's when you dream while you're awake."

"How can you dream while you're awake?"

"Your mind travels. It goes to other places, but I think you can harness the fantasy somehow."

Ava shook her head. "I don't get it."

"My grandma says it's all part of the mystery of human consciousness." Goosebumps suddenly rose along his arms. *Solve the mystery.*

Had Professor Yang wanted him to solve the mystery of human consciousness?

"So," Ava pressed him. "What happened with the deer?"

He couldn't answer because Professor Yang kept whispering in his ear: *Solve the mystery. Solve the mystery.*

The sound of footsteps turned both their heads. Wearing a clean pair of tan slacks and a black t-shirt, Chris strolled toward Aiden and Ava. His typically wild hair was neatly combed. "Well?" He turned in a circle before them.

"You look downright respectable." Aiden grinned.

Ava paused to sniff the air. "Do you smell something?"

"Ha ha." Chris smirked. "I'm washed, okay?"

"No, there's..." Ava looked toward town, and the two men followed her gaze. Above the trees, the sun had gone a vivid orange, and smoke drifted into the clearing.

CHAPTER 32

Crackling fire devoured Ava's neighborhood. Residents ducked and ran as homes exploded into flames. Above the street, high-tension power lines snapped like thread, and roiling black smoke consumed the sky. Chris ducked from orange embers that fell like hellish rain.

He strode down the fiery street. "What happened? What started it?"

A man clasped panicked hands on his head. "I did what you said! I collected wood and made a fire in my living room."

"In your living room?" Chris repeated. "In the fireplace?"

"I made a rock ring on the carpet, just like you said to do."

A coughing woman shook a finger at Chris. "This is all your fault!"

"Ah, shut your pie hole," Chris barked. He wasn't about to take their abuse like Govind Lal. "I didn't teach you how to make a fire to burn down your houses. Where's the good sense God gave you? Who sets a fire on their living room carpet? Your brains are mush. Don't you see that?"

"What do we do?"

Chris shrugged. "Get some marshmallows and start roastin.'"

The windows of one house exploded, making them cringe with the sound of shattering glass.

"This isn't funny! We're losing everything! Do something!"

"What do you want me to do? Take a piss on it?"

They had no choice but to stand back from the inferno. The people who didn't run stood on the shimmering asphalt in disbelief, unwilling to grasp that yet another catastrophe had befallen them.

A buffer of Coast Live oak trees stood between the community and the summer-dry pine needles of the forest. With their leathery leaves, the hearty oaks battled the onslaught of flames, but the wind pushed the fire forward.

Ava used her super optics to track pockets of flying embers and directed people here and there to stomp out smoking hot spots, but they couldn't get to every one. With disheartened eyes, the people of Sierrawood watched the flames set the forest afire. It moved onward like a ravenous dragon, roaring and spurting flames.

Within an hour, the conflagration ate up most of the homes in Ava's neighborhood, including hers, and left behind warped metal twisted in artful shapes against a dreamlike sky of yellow-orange. The surviving homes suffered heat damage and smelled like a chemical campfire.

Ava held hands with her mother as they sat slumped on the sidewalk that fronted the charred remains of their home. Tiny black bits, the remnants of their possessions, peppered their hair and clothing. White smoke cloaked the streets in an acrid gauze that dried out their noses and stung their eyes. The dusky orange orb in the sky seemed the only familiar object in the world, and even that seemed distant, too far from the beleaguered population of Sierrawood.

Aiden knelt beside Ava. "Come. You two can stay with me."

She didn't respond. Her eyescreens were ash-gray. Blank. Clyde stood with his father before the smoldering remains of their house, and Clyde's dad shouted his frustration to no one in particular. As Aiden surveyed the anguished people, an idea came to him, and he stood up.

"Everyone listen. We can set up temporary quarters in the high school gym. It can hold a lot of people."

No one responded.

"Look, it's somewhere to go, at least. Those of you with homes that didn't burn, please share blankets and any bedding that's undamaged. Come on. Let's get there before nightfall."

THE STRAGGLERS BUSTED into the high school gym. They set up makeshift beds using couch cushions, rugs, and anything they managed to drag inside. They closed the entrance they made by using a pair of wallscreens, but cool air wafted inside from an open skylight in the roof. Chris told Aiden and Tash they were lucky.

"We can build a fire ring right below." He fingered his beard as he contemplated the skylight. "But we'll need a hood and a chimney to draw up the smoke."

The sight of the wildfire alarmed the town, and many people, including Govind, Lizzie, and Doug, arrived at the gym to find out what happened. They feared an enemy force had attacked them again.

"Don't just stand there staring," Chris told the new arrivals. "Do something to help."

"Like what?" Doug shrugged.

"These people lost their homes. What do you think they need? Use your brains."

The visitors surveyed the bereft souls sitting on the gym floor.

"Beds?" Doug asked. "Clothes?"

Chris tapped his forehead. "That's using the old noodle, Dougie. Bedding, towels, toiletries, you name it."

Tash pulled Aiden aside. "I'm going to bring my parents here."

"Why?" Aiden asked, perplexed. "Your home didn't burn."

"This place seems safer than the complex. Besides, my folks don't like climbing the fence. They're imprisoned there."

Tash took off, and Aiden, again, invited Ava and Z'ier to shelter at his house.

"It's too much for your family," Ava told him.

"No, it's not." He couldn't think of anything better than to share his room with Ava.

She slid her eyes toward her mother, who wore the despairing but determined expression of someone about to step off a high cliff.

"No," Ava repeated dully. "We're fine."

She doesn't want to bring her mom around my family, Aiden decided. He smoothed her sooty blonde hair. "I'll stay here tonight with you then."

He sat beside her on the wood floor, and she leaned her head on his shoulder. "You're a good friend, Aiden."

The words stabbed his heart. Ava considered him a friend and nothing more.

CHAPTER 33

The following morning, volunteers arrived with clothing, water, and bedding. Grandma Rosie requested Doug's assistance in walking to the gym, and upon arrival, the older woman assumed command. Aiden proudly observed his grandmother orchestrate the organization and distribution of the donated items. For someone who had relied heavily on Roland II, Rosie displayed remarkable inner strength.

The fear and anguish of the gym-dwellers had clung to him like a sickly film during the night, and their discomfort was still palpable this morning. Families huddled together, and people avoided interacting with one another.

Then, a magical thing happened. Rosie and her helpers laid out breakfast: elderberries, oyster mushrooms mixed with canned tomato sauce, dandelion flowers, and purslane. The lure of food brought the gym-dwellers to the table, where the nourishment fed more than their bodies. They began to talk.

"Did your house burn?"

"Yes. I lost everything."

"I did, too."

"I can't believe everything I own is gone."

"I know. I don't know what we're going to do."

As the conversation flowed, the room's atmosphere shifted. Aiden's sensory perception had heightened since the blackout, and he could almost see the mood change. Through the gray desolation, a yellow glimmer of sunshine emerged. Although the gym-dwellers commiserated, their small connection created a spark of positive energy. Aiden felt the prickling of that spark and wanted to see what it could ignite.

Meanwhile, Grandma Rosie received a lot of compliments for her food donation. Aerta, Aiden's neighbor, urged her husband Mac to return to their home to retrieve a stack of clothing to give away. She undoubtedly wanted to earn similar recognition and commendation as Rosie.

However, when Aerta offered Z'ier Durand her cast-off clothes, she burst into unexpected tears. Ava's mom was taken by surprise and left speechless as the stout woman grabbed her in an embrace.

Aiden smiled as he witnessed the spectacle, but Lizzie confronted Aerta.

"You didn't lose your home," she said. "Why are you crying?"

The woman released Z'ier and wiped her eyes. The heavy makeup she wore ran down her face. "I don't know. I just feel good."

"You're crying because you feel good?"

Sniffling, Aerta ignored Lizzie and ushered Z'ier to a secluded spot. While Aerta held her plus-sized dresses, shirts, and pants against Z'ier's rail-thin frame, she rambled on and on. A floodgate had opened within the privileged woman, and she poured out her fears, self-doubts, and dreams to Ava's mother. Like a not-so-fragile gourd, Z'ier remarkably absorbed the flood.

Aiden, still grinning, walked over to Lizzie. "Look at that. All kinds of emotions are opening up. Pretty amazing, isn't it?"

Lizzie's posture stiffened, and she narrowed her eyes at him. Her fierce expression caught him off-guard, and Aiden searched her eyes, trying to deduce the source of her anger. He picked up on nothing.

Unnerved, he stepped away from Lizzie and spent the rest of the morning helping Z'ier and Ava set up their shelter.

The other gym-dwellers erected private living quarters as well, and soon, the gym filled with tents, hanging tarps, and propped-up wallscreens.

Chris arrived, accompanied by the rest of the grid-skippers. They'd decided to move into the gym, but knowing how the townsfolk viewed them, the ragged group assembled in a far corner.

Tash offered to help Chris set up his shelter and, as they worked, he said, "I was thinking about your fire ring and how we could draw out the smoke. Well, there's a big ventilation pipe at DAPHNE's bunker. If we could pull it out somehow, I'll bet we could use it as a chimney."

Chris paused to admire the bright young man. "Ingenuity. God love it. You go for it, Tash."

WHILE TASH ASSEMBLED a team of able-bodied volunteers to trek to the old army base, Aiden led a group into the forest to assess the fire damage. Insects, animals, and plants should have radiated green life under the sun's warmth. Instead, the black skeletons of trees poked from a gray carpet of ash. When Aiden stumbled upon the charred carcass of a fawn, he turned on his followers.

"All it would have taken was a little respect," he hissed. "A little consideration for something other than yourself. What does the earth ask of you? Nothing. Just don't hurt it!"

The people accompanying him exchanged sheepish glances. Aiden sighed, knowing no one had meant to start the blaze. Thankfully, the wind had driven the fire in one direction, and a good portion of the flora remained undamaged.

LIZZIE CHEWED THOUGHTFULLY on the side of her lip as she observed Chris organize the books in his wheelbarrows. She hesitated momentarily and then wandered to where Clyde Parrish and his father constructed their shelter. She addressed the son since Mr. Parrish seemed more focused on swigging from a whiskey bottle.

"I see you're using store displays as walls."

Clyde tossed her an indifferent look.

"Very smart," she said. "They stand up by themselves, but they'd be stronger if you glued them together. I have some glue and could show you how to do it, if you like."

"Whatever."

"It's wise to put up walls. You'll want to hide what you have since they've moved in." Lizzie pointed to the corner where the grid-skippers were rebuilding their shanties.

That got Mr. Parrish's attention. "What are they doing here?"

Lizzie shrugged innocently.

Clyde's dad lurched to his feet and stumbled across the floor, sloshing liquor. He halted and swayed in front of Chris's newly erected tent.

"You and your kind... Get out."

Chris carefully laid a tarp over one wheelbarrow. "This isn't your gymnasium."

"Get out." Spittle flew from Mr. Parrish's mouth. "You're stinking up the place."

"I'm clean. You stink. You stink of cheap booze. What did you do? Raid all the liquor stores by yourself?"

Mr. Parrish kicked over the wheelbarrow.

Chris fumed to see his precious books tumble to the ground. "You think you're so tough." Pushing up his sleeves, he lunged at Clyde's dad.

The two men grappled with each other and threw punches. Clyde and Pete egged them on, which brought curious people to the sidelines.

AIDEN ELBOWED HIS WAY through a boisterous crowd surrounding Chris and Mr. Parrish. The two men had squared off and were fighting. Clyde's dad, although bigger and stronger, staggered from the booze. Even still, he managed to smack Chris in the nose. Seeing blood spurt from his friend's face, Aiden shoved Mr. Parrish aside, yelling, "Leave him alone!"

The crowd booed Aiden for disrupting the entertainment. A couple of men helped Mr. Parrish back to his shelter, where he promptly passed out.

Clyde stepped into the circle and spun Aiden around. "Baylor, I've wanted to give you this for a long time."

Stars jumped in Aiden's vision as Clyde's fist slammed into his mouth. As he fell to the ground, he heard Tash's angry voice.

"Get back, all of you! Move!" Tash knelt at Aiden's side with the ax gripped in his hand. "Are you okay?"

Aiden spat blood into his hand.

Jill ran into the circle, brandishing a knife. "Anyone else so much as touches my son, I will stab you in the neck!"

"Jill..." Doug pulled his wife away.

Tash stood up and addressed the crowd. "It's over. Get back to what you were doing." To Aiden, he said, "You sure you're all right?"

Aiden nodded. "You got the pipe?"

"Just outside. We're gonna haul it up now." He looked up at the skylight. "I hope it works."

"It'll work."

Chris held a hand over his bloody nose and said to Aiden, "We've got to get some kind of order in here."

Lizzie meandered over, handed Chris a cloth, and smirked at Aiden. "All kinds of emotions are opening up."

Aiden rubbed his sore jaw in response.

"You're a fool," she told him. "Do you think these people will come together? Without DAPHNE to manage them, they're going to tear each other apart."

Up on the roof, Tash and his crew suspended the pipe from the open skylight. When they secured it, they used scrap metal to build a hood at the bottom. Since Tash could not weld the hood to the pipe, he fashioned supports on the floor to hold the hood in place.

Once he finished, the grid-skippers built a rock ring under the hood, brought in wood, and lit a fire. Tash smiled to see the smoke travel out of the skylight via the new "chimney."

Chris pulled up a chair near the crackling flames. Other gym-dwellers copied him and jostled with each other to claim the prime spots.

Aiden watched them squabble, and, thinking about what Lizzie said, moved over to Chris. "We need a leader. You should lead us."

"Are you kidding?" Chris pressed the cloth against his bruised nose.

"You're the only one who knows how to live off the grid."

"Forget it."

Aiden put a hand on his friend's arm. "You once told me human beings need a purpose. You chose to live on the streets because the job you worked gave your life no meaning. Well, take this job. This job has meaning."

Chris shook his head.

"Show us how to live without power or—," Aiden nodded at Chris's wheelbarrows. "At least lend us some books so we can teach ourselves."

Chris gazed at Aiden. A couple of minutes passed, and he stood up and loudly snapped his fingers. "Okay, dummies, listen up. It's time to learn something other than how to watch a commercial."

The gym fell silent. Not all eyes were friendly as they settled on Chris.

He cleared his throat. "I'll let you borrow my books if you treat 'em better than your kids."

"What good is a book gonna do me?" one woman sneered. "Can it rebuild my house?"

Chris gazed at her with compassion. "'There are times when dreams sustain us more than facts. To read a book and surrender to a story is to keep our very humanity alive.'"

"Ah, shut up," someone else grumbled.

Chris cracked his neck in an attempt to control his temper. "Long ago, a woman named Helen Fagin wrote those words in a letter. She was a Holocaust survivor who taught Jewish children in the Warsaw ghetto, where books were forbidden. You're not the first people to run into a rough patch, but you may be the first to have forgotten how to dream."

A young mother holding a toddler approached the wheelbarrow. Settling the child on her hip, she picked up a book and examined the cover.

"That's right," Chris told her. "It's a book. You hold it in your hand and hit yourself really hard on the head with it."

Aiden crossed his arms. "Chris."

The grid-skipper shrugged. "Knock some sense into their skulls."

"Say something else."

"Like what?"

"Teach 'em like you taught me."

Chris contemplated the floor for a minute. At last, he smoothed the plaits of his blood-speckled trousers and addressed the company. "Many centuries ago, the Sierra Miwok settled this area. Miwok blood runs in my veins. My ancestors were indigenous people who knew how to live off the land. They respected the earth, and it nurtured them. I suggest you listen to Aiden here who has studied up on the subject. The ancient people created a roundhouse or *hun'ge* to be their ceremonial and social center. This gym will be our roundhouse, our gathering place. These books will be your library. Educate yourselves." He glanced at Mr. Parrish, who snored on a cot. "Learn things essential to our survival. We will survive if we work together, but only if we work together."

Chris then plopped down on the floor and gave Aiden a weary look that asked, *is that good enough?*

Slowly, people began to approach the wheelbarrows of books. Some surrounded Chris, asking him how people lived before the Digital Age. Aiden nodded in satisfaction, knowing that, at that moment, Chris had become the Chief of Sierrawood.

CHAPTER 34

As the forest grew fragrant with summer, more and more people opted to move out of their homes and into the gym or the surrounding classrooms. They felt safe from the wildlife around other people, but, more than that, they seemed to recharge on the energy surrounding the communal dining table. The gym-dwellers also shared the information they read in books, which led to lively discussions that further invigorated them.

As a frequent visitor to the gym, Aiden received an invitation from Z'ier and Ava to share their shelter. When he informed his parents he wanted to move in, Jill agreed, but under the condition that Z'ier keep a watchful eye over the two young people. Although it hurt to admit it, Aiden reassured his mother that Ava had no interest in him beyond friendship.

On his first night in the shelter, he watched Ava sleep. He wished the moonlight streaming in through the windows would illuminate her more. He longed to hold her, and it killed him that he could only do so in his fantasies.

Aiden, like everyone else, fell into a routine. An abundance of chores awaited the gym-dwellers each day, primarily focused on acquiring food. Chris insisted everyone maintain a clean and orderly living space, an unusual demand for a guy who used to wear dirty clothes and live on the street. Nevertheless, Aiden observed that almost everyone respected his guidance because they knew Chris had thrived without power.

The gym-dwellers seemed to split into different groups during their idle moments. Some, like Aiden, Chris, Ava, and Tash, proactively planned for their survival. Others, whom Chris nicknamed "The Depressionists," wrung their hands and cried over their predicament. Another group, fondly labeled "The Aggravationists," gathered in frustration and assaulted Govind with complaints whenever he visited. Clyde and his dad played central roles in this group and seemed to derive pleasure from inciting others to anger.

Lizzie conducted daily meetings with her team in one of the classrooms to discuss ways to revive DAPHNE. The Depressionists and Aggravationists attended and clung to her every word as though she were a prophet who could connect them to AI heaven.

Aiden dreaded DAPHNE's return. Curious about Lizzie's plans, he attended one of her meetings.

"We're going to need at least ten megawatts of power to run DAPHNE again," she stated.

Professor Feinstein crossed one casual leg over the other and lit his pipe with a flaming twig. "What about collecting all the fallen drones, robots, and androids and harnessing their leftover charge?"

With his fake, broken spectacles, the teacher looked the part of a distinguished, if eccentric, scientist. Aiden, now adept at reading a person's fears and desires, clearly saw through Feinstein's facade of academic importance and could tell his former teacher felt totally insecure.

"To amass ten megawatts of power? Don't be ridiculous." Lizzie turned her back on the defeated man and addressed her team. Vivica attended the meeting but didn't appear too interested. Her eyes continually wandered to the window and the bright daylight.

"I want all of you to use your brainpower," Lizzie said, "and come up with another source of energy. Even if we have to rekindle every single advancement of human evolution, we're going to bring back DAPHNE's technology."

Aiden had heard enough. He assembled his group of food gatherers and, this time convinced a few of the Depressionists to come along.

The team walked through the sunlit forest, which welcomed them by offering a bounty of wild and sweet blackberries, raspberries, tender miner's lettuce, and a host of other edible plants. Aiden urged those with torn spirits to see the environment as a friend, not an enemy to fear.

He taught the food gatherers how to peel back the bark of pine trees to expose the inner, edible layer. He also showed them how to lay sheets under the trees to catch the cones that shed nuts and how to collect pitch from the pinyon trees. He'd found that when he melted the sap with oil, it cooled into an excellent skin salve that stopped itches and healed minor cuts and bug bites.

As Aiden stood beside a pinyon pine, he pulled a plug of the honey-like sap from its bark and rubbed it between his fingers. Indeed, the resin seemed like a live, bodily fluid. Contemplating the wound in the pine's trunk, he whispered, "Thank you for sharing your blood with us."

A crack in the nearby brush made him turn around. Dr. Lizzie Appel appraised him with tight lips and a raised eyebrow. Apparently, she'd decided to check on him like he did on her.

"Who are you talking to, Aiden?"

He placed a bold hand on the tree trunk. "This is a living being. A living being that's helping us."

"Do you think it speaks to you like the voice in your head?"

"In a way. I also believe it listens. That's why I talk to it." He focused on her face, trying hard to read her. Only an unrelenting hardness lay behind her eyes.

"Why are you so interested in me, Lizzie?"

She didn't reply.

"Is it the voice in my head? Are you worried it's real?" She turned and walked away, but he called after her, "Why does it frighten you?"

UPON RETURNING TO THE gym, Aiden took a cue from the book on tribal life and mixed the sap he'd collected with ash from the fire pit. The mixture created a strong and effective glue. Tash tried to adhere the fire ring's hood to the pipe with the 'glue,' except the heat melted the sap, turning it into a crystalline, sticky mess.

The food gatherers returned with a host of plants, including cattails, all parts of which, according to Aiden, were edible. The rhizomes, the nutrient-packed stems that grew horizontally underground, tasted especially good. The soft, white tails were highly absorbent and made good padding for bedding and diapers.

The cooks, led by Rosie, took possession of the various plants, and not only used them for food but learned about their medicinal uses. As the days of June passed, the cooks/pharmacists found that the chokecherry fruit soothed sore throats and irritated eyes. Arnica flowers soaked in olive oil helped with muscle soreness, and California Spikenard eased coughs. Syrup made from Wild Ginger rhizomes relieved gas and stomach cramps, and the bark of the black oak, when pulverized and mixed with baking soda and peppermint, created a tasty toothpaste.

As Aiden observed the cooks dabbling with nature's magic like magicians discovering new tricks, he could see that none of them had realized the earth was a garden from which they could draw sustenance.

The book on Native American life claimed that none of the flora offered more sustenance than the proud oaks, whose cheerfully capped acorns held the secret to life. Since the nuts were so plentiful, they'd been a staple of the early people's diet. Aiden pressed the gatherers to collect as many acorns as possible, but everyone grimaced at their terrible taste.

Professor Feinstein blamed the bitterness on tannins, a compound found in plants, and suggested the cooks boil the acorns.

When the water turned the color of strong tea, the cooks strained the nuts and dropped them into a second pot to boil. They repeated this process until the water turned clear. Afterward, the cooks roasted the nuts and conducted a taste test. The acorns now had a sweet and nutty flavor, comparable to potatoes, definitely edible! The roasted nuts were fine by themselves but the cooks wished they could do more with them.

They got their wish within the week.

WHILE HIS TEAM FORAGED in the forest, Aiden mentioned to Ava how the cooks wanted to craft better foods. Within minutes of having this discussion, he felt an urge to wander away from the group. He hiked along a stream and stopped at a boulder half-hidden by the leaves and blue flowers of a buck brush. *There,* he thought. *Something lies there.*

Ava, curious, followed him and tilted her head in confusion as she watched him tear away the foliage.

"What are you doing?" she asked.

"I'm not sure."

He pulled and tore at the buck brush until his efforts revealed a long, flat rock pitted with holes.

Ava inspected the Swiss cheese surface. "Weird. It looks like a drone attacked it, but why laser a rock?"

Aiden didn't know. Again, he wished he could learn more about the Great Source. He knew to follow its direction but never knew where the direction would lead."

Unable to make sense of the rock, Ava and Aiden brought Chris over to inspect their discovery.

"A drone didn't make these holes," Chris told them. "This is an old *metate*, or grinding rock. The indigenous people used this place for grinding acorns into meal." He searched the surrounding grasses until he discovered a smooth, elongated stone about the size of his hand. He displayed it to Ava and Aiden and said, "You can use this as a pestle. Put acorns into the hole and use the pestle to mash them. Ava, can you use your optics to locate other rocks like this?"

She nodded and then turned to Aiden. "How did you know where to look?"

He shrugged. If he told her about the Great Source, he might lose her friendship.

Ava's eye screens displayed question marks. Still, Aiden would not answer.

AS THE DAYS OF JUNE passed, the grinding stone became another area for social gatherings. The human chatter, blending with the rhythmic crunching of pestles, created a lively ambiance. The people worked, conversed, and drank tea made from pine and fir tree needles, which cheered them because their breath smelled like Christmas trees.

The Pulverizers (as they called themselves) transported the ground acorn meal back to the roundhouse, where Grandma Rosie taught the cooks how to prepare pound cake, pasta, and chips, which tasted like graham crackers. Like the ancient tribes before them, the acorn meal became an essential part of the Sierrawood people's diet.

The lake was another gathering place, serving as a vital water source, bathing area, and fishing hole. Doug taught the people how to fish because Aiden refused to kill something, even if it was for food.

THE DEMANDING TASKS of the day exhausted the gym-dwellers, and the conversation around the campfire dwindled. The flickering firelight on their faces revealed the truth about their situation: a relentless struggle for survival and a wish to return to an easier way of life.

Observing their weariness one evening, Aiden decided to try something to lift their spirits. He brought his guitar to the gym and began to play. The music had a profound effect on the gym-dwellers. Some listened with tears welling in their eyes, while others tapped their feet or hummed along. At first, their feet tapped awkwardly, but then their bodies fell into a shared rhythm. Aiden thought up lyrics to complement the melody and began to sing. He persisted despite a couple of Aggravationists shouting at him to be quiet. In fact, he encouraged those listening to sing along.

Initially, no one did until Ava stood up and belted out the lyrics. When her voice cracked, she laughed, aware she was no diva, but her confidence encouraged others to join in. Aiden felt energized as the gym filled with human voices, and he wasn't the only one who felt buoyant. The high spirits quieted even the most vocal of the Aggravationists, including Lizzie, who witnessed the singalong with perplexed eyes and pursed lips.

CHAPTER 35

The following day, Tash proudly showed Aiden a drum he'd fashioned out of a barrel and a stiff leather jacket.

"Chris told me the ancients considered the drum 'good medicine' because it mimics the human heartbeat." His eyes searched Aiden's. "Do you think the medicine will work on my blood cells?"

Aiden noticed more white and less yellow in his friend's eyes. Their diet of mostly vegetables and fruit seemed to be helping Tash.

"It's sure to work," he said. "Let's try it out tonight."

The gym-dwellers enjoyed Tash's rhythmic contribution. One of the listeners had collected antique musical instruments and offered to make a donation to the band. The next day, guitars, bells, tambourines, a piano, and even a vibraphone filled an adjoining classrooom. Vivica decided to teach herself to play the vibraphone, and Tash joked that she wanted to join the band only to get closer to him.

"Keep thinking that." She tossed him a sassy grin as she tapped the mallets on the tone bars. "I'm sure it boosts your overcharged teenaged ego."

Each night, the central fire burned, and music filled the gym. No one complained about the band, whose sound starkly contrasted with the spiky electronic tones of vocaloids like Kiko. Aiden's guitar chords carried an earthy quality, resonating at one's core, and the mellow warmth of Vivica's vibraphone lulled many into a sound sleep. No ghost of anxiety haunted the roundhouse, as the music acted like an antidepressant. The energy from the singalongs often moved people to tears.

When Aiden explained this phenomenon to his mother in the hope she would move into the gym, Jill refused to leave the privacy of her home. "Why would I want to sleep with a bunch of strangers?"

Govind, Lizzie, Oreanna, and Doug also shunned the idea of communal living, but Grandma Rosie and Grandpa Harry opted to move. The two had outlived most of their friends and lived in daily fear of losing each other. Harry grew increasingly depressed with each passing day because his Smart Legs continued to malfunction. Some days, he could walk around, but most days, he had to sit in a chair. Rosie hoped the activity in the roundhouse would rejuvenate her husband.

The longer days and balmy evenings of summer allowed Govind and Lizzie to stay and watch the band before returning to the Baylor home. One evening, as they trekked back to Jill and Doug's, Govind asked, "Did you see them dancing? I never thought I'd hear laughter again, let alone see people dance."

Lizzie shrugged under the crescent moon.

He casually slung the sturdy protective stick he carried over his shoulder. "We're surviving without DAPHNE. It's amazing. Her intelligence guided me my entire life, but now I wonder why we invented her in the first place?"

Lizzie gawked at him. "Are you serious? Do you think those people are happy? They may be surviving, but surviving is a far cry from thriving."

"Were we thriving with DAPHNE?"

She tucked in her chin and regarded Govind as though he were a child. "Let me ask you a question. Why do you think we developed the washing machine?"

"To make our lives easier."

"Exactly. People didn't want to wash clothes in a river."

"Ah, but there was a price to pay for that convenience," he countered and flinched at the sudden screech of some animal. "The factories that make those washing machines polluted our skies. Who knows what that poison did to our health and the planet's over all these years?"

She remained firm. "Yet, technology extended our lifespans. Go ahead and ask the people, Govind. Ask them if they'd rather wash their clothes in a river to save the planet or use a washing machine. Human evolution led to technology, which led to DAPHNE. It's meant to be."

Govind didn't respond. He knew the people of Sierrawood considered this current crisis temporary. They only had to survive until DAPHNE powered up and got all the machines running again.

"HERE, GRANDPA HARRY," Aiden said as he handed the older man a cup of tea in the morning. "Grandma read that the leaves and twigs of the chokecherry bush ease arthritis."

"Thanks, Rebel."

Grandpa sat on an armchair gazing at the dancing flames of the central fire. Aiden had plucked two armchairs from the Baylor living room and placed them close to the fire ring, a prime piece of real estate.

"You've got a gift," Harry said to his grandson. "Everyone likes your music. It makes them feel better."

Lizzie arrived at the gym, and Harry begged her to examine his legs. "Is there anything you can do? I think they've completely died."

"I'm sorry, Mr. Katz, but even if we could recharge them, they'd have no guidance, not without DAPHNE."

He sighed and shook his head. "It's a shame. Right before the blackout, I ordered the new version of Smart Legs. Those models don't need to be recharged because they run on a person's kinetic energy."

Aiden blanched at the mention of kinetic energy and remembered Professor Yang. In his dream, she'd asked him to solve a mystery, which he'd assumed was the mystery of human consciousness. But what did human consciousness have to do with kinetic energy? Aiden couldn't see any connection.

Lizzie placed a reassuring hand on Harry's shoulder. "It's my team's goal to get DAPHNE powered up as soon as possible. Then, you'll get your new legs."

Grandpa Harry's shoulder drooped under her hand. "I doubt you'll do that anytime soon, Dr. Lizzie."

It saddened Aiden to see his grandpa's youthful outlook dampened, and he begged Tash to return to the Katz's apartment to search for tools.

"You're so good with building things, I thought maybe you could build something to help him get around."

Tash glanced at the elderly man sitting miserably in his chair. "I'll do anything to help Grandpa Harry."

When Aiden's classmates got wind of the plan, they asked to come along. With no school or VR games to occupy their time, the young people yearned for entertainment. Exploring Harry and Rosie's treasure trove sounded fun, and the elderly couple readily granted permission. They were pleased that their hoarding now served a good purpose.

When Clyde and Pete asked if they could join the expedition, Aiden gave a self-important shrug. "Sure. You can tag along." He secretly hoped the shared adventure would soothe the tension between him and Clyde.

On the way to the apartment complex, Aiden walked beside his nemesis with his chin held high. He tried to get the burly young man to open up, but Clyde didn't talk much except to admit his parents divorced years ago, and he didn't see his mom at all. He refused to discuss life with his father, but Aiden imagined it wasn't much fun. Mr. Parrish was as much of a bully as his son.

After the young people scaled the security fence, Tash grabbed Aiden's arm. "You know those assholes are just using you, right?"

Aiden jerked away and hurried to catch up with Clyde and Pete.

MANY TENANTS, LIKE Tash's parents, had moved out because they grew weary of tackling the outside fence. With few inhabitants to intervene, the building fell prey to the encroaching forest. Weeds sprouted across the once-manicured lawn. The fountain stood dry and cracked. A buzzing beehive hung over the lobby doors, and mice, squirrels, and chipmunks ran amok inside the building. Dirt, trash, and abandoned furniture filled the halls. The place resembled a gothic ruin.

Rosie and Harry's apartment had weathered the abandonment pretty well. The young people discovered hammers, files, saws, and packets of screws and nails. Busty Trina pulled a few cobwebbed brooms from under Jill's old bed while Clyde and Pete discovered a box of knives in L'Eren's former room. Clyde took one of the brooms, sawed off the brush, and, using a cord, secured a butcher knife to the end to make a spear.

Admiring his friend's handiwork, Pete said, "That's so plus, Clyde! That bear can't mess with us now. We've got protection."

"Screw protection." Clyde tested the weapon in his grip. "I'm going to kill that bear."

A girl found a small box that rattled when shaken, and Aiden's pulse hiked. He knew the box contained bullets from his great-grandmother's gun. Relief washed over him when the girl tossed the container aside, which Aiden quickly hid away. With

Clyde on the warpath, the last thing Aiden wanted was to introduce him to firearms, even antique ones.

Aiden and Tash found a bicycle and a defunct Roland in the hallway outside the apartment. They spent the rest of the afternoon hollowing out the boxy, wheeled robot to create a wheelchair for Grandpa Harry.

That evening, when the two boys proudly presented the makeshift wheelchair to Grandpa Harry, Aiden's face fell to see the once spry gentleman lowered into the seat like an invalid. Catching Lizzie's knowing eye, Aiden knew what she was thinking. Without technology, Harry would take one step closer to the grave.

CHAPTER 36

One warm morning in July, Clyde asked Aiden if he and his friends could come along on the daily food-gathering expedition. Hope radiated in Aiden's chest. Perhaps he had finally made headway with his nemesis. However, it quickly became apparent that Clyde and his gamer pals had no interest in picking plants.

The group carried homemade spears as they prowled the forest and itched to meet up with an animal. Aiden felt pretty confident the wannabe hunters would never get the chance; they didn't realize their clomping, stomping footsteps scared off the wildlife.

Still, the hunters persisted and continued to join the food gatherers. As they paused at a stream to drink and rest one afternoon, Aiden decided to raise the subject of hunting with Clyde. He strolled over, thumbs hooked into the pocket of his jeans, and watched Clyde chuck his spear at a downed tree.

"You're getting good," Aiden commented.

Clyde ignored the compliment and retrieved his spear. A chipmunk chattered and scolded him from a nearby rock. Clyde returned to his spot and took aim again.

"What are you trying to hit?" Aiden squinted his eyes at the tree.

"That gap right there." Clyde pointed to a deep crevice in the wood.

Aiden didn't know what to do with his arms, so he crossed them. "You're not really gonna kill anything, are you?"

Clyde threw the spear, and it landed perfectly in the gap.

Walking over to his weapon, he said, "You know, Baylor, you think you're hot shit now, but you're still the same geek you always were." He yanked the spear from the wood.

Aiden kept his arms crossed and swallowed. To his relief, he heard his name called and saw his father running up the path toward him.

"Aiden!" Doug yelled. "Come home. Aunt L'Eren is having her baby!"

GOVIND WANTED HIS WIFE to deliver in the hospital because of the more accessible access to medications, but it happened that L'Eren chose to walk to the roundhouse, where the noise and people might take her mind off her discomfort. The long walk, however, induced her labor, and Govind panicked because they had no choice but to have the baby in the gym. Z'ier Durand, watching the couple struggle, offered L'Eren her bed.

The prospect of a new life gave the gym-dwellers something joyful to anticipate, and many of them huddled outside Z'ier's shelter, whispering and cringing every time L'Eren screamed.

Behind the mounted wallscreens that gave them privacy, Govind gripped the edge of the bed where his wife lay. Jill stood shamefaced, her fist pressed against her mouth. It had been her idea to encourage L'Eren to walk to the gym. Standing beside Jill, Oreanna winced with each cry that escaped her aunt's lips.

"Help me," L'Eren pleaded. "Something's wrong."

Rosie entered and put a cool cloth on the suffering woman's forehead. She eyed Jill in worry. "The baby should have come by now. I don't know why it's not."

Panicked, Govind rushed out to find Lizzie. He located her sitting in one of the classrooms, holding a strategy meeting with her team of engineers.

"Please," he begged, "you have to help L'Eren. She's having her baby, but it won't come out."

Lizzie seemed annoyed at the disruption. "I don't know a thing about births, Govind. I'm sorry." She refocused on her group.

"Please. Rennie might die."

Lizzie sighed at her followers. "Someday, there won't be a need for a uterus. With exogenesis, all babies will be grown in biobags."

Govind stared at her, horrified. "Who cares about that now?"

He heard a commotion in the gym and raced back inside. There, he saw Ava pushing her mother through the crowd of people.

"LET US THROUGH!" AVA shouted. "My mom once worked as a nanny."

Z'ier tried to backpedal. "As a nanny, Ava, not a midwife."

Ava prodded her mother forward. "You said you watched over an infant."

"Watched him, not delivered him!" Z'ier tried to duck away, but Ava pushed her through the tarp that served as their door.

L'Eren shrieked, which made both Ava and Z'ier jump. Govind hustled inside.

"Please," he said to Z'ier. "Can you help her?"

Ava's mom gazed at L'Eren. She didn't know what to do, but something inside Z'ier told her to try. A moment passed, and she said to Oreanna, "Bring me some warm water and towels." Z'ier then put her hands on L'Eren's stomach. "The baby seems off-center. I'm going to try and move it."

She pressed her hands this way and that, and L'Eren shrieked in pain. At last, Z'ier helped her sit up. Positioning herself between the laboring mother's legs, Z'ier said with relief, "The baby is crowning. It's almost here. Take a deep breath, L'Eren. Bear down. Push. Push with all your might."

A guttural yell issued from L'Eren, and those beyond the tarp bit their fingernails or held onto each other. The Depressionists told each other that L'Eren would probably die. At the same time, the Aggravationists slammed their fists against the walls and shouted for the women to shut up. Inside the shelter, Rosie continued to wipe L'Eren's face with the cloth, and Jill massaged her sister's shoulders and murmured encouragement.

"That's it. Push again." Z'ier smiled. "My gosh, you're almost there."

Oreanna, pale and trembling, patted L'Eren's arm. "Almost there, Aunt Rennie."

"Will she be all right?" Jill squeaked.

Z'ier couldn't reply, for emotion choked her throat, and tears streamed down her face. Suddenly, she cradled a brand-new baby in her hands. "It's a boy," she whispered.

"He's not breathing," Govind said.

Z'ier, gazing at the newborn, hadn't been aware the new father knelt beside her.

Wiping her eyes, she laid the baby facedown on a blanket and firmly rubbed her hand up and down his back. She tried to ignore the waves of panic rippling off of Govind. Silently, Z'ier prayed, *Please don't let my fumbling hands kill this baby.*

Carefully turning the infant over, she rubbed his chest. Where the idea came from, Z'ier didn't know, but she massaged him with quiet determination. A gasp suddenly bubbled from the baby's mouth, and L'Eren let loose a cry of relief. Govind's shoulders released, and he laughed as his newborn son began to bray loudly. Z'ier couldn't take her eyes off the squirming life in her hands. *I did it.*

"Can I hold him?" Govind asked, which snapped Z'ier back to reality.

She gently placed the baby in his arms and told Jill, "Help me deliver the placenta."

Z'ier held a towel against L'Eren, told her to push, and the afterbirth slipped out. "Can someone find a pair of scissors or a sharp knife? We need a tiny bit of twine or some thread too."

Oreanna scrambled under the tarp and returned with Grandma Rosie, who handed Govind the scissors and Z'ier the thread. Govind cut the umbilical cord while Z'ier clamped off the baby's belly button. After Jill gently cleaned her nephew, Z'ier swaddled him. When she handed Govind his son, he leaned forward and kissed Ava's mother on the cheek.

"Thank you," he gushed. "Thank you with all my heart." He brought the baby to L'Eren.

Z'ier twisted the hem of her blouse as she watched the new family enjoy a blissful moment. Ava nudged her mom. "How did you know what to do?"

"I-I must have seen it on a show, I guess." Z'ier's face suddenly screwed up, and her shoulders quaked as she began to sob.

Ava, embarrassed, patted her mother's shoulder. "Don't cry, Mom. You did great."

"I don't know why I'm crying." Z'ier wiped her eyes with her sleeve and gazed sadly at the infant. "Isn't a new life beautiful? He's got all his chances ahead of him."

Grandma Rosie pulled Z'ier into a hug. "Every life is beautiful, honey, including yours. Look what you just did."

Z'ier sniffled, and Jill, wearing a rare smile, handed her a box of tissues. When Z'ier exited the shelter, people cheered and patted her on the back. Some even embraced her. She took a seat near the fire and gazed at the flames, overwhelmed by emotion. A woman with a small baby bump under her shirt knelt beside her.

"I didn't know you were a—," the woman searched for the word. "A midwife, right?"

"I didn't know either." Z'ier blew her nose into a tissue.

"Will you please help me when my time comes?"

Z'ier hesitated a moment and then nodded.

In the future, when Z'ier Durand would count many summers and births behind her, she would tell people that the day she first delivered a new life into the world, her life began anew.

THE GYM-DWELLERS TREATED L'Eren and her baby boy, whom she and Govind named Kimber, like royalty. The new mother basked in the attention. Grandma Rosie and her fellow cooks made acorn cakes to celebrate the birth and decorated them with donated (looted) frosting. Doug and his fellow anglers brought in baskets of fresh trout from the lake for the party, and Ava and Z'ier made a salad of wild greens. Aiden's band played for hours while people danced. Vivica's mallets tapped across the vibraphone board, and she smiled at Tash as he sat behind his ever-growing drum set.

Pete Farmington approached Aiden with a tambourine and a harmonica in his hands. Shyly, he asked if he could join the band, and Aiden welcomed him.

When the band took a break, Ava told Aiden how much she loved watching his fingers move along the strings. What she didn't tell him was how much his moving fingers attracted her, how she wondered what his touch would feel like on her body.

Aiden watched Ava dance but didn't tell her that she inspired his music, that the melodies he created echoed the chords of his heart.

From his shelter, Clyde Parrish watched Ava dance as well. His face betrayed no emotion, but he didn't take his eyes off her. Near the crackling fire pit, Oreanna sat beside Grandpa Harry to keep him company but couldn't take her eyes off the brooding, muscular Clyde.

CHAPTER 37

July became August, and the young people stole moments of fun when they could. The earth served as their playground and threw confetti at them in the form of gold leaves. Aiden, Ava, Tash, and Vivica used the casings of robots to float on the river and yelled in excitement when they bounced over rapids. *Jungle Flight* flashed in Aiden's mind as he gripped the bobbing, hollowed-out robot and prayed he wouldn't fall out. As the water spray hit his smile and adrenalin hit his heart, Aiden knew that virtual reality had nothing over a real adventure.

One sultry afternoon, the friends pulled their makeshift rafts from the cool water and ate a picnic of salal berries, chanterelle mushrooms, and a bag of potato chips. They drank a coffee substitute prepared from roasted dandelion roots. While they ate, Aiden decided it was time to share the Great Source with his friends.

"I'm trying to figure out what it is. God? Aliens?" He munched on a chip and hoped they wouldn't judge him too harshly. "The Lakota mentioned something called 'Wakan Tanka,' a lifeforce that flows in all things. A scientist once told Ava and me about a 'lifespark.' Maybe the two are the same. The Great Source exists, and whatever it is, I'm communicating with it. I think we all can."

Ava's foot gently kicked his leg. "Did you use it to read my mind that day on the bus?"

"You mean when we talked about the Spotted Towhee?" Aiden considered that. "I think so. The bird just popped into my head like the words do."

Vivica reached an excited hand into the chip bag. "Wow, maybe we could use the Great Source like a WeConnect. You know, talk to each other that way."

Aiden frowned at the mention of the hated device. "The communication with the Great Source is organic and beneficial. It won't spy on us like DAPHNE did to make Ophidian rich."

"Didn't your dad work for Ophidian?" Ava asked.

"Yeah, but he wasn't happy about it."

"His job gave you a nice home."

Aiden's home had been comfortable, but he never felt important there. To himself, he said, *The money never benefited me.*

But you could afford anything you wanted, Ava's answer surfaced in his head. *Some of us don't know what that feels like.*

"Well, no one knows what it feels like now," Aiden said aloud.

Tash exchanged glances with Vivica. Ava's eyescreens showed an emoji face with its mouth falling open. Aiden leveled his gaze at her. *Ava, can you hear me? Say you can.*

She didn't respond. Why didn't the communication work all the time?

"You heard my thoughts," Ava told him. "How?"

"I don't know." Aiden shook his head in frustration. "It's the mystery of human consciousness. I can't figure it out. I had this dream where Professor Yang told me—"

"Professor Yang?" Tash interrupted. "She's dead."

"I don't think so." Aiden gazed at their surprised faces. "I saw her as clear as I'm seeing you."

"In a *dream*," Vivica reminded him.

"But she gave me a message. She said I had to solve the mystery, and I think it's the mystery of human consciousness. What else could it be?"

Tash furrowed his brows. "Why do you have to solve it?"

"She said our survival depends on it. I can't do this alone, you guys. I need help."

"Aiden," Vivica began, "if you've discovered some new power source, it's a game-changer."

He nodded and stood up. "Let's try an experiment. Let's summon the Great Source. Ava, you go one way. Tash, you go another. Create a mind-drift—I mean, a fantasy about the place you're at. Dreaming when you're awake creates something. Vivica and I will try to find you with clues that come into our heads."

Although they traded doubtful looks, Tash and Ava jogged away from the river.

Tash disappeared up a hill, and Ava hiked a different path until she reached a sunlit meadow containing an old wooden cattle ramp. Oaks bordered the field along with maple trees, whose leaves had become scarlet. Chris had told Ava that gold miners imported non-native trees to the Sierra Nevadas because they missed their homes in the east. The prospectors had died long ago, but their maples remained as a living testimony to their nostalgia. Leaning against the dilapidated wooden rails, Ava tried to implant the scene firmly in her mind.

I'm standing next to a splintery wood structure, gazing at red leaves. The grass is soft and yellow under my sneakers, and the sun makes the trees glow like angels. I'm here. Find me.

Try as Ava might to concentrate on her surroundings, her mind wandered to her father. Was he still alive? Montana boasted wide-open spaces with lots of natural resources, so she thought he might be okay. On one hand, she loved her dad. On the other, she resented him. Why hadn't the family he'd had with her and Z'ier been good enough? Did that mean he loved his new kids more? The usual lousy brew of sorrow and anger began burning Ava's stomach. *I will never love anyone without holding up a shield.*

Her shoulders sagged, and she looked around with a sigh. She saw no sign of Aiden, but a buck trotted into the clearing with an arching, thick set of antlers. Ava kept stock-still as the beautiful animal drew close to the cattle ramp to eat some clover. *Please don't go,* she prayed. *Please don't run away.* Her dad momentarily surfaced in her mind.

The buck lifted his head to appraise Ava and returned to his foraging. She spied some acorns in the grass, picked them up, and held the nuts in her damp palm.

The buck meandered closer. *Drop the shield, Ava.*

The words came but didn't seem to be hers. *Let go and let yourself love.*

Ava shut down her eyescreens so their glow wouldn't scare the animal and held out the acorns. Unable to see, she envisioned petting his coat, hugging his neck. *Love me,* she begged. *Love me as I love you.*

Just as her arm began to tire, warm breath wafted on her palm, and Ava felt a nibbling mouth. She quickly reactivated her optics to see the buck eating from her hand. Incredible joy cascaded over her pitted heart and soothed it like honey.

"YOU'RE RIGHT," SHE said to Aiden when the four friends reunited.

"What do you mean, 'I'm right'?" he scratched his arm in annoyance. "We searched all over for you and Tash, and I ended up running into poison oak." He displayed red welts on his arm. Vivica hid a grin and winked at Tash.

"Something inside me spoke," Ava said.

Vivica pulled a thistle from her sock. "Was it the Great Source?"

"I don't know, but it helped me."

"How?"

Ava hesitated but then remembered the advice she'd received about dropping her shield. As they hiked back to the school, she took a deep breath and confessed how hurt she felt about her father's new life. To Ava's relief, the others didn't judge her. They validated her feelings, which lifted a weight from her.

Vivica took her hand, which felt strange and wonderful. Ava couldn't remember the last time she held someone's hand.

"I'm sure your dad loves you," Vivica said. "But you still have every right to feel rejected. Problem is, it doesn't change anything. You're never going to be a family again. You'll have to live with it somehow and move on."

Ava considered the truth in the other girl's words. Move on. She never considered moving on. Could she actually choose not to sit in misery? Snapping off a dandelion, Ava chewed on the root as she walked and realized she'd never had good friends like these.

"Tell us exactly how the Great Source helped you," Aiden pressed her. "Maybe if we can understand how it works, we can find out what it is."

"I can't say exactly. It opened a door somehow." Ava shrugged. "Just having this conversation is helping."

LIZZIE WITNESSED THE four friends entering the gym, talking about an encounter with a deer, which aided Ava in some symbolic way. Although she couldn't catch everything they said, they mentioned the Great Source, which snagged Lizzie's attention.

She wandered closer and gasped to see Vivica holding Ava's hand.

"We've got to tell the others," Vivica said.

"We can't." Aiden shook his head. "Not until we have more proof."

"But the Great Source helped Ava," Tash argued. "It can help other people, too."

Apparently, the elusive voice in Aiden's head had transcended him and was now influencing others. Being sensible and resourceful, Lizzie surmised that whatever type of power source this was, it became infectious when people congregated. She'd need to halt the spread of the Great Source before it went viral.

CHAPTER 38

Lizzie got her chance with the coming of autumn. Despite the drop in temperature during the nights, Rosie and her group of self-appointed nurses were surprised to hear a few gym-dwellers complain of feeling hot.

After feeling their foreheads, Rosie declared they had a fever. The symptoms quickly worsened with nausea, vomiting, and diarrhea. Lizzie made a more careful examination of the sick individuals and pulled Govind aside.

"We've got an outbreak of cholera," she said.

He paled. "How? What caused it?"

"It's usually brought on by unsanitary conditions."

Govind looked around the gym—at the clutter of makeshift homes, the central fire ring, and the long dining table. "Where?"

"I don't know," Lizzie told him. "But everyone will have to quarantine immediately."

The two informed Chris, who announced the emergency to the entire gym. The people eyed each other in fear.

"Don't panic," Lizzie told the assembly. "Shelter in the adjoining classrooms by family only. Keep apart. You must isolate from each other completely or you will all get sick."

People immediately began packing up, which greatly dismayed Aiden. He hustled over to Chris. "We're all learning to live together now, to trust each other. Is isolating really necessary?"

Lizzie interrupted their conversation. "It's absolutely necessary. The people will have to stay confined until we figure out what caused the outbreak."

Professor Feinstein approached them and cast a wary eye at Lizzie. "Excuse me, but I believe cholera isn't contagious unless one is exposed to the bacterium, usually through contaminated water, so perhaps we don't have to—"

"Do you want to see people die?" Lizzie faced him. "Do you want to be blamed for giving them the wrong advice?"

Aiden could tell she'd successfully pressed Feinstein's buttons. The professor shook his head, stuck his pipe in his mouth like a pacifier, and slunk away.

Aiden could do nothing but watch as Chris assigned families classrooms to shelter in. He instructed the cooks to continue preparing food, but they would package it for individual distribution. Eating at the communal table and gathering to hear music was strictly prohibited. In fact, nobody would be allowed into the gym except the cooks, sick folk (housed in a far corner), and their care persons. The feeling of camaraderie and the enjoyment of working together unraveled in one night.

Aiden had no choice but to move back home. In the Baylor's large, frigid house, he huddled under his blankets to stay warm and slept a lot. He longed for the cheerful ambiance of the roundhouse with the central fire's comforting crackle. He missed playing music with Tash, Pete, and Vivica. Most of all, he missed Ava.. People would withdraw into their secluded little worlds, which reminded Aiden of life with DAPHNE.

SEPTEMBER BROUGHT FALLING leaves and breezes, and the oak branches outside his window scratched at the glass like a mournful ghost begging entry. One particularly restless night, Aiden tossed and turned in bed in the grip of a terrible dream.

I'm alone, sitting at my pod in Professor Feinstein's class. The gramophone sits on my deskscreen with the horn pointing in my face. The record spins, and a man's tinny voice sings, "Please let Beth know I discovered it. I found what she is searching for, and she can only find it in—" *My eyes seek the window and view green grasses swaying under a spring sky. I yearn to walk in the forest, but I can't move. Looking down, I see my arms bent at the elbows, my forearms jutting forward, and my hands clenched into fists. They seem frozen. They seem like armrests. My arms are armrests. My legs... My legs are bent sharply at the knees with my feet firmly rooted to the floor. Professor Feinstein stands at the door and speaks to someone in the hall beyond my sight. "You can sit right there." He points to me and then narrows his eyes. "Is it still alive?" Yes! Yes, I'm alive. Don't leave. Come back!*

Slosh-slosh-slosh. I muster all my strength to move my eyes to the left. Ava mops the floor a few feet away. She's faded, worn-out. Matted hair. Pallid skin. She swivels her head towards me. She no longer has a face. Only a screen that displays nothing but static. Slosh. Slosh. The sound of the mop fades away as a buzzing sound fills the room. A drone has replaced Feinstein in the doorway. It suddenly whizzes toward me and lands like a spider on my chest. I can do nothing but watch one of the drone's sharp claws plunge into my chest and rip out my—

"Aiden, wake up."

Tash stood over him.

The morning sun made Aiden squint. He wiped his upper lip, which was damp with fright. "What's the matter? What are you doing here?"

"You need to come to the gym. There's something you should see."

TASH BROUGHT AIDEN and Chris into the men's bathroom. "I think I've found our problem." He opened the door.

Aiden gagged at the stench and slapped a hand over his nose and mouth. Bugs ran over the tiled floor, and the toilets and urinals overflowed with human waste.

Chris grimaced. "What pigs. I assumed people were doing their business outside."

"Most of us go outside," Tash answered and coughed into his elbow. "Apparently, others haven't been."

Aiden pushed the door closed with his foot. "What are we going to do? What did the grid-skippers use as a bathroom?"

"Compostable toilets. Basically, big buckets with a mixture inside that turns waste into compost." Chris eyeballed Tash.

"Oh, come on..." The young man raised his hands in defense. "You want me to design toilets now?"

"It's a matter of life or death."

Tash rolled his eyes. "Fine, but I am *not* heading the bathroom cleanup committee."

THE HEALTHY GYM-DWELLERS were anxious to solve the problem and wore masks and gloves to clean the bathroom. Meanwhile, Tash, Vivica, and other volunteers collected as many large buckets as they could find.

"The most important factor in composting is aeration," Chris told them. "If the toilet sits in a bathroom, a confined space, you have to connect a pipe to the bucket to let in fresh air. The drier things are, the less the bacteria grows."

"It's a toilet." Vivica grimaced. "How can we possibly keep things dry?"

"Liquids go one way and solids another."

Tash sighed. "I'll design some sort of divider for the buckets."

"Remember," Chris said, "you've got to fill the bottom of each bucket with moss and dry leaves. Folks will have to add more each time they go."

Professor Feinstein approached Tash and Chris. After scanning the area to make sure Lizzie wasn't around, he said, "You'll need high-carbon material. Human waste contains nitrogen. The carbon neutralizes it and promotes decomposition. Wood ash has carbon, and we make plenty of that."

Chris slapped the professor on the back. "Thanks, doc."

"Oh, no. I'm—I'm not a doc." Feinstein waved an embarrassed hand in the air. His cheeks flushed, which caused his spectacles to steam slightly. "I never got a doctorate degree. I *should* have, my parents wanted me to get one but—"

"You seem pretty smart to me." Chris addressed his volunteers. "Rip the toilet seats from other bathrooms. Create frames around the buckets and secure the toilet seat to each frame. Put a big container of ash and sawdust next to every toilet with a sign that says 'Add Me!'"

"But what do we do with the stuff in the bucket once it fills up?" Vivica asked.

"Bury it," Chris replied. "It's too toxic to put on plants."

Feinstein cleared his throat and whispered, "I believe if we let the mixture cure for a –"

"What?" Chris cupped a hand to his ear. "I can't hear mumbling."

Louder, Feinstein said, "If you let it compost for a year or two, the pathogens will die. Then, we can use the humanure as fertilizer."

"Humanure," Chris repeated. "I like that."

Encouraged, the professor removed his fake, cracked glasses. "If we clean out a few old dumpsters, we can throw the compost in them. After a year or so, we can use the stuff as fertilizer. Tash could design a valve of some sort at the bottom that will release the cured humanure."

"A year?" Vivica inhaled with concern. "Do you think we'll still be like this in a year?'

The men traded looks. No one could say.

WITHIN A WEEK, THOSE stricken with cholera had recovered, and Aiden encouraged everyone to return to the roundhouse. Some families chose to remain in private classrooms, but most moved back. Aiden, especially, wanted to return because bad dreams didn't plague him when he slept near Ava. Still, he couldn't shake off the haunting memory of his recent nightmare, in which he was paralyzed and transformed into a piece of furniture, an object to use or exploit. Worse, the nightmare didn't feel like a dream. It felt like a warning.

As they reconstructed their shelter, Ava pressed him to let her share her experience with the others.

"They'll think you're crazy if you talk about a voice in your head," he warned. "Trust me, I know." Aiden couldn't tolerate the idea of people making fun of her.

"I don't care." She seemed to sense his anxiety and relented. "Fine. I won't mention the Great Source. I'll tell them only about the deer and what he meant to me."

CHRIS HAD BEGUN HOLDING nightly meetings following supper, offering the gym-dwellers a chance to express their concerns or propose ideas for enhancing life within the roundhouse. These gatherings also served as a forum for Lizzie to provide updates from her technology team.

That evening, Ava stood up before the assembly. "Something interesting happened to me. A buck, a male deer, ate from my hand."

An Aggravationist rolled his eyes. "So?"

"He'd been shy," she went on, unthwarted. "I used a fantasy to get him to trust me."

That statement brought curious looks.

"I visualized what I wanted, and it worked."

"You used your optics?" Jill interrupted.

"No, I imagined in my head that I was petting him, that we were friends. I think my fantasy communicated my feelings to him." She let the people absorb that and then grinned. "But that wasn't the best part. When we connected, the buck helped me discover something about myself."

Busty Trina waved her off. "Shut up, Ava."

Mr. Parrish growled at Chris. "I thought these meetings were held to discuss our survival." He rolled his eyes at Ava. "Listen, girlie, why don't you go pick weeds or something?"

Tash piped up. "Let her talk."

"When the deer ate from my hand," Ava continued, "I felt... I felt something hard break inside of me and realized I'd been holding back from allowing myself to love."

Aiden could only admire her bravery.

Lizzie stood up. "What an endearing story. I'd like to give my update now. The team feels that if we can find a way to make metal again, we could repair the housing on—"

"I'd like to hear the rest of the endearing story." Chris eyeballed Lizzie, and she reclaimed her seat, glowering. He smiled at Ava. "Go on."

"I knew I felt hurt," she said. "I just didn't know how badly the hurt had affected me."

Chris nodded. "They say 'you can lead a horse to water, but you can't make him drink.'"

"What horse?" Mr. Parrish scowled. "I thought she was talking about a deer."

"It's an old saying," Chris explained. "The horse doesn't drink because he doesn't realize he's thirsty. Do you get it?"

People traded looks. They did not get it.

Chris slapped his thighs in exasperation and stood up. "We're thick as bricks when it comes to self-awareness. We usually need a message that hits us hard to see something we've been blind to. That buck triggered something in Ava and gave her an important insight, which is great because the insight brings her one step closer to being a happier person. A famous psychologist, Carl Jung, once said, 'Until you make the unconscious conscious, it will direct your life and you will call it fate.'" He sat down again. "I don't know about the rest of you, but I'd like to hear more about Ava's use of fantasy to communicate with animals."

Ava opened her mouth to speak, but Aiden shook his head in warning. She took the hint and fell silent.

Vivica, however, grinned at Ava and blurted out, "We're unlocking the mystery of human consciousness!"

Dread radiated through Aiden, and he glanced at Lizzie, who stared at him with a predator's bright, menacing eyes.

THE FOLLOWING MORNING, Ava trekked alone into the forest to collect the last of the summer raspberries. A cool breeze rippled the lake water, and the maples and aspens shed red and gold leaves.

As she wandered, she asked the Great Source, "What do you look like?"

Nothing replied. Ava supposed if anyone heard her asking the trees questions, they would consider her insane, but nobody was around.

Close your eyes, and you will see.

A tingle ran through Ava's body. The voice spoke! She parked herself on a fallen log, put her eyescreens into "sleep" mode, and waited for something magical to happen. She expected fireworks, but nothing lit up behind her eyes except the image of a deer. *Her* deer. Ava could clearly visualize the curve of the buck's antlers, the white patch at his throat, and his gentle brown eyes.

The minutes ticked by, and nothing happened. Ava reactivated her eyescreens and looked around. A black-capped mountain chickadee whistled "skiddledee-dee-do-do," and the breeze made a few leaves dance at her sneakered feet.

A little disappointed, she headed back to the gym. To her joy, she spied the buck grazing alone in the field outside the school as if he'd been waiting for her. A powerful longing swept through Ava at the sight of him. She wanted only to care for the animal, and happiness flooded her, knowing her heart could feel love.

"Hi," she said gently as she approached. "You came to see me."

The buck allowed Ava to stand right next to him. He had a musky scent, not offensive, and she considered it miraculous that this wild animal trusted her. Dipping her hand into the basket, she held out some raspberries. The buck ate from her hand, and Ava wanted to weep.

Suddenly, she heard a whooshing sound and gasped to see a heavy spear hit the deer's shoulder. The buck went down with a grunt. Ava's lower jaw fell open. As the animal kicked and struggled to right itself, Clyde and Pete materialized from behind a building. Clyde ran forward and stabbed the buck with a butcher knife.

Ava put shocked hands on either side of her head. "What—what are you doing?"

Clyde stood up, gripping the bloody knife. "I thought you made it stay on purpose to give me an easy shot."

Ava, stunned, dropped her eyes to the dead animal at her feet. She let loose a savage scream and pushed Clyde. "You piece of shit!"

Clyde stumbled backward and gaped at her.

"He trusted me!" Ava shouted. "That's why he came here! How could you?"

"We need its meat."

"He was my friend!" She shoved Clyde again. Hard.

Drawing himself up to his full height, he sneered. "Well, now he's dinner."

Ava's throat constricted because she couldn't cry. Instead, she bit her knuckles and made a mewling sound.

Pete scratched his head as he inspected the deer. "How do we get to the meat?"

Clyde didn't reply. He eyed Ava and yanked his spear from the buck's body.

AIDEN AND CHRIS, HAVING heard Ava's scream, ran toward her and skidded to a halt upon seeing the downed buck. Aiden looked at Ava and then at the bloodied weapon in Clyde's hands.

"What did you do, Clyde?"

"What does it look like?"

"It looks like murder."

Clyde began cleaning the spear with a rag. "You want to make something out of it?"

Aiden knew what the buck meant to Ava and balled his hands into fists. Yes, he would 'make something out of it.' Clyde threw the spear on the ground, and the two young men faced off.

Ava found her voice. "Forget about it, Clyde."

"No." He grinned. "I don't want to forget about it. I want to beat nature boy's ass into the ground."

Aiden would take it. For Ava, he would take it. He raised his fists and noticed how slight he seemed next to Clyde. Just then, Chris inserted himself between them and addressed Clyde.

"You did good."

Aiden's mouth fell open, but Chris ignored him. "You did real good. But hunting is more fun than killing someone's pet, don't you think?"

Clyde's shoulders relaxed, and he lowered his hands. His eyes dropped to the buck.

"Next time," Chris said, "make a sport of it. Challenge yourself. A guy like you doesn't need to be handed a win, does he?"

Clyde scratched his chin and glanced at Ava. "Sorry."

Her lower lip trembled, and she ran into the forest.

"Ava!" Aiden called, but she kept on running.

Gripping his spear, Clyde walked back toward the gym with Pete on his heels. Aiden spotted Lizzie waiting for them at the entrance and frowned.

"She did this."

Chris contemplated the dead buck. "Who?"

"Lizzie. She knew what this deer meant to Ava, and she told Clyde to kill it."

"You don't know that."

"I do, Chris."

The two watched Lizzie disappear into the gym with Clyde and Pete.

"Well, you can't prove it."

"She's out to get me. I'm not sure why, but she is."

"Why would she be? Dr. Lizzie has only helped us."

Aiden faced Chris. "You call me a medicine man. Maybe she's a doctor who doesn't like my brand of medicine. And another thing: I can't read her. There's something about Lizzie that's different." He lowered his voice to a whisper. "Could she be a cyborg?"

"No. You know as a well as I that cyborgs and robots can't run without power, nor do they have any intelligence without DAPHNE." Chris gazed at the dead animal. "Maybe Lizzie is a person devoid of feelings, which almost makes her worse than a cyborg. There are people who lack empathy, Aiden. Sociopaths, psychopaths, megalomaniacs... They may be heartless, but they are still human beings." He put a hand on the young man's shoulder. "We'll keep an eye on her, okay?"

Aiden nodded but didn't feel comforted.

CHAPTER 39

Nobody knew how to butcher the meat. A thorough search through Chris's library produced a book about a hunter's exploits, which provided some instruction.

Volunteer butchers, including Clyde, assembled on the field and listened to Chris read from the book.

"Okay, turn the animal on its back and place small logs on either side to keep it steady." Chris sighed at Aiden. "I don't think you should watch this."

Aiden remained where he stood. He felt a sense of obligation to the animal and to Ava, who sat in silent misery in their shelter.

Chris nodded to Clyde. "You've got to get rid of the guts. Use your knife and make a circular cut around the anus. Cut the skin and tendons connecting the anus to the body so the colon will slide out along with a bag of guts."

One of the hunters gagged. "This is disgusting."

"Maybe so," Chris said. "But you can't buy a shrink-wrapped steak anymore."

Pete sniffed. "We owned a bio-printer and made our own."

"Good for you." Chris directed Clyde to make an incision from the paunch to the rib cage. "It says to cut through the ribs all the way up to the base of the neck."

Clyde did as he was told.

Chris nodded. "Push the diaphragm off to the side and coax out the stomach and intestines."

A wave of nausea rolled through Aiden, but he refused to look away.

After Clyde disemboweled the animal, Chris told him to make skinning cuts on each leg. From these cuts, Clyde pulled the skin up and hung the animal from the schoolyard's parallel bars with sharp wire through the hind legs.

"Now, pry the skin away from the muscle until you can get your hands underneath to grip the skin."

"It's actually easy." Clyde pushed in his fist to get under the hide. The sight of his bloodied hands forcing the hide down and off the body reminded Aiden of his dream where a drone ripped out his heart.

"Now, what do we do?" Clyde asked.

"Cut off the head."

Pete came forward with a saw. When the head with its artwork of antlers came away from the body, tears pressed at Aiden's eyes. He should make them pay homage to the desecrated animal. Shaking his head, he walked away and heard Chris recite to Clyde how to quarter the animal. Clyde's fellow hunters rushed past Aiden to get the tenderloins, shoulder roasts, and hindquarters to the cooks.

TO HIS DISMAY, THE gym-dwellers relished the hearty meat dishes prepared by the cooks. The plants provided only so much by way of food, and the enticing aroma of cooked meat attracted the residents like a magnet.

More and more people abandoned their homes to reside in the gym, where warmth, company, and now the stomach-satisfying protein were shared. Crude shelters spilled into the hallways and filled the adjoining classrooms.

L'Eren pressed Govind to move in as well. Besides the opportunity to eat more protein, the gym offered L'Eren a host of babysitters, which afforded the new mother plenty of nap time.

"Rennie," Govind argued, "no one expects us to live with... Well, like everyone else."

She furrowed her brows at her husband as they huddled before the fireplace in the Baylor's living room. "Do you think you're better than them?"

"No, of course not."

"You do." L'Eren cradled her sleeping son. "We're all in trouble, Govind, and that makes us equals."

The following day, Govind, L'Eren, and Kimber made a home in one of the classrooms. Worrying they'd miss out on the new food source, Doug, Jill, Oreanna, and Lizzie moved into the school and took Kif, the cat.

CLYDE TOOK TO HUNTING like a duck to water. He and his crew painted themselves like ancient warriors and crafted a variety of spears. The animals had grown complacent because generations of humans had left them in peace, and Clyde took his advantage. The hunters learned to sneak about the forest quietly, camouflage themselves with leaves, and ambush their prey. It paid off.

Hunting provided the young people with both adventure and praise. Each day, the bloodstained warriors would return from hunting carrying a carcass of some sort, such as a rabbit, squirrel, duck, bighorn sheep, mule deer, and even the occasional elk.

To prepare for winter, the cooks salted the meat to preserve it. When one of the hunters discovered a cave in the hills, the cooks made it into a smokehouse. Clyde's popularity grew.

Aiden protested to Chris about the hunting frenzy. "This is just a game to Clyde and his friends, but the animals have a right to live in peace. Put a limit on the hunting."

Chris tried, but the burly young man paid no attention. Instead, Clyde begged Ava to join them, to use her eyes to ferret out the game. She refused. As well, neither she nor Aiden would eat the cooked meat.

Oreanna, on the other hand, grew excited by the prospect of a hunt. She had ranked high in the online gaming world and believed she could easily ace this new form of entertainment. Besides, she had trimmed down since the shutdown and now felt she could redeem herself in the eyes of her judgmental peers. She could never forget that Clyde labeled her 'revolting.'

She wanted to prove her worth to him and joined his team of hunters.

One morning, when the group came upon a rushing river, many hesitated to swim across. Oreanna, remembering how easily she maneuvered among the swinging vines in *Jungle Flight,* grabbed the branch of an overhanging tree.

"Watch me!" she shouted. "We can get across this way!"

Holding tight to the branch, she pushed off the bank and flung herself toward the opposite side. Unfortunately, the tree branch snapped, and Oreanna fell into the water. The others enjoyed a good laugh as they moved on and left her soaked and humiliated.

On another expedition, the hunters pursued bighorn sheep along a rocky crag. Oreanna tried impressing Clyde by speeding past the group, but she tripped on a rock and fell flat.

As the others sprinted off, Oreanna curled into a ball and held her bruised ankle while tears coursed down her face. Suddenly, a hand reached down. Pete Farmington, also not much of an athlete, helped Oreanna to her feet.

"Your ankle is swelling." He dropped shy eyes to the ground. "Want me to help you walk back to the roundhouse?"

Sniffling, Oreanna shook her head. She remembered how Pete had primed her for Clyde's Big Insult and limped home alone.

WHEN OREANNA RETURNED to the gym, Lizzie advised her to rest and elevate her sprained ankle. Chris gave the girl a book on rocks and minerals to pass the time, and Oreanna lay on a chaise lounge and read to keep from weeping. She wished she could go back to the time of DAPHNE and live entirely in a virtual world.

Then, the glittering treasures found in the earth began steering Ori from her self-pity. Crystals with captivating, delectable names such as chocolate dolomite and watermelon tourmaline fascinated her. Oreanna's gaze followed the shimmering, intricate pathways of the minerals, which guided her into an enchanting realm of their own. She read about practical applications of other minerals like halite used for salt, fluorite, a component of toothpaste, and copper, silica, titanium – so many minerals with so many uses!

Oreanna was asking Chris if he had a second geology book when the hunters returned home at dusk.

Clyde arrived, hefting a ram over his broad shoulders, and the gym-dwellers mooned over him as their hero. Oreanna watched Busty Trina and her girlfriends drag buckets of lake water to the fire ring. They then marched the buckets to the boy's locker room, where they poured hot water into a tub so Clyde could enjoy a hot bath. What a luxury!

Later, when Clyde emerged, clad in nothing but a towel tied around his waist, Oreanna gasped. The sight of his wet, flexing muscles, tanned by the summer sun, took her breath away. When his eye chanced to fall on her, a delicious warmth bloomed in the lower part of her body.

CHAPTER 40

Aiden resented Clyde's celebrity. It diminished his importance. Aiden was a medicine man, a conduit to the Great Source, and the leader of their important food-gathering missions. Clyde, the bully, the animal killer, had successfully shoved him out of the spotlight.

The voice of the Great Source went dead, and Aiden knew why. He imagined his jealousy of Clyde cut the connection with anything positive. He didn't realize how much he stewed in his rotten juices until Z'ier Durand approached him one cold, windy night. Immersed in self-pity, Aiden sat outside on a folding chair, staring at the stars while the wind buffeted him.

Z'ier, wearing one of Aerta's thick coats, handed Aiden a book.

"I think you should read this. I found it in Chris's library. It's called *A New Earth: Awakening to Your Life's Purpose*, by Eckhart Tolle."

Aiden took the book and promptly dropped it on the grass.

Ava's mother didn't appear daunted. "It's okay. I memorized a quote for you. '*All we can perceive, experience, think about, is the surface layer of reality, less than the tip on an iceberg. Underneath the surface appearance, everything is not only connected with everything else, but also with the Source of all life out of which it came.*'

She gave him an eager smile. "Ava tells me that you two have connected with a Great Source. What is it? Can you share it?" A wind gust pushed her forward.

Aiden looked heavenward. With no light pollution to drown them out, the stars poked through the black, velvety sky like diamonds. Each one, a Sun. Didn't it follow that one or more suns warmed a planet crawling with life like Earth? Perhaps the Great Source resided in one of those distant worlds.

How brazen of DAPHNE's countless electric lights to dim the stars, to rob human beings of the ability to imagine other worlds. Ophidian had done all the imagining for them and provided fantasies through the company's virtual worlds and games. But Aiden had glimpsed behind the curtain of human consciousness. There, in the dark matter of the brain, lay incredible light. If he and Ava had made a connection to God, a Great Source, a collection of souls, or even to aliens thriving on a distant planet, they needed to share their discovery.

Aiden looked at Z'ier. The good color of her complexion. The bounce in her step. No longer a punctured tire, life filled her now. The Great Source was at work in the roundhouse, and Aiden knew he needed to get past his bad feelings to enlighten the others. He just wished he knew how.

WITH WINTER ON THE horizon, Chris suggested they make use of the animal hides since no one could buy new clothes. Most vulnerable were folks who'd lost all their winter wear when their homes burned.

To create clothing from the hides, volunteers had to scrape the skins clean of fat and tissue with shrapnel, knives, or the toothless side of saw blades in a process called "scudding."

It was hard work, and no one wanted to do it, but the fear of cold weather made a "scudder" even out of the most disgruntled Aggravationist.

Grandma Rosie reserved some of the fat for cooking and put the rest into jars. One afternoon, when she spied Jill napping next to Harry near the firepit, Rosie dropped a box of jars on her daughter's lap.

Jill awoke with a cry and shouted, "What did you do that for?"

"Everyone has a job except you." Rosie planted firm hands on her hips.

"I'm keeping Dad company."

Harry shook his head at his daughter. "Don't get me into this."

"You can't keep pining for DAPHNE," Rosie said. "Make yourself useful."

"Oh, Mother, leave me alone and take these disgusting jars with you." Jill tried to return the box to Rosie, but the older woman refused.

"We need light," she insisted. "Long ago, human beings made candles from tallow."

"Is this tallow?"

"It's fat. You figure out how to make it into tallow."

"Are you kidding? How do you expect me to ma—"

A sharp cry interrupted Jill. The two women witnessed Ava stumble dangerously close to the fire ring. Flailing her arms, the girl tripped again and nearly fell into the flames. Jill, happy to set down the box, rushed over to her.

"What is it, sweetheart?"

Ava jerked away and raced across the gym. "It's dark!" She spun around and knocked over a lean-to. She careened into Mac and Aerta's shelter and began to claw at her eyescreens. They'd gone black.

"Get Aiden," Jill shouted to those watching.

Blood pooled under Ava's fingers. Some gym-dwellers tried to catch her, but she recoiled from their touch and dashed away. Aiden rushed into the gym.

"Ava!" He grabbed her hands. "What's wrong?"

She struggled to free her hands and let loose a banshee shriek that rattled the onlookers.

"Ava, it's me! It's Aiden."

"Aiden, I can't see! Take these things off!"

He viewed her face, the dead eyescreens, those black ovals where her eyes should have been now circled by red scratches. She sunk to the ground with a long, eerie moan.

Tears embody our pain, Aiden thought, which we can then shed. Ava's pain, he knew, had no such outlet. Kneeling down, he held her close and didn't know what to do except let the wind of her wailing blow cold in his ear.

CHAPTER 41

Ava's blindness took second place to a more urgent matter. The temperature had dropped considerably overnight, and the people of Sierrawood needed to deal with the reality of a mountain winter.

The shorter days left less time to work, and the scudders toiled overtime to prepare the hides for use as clothing. They kept the fur on some but scraped other hides. Once cleaned, the coats had to be "cured" or salted to prevent bacterial growth. The hunter's book advised 'brine-curing,' or agitating the hides in a saltwater bath. The problem was, where would they get enough salt? The cooks needed the precious few shakers the gym-dwellers brought from their homes for flavoring meals and preserving the meat.

Chris remarked how his Miwok ancestors filled basins with water from a salt spring, allowed the water to evaporate, and then traded the salty residue with other tribes. Aiden wasted no time leading the scudders to the salt spring, where they collected enough water to soak the hides. Afterward, they bathed the hides in clean water to remove the salt. Unfortunately, the resulting material was too stiff to use.

Chris brought up the issue of the tough hides at the nightly meeting.

"Doesn't anyone know how to soften textiles?" Chris asked the group and looked beseechingly at Professor Feinstein.

Aiden emerged from Ava's shelter to join the meeting. He'd left her sleeping – again. Ava wanted only to sleep and escape the perpetual night in which she lived. Aiden begged the Great Source to offer him advice on how to help her, but the words of wisdom remained silent.

"Nobody knows anything about making leather?" Chris asked. "Come on, people, we're gonna need coats, blankets, and rugs."

At last, Professor Feinstein raised a timid hand and flashed an eye toward Lizzie, who sat among the others. "You need to tan the hide and alter the protein structure of the skin." When Lizzie didn't correct him, he continued, "I know something about chemistry. I can give it a try."

AIDEN, GOVIND, AND Lizzie followed Feinstein and his volunteer tanners as they chose a workplace. Historically, tanning created noxious odors, so they settled in the cement parking lot at the far side of the school. Feinstein finally looked the part of a true eccentric with his gloves, apron, and cracked spectacles for protection. The only difference was that his hair had grown out a beautiful copper color. The professor stated they needed tannic acid, and Aiden suggested using the dark water leached from the acorns.

"Don't the tannins make the nuts bitter?" he asked.

"Great, idea, Baylor," Feinstein said. "I believe before using chromium products, people used to process hides with plant acids."

The cooks rushed to give the dark water to the tanners, and they soaked the hides in it.

Govind grinned and put a hand on Lizzie's shoulder as they walked toward the gym. "Look at how our minds are working. Look at how we experiment and refuse to give up."

Lizzie clucked her tongue. "This isn't magic, Govind. The human brain consists of about 100 billion neurons, making on the order of 100 trillion connections. It's no different from a computer. Neurons are wired into complex circuits to process information. What you're seeing are electrical signals at work, nothing more. The people are using their computing powers to figure things out. Geez, you're beginning to sound as bizarre as Aiden."

Govind blew on his hands as they passed the scudders laboring on the hides. "This is more than neurons making connections, Lizzie. It's inspiration. It's intuition. How can you be sure they haven't subconsciously tapped into a Great Source?"

"You mean the voice in Aiden's head?"

Lizzie's eyes drilled holes into him, and Govind wondered why the subject bothered her. "What if there is a mysterious, higher power we can access?"

"Then, why haven't we used it?"

"Maybe we did once." Govind's breath came out in a cloud. "Maybe we've forgotten it."

The sound of arguing interrupted them. Aerta, who scraped hides next to her husband, stood up and pointed at the knife he used. Her calloused finger protruded from a hole in her glove. "I'm telling you, Mac, that knife you're using is gonna cut you."

"Leave me alone, woman," her husband groused. "Why are you hassling me?"

"The knife is going to break!"

Govind wandered over to them. "What's wrong?"

"His knife is bad." Aerta pointed at the blade in Mac's hand. "But he's too lazy to find a new one."

Govind observed that weeks of eating a simple diet had trimmed Aerta into a petite woman he barely recognized. Her hair had grown out gray, but without the loud makeup she used to wear, her face looked younger. "How do you know it will break?"

She blew a lock of hair from her face. "I just know. I got scared all of a sudden." Aerta pointed again to the knife. "I got scared of that. Tell him to get a new knife, Dr. Lal."

"Fine!" Mac shouted. "Drive me crazy! As if we don't have enough trouble in our lives!" Muttering, he stormed off, threw down the knife, and the wood handle broke off as soon as it hit the cement. Mac paused to gaze at the exposed blade.

Govind picked up the two pieces. "If this broke in your hands, it would have cut you."

Mac eyed his wife and bit his lower lip. A spooked Aerta chewed on the nail of her exposed finger.

Govind held up the broken blade to Lizzie. "Did a wife's bad feeling about this particular knife come from a computing power?"

AFTER MUCH TRIAL AND error, Feinstein devised a way for the skins to absorb the tannic acid even faster. "Soak the hides in a baking soda and water solution first," he told the skudders. "The baking soda will raise the pH of the collagen, which should speed up the reaction time."

The experiment worked. The tannic acid softened the pre-treated skins in record time. Skins dyed with tannins turned a dark brown. To avoid darkening the lighter-colored furs, the tanners only applied the acid to the skin side.

The light-colored furs inspired Vivica to rifle through Chris's books to learn what plants people used to dye material. She missed her once vibrant hair color and figured that what worked on animal fur might also dye her ash-blonde locks.

She collected blue and red elderberries and mixed the juice with various ingredients. When she added vinegar, the berry juice turned pink. A dash of baking soda created a gray hue. The flower heads of the yarrow plant produced a yellow dye when boiled. If Vivica placed the yellow material in an iron bath (made with rusty nails, vinegar, and water), the yellow turned olive green. Vivica searched the ground for ocher, clay that provided burnt orange, beige, brown, red, and violet pigments. She even climbed oak trees to extract wasp galls.

When wasps laid their eggs in newly formed leaf buds, the plant hormones combined with the insect's chemicals and produced a woodsy ball that served as a crib for wasp larvae. Vivica plucked the brown galls, pulverized them, and then let them ferment in glass jars filled with scrap metal and rusty nails. The resulting pigments ranged from brown to jet-black, which the townspeople used as writing ink.

Vivica experimented on herself and soon resembled a cute mad scientist with her stained fingers and multi-colored tresses. She dyed the hides of rabbits and deer all sorts of hues, which earned her the nickname 'The Color Queen.' Vivica had found her calling.

CHAPTER 42

The gauzy tendrils of rain dangling from black clouds heralded winter's arrival. A streak of bright white cut across the horizon every few minutes, accompanied by a loud drum roll. Animals disappeared into burrows, and the soft water from the sky blanketed the trees so they could sleep. The gym-dwellers built a waterproof cap over the skylight that allowed the smoke to escape but prevented the rain from falling in.

Ava sat, listless, in the shelter she shared with her mother and Aiden and listened to the patter of raindrops on the roof. Z'ier had tied a torn, plaid shirtsleeve around her daughter's head to cover the eyescreens because they looked like black holes and frightened the children.

Ava had become like her mother—a half-person incapable of experiencing joy. She yearned for her former life when she saw things invisible to others. She wished she had tear ducts, then she could cry. The only respite came when Ava slept, for in her dreams, she could see.

Reaching out a hand, Ava felt the smooth wood surface of Aiden's guitar. He serenaded her often because his gentle strumming lessened her panic attacks.

"May I come in?"

Chris's voice.

"Sure," she answered.

She heard the rustle of the tarp and felt him sit beside her. He smelled of damp wool.

"My dear, you may have lost your sight, but you're still vital to this community. Come out and join us."

"Everyone here has a purpose, Chris. Mine died with my eyes."

"You'll find another purpose."

"I can't find my way to the bathroom."

"This is your challenge, Ava," he said. "Don't hide from it. When I was in college, I learned about Helen Keller, who was both blind and deaf. She said, 'The best and most beautiful things in the world cannot be seen or even touched, but must be felt with the heart.' Maybe that's where your purpose lies. To remind us what our feelings can do for us."

Ava thought briefly of the buck and how she let herself feel love. Then, she remembered her beautiful friend was butchered, dead—along with her sight.

"If this is what having feelings is like I don't want them," she murmured. "I was happier when I played in a metaverse and my heart felt nothing."

Chris bristled beside her. "If that's true, you've got bigger problems than going blind. Maybe you ought to think about that."

Why bother? Nothing mattered in the darkness. Ava choked on her breath whenever she remembered she'd never again see the light.

AIDEN HAD KEPT HIS grandparents' gramophone a secret but decided to share it with Ava. He had to do something to make her smile. Without telling her where they were going, he helped her into a raincoat, donned one himself, and carefully led her down the wet, deserted streets of Sierrawood. It encouraged Aiden to watch how easily Ava climbed the security fence, slick as it was with rain, but then, she'd always been athletic.

The first thing he noticed when he slipped through the opening to his grandparents' apartment were muddied footprints all over Rosie's beige carpet.

Fury sizzled in his chest. It wasn't enough that Aiden had welcomed his classmates for a special excursion. Apparently, some had returned to rifle through his grandparents' possessions. Worse, whoever did it had no remorse because they'd trashed the apartment.

"What is it?" Ava asked.

"Nothing."

Bookcases had fallen over. Yellowed newspapers and magazines littered the floor. Stuffing poked out of the couch, although Aiden couldn't be sure an animal didn't commit that offense. Rainwater stained the wall under a cracked window, and the whole place smelled musty. He gazed at the damage and felt bruised, violated, just the way he felt when Clyde used to beat him up.

"It's something," Ava murmured. "I can tell."

Aiden kicked debris out of the way and guided her across the living room. Thankfully, the polished wood box of the gramophone was intact.

Sitting Ava on the couch, he placed a hand on her shoulder. "Wait here."

Rain tap-tap-tapped against the window as he thumbed through the dusty box of 78 recordings. Aiden had no idea which record to choose until his fingers paused on one that boasted a red label imprinted with the title 'Always' and, underneath it, the name 'Irving Berlin.'

This one. Aiden felt the familiar tug, and his heart gladdened with relief. He'd reconnected with the Great Source. But why now? Perhaps his purpose here had something to do with it. If vices like jealousy could damage the connection, maybe doing something nice strengthened it.

Removing the black disc from its brittle paper liner, he positioned it on the turntable and cranked the handle. As the record began spinning, he placed the needle at its edge and returned to Ava's side. Static filled the room. A tinny-sounding intro played, and a long-ago man who trilled his *R's* sang,

"Everything went wrong
And the whole day long, I'd feel so blue
For the longest while I'd forget to smile
Til I met you."

Aiden's heartbeat quickened at the lyrics, and he glanced at Ava.

"Now that my blue days have past
Now that I've found you at last...
I'll be loving you, always
With a love that's true, always."

The words mirrored his feelings exactly. He silently thanked the Great Source for leading him to this record. If only Ava could see his expression. She'd read the shy hope in his eyes.

"When the things you've planned
Need a helping hand
I will understand – always."

Ava's hand lifted to his face. Her fingers skimmed along his flesh, and Aiden closed his eyes under her gentle exploration. Could she sense the longing behind his half-open lips?

"Days may not be fair, always
That's when I'll be there, always
Not for just an hour
Not for just a day
Not for just a year
but always."

When the instrumental played, he rose to his feet and tenderly stood her up. The two swayed together as the music transported them from their fearful existence to the warmth and affection found only in human arms.

When the record ended, the needle bumped in slow repetition against the red label. The two young people didn't notice. Their lips met, and their hands traveled over each other's bodies. Aiden explored Ava's curving landscape of flesh, not in a fantasy but in an abandoned building surrounded by ruined furniture and moldy artifacts. Eventually, the turntable quit spinning, and the gramophone went silent. It didn't matter. Aiden and Ava had created their own virtual reality, where they saw and heard only each other.

CHAPTER 43

The November gales blew through the mountains, and the wind wailed a lament to the trees. Aiden listened and sensed a warning in the air. Ever since he and Ava had made love, melded in a way he could never have imagined, he felt his perception ripen within him, reaching full flavor. Nightmares no longer plagued him, not around Ava, but the wind promised trouble. What did he miss? What didn't he see?

Clyde Parrish considered the wind his ally, for it carried away the hunters' scents. His rough hair had grown past his shoulders and sailed behind him like a tawny flag as he searched for prey with his fellow hunters.

One morning, when the tree branches danced to the wind's song, Clyde stopped short and lifted a fist. In response, his crew stood motionless behind him. In the distance, a black bear picked at the ground, searching for the extra calories it needed to hibernate. Clyde readied his spear. With a silent promise to send the bear into eternal hibernation, he flung the weapon with all his might. It stabbed the bear's side, and the creature uttered a guttural yelp and fell over. The young man, confident, proud, and imbued with a hunger for a kill, approached with an upraised butcher knife. The hunters loomed near him to help, but Clyde ordered them to stay back.

"This girl is mine," he said through gritted teeth.

The bear struggled to stand up and bared its teeth to Clyde with a throaty growl.

With a warrior shout, he rushed forward. He thrust the knife at the animal's heart, but not before the bear snarled and clawed him. Three bleeding rivers made tracks across his brawny chest.

When Clyde returned to the roundhouse, bloody and triumphant, he received a hero's welcome. The scudders whisked the bear outside for dressing, and Lizzie stitched up his wounds. Feinstein offered Clyde a bottle of scotch to ease the pain.

Inside the shelter she shared with her parents, Oreanna decorated a table with rocks of various colors. She'd learned quite a lot from the geology books and collected as many gems as she could find. Not only could she identify many rocks, crystals, and minerals, but Oreanna had read up on the healing properties associated with them. She loved touching them, polishing them, and wearing them. She even gave them away as gifts. The rocks represented a tangible kind of magic to her, which Oreanna hoped would empower her.

Hearing the commotion outside, she lifted the tent flap to observe the mighty warrior of Sierrawood. Instantly, she felt a stirring in her body. Tucking a piece of glittery pyrite into her shirt for willpower, Oreanna meandered over to the group of hunters.

Some were male, some were female, and others were non-binary, but all oozed confidence. The young, mighty hunters gave Oreanna the once-over but then ignored her, which suited her fine. She hung around with them as if she belonged and tried to calm her heart, which quaked each time Clyde Parrish caught her eye.

JILL STUDIED A BLOCK of hardened fat. Her mother had continued to nag her about making candles, and Jill finally relented. Still, she didn't know where to begin. She'd heard that quack teacher, Feinstein, mention that tallow went into soap, skin balms, candles, and even wood polish. Maybe he'd know what to do.

"I need to make candles and soap," she told the professor and lifted a defensive hand. "What I don't need is one of your useless lectures, so just tell me how to turn the fat into tallow."

"Well, Mrs. Baylor, everything boils down to chemistry." He winked, puffed on his pipe, and rocked on his heels. "Pun intended."

Jill gave him a blank stare.

Feinstein ceased his rocking. "Get it? Boils. Boiling. Changing the composition of something."

Jill crossed her arms. "Quit acting smart and tell me what to do."

"Boil the fat," he replied dully. "It will render it. Skim off the top impure layer and use the rest to make a candle."

"What about making soap?"

Feinstein rubbed one ear in contemplation.

She sighed in exasperation. "Don't you know? Aren't you a teacher?"

"The fatty acids need to react with something. I think you'll need to make lye."

"Lye? What's that?"

"Something caustic, like your personality."

FEINSTEIN HELPED JILL create a workshop in a shed on the school's property. To make candles, she shredded the animal fat and melted it on low heat. Eventually, the impurities rose to the top, which she strained off. Then, Jill used two twigs to hold a wick made from wild rushes in a clean jar. Carefully, she poured in the rendered liquid fat. After the fat hardened, she tried lighting the wick. It worked! She'd made a candle.

After making several more and delivering them to Rosie, Jill tried her hand at making soap.

On Feinstein's advice, she donned a pair of goggles and rubber gloves to protect her skin from the harsh lye. First, she boiled oakwood ash in rainwater. The professor told her that soft water, like rain, contained fewer minerals, which would enable them to extract more lye. After the ashes settled at the bottom of the pan, Jill skimmed the lye water off the top and stored it in a glass container.

When she added the lye water to regular water, the mixture turned cloudy and steamed. Wide-eyed behind her goggles at the magic of chemistry, Jill carefully poured the liquid into the tallow and blended it to a pudding-like texture.

It hardened into soap. Excited, she ran into the gym, calling out for scents. "Rosemary!" she yelled to the gym-dwellers.

"Who?" L'Eren asked as she nursed baby Kimber.

"Not who! I need rosemary! Oreanna, find me some sage! Does anyone have any sage? What's wrong with you people? Why are you staring at me like a bunch of idiots? Get me some scents!"

Jill embraced her new career and disappeared into her shed almost daily. Doug asked Tash to build a cookfire in the old school cafeteria, where Jill could stay warm and utilize the long steel dining tables. In her new cafeteria workshop, Jill fashioned candles and poured soap into old loaf pans. When the soap hardened, she cut the loaves into bars with a ridged knife.

Jill brought Kif, the cat, into the cafeteria to keep her company. She carried on lively conversations with the feline as she handcrafted molds in the shape of flowers and animals. Jill's artistry provided an effective outlet for her anxiety. Sometimes, Aiden even caught his mother nuzzling Kif's white fur, a display of affection the cat didn't seem to mind at all.

CHAPTER 44

Long before Aiden was born, the snow came to the mountains as early as October, but the earth's winters were much shorter now. Although the people needed the snowfall to feed their water supply, they were grateful for the extended autumn because no automated snowplows would clear their streets, and no central heating would keep them warm. They would find no food in a forest covered in white.

Aiden had read that many Native American tribes left the mountains to winter on the coast. He suggested this to Chris, who brought up the idea at their nightly fireside meeting.

"We must decide what we're going to do," Chris addressed the assembly. "The ancient people used to migrate in the winter."

"Then, we should too." Doug placed a log on the fire. "We could go to Fresno or San Francisco. There's no snow there."

Lizzie raised her hand. "Bad idea. Tell them, Govind. Tell them why we should avoid the cities."

Govind shrugged. "I... I can't imagine how the people there are surviving without any resources. We could face a worse predicament if we join them."

Aiden watched the gym-dwellers absorb the idea of dealing with starving, desperate strangers in a ruined city.

"DAPHNE's headquarters are here," Lizzie said. "If we leave, we can't work on her."

Rosie adjusted a blanket over her lap. "Stay here through the winter without proper heat? We won't survive."

"DAPHNE is the main brain of the United States." Lizzie pointed to her followers. "Every day, these people go underground to repair her. They use torchlight that competes for the little oxygen they have, but they go every day for you and every other person in this country. What kind of patriots are you if you leave? Isn't there one hero among you?"

Aiden resented the guilt trip Lizzie threw on them, but DAPHNE's devotees began to clamor in support of her.

"I'm not afraid to give my life," someone shouted, "if it's for DAPHNE."

"Anyone who doesn't is a coward!" Mr. Parrish pointed a bottle at the audience, sloshing booze on the floor. He and a few of his fellow Aggravationists had fermented acorn mash to make liquor. By adding juniper berries for flavor, they'd crafted a harsh gin. Their drinking didn't do anyone any good, in Aiden's opinion. Only yesterday, Mr. Parrish accidentally dropped the rope he was using to lower one of Lizzie's engineers into the underground bunker because he was drunk. Fortunately, the engineer only suffered a sprained arm.

A Depressionist wildly shook his head. "I don't want to freeze to death."

A woman grabbed him by the shoulders. "Can't you see we're blessed? We are the guardians of DAPHNE. Only we can resurrect Her. We are apostles, charged with spreading Her intelli—"

Aiden slammed his fist on the floor. "DAPHNE is not a god! She-*IT* is a machine. We don't have to risk our lives for a machine."

"You unpatriotic little shit!" Mr. Parrish dropped his bottle and lunged at Aiden. Grabbing him by the throat, he hauled Aiden to his feet. "Di'n't you hear what Dr. Lizzie said? We're trying to bring DAPHNE back, but you want us to live in the dark forever."

As Doug, Jill, and Tash rushed toward them, Mr. Parrish began shaking Aiden by the neck like a coyote on a rabbit. Aiden struggled, but Parrish wouldn't let go. The central fire suddenly popped like a firecracker, spitting sparks toward the skylight and settling into a symphony of crackling. Aiden's vision blurred until, on the edge of losing consciousness, he could discern nothing but the reddish-orange flames. At that moment, Clyde's father yelped and dropped Aiden.

He gaped at his hands. Aiden rubbed his throat, shaken. His parents landed at his side, and Doug helped him to his feet. Tash, gripping the ax, stood in front of Clyde's dad. Daring him.

Mr. Parrish picked up the gin bottle. "He burned my hands."

"You're drunk," Tash growled.

Parrish shook his head. "He burned my freakin' hands!" Viewing the congregation, he yelled, "How come no one asks how he knows the things he knows?"

Mac waved him off. "Go pass out, Parrish."

Clyde's father pointed the bottle at Aiden, who self-consciously stepped away from his protective parents.

"I wanna know. I wanna know how he burned my hands."

"Shut up," Tash warned.

"I will not shut up." Mr. Parrish swayed on his feet. "Know what I think? I think he's evil. Yeah." He looked past Tash to Aiden. "You're a demon hell-bent on our destruction. That's what you are." He swallowed more gin, then whirled around to face the crowd. "We should burn him into ash!"

"Parrish!" Chris barked. "Sit down."

Clyde's father began sniggering. "Burn him into ash and toss him in the toilets." He laughed, a wicked bray, which soon faded into heavy breathing. Then, the man slid to the floor. Doug and Mac lifted him up and carried him to his shelter.

Aiden locked eyes with Lizzie, who hid a smile. He didn't need to be psychic to see she enjoyed having an ogre as her ally, but why?

Feinstein cleared his throat and stood up. "I think we should get back on track."

"Good idea," Chris said.

Jill put a protective arm around her son, and the two took seats near Ava. Feinstein nodded at Aiden and continued, "This gym was built for central heating and isn't well-insulated. We need to figure out where we're going to shelter if we stay." He lit his pipe and glanced at Lizzie.

Vivica tossed her long hair, which she'd dyed in stripes of blue and green, a style she called Forest Mermaid. "We'll have to chop down trees in the snow to keep the fire burning all winter."

"What about coal?" Rosie asked. "People once used coal for heat. Can we make some?"

Lizzie shook her head. "Not without a blast furnace."

AVA, SITTING NEAR AIDEN, listened to the discussion. Her hearing had sharpened, and when someone coughed, it sounded like an explosion. She could not see the firelight but felt its heat. She could also feel Aiden's distress as if it stung her. If only she could see. She would have thrown something heavy at Clyde's father.

Ava heard Chris's firm tone. "Let's take a vote. Who wants to migrate? Raise your hand."

She heard the rustle of clothing and sensed a lot of fidgeting in the crowd.

"Who wants to stay to repair DAPHNE?" A moment passed, and Chris said, "I guess you win, Lizzie. We stay."

Ava felt Aiden sigh heavily, and she elbowed him. "Play some songs. You'll feel better if you play."

"No."

"Please? I'd like to hear the music. I'm sure everyone else would, too."

"You sure you'll be okay?"

"Of course," she lied.

Cool air replaced him, and Ava felt a flash of angst at his departure. Ever since they'd made love, she wanted Aiden near her—*always*. Ava smiled at the memory of the gramophone song as the flames from the fire ring heated her cheeks.

She heard Jill say, "Lean back, Ava. You're too close to the fire."

She sat back.

"HOW ARE YOU FEELING, AVA?" Mac bellowed as if she were deaf.

"I'm fine."

Someone else took Ava's hand. She recognized the soft, slender fingers that smelled like rich earth and perfumed flowers. "Hi, Viv."

Two soft lips pecked her cheek. Ava supposed she should feel lucky with everyone looking out for her. Still, their watchfulness annoyed her.

"Where's Tash?" she asked Viv.

"With Aiden. We're about to play." Vivica squeezed her hand. "Let me bring you to the dance floor."

"I don't feel like dancing."

"You used to love it," Vivica pressed. "Come on. How 'bout if Trina brings you over later?"

Ava shrugged. Vivica departed with another squeeze of her hand. A homey, sugary smell filled Ava's nostrils as somebody small shuffled next to her.

"Is your eyes not wooking?"

A little boy's voice. Ava imagined the tot staring wide-eyed at the shirtsleeve tied around her head.

She smiled at the child she couldn't see. "Nope, not working."

"Is you sad?"

Ava nodded.

"Hehr."

She felt something mushy press into her hand.

"Meina," a woman's voice admonished, and footsteps hurriedly approached. Ava caught the herbal scent of Jill's soap. "Ava doesn't want your half-eaten cookie."

A cloth briskly rubbed against her hand. "Sorry."

"It's okay. Thank you, Meina, for sharing."

The cookie aroma disappeared, along with the herbal scent.

She tugged at the plaid cloth that covered her eyescreens and waited for Trina to drag her to the dance area. People danced when they had something to celebrate. Was she supposed to celebrate going blind?

Now that your eyes are closed, you will see.

The voice inside her mind spoke. Swallowing, she asked silently, See what?

Light.

The thought excited Ava. How? Where? Where will I see it?

Everywhere.

What kind of light? Sunlight? Starlight?

The deer.

The deer? What connection could the buck possibly have with seeing light? She thought about her animal friend. He'd provided her with a trustworthy avenue to experience affection; for that, Ava would always be grateful. Without that experience, she wouldn't have been able to cultivate the beautiful relationship she now cherished with Aiden. Simply put, the buck had made Ava realize she could love.

Silently, she asked, 'Is that what light looks like? Like a deer?'

The reply came instantly. *It looks like the realization.*

CHAPTER 45

As Aiden removed his guitar from his case, he saw Professor Feinstein loitering around the "bandstand," a raised platform made from the roof of an airbus. The professor paced about with his hands clasped behind his back and chewed on the stem of his unlit pipe. Despite Feinstein's posture of scholarly contemplation, Aiden sensed intimidation and frustration rolling off his former teacher.

Catching Aiden's compassionate eye, Feinstein pulled the pipe from his mouth. "She's wrong, you know."

Aiden knew to whom Feinstein referred, but he asked, "Who's wrong?"

"Lizzie. You can chop up hardwood, put it in a container like a small tin garbage can, and cover it with a lid. If you put that on a bonfire, it'll cook the wood."

"What are you talking about?"

"Coal. Charcoal. The wood will cook right into lump charcoal without needing a blast furnace."

"Then why didn't you say so?" Aiden asked.

"I didn't want to cross her." The pipe returned to Feinstein's mouth.

"Why not? What is it with you two?"

"She's a genius. Absolutely brilliant."

Aiden huffed. "You're the one with the good ideas, Professor. My mom's a new woman because of you."

Feinstein pulled on Aiden's sleeve to bring him close. "Compared to Lizzie Vasquez, I'm a drooling idiot. We all are."

"Her name is Lizzie Appel."

"That's her married name. The Vasquez family pioneered artificial general intelligence. You can list them along Turing, McCarthy, Newell, all the historical masterminds behind AI. Who wouldn't be intimidated by her?"

Feinstein moved off to leave Aiden wondering where he'd heard the name Vasquez before.

THE BAND BEGAN PLAYING, and the music had an immediate calming effect on the crowd. Some even got up to dance, among them, Ava.

Across the gym, Oreanna gazed at Clyde Parrish. Seated upon his throne of fur and hides, he exuded an animal magnetism that ignited a fire in her. His lion's mane of tawny hair, the stains of warrior paint on his face, those overpowering, flexing muscles he used to provide sustenance to the entire community... Oreanna could no longer tamp down the blaze burning within her.

She wandered over to where the cooks were preparing supper and asked for some arnica gel. The cooks fiercely protected the precious medicines they crafted but spooned a little into a cup for her. Oreanna swallowed her fear and drifted over to Clyde's throne. Busty Trina, Pete, and a few hunters surrounded the great warrior, who watched the band and the dancers.

Holding the gel with one hand, Oreanna fingered the bleached straight ends of her kinky dark hair with her other hand and chewed at her lower lip. Pete smiled at her, but a hunter shouted, "Move! We can't see!"

Oreanna timidly held out the arnica gel to Clyde and tried to speak, but no words came.

"Get lost, fatty," Trina told her.

The cruel moniker no longer applied to Oreanna; no one could call her overweight. Still, defeat lowered her arm. She turned to leave but heard Clyde ask, "Whatcha got there?"

She blushed at his wry grin. Clyde took a swallow from the bottle of scotch, and a few of the hunters snickered. Busty Trina put a possessive hand on Clyde's muscular thigh while Pete Farmington bowed his head and averted his eyes. The crackling flames tossed sparks into the air as the musicians played.

Oreanna lifted the little bowl of gel again. "I thought I'd bring you some arnica for your cuts. It's... It's really plus how you handled that bear."

Busty Trina rolled her eyes. Clyde drank more liquor and settled his gaze on Ava, who swayed in the steamy air as one might undulate against a silken sheet. Oreanna followed Clyde's eyes as they traveled from Ava to Aiden, who played his guitar with a broad smile. Why wouldn't he smile like that? Aiden knew Ava danced only for him.

At last, Clyde slid his steel-gray eyes over to Oreanna. "You can rub that gel on me. Move over, Trina."

Busty Trina tossed her long dark hair but moved aside to let Oreanna sit beside Clyde. Pete made room, too; only his eyes flickered wistfully. Carefully warming the gel between her hands, Oreanna smoothed the salve over the rugged ridges of Clyde's muscles, around his bulging biceps, and over his broad chest where the stitches poked hard and black. Touching him made her feverish, and her breath hitched. Clyde, however, didn't notice. He seemed fixated on Ava.

When Oreanna spread the gel down his torso, over the sparse, wiry hair on his taut stomach, Clyde gripped Oreanna's hand and angled his face toward her. A bolt of fear flashed in her, thrown down by a thunderstorm in the brawny boy's eyes.

"You wanna hang out?" The question came out in a hiss.

Trina suddenly rose to her feet and left. Perplexed, Oreanna watched the other girl's departure and fretted over what silent cue she missed. Pete opened his mouth to say something, but a glance from Clyde shut him up.

"Well?" the mighty warrior asked.

"Sure," she squeaked.

Clyde got to his feet. Oreanna also stood up, although she didn't know why they'd need to leave the gym to 'hang out.' Still, she followed Clyde obediently out the door toward a darkened part of the school.

CHAPTER 46

The following morning, the gym-dwellers woke to see ice framing the windows. More and more people crowded around the fire pit. They wore old winter jackets, hides, blankets—anything to keep warm.

Vivica bundled Ava into a nanofiber jacket and gloves and led her to the ball field. "You're going to help Tash and me today," she said.

Ava appreciated her friends' kindness. Helping Tash and Vivica made her feel useful and less of a burden on the community. She knelt on the grass and helped Vivica steady an old barbeque drum.

"What are you building, Tash?"

"A forge." He grunted as he worked. "I'm drilling a hole into this thing so I can insert a pipe into it. Lizzie says the pipe is called a *tuyere* and works like a nozzle."

Vivica added, "Lizzie says that if we pump air through the nozzle, it'll make flames inside hot enough to melt metal. Then, we can make potbelly stoves."

"What's a potbelly stove?" Ava asked.

"Something we can cook on," Vivica replied. "Something we can put in every room so everyone can stay warm. Lizzie also says that once we become real good at working with metal, we can make tools to bring DAPHNE back."

Ava held tight to the drum. She wanted to be a good helper. "Do you both want DAPHNE back? Aiden's kind of against it. He thinks all our work with the Great Source will end if she returns."

"Yeah, but if DAPHNE comes back, you'll be able to see again," Vivica said.

Ava lay her cheek against the cold metal. She'd be able to see again...

A few minutes passed. Because the sights of the outside world no longer captured Ava's attention, her mind easily drifted off into an inner world. She gripped the drum and imagined she flew through a cloudy sky.

Sunbeams are breaking through the sky, and a brilliant rainbow arches before me. I glide between misty strips of red, orange, green, blue, indigo, and violet. I grow light-headed, surrounded by so much color, but I want to drink it in; it's so beautiful. I see the forge below the rainbow, and Tash feeds metal into the flames. I know that, soon, I'll be able to see again.

Ava couldn't wait to tell Aiden about the forge. She didn't know that her mind had already told him.

IN THE GYM, JILL APPROACHED Aiden, where he sat under a shaft of morning sunlight, trying to catch its meager warmth.

"Have you seen Oreanna?" she asked. She wore a coat over her old nanofiber tracksuit and a donated beanie with a San Francisco Giants' logo.

"Not since last night." Aiden stirred melted pinesap with tallow to make a skin salve. He needed to work quickly before the sap hardened and didn't mind when drops of the hot liquid burned his fingers. At least it felt warm.

Jill, distracted, reached under the beanie to scratch her scalp. "I need her help with my candle molds. Someone said she was with Clyde."

Aiden stopped stirring. "With *Clyde*?"

Jill sighed. "I'll have to find someone else. Maybe Z'ier..." She wandered off, absorbed in her quest.

Aiden scanned the room with his eyes. These days it wasn't easy to see the entire gym with so many workstations and shelters crowding the place, although he did catch Lizzie's curious eye. Aiden ignored her and continued searching for Oreanna. Was his sister really hanging out with Clyde Parrish?

Aiden!

Ava called him, but he couldn't spot her.

Aiden!

She sounded far off, yet he heard the call clearly above the cooks' din and the gym-dwellers' conversations. A wave of joy suddenly splashed him, and a rainbow flashed before his inner eye. An instinct told him to focus on the pleasurable tingle in his chest, and the airy elation in his head, but how could Aiden possibly feel happy when the news of Clyde and Oreanna vexed him?

A scene suddenly lit up in his brain: an image of Ava and Vivica observing Tash as he built something on the ball field outside the gym. Perplexed, Aiden abandoned his task and headed toward the exit.

He noticed Lizzie trailing behind as he crossed the field under a heavy pewter sky. After walking past the scudders and the tanners, he spied his friends.

"Hey." He squatted next to Ava, who clutched a steel drum.

She grinned under her blindfold. "I was just thinking about you."

Aiden regarded Tash, whose muscles flexed as he twisted an antique auger into the drum. "What are you doing?"

"Making a forge."

"What's a forge?"

Vivica handed Aiden two pages torn from a book. "Lizzie found these in a book from Chris's stash."

One page showed a black and white drawing of a brick hearth covered in ash with a row of long tools hanging nearby. A man sporting a handlebar mustache and a leather apron aimed a hammer toward an anvil that held a metal rod. The next page featured a drawing depicting a quaint parlor from a bygone era.

Vivica pointed to the parlor picture. "See that round container with a fire in it? It's called a potbelly stove."

Aiden returned the torn pages to her and gazed at the metal drum. "But why do you need a forge?"

Lizzie stepped up to their group. "A forge is a furnace that heats metal, allowing you to shape it into objects like a stove." She eyed him. "I hope you don't hinder our progress, Aiden."

"Why would I?" he asked, offended.

"You don't seem to be a big fan of DAPHNE's."

"What does DAPHNE have to do with making a forge?"

"Well..." Lizzie's lips curled into a wry grin. "We're witnessing the course of human development here in Sierrawood. First, we entered the Age of hunters and gatherers. Now, we're experiencing our very own Iron Age. In time, we'll plant crops and usher in the Age of Agriculture. Then, we'll create a steam engine for power, just as they did in the Industrial Age. The good news is, we already have a roadmap to all these developments: History." She locked eyes with Aiden. "When we return to the Digital Age, we'll see our destiny unfold."

Icy fingers gripped his heart at those words, and, again, he searched Lizzie's eyes. They gave up no secrets, but to him, her dark irises resembled black holes, dead stars that drew the one gazing upon them into oblivion.

WHEN THE SKY TURNED a vivid orange and red, Aiden, Ava, Tash, and Vivica walked toward the roundhouse for supper.

Aiden, holding Ava's hand to guide her, squeezed her gloved fingers. "You called me. I heard you as clearly as if you stood next to me. I also saw what you were doing."

Vivica smiled. "That's so cool. You guys communicated without a WeConnect. Tell us how to do it."

"I wish I could." Aiden rubbed the nape of his neck in frustration. "I don't know how."

"Let's review what we know," Ava said. "I used a fantasy to communicate with you, just as I did with the deer."

Tash stretched his sore muscles as he walked. "So, all we need to do to send a message is picture something in our heads." He caught Vivica's eye, winked, and flexed his bicep. "Picture this."

She elbowed him with grin and slid her arm through his.

Aiden shook his head. "We tried doing that, remember? It didn't work."

"Maybe it takes more than envisioning something." Ava squeezed his hand. "Tell me exactly what popped into your mind?"

"I saw a rainbow and felt happy for no reason." Again, he thought of Clyde and Oreanna.

"I *was* happy, and I did imagine a rainbow."

The breeze shifted her blindfold, and she adjusted the fabric. "Maybe the feeling has something to do with it. Maybe our emotions deliver our thoughts like taxis carry people to a destination. When I heard about the forge, I was really happy and wanted to tell you about it."

Tash looked doubtful. "If the communication rides on emotion, then the Aggravationists and Depressionists should be the most intuitive of us all."

"That's right." Vivica giggled. "They express a lot of emotion, and none of it good."

"We all feel things," Tash insisted to Ava. "So, why can't all of us communicate like you do with Aiden?"

Ava chewed on her lower lip, thinking. "Maybe it works only with someone receptive to your feelings. Aiden and I love each other, so maybe that's why we're able to send each other our thoughts."

A smile broke across Aiden's face. She loved him. Clearing his throat, he asked, "Why would a forge make you so happy?"

"Vivica says it'll help me see again."

"But you are seeing, Ava." He paused to put his hand on her cheek. "You have incredible insight." Just then, he spotted Oreanna entering the gym.

AIDEN SETTLED AVA IN their shelter and then searched for his sister. He found her heading toward the women's restroom with a towel, soap, and bucket of hot water. He rushed up to her and put a hand on her arm. "Where have you been?"

The girl grinned and chewed on a stubby fingernail. Her curly hair appeared mussed, and she wore her shirt backward.

A sense of dread flooded Aiden. "Were you with Clyde?"

She giggled, and he squeezed her arm. "What were you doing with Clyde?"

Oreanna jerked away, which caused her bucket to slosh water. "None of your business."

"Did he hurt you? What did he do to you?"

"What do you think?" She left Aiden fuming in the hall and sauntered into the bathroom.

AIDEN FOUND CLYDE AND a few of his hunter friends talking to Lizzie about the forge and the possibility of making better weapons.

Without a word, he stormed up to his nemesis and pushed him hard. Clyde's lips curled, but he said nothing. Activity halted in the roundhouse.

"Stay away from my sister," Aiden seethed.

"Kick his ass, Clyde," urged one of the hunters.

Aiden pointed a finger in his face. "Stay away from her."

"Make me." Clyde held out his knife. "Go ahead, Nature Boy. Teach me a lesson."

Aiden stared at the proffered blade. He should do it. He should grab the knife and... What? Kill Clyde? Aiden glanced at Lizzie, who wore an interested grin. She seemed to want the two young men to fight. Maybe she knew Aiden would end up dead. Unwilling to gratify her, he stepped back.

"You wimp." Clyde sheathed the knife in disgust. "What the hell does Ava see in you?"

CHAPTER 47

Doug had developed an affinity for woodworking and dedicated a week to carving a bellows out of wood and leather. Lizzie told him bellows would blast air through the tuyere into the furnace. She also encouraged Doug to immerse himself in the knowledge and skills required to become a blacksmith.

Meanwhile, Tash's construction team collected fallen bricks from the city center to build a hearth around the new furnace. When he completed the forge, everyone gathered around Doug to watch him burn metal until it glowed white-hot. Wearing oven mitts and using tongs, Doug removed the metal scraps from the forge and placed them on a flat steel block. On this substitute anvil, he hammered the hot metal into various shapes.

He practiced and experimented over the next couple of weeks and discovered he could create an extra hardy tool if he heated the metal to the highest temperature and then rapidly cooled it with water. The metal turned out even more robust if he used oil to cool it. Despite the scratches and burns he received, Doug relished his new role as a blacksmith. Metalwork signaled a tremendous technological advancement for the people of Sierrawood, and Doug took pride in being the one man to deliver it to them.

Lizzie declared an industrial revolution right around the corner and suggested they try building a steam engine next. If they could make a motor run, they could find the means to power up DAPHNE.

AIDEN COMPLAINED TO Grandpa Harry one day as he wheeled the older man around the school's parking lot to take in some fresh air. "Lizzie turned my own father against me."

"That's not true, Rebel," Harry reassured him. "Your father is your biggest fan."

"She's smart, all right. Of all the people she could have trained as a blacksmith, she chose my father, knowing his work will undermine me."

"I don't get it." Harry furrowed his brows. "What do you have against progress?"

"Grandpa, I know how much technology will help you and Ava." He sighed, and his breath came out in a cold mist. "But we're onto something powerful that isn't outside of us like DAPHNE. It's inside of us. Don't you think we should explore it? We'll never get the chance under DAPHNE."

Harry struggled to wrap his scarf more securely, and Aiden crouched in front of him to help. As he tied the scarf, he met his grandpa's eyes and saw doubt.

"You probably won't believe me," Aiden began, "but when Clyde's dad tried to choke me, I didn't push him away. I was scared, but I focused on the fire and imagined his hands going up in flames. Next thing I know, he jumped away. I used the Great Source to help me, and whatever its powers are, we can all tap into it now because DAPHNE isn't around."

When Aiden stood up to push the wheelchair again, Harry grabbed his hand. "Maybe humans aren't meant to have that kind of power, Rebel. If people don't come from a place of compassion and love, that kind of power can be abused. That's why we need something greater than us to manage us, something like DAPHNE."

"Are you serious?"

"Dr. Lizzie is the smartest person I know. If she says we need to bring DAPHNE back, then that's what we should do."

"I don't care what she says." Aiden pulled his hand away and steered his grandfather toward the gym. "There's something wrong with her."

The older man guffawed. "There's nothing wrong that I can see. The woman is probably the most perfect person I've ever met; brilliant, beautiful, resourceful... We wouldn't have survived without her."

As they neared the entrance to the gym, Aiden spied Oreanna trailing after Clyde like a servant, carrying buckets of hot water for his bath. Once again, his sister had created a new persona. She'd convinced herself she was Clyde's girlfriend when, in reality, he treated her like shit.

Maybe Grandpa Harry was right. Maybe all of them needed DAPHNE to control them.

LONGING FOR PEACE, Aiden hiked to the clearing near the lake. Something his grandfather said nagged at him, something about Lizzie. What was it? He couldn't remember. He felt too depressed.

When he arrived at the lake, he found the place buzzing with activity. Someone had built a fire ring on the bank so people could heat their water without dragging buckets back to the gym. Bathing shelters and clotheslines dotted the entire shoreline. Chipmunks and squirrels raced between the huts to beg for snacks. Aiden's meditative haven no longer existed.

Nearby, Chris and Professor Feinstein explored the clearing for domesticated plants. As Aiden sulked on a nearby log, he overheard their conversation.

"People once swarmed to the gold camps here in the 1800s," Chris explained. "They did logging, planted crops, and made settlements. I'll bet you this whole area was once cleared for crops. Keep your eyes peeled, Doc. When spring comes, we've got to look for any small green, glossy leaves. They might be leftover wheat seedlings from the old days."

The two men began walking in the direction of town. "If we can find the seedlings," Feinstein said, "we can replant them and create a stable food supply."

Chris clapped the teacher on the back. "Exactly what the Age of Agriculture did for humankind."

Seated on the log, Aiden put his head into his hands. His brown hair, so much longer now, fell between his fingers.

"What's up, son?"

Doug sat down. Working in the forge had made him leaner and more muscular. "You have that sad, confused look on your face I haven't seen in a long time." He gently elbowed his son. "What is it? It's going to worry folks when they see their spiritual leader acting depressed."

"Nobody believes in me."

"You'd be surprised."

"Doug!" Jill stumbled down the dirt path toward them. She wore a hood with netting, thick gloves, and a baggy plastic jumpsuit. She looked like an astronaut. "I've been looking all over for you. You said you'd help me make an apiary." She nodded at her son. "Hi, Aiden. You okay?"

"All good," he lied.

"Great." Jill nodded under her hood and then eyeballed her husband. "I'm waiting."

"Be right there, sweetheart."

Jill marched off, a woman on a mission. Aiden looked at Doug. "Mom's keeping bees now? She used to be scared of our cat."

"She's changed." Doug stood up and adjusted his loose trousers. "For the better, I might add. You keep shining that light of yours, son. It'll illuminate a path for us. You'll see."

When his father left, rain began falling, but Aiden felt the now-familiar tug. Instead of heading home, he walked uphill, following a narrow trail made by animals. He continued upward where the groves of trees thickened and rocky crags jutted from the earth. Against one such bluff, he spied the open mouth of a cave. *Go in.*

Aiden hiked up to it and entered an immense cavern. He'd heard rumors about local caves, but no kids he knew ever explored them. Why would they? In the days of virtual reality, who needed a mountain cave when one soared over a gorge in *Jungle Flight*?

Aiden explored the interior and discovered multiple 'rooms.' Thousands of years ago, the area's many volcanoes erupted with lava. The molten rock flowed in channels, and the cool air made the outer layers crust over, creating a tube or cave. If the lava branched off in different directions, offshoot tubes formed and created 'rooms' off the main cave.

Daylight streamed through holes in the rock 'roof.' The holes didn't allow much rain to fall inside, which gave Aiden an idea. He'd tell the people to move in here when the snow fell. The thick rock walls would insulate them. The potbelly stoves would warm them, and they could send ventilation pipes through the holes in the roof.

Returning to the main cavern, he tried to measure the expanse. As he surveyed the space, drawings on the cave wall caught his eye. Aiden moved closer to inspect them.

Pictographs. Ancient paintings in black, red, and blue pigments. One drawing depicted a bighorn sheep. Another, some sort of bird. Aiden smiled. The entire cave was decorated. He traced his finger along something that resembled a snake and peered at a series of geometric blocks. He had no clue what they symbolized. Then, his wandering gaze halted on a crude rendering of two human figures holding hands with two other beings, similar in shape to humans but taller and wider. Wavy lines emanated from the heads of the giants. In his heart, Aiden heard, *Hello.*

CHAPTER 48

Aiden brought Chris, Tash, Lizzie, Govind, and Ava to the caves. They all agreed the caves would serve as effective shelters during the winter.

Tash pointed out several crevices in the rock. "People can use these as sleeping areas."

Aiden walked over to the pictographs. "Look at these."

The others wandered over to examine the drawings, while Aiden described to Ava the drawing of the human figures holding hands with the giants.

Doug crouched down to peer closer. "The wavy lines above their heads are interesting. What do you think they mean?"

"Could it denote thinking?" Govind rested his chin on his fist. "Perhaps the smarter homosapiens leading the Neanderthals to a more enlightened life?"

Ava grinned. "Maybe it represents something more spiritual."

Chris nodded in thought. "The early people believed they could walk arm in arm with their spirit guides. Although they couldn't see them, the spirit guides were always close. The people tried to visualize them, often with the help of a shaman." He winked at Aiden. "Maybe this is a drawing of someone's vision."

"Early people didn't know any better." Lizzie leveled her gaze at Aiden. "They filled their world with mysticism and magic because they had no understanding."

Aiden met the challenge in her eyes. "How do you know they had no understanding?"

"Do you think this drawing proves your theory? There is no god, angel, or spirit guide trying to communicate with you from some other dimension. There is no need for a god because everything can be explained. *Everything*."

"People still get scared," he told her. "Don't you ever need comfort?"

"Fear is an obstacle to personal expansion. I don't let myself feel it."

Aiden traded looks with Chris and said to Lizzie, "You talk like a sociopath."

"You're a fine one to accuse me of having a mental disorder."

"Lizzie..." Govind began.

"Early people didn't understand the diseases and natural disasters that befell them," she said. "They didn't know what the stars were or why the sun lit the day. Hurricanes and earthquakes terrified them, so they created myth and folklore to explain that phenomena. We're fortunate to have science and technology to understand our world."

Aiden left Ava to move protectively in front of the pictograph. "The ancient people may not have known what caused a hurricane, but they believed they had the power to appease a deity. They made sacrifices, performed good deeds, maybe they prayed, maybe they did a frigging rain dance during a drought, but they did these things because they *believed* doing them would help."

Lizzie arched a mocking eyebrow. "And did it?"

"Who's to say it didn't?"

"Gee, I don't know." She laughed. "Did a rain dance eradicate polio? Tell me something, Aiden, would you prefer to believe the world is flat?"

Govind tried to take Lizzie's arm. "Leave the kid alone."

She jerked from his grasp and stayed on Aiden. "Would you purposely stay stupid, or would you eat the forbidden fruit if you could?"

"You want to talk about the Bible?" He tucked his hair behind his ear with an eager hand. "Adam and Eve had the entire Garden of Eden at their disposal. They ate the forbidden fruit and were cursed with the need to know everything. And it is a curse, Lizzie, because knowledge has robbed us of our ability to imagine."

"That is the most ignorant statement I've ever heard."

WHILE LIZZIE AND AIDEN argued, Ava leaned her head against the rock wall and reached in her pocket for a piece of quartz that Oreanna had given her. Ori said the strong mineral could transform energy from one form to another. It might have been Ava's imagination, but energy seemed to radiate off the rock next to her. In the dark setting of her blindness, it was easy to shut out the shouting voices and disappear.

Ava sighed and imagined the rock wall absorbed her like a sponge. She melded with the granite and felt every stage of its creation, all the way back to the magma from which it crystallized countless years before.

LIZZIE SHOOK HER HEAD with an exasperated grin. "Do you know what imagination is, Aiden? Everything you feel, every emotion, even this sixth sense you go on about, can be explained physiologically. Special neurobiological features of a complex nervous system create consciousness. That's it. That's all there is to it."

"I don't believe that."

"Then, you're deluding yourself. An animal that uses complex senses to create a map of its body and its world is capable of creating mental images. Every thought that crosses your mind, every emotion your feel, and every belief you hold sacred is nothing more than the dynamics of your brain chemistry, a conglomeration on the molecular level of every human experience dating all the way back to the Big Bang."

"I'm talking about feelings."

Lizzie lifted her shoulders. "So am I. An animal that shows complex operant conditioning, which means it learns from experience based on rewards and punishments, possesses positive and negative feelings."

"I'm not talking about that kind of feeling," Aiden insisted. "I'm talking about a gut feeling. Intuition."

AVA OPENED HER EYES. Suddenly, she had eyes and could see. She was no longer in the cave.

I'm standing on a wood floor in a simple room adorned with bare wood walls. Outside a window, a windmill turns over a field of pink tulips. A long-haired man wearing hose, breeches, and a tunic bordered in fur, sits at a table, hunched over a single-lensed microscope. He doesn't appear to see me. Where am I?

"In this rainwater," the man says to himself, "I can see shapes moving about. They seem to be alive." He scratches his head, frustrated, and peers into his microscope. "What are these little animals?"

"Protozoa," I tell him.

The man pauses for a moment, then smiles. "Protozoa. I shall call you protozoa."

Ava felt the rock wall against her body again and heard Lizzie's voice berating Aiden.

"The intuitive mind is nothing more than the teachings and warnings from thousands of years of human evolution."

CHRIS LIFTED HIS HANDS. "Okay, you two. Enough. It's getting cold. Let's—"

"If I'm traveling on an unfamiliar trail," Aiden countered, "and I hit a fork in the road, how do you explain the pull, the tug, that points me in one direction, which happens to be the right direction. Is that thousands of years of evolution?"

"Yes." Lizzie nodded emphatically. "It's rationalization happening in the dark matter of your brain."

"You're wrong."

"I'm right."

"Then how do you explain Ava and I speaking to each other without saying a word?"

The present company fell quiet, including Lizzie.

Aiden nodded. "That's right, Lizzie. We communicate without speaking."

"How?"

"Call it what you will, the Great Source, the Lifespark..." He nodded to the cave drawings. "Maybe they were trying to understand what it was, too."

"Your Great Source," Lizzie repeated dully.

"Not mine. Everyone's. It exists, it's everywhere, and it's not DAPHNE. It's been in our consciousness all along. DAPHNE blotted it out, and you want to do the same. Why?"

Lizzie swallowed, straightened her shoulders, and walked toward the cave entrance. There, she halted and eyed the interior of the cave. "This place suits you, Aiden, because you think like a caveman."

CHAPTER 49

Almost immediately, volunteers began furnishing the caves. They cleared the earthen floor of fallen rocks and laid down hides or woven mats. As Tash had pointed out, the natural crevices in the rock walls made decent sleeping areas under which small hearths were lit for extra warmth. Some industrious souls propped up wallscreens to cover the cave entrances and inserted pipes into the screens to allow ventilation.

Doug made potbelly stoves for the caves, and people living in private homes and the school's classrooms also requested them. Sierrawood's blacksmith made so many in one week that he gave up washing the metal dust and soot from his person, which made him resemble something crafted in a forge.

The gatherers built a granary to store acorns. It stood eight feet high and looked like a large basket on poles. Like the Miwok before them, the gatherers lined their storehouse with pine needles and wormwood to repel insects and rodents. They placed a thatch of cedar boughs on top to keep out the rain and snow.

Clyde and his hunters stepped up their game and hunted black-tailed deer, elk, mountain goats, and bighorn sheep. Rosie and her cooks salted as much of the meat as they could. The prospect of starving in the snow motivated one and all.

During Kimber's naps, L'Eren offered to teach other youngsters to read. Govind instructed them in math. Feinstein revived his science classes, and other community members made "guest appearances" to introduce the children to various specialties. Jill gave a soap-making lesson in the cafeteria. Oreanna lectured on geology, which did wonders for the girl's self-esteem. Doug toured the children through his blacksmith shop, and Tash spoke on architecture and structural engineering. Vivica introduced art and color to the children.

One evening, when the hunters arrived with several wild turkeys, the people decided to hold a holiday feast. Tables extended out of the gym and into the hallway to support the large communal meal. Children searched the classrooms for craft supplies and made centerpieces. In addition to barbequing the turkeys, the cooks prepared acorn dumplings, wild mushroom gravy, and bowls of dandelion and clover salad.

Aiden observed Clyde at the table. Oreanna sat next to him, but he completely ignored her. Still, she ate and drank with gusto and chatted up Clyde's friends as if she were one of their crowd. Only when Oreanna met Aiden's eye did he glimpse her desperation to belong, be accepted, and clutch at something barely in her grasp.

Ava had insisted on sitting next to Lizzie at the table, and Aiden wondered why.

As they ate, Ava asked Lizzie, "Who first studied things like bacteria?"

"That's an odd subject to bring up during a meal." Lizzie merrily twirled her fork.

"I'm thinking of someone who would have lived near windmills and tulips."

Lizzie put down her fork and paused, thinking. "Antony Van Leeuwenhoek. He was Dutch, so I'd say there were tulips around. Van Leeuwenhoek had no formal training, but many consider him the father of microbiology. In 1677, he wrote a famous paper that gave the first detailed descriptions of protists and bacteria. It was called 'Letter on the Protozoa.' Why do you ask?"

"No reason." Then, Ava whispered to Aiden, "Except that I gave him the name."

AFTER SUPPER, AIDEN brought Ava into their shelter and begged her to explain.

"I had a mind-drift when we were in the caves," she whispered. "I went somewhere, and I could see again. I saw a man, but he didn't see me. His room, the strange microscope he used, it looked ancient. He was trying to figure out what to call the living things he saw in a drop of rainwater."

"Were you scared?"

"Not at all. I thought I was daydreaming. I said 'protozoa,' but the man figured he came up with the word. Tonight, Lizzie told me the guy was real. He was a scientist who lived a long time ago, but I visited him."

Aiden's breath hitched in his throat. "Are you saying that when we get inspired, someone from another place or time advises us, stands next to us like a ghost?"

"Not a ghost." Ava smiled. "A guide. Remember what Chris said in the cave? How the ancients felt they could hold hands with their guides? What if the Great Source really is where the past, present, and future come together? Where the dead don't sleep. Where we get our inspiration from. What if we can step into the Great Source through our dreams and fantasies and step out to help someone else?"

Aiden contemplated the idea. "If that's true, there are no boundaries between time and space."

"Don't forget how you defended yourself from Clyde's dad. You did it without touching him. Can you remember how you did it?"

He shook his head. "It's so frustrating."

She reached for him and kissed his lips. "Don't think about it anymore tonight." She kissed him again and sent him a thought that made him blush.

LIZZIE HID OUTSIDE their shelter and listened to the couple kissing. Coming together physically. The physical bonding didn't bother Lizzie. All animals procreated. It was the mental bonding that worried her. Having heard enough, she slipped away.

LIZZIE WALKED PASSED L'Eren, who sat by the fire pit reading poetry to her class. When Kimber began to cry in Grandpa Harry's arms, L'Eren glanced at her father. "Dad, hold the baby tighter. He's slipping."

Harry didn't respond. His eyes were closed, and his mouth was open.

"Dad?" L'Eren rose from the chair, picked up her baby, and gently shook her father. "Dad."

Harry didn't move.

TASH WIPED TEARS AWAY as he constructed Grandpa Harry's coffin. The man had, after all, given him the ax that had strengthened him. Aiden helped build the coffin and worked in disbelieving silence. When Rosie asked Aiden to preside over the funeral, he refused, saying he'd choke up.

"You won't," Rosie assured him. "You're a professional now." The older woman pulled a cloth from her apron and wiped her eyes. "Isn't life strange? I always thought I'd go first. Your grandpa was such a lively man. What will I do without him?"

Aiden's heart went out to her. Rosie had overcome personal ailments to see that the entire community ate cooked food. Although her back was crooked, she volunteered as a nurse for the sick and infirm. If she could conquer her weaknesses, he could, too.

What could he say at the funeral? Aiden felt obligated to speak of the man and his accomplishments but kept circling back to what Harry had inspired in him. After all, what greater feat can one accomplish than making another person's life better? It is the kind of accomplishment that lives on after one is gone. At last, he figured out what he would say.

They buried Grandpa Harry in the cemetery near the hospital, and the clouds draped the crowd of mourners in a soft, fluffy gray cloak. Aiden held onto the well-worn book about the Native Americans but no longer needed to read it. He'd memorized every word.

"Oh, Great Spirit, whose voice I hear in the wind, whose breath gives life to all the world. Hear me; I need your strength and wisdom." Aiden's gaze settled on the mound of rich, brown earth. "Let me walk in beauty, and make my eyes ever behold the red and purple sunset. Make my hands respect the things you have made and my ears sharp to hear your voice. Make me wise so that I may understand the things you have taught my people.

"Help me to remain calm and strong in the face of all that comes towards me. Let me learn the lessons you have hidden in every leaf and rock. Help me seek pure thoughts and act with the intention of helping others. Help me find compassion without empathy overwhelming me. I seek strength, not to be greater than my brother, but to fight my greatest enemy, myself." Aiden's face twisted with emotion. "Make me... Make me always ready to come to you with clean hands and straight eyes. So when life fades, as the fading sunset, my spirit may come to you without shame."

He sniffed and wiped away a tear. "That was the Akta Lakota prayer to The Great Spirit." Regarding the grave, he said, "Grandpa Harry, pass into the land of dreams without regret. Your spirit goes without shame."

JILL DEALT WITH HER grief by throwing herself into work as a beekeeper. She donned a protective suit and prodded a hive of bees to fall like a writhing blob into a cardboard box. She placed a framed window screen atop the box, turned it over, and waited for the rest of the bees to return to their hive. When the late arrivals crawled through holes in the screen to join their brethren, Jill covered the screen with a towel and placed the hive in her homemade apiary. The gym-dwellers joked that the bees wouldn't dare sting Jill because she might sting them back.

Doug fashioned a honey extractor for his wife by welding a spinner into the hollowed-out torso of a robot. When Jill turned a crank outside the extractor, it spun honey from the honeycomb. She gave the sweet honey to the cooks and kept the beeswax to enhance the products she made.

Per Feinstein's instructions, Jill wrapped the wax in cheesecloth and added it to boiling water to break it down. She then poured the oily water into a container and allowed it to solidify. The bright yellow beeswax made an excellent addition to her moisturizers, lotions, wood polish, lip balms, and candles. Jill worked nonstop and, in one week, had filled her apothecary. It was then she decided to sell her surplus products.

CHRIS HEARD ABOUT JILL'S fledgling business and made her shut it down. Outraged, Jill demanded a discussion at the fire ring. A large crowd attended the meeting because everyone wanted to know if they'd need money in the roundhouse. This would be a problem because no one had any.

"I don't understand why I can't sell the extra stuff I make," Jill argued.

Chris leaned forward in his chair with his hands on his knees. Despite being near the fire, a blanket printed with various birds covered his shoulders against the cold. "We live as a community here, where every person contributes something for the common good. That's how we've survived and will continue to survive."

Jill crossed her arms in defiance and to keep warm. "But why should I give away everything I make for free?"

"Did you purchase the ingredients you use?" Chris asked.

"No."

"Are you willing to pay the scudders who stripped off the fat you use for tallow?"

Jill eyed Mac and Aerta, who frowned at her in resentment.

"Are you willing to pay Vivica for the flowers you use for your scents?"

Jill pursed her lips together.

Mac stood up. "Maybe I should charge for my services." He shook his fist at Jill. "How would you like to scrape fat and capillaries off hides all day long? At least your job smells good. Do you have any idea how a hide begins to stink after a few hours?"

Chris threw a log on the fire, which sent up flying embers. "Nobody gets paid. Nobody sells anything. If we introduce money into our roundhouse, things will get complicated fast." He looked at Jill. "Leave your greed outside, Mrs. Baylor. If you want a little more of something, ask nicely for it. Chances are, you'll get it."

Jill reddened in shame and blew out a big breath. Doug took her hand, and L'Eren pulled her sister into a chair.

Lizzie shook her head. "It's not sustainable."

"What's not?" Chris asked.

"This communal living. It's not sustainable. None of you will be able to 'leave your greed outside.' Don't you see? It's human nature to compete. When you all have more than you need, you'll want to sell your wares like Jill."

Chris fingered his long beard and gave her a long, hard look. "Then, I guess it's convenient that we do NOT have more than we need. Not by a long shot. You'll realize that when the snow falls."

An uncomfortable silence dropped on the crowd, but Lizzie smirked. "Maybe we should ask the Great Source to help us. What do you think, Aiden?"

His mouth fell open as all eyes settled on him.

"Tell them," she pressed. "Tell them about the power stronger than DAPHNE."

The audience members traded doubtful looks, but some seemed interested and hopeful. Aerta raised her hand. "Can it power up the heat? Can it restart the Rolands?"

"No," Lizzie answered. "But you can communicate without a WeConnect. Aiden says he and Ava speak to each other with their minds."

A murmur rolled through the crowd.

Before Aiden could speak, Ava got to her feet and faced the crowd she couldn't see. "We do communicate without speaking. We do it through our emotions."

Busty Trina broke out in giggles, and the Aggravationists rolled their eyes.

Grandma Rosie raised a hand, shaky with tremors. "Let her finish. Years ago, before the WeConnect, I'd think about someone I missed a lot, and that person would call me out of the blue. I always wondered how that happened."

Lizzie grimaced. "It's called a coincidence."

"What if it's not?" Ava countered. "What if it's an ancient form of communication?"

Z'ier called out from her seat, "Tell us about the Great Source, Ava. Tell us how how it tells you things."

"Wait," Jill interrupted. "Is the Great Source the voice my son hears in his head?"

Mr. Parrish and the Aggravationists roared with laughter. Aiden's cheeks flamed up.

Ava, however, stood her ground. "I hear it, too. The Great Source speaks to us with wisdom, insight, and guidance."

"Why don't we hear it?" Aerta asked.

"You did," Ava told her, "when you knew the knife would break in your husband's hands."

Pete asked, "What does the Great Source look like?"

Ava rubbed her lips with thoughtful fingers. "Let me try to visualize it."

Some people elbowed each other in amusement, but many leaned forward with interest.

Ava shook her head. "The only image I'm receiving is a bunch of black and white pixels."

"Static," Chris said.

"Static?" L'Eren bounced her baby on her lap. "Static is the source of your insight? I'm too tired for this nonsense. Kimber and I are going to bed." She traded "goodnight's" with everyone near her and headed toward the shelter she shared with Govind.

Chris reached for some breath-cleansing sage leaves. "In the days of analog television, static filled the screen if the antenna received no transmission signal."

"What exactly is static?" Mac asked.

"Electromagnetic noise. It looks like black and white pixels." Chris gazed at the fire in contemplation. "I wonder why you would receive an image of static? What signal isn't transmitting?"

Lizzie threw her hands into the air. "Who says she received something? This is lunacy."

Chris placed a sage leaf in his mouth in response.

All at once, Aiden realized what the image of static signified. Silently thanking the Great Source, he stood up. "Ava and I have asked ourselves why other people can't access the Great Source. The transmission is blocked."

Everyone gave him blank stares.

"Don't you see? The pixels represent us, the soul of every human being. We're not connected with each other, not how we should be. All of us are part of the Great Source, part of a big picture, but we can't see it clearly, so we don't use it."

"What would block the signal?" Govind asked.

"We're blocking it. To use the power of our minds, we must come together like pixels in an image."

"Why are we listening to this?" an Aggravationist yelled. "Don't we have more serious matters to discuss?"

"Yeah," another one said, "Like our survival."

Z'ier clenched her hands into fists and faced the Aggravationists. "This is serious. This is important, and people like you block the transmission!"

"Shut up, you stupid witch!" Mr. Parrish yelled.

Govind jumped to his feet. "Don't you dare call her that."

"Yeah? What are you going to do about it, Mr. Useless Secretary?"

The audience erupted then, with some siding with Aiden and others heckling him.

Chris raised his hands. "Everybody calm down. Dr. Lizzie brought up this subject. Let's finish it and move on."

"Why don't we try to tap into the Great Source?" Pete asked with hope. "Let's test it and see if it really works?"

Aiden gazed at the former bully. Pete Farmington had softened since the days of DAPHNE. Aiden had noticed him offer to help Oreanna with her chores and inquire about her growing collection of rocks.

"It won't work," Aiden told Pete gently. "It won't work because we're not connected. Each of us is focused on our individual needs and wants." He eyeballed his mother, who hung her head. "And the noise we create makes it worse." He glanced at the red-eyed Mr. Parrish. "Noise distracts us. It won't let us get quiet so we can listen to our guides."

Pete looked confused. "Who?"

"We have guides?" Aerta piped up. "Where do they take us?"

Aiden chose his words carefully. "Guides come from the Great Source to help us work out our problems so we can be more positive. Positive people are more likely to bond with others. When we finally connect, our human consciousness will become as clear as a picture and won't be a mystery anymore."

Remembering Professor Yang, he added silently, *our survival depends on that.*

Feinstein sighed at his former pupils. "I think you two have been eating the funky kind of mushrooms."

The gym-dwellers broke out in laughter. Aiden pointed a decisive finger at Feinstein.

"You taught us that the computer emulates the human brain. If you believe that, then is it so farfetched to think that people created an online Internet to emulate another, more organic network? Think about it. A worldwide web of souls. A universal consciousness. Maybe the Great Source is all of our minds working as one in a space where the past, present, and future come together." He regarded Lizzie. "A space that offers something far greater than knowledge."

"If this Internet of the mind exists," Feinstein asked, "how come we can't use it? It should be as natural to us as breathing."

Ava took over. "We keep telling you. We're lost. Separated like pixels in static. We've lost the signal, so we only access the Great Source in bits and pieces."

"You mention guides who come from this power source." Feinstein lit his pipe. "Name one."

Although unsure, Aiden replied, "Maybe Grandpa Harry is one of them now."

Suddenly, an idea struck him like a thunderbolt. Aiden could almost believe his grandfather sat beside him, giving him a cosmic nudge.

"Grandpa Harry once told me we have to come from a place of love. While having a positive outlook is the first step in connecting with each other, we need to love each other."

"Really?" Mac laughed. "Why not ask for the moon?"

"It's a safeguard," Aiden told him, "so people won't abuse the power of the Great Source. Ava and I love each other, so we would never harm each other with our abilities."

Aiden caught Clyde's face darkening with anger. Oreanna tried to snuggle against him, but his powerful body appeared to harden like a block wall.

"Well!" Lizzie slapped her thighs. "All we have to do to tap into this power is be positive at all times and love each other no matter what." She grinned. "I'd say using the WeConnect was a hell of a lot easier."

Aiden gazed at her. "We don't need a WeConnect, Lizzie. *We* just have to *connect*."

She took a deep breath and addressed the assembly. "You have a choice. You can follow the Great Band of Static or follow me to bring DAPHNE back. Choose."

"I'm with you, Dr. Lizzie," Mr. Parrish said, and many others voiced their agreement.

Aiden sat back down, averting his eyes from her smug smile. She knew that unveiling the Great Source to the public would be catastrophic, that it would snuff out the idea before it had a chance to flourish. She really was brilliant.

CHAPTER 50

During the night, the gentle thrumming of rain gave way to an opaque quiet. Aiden awoke in the morning, pulled on his nanofiber jacket, and trudged outside. His footfalls made crunching sounds on a plush ivory carpet as he walked. The tree branches held white bundles, and snowflakes fell from a gray sky. He lifted his face and let the lacy bits melt on his skin.

Winter had arrived.

People spent the day moving the hospital patients into the roundhouse. The hospital was across town, and few volunteers would trek there in the snow. Since the elderly and the infirm had first rights to the fire ring, the former "tenants" were pushed out.

Tash's potbelly stoves could effectively warm the smaller classrooms but didn't provide sufficient heat for the entire gymnasium. As the temperature fell, the distant corners of the room grew too cold to inhabit. Chris announced that it was time for the younger and hardier souls to move into the caves.

Those remaining in the gym and the classrooms mourned the separation. People had grown accustomed to spending time together.

Before Aiden joined Z'ier and Ava to hike up to the caves, he knocked on the classroom that Lizzie had claimed as her shelter.

"Yes?" She sat at a desk, engrossed in drawing.

"Is that paper?" he asked, incredulous.

"Paper and pencils, courtesy of your Grandma Rosie."

He'd never seen paper or pencils used before. "Wow. We should introduce them to the kids."

Lizzie sighed but didn't lift her gaze from her work. "What do you need, Aiden?"

Irritated by her coldness, he said curtly, "I'd like to talk to you."

She chuckled. "About what? Your Great Band of Static?"

Aiden walked closer and examined her drawing. It depicted what seemed like a rotor attached to a shaft, which was connected to a lengthy tube.

"What are you drawing?"

"A generator."

In response to his raised eyebrows, Lizzie displayed the paper to him. "More specifically, a wind turbine. You see, once we make steel, we can create this. The wind turns the blades of the rotor, which spins a rotor shaft connected to a stator." She pointed to the tube. "The stator is basically a coil of wire housed inside an engine case. A magnet on the shaft spins within the stator and creates an alternating current or AC. The current travels along the heavy gauge wire through the case and into a regulator, which converts it to DC power. If we can create a power grid from a few turbines, we can power up DAPHNE."

She pursed her lips at the sketch. "Unfortunately, we need a way to start them up. If I could find a way to generate enough electricity to get the turbines operational..." Wearily, Lizzie regarded him. "What do you want?"

"I want to know why..." He paused. He'd intended to confront Lizzie, ask her why she continually resisted the idea of a Great Source, but a different question pressed against his lips. Aiden had learned from experience to release his words. Although the subject was off-topic, he believed Lizzie, the top scientist among them, would know the answer.

"Has kinetic energy technology been used for a purpose other than powering appliances with nanofibers?"

He expected Lizzie to criticize him for wasting her time but, instead, saw her face visibly pale. Then, she collected herself and returned to her drawing.

"Why would you ask me that?"

He told the truth. "The Great Source gave me the question."

Her pencil slipped, and the lead broke off. "Let me tell you something, Aiden. We're bringing DAPHNE back, and when she's fully operational, you and your Great Source will become nothing more than an indecipherable drawing on a cave wall."

"You didn't answer the question."

"About kinetic energy?" She smiled at her sketch. "I believe you've found the solution to my problem. I ought to thank you. We'll harness the electricity from every piece of nanofiber material we can find, then use that electricity to power up the wind turbines."

Aiden felt his pulse hike. The walls seemed to close around him, and he left the room as Lizzie called out, "I'll make sure to credit the Great Source for bringing back DAPHNE."

AIDEN FLED TO THE CAVE he would share with Z'ier and Ava. How could he have been so dumb? Why would the Great Source prod him to ask Lizzie about an energy source?

He threw himself into making his new home habitable to forget Lizzie's triumphant smile. He set up a potbelly stove and ran its pipe through a fist-sized hole in the cave roof. Then, he built a chimney cap above the hole to keep out the weather.

Meanwhile, Z'ier dragged in rugs and bedding, and Ava set up a little table with dishes and cups for an eating area. They soon transformed the small cave into a cozy room where Aiden could find peace, not only because he roomed with Ava but because one wall boasted ancient petroglyphs. The crude etchings appeared to represent a shamanic underworld or spirit realm filled with animals and gods and seemed custom-made for him.

WHEN IT WASN'T SNOWING, the cave-dwellers hiked down to the gym to eat at the communal table, visit with people, and collect more rations. Aiden took these opportunities to continue his dialogue about the Great Source. He needed to attract more followers before Lizzie got her wind turbines up and running.

By mid-December, the size of his audience had more than doubled. More and more people were interested in the hidden power of the mind.

One afternoon, when a cold sun made the snow glisten, Clyde and his crew of hunters dropped in. They sat among the crowd and sharpened their knives with stones. Even Lizzie dropped in. Aiden felt encouraged to see them.

"The biggest thing that prevents people from feeling positive is a lack of love." He glanced at Clyde and then at Lizzie. "To feel relevant and included opens the door to self-worth and the positive feelings we need. Remember, negativity separates us—drives the pixels apart. How can you connect with others if you're jealous of them? How can you value someone else if you can't even value yourself?" He met Oreanna's eyes. "You can always pretend, but acting won't help you."

"We must find a way to work through our issues, become more positive, and love each other, care for one another, so that each of us feels valuable. That's when we'll truly bond together and see the bigger picture. Then, we can all access the power waiting in our consciousness."

He glanced again at Lizzie, who sat stiffly in her chair and appeared to be counting all the attendees. *She looks worried,* he mused.

Vivica rested her multi-colored head against Tash's broad shoulder. "When you say love, do you mean romance?"

"I mean love on the deepest level. That can include friendship or the way you love your parents or child."

"But it can be romantic, right?" Vivica winked at him. "Like you and Ava."

A wave of hatred suddenly steamrolled over Aiden and made his skin prickle. His eyes roamed the audience and settled on Clyde. Blood ran from the warrior's hand – his knife must have slipped – but Clyde remained oblivious, fixated on Aiden. One of the hunters elbowed Clyde and gestured toward his wound. Clyde glanced at the cut and trudged out of the room.

Oreanna's desperate eyes followed him but then fell on her brother.

Stay, Aiden pleaded to her in silence. To his surprise, she remained seated. Lizzie, however, followed after Clyde.

CLYDE WALKED OVER TO where the cooks were making lunch and asked for a clean cloth. He tried to bind his hand with it, but the rag slipped.

Lizzie retrieved it for him. Taking his hand, she expertly bandaged his wound.

"A lot to take in." She indicated the crowd seated around Aiden.

Clyde sulked and said nothing.

"I didn't notice Ava in the group." Lizzie combed her dark curls with her fingers. "She must have stayed at the cave. Didn't you two used to be good friends?"

Clyde eyed her.

"Maybe you should try to reason with her. You know, Aiden used to see a psychiatrist, and he still needs one, but Ava seems to be a sensible young lady. She shouldn't associate herself with someone who might be psychotic. I wonder if you could make her see the light."

AVA SAT CROSS-LEGGED in her cave, facing a rock wall. She was alone because Z'ier had left to check on a pregnant woman in one of the other caves. Ava didn't mind. She wanted to be alone to create a special surprise for Aiden.

She shivered where she sat. The warmth from the stove didn't reach this far, but this wall was the only one, according to Aiden, not already adorned with drawings.

Her cold fingers felt on the ground for a piece of charcoal. Ava wanted to draw a message about kindness. She'd noticed how the more she opened her heart, the better the transmission signal she received from the Great Source. But how did one illustrate a positive feeling? She wiped her cold nose with her sleeve and lifted the charcoal to the stone. Steadying her hand, she asked the Great Source to send her an image symbolizing kindness.

Just then, a soft fur wrap draped over her shoulders. She smiled. Aiden always managed to anticipate her needs. As well, the Great Source had answered her. She would draw one person shivering with cold and another soul offering warmth.

Nuzzling her cheek against the fur, Ava murmured, "That feels nice. It's—"

Suddenly, she stiffened.

"Aiden?" she asked, knowing it wasn't him.

"No," Clyde replied.

Ava dropped the charcoal, jumped to her feet, and let the fur drop. "What are you doing here?"

A slight wisp of air swept by her as Clyde retrieved the fur.

"You're cold," he said. "Take it. I had my bitches scrape it extra clean for you."

"Your bitches..." Ava swallowed. "Get out, Clyde. I don't want any gifts from you."

"What's wrong?" he asked. "We used to be friends. Is it because you're blind?"

An angry vein throbbed in her neck. "Can you just leave?"

She heard a crunch on the reed mat as he approached her. Ava crossed her arms.

"What are you scared of?" Clyde asked. "Are you scared of me?"

"No."

She jumped a little as the fur draped over her once more, only this time, Clyde's hands remained firm on her shoulders. Ava's heart began to pound.

"I guess you're scared 'cuz you're blind."

Clyde's hands felt powerful on her shoulders, strong. Ava's body went rigid.

"I'm not scared. I just don't want you here. Please leave."

His grip on her tightened. "What's your problem?"

She jerked away, but her neck whiplashed as he yanked her back. She felt the fur wind fast around her, and Clyde crushed her in his big arms. Ava's body, at odds with itself, welcomed the warmth but shook with panic. She quickly visualized something scary—falling into a deep hole and screaming as she hurtled downward. *Aiden!*

"Let go of me, Clyde!" She smelled animal blood on him and felt his breath hot on her face. She visualized him squeezing the life from her. *Aiden, I'm in trouble!*

"Is it Baylor?" Clyde hissed in her ear. "What the hell, Ava? Why would you lower yourself?"

"Get out of here!"

"Baylor's a wimp," he said. "A pussy. I know you're scared, but who do you think can protect you better? Aiden? He won't even squish a bug."

"Leave me alone." She struggled to free herself.

Ava felt Clyde's lips crush against hers, and she angled her face away. "Stop it!"

He forcibly pressed his lips against hers again, but she retaliated by biting him. He recoiled slightly, allowing her to free her leg, and she promptly delivered a powerful kick. Clyde's grip on her weakened, but her momentary sense of satisfaction turned into searing pain as his fist struck her stomach, leaving her breathless and unable to speak.

Then, he was on her. She grabbed his hair and pinched his skin. He felt heavy, like a pile of rocks, and she couldn't push him off. She could barely breathe. Ava managed to shove a knee into his groin, and Clyde howled. She quickly crawled away, but he grabbed her foot and dragged her back under him.

Then, a refreshing energy flooded the cave. Clyde grunted in pain, and suddenly, Ava was free. She slid away but heard a violent scuffle. The scuffling stopped, and Clyde hissed, "I'm gonna kill you, Baylor."

A crash rang out as the table and its dishes overturned. Ava heard Aiden gasp.

"Leave him alone, Clyde!" She tottered to her feet and tried to discern where they were fighting. If only she could see. The two young men kept darting around. Ava lunged in the direction of smacks and punches but tripped over the table and went down on a rock.

Holding her knee, she shouted, "Clyde, stay away from him!"

All at once, the granite floor seemed to buzz beneath her. She could swear static electricity lifted the hair on her head. The cave walls trembled, and Ava's heart pounded harder. Was it an earthquake? Then, a loud crack sounded, followed by a CLUNK. She felt a whoosh of air as a body thudded to the ground beside her. She knew Clyde lay there. She could smell his musky scent.

Everything went quiet. A rivulet of wetness meandered from Ava's knee to her ankle.

"Aiden?" She tried to get a bead on where he stood.

All at once, the air surrounding her lightened, and she melted to feel his arms wrap around her.

"I'm sorry." His words sounded slurred. "I'm here."

Her fingers explored his face, his swollen lips, and the knob on his forehead.

"You're hurt."

"I'm fine, but your leg is bleeding." He disappeared momentarily, and when he returned, she felt a cloth pressed against her cut.

Another person with a heavy tread burst into the cave. "You guys okay?" It was Tash. "Wow. Look at the meathead. He's out cold."

Ava heard the ax slide into its sheath as Tash paused over Clyde's body. "I knew something bad was going down when you ran out like that, Aiden."

Tash groaned as he hoisted the unconscious man on his shoulders.

"I'd better get Mr. Personality out of here," he said. "He's gonna be one angry shitbag when he wakes up."

Tash's heavy footsteps departed, and Ava rested her head against Aiden's chest. "You came. You heard."

She felt him nod and press his body against hers. She wished they could meld beyond the barrier of their flesh.

CHAPTER 51

Clyde suffered a concussion and a bruised ego. No one had ever gotten the better of the famed hunter, but now everyone could see that Aiden, the Nature Boy, had bested him. It was humiliating.

He'd had Aiden by the throat! He was about to snap that scrawny neck, but then the hairs stood up on his arms, and goosebumps rippled over his body. The air seemed to sizzle and grow hot, and, just like that, a piece of rock broke off from the cave roof and hit him on the head.

As he stood before Chris and the rest of the townsfolk at a special meeting, Clyde still couldn't believe what happened.

"You need to learn to respect others," Chris told him, "and keep your hands to yourself."

Clyde's lips remained in a tight, thin line. He wanted to snap the grid-skipper's neck, too.

His dad stood next to him, sober—surprisingly.

"What about Baylor?" Mr. Parrish asked. "He hit my son with a rock."

"Aiden was defending himself," Doug yelled. "Ava is his witness."

"How can she testify? She's blind!"

"She says Clyde tried to attack her."

Mr. Parrish waved a dismissive hand in the air. "She's lying. My son is a hero. He feeds all of you. That girl does nothing but spout off fairytales."

"Shut up, you drunk," Jill yelled from her seat. "I wish I'd been there. I'd have dropped a dozen rocks on your son's skull."

Mr. Parrish gave her a smug grin. "That's because you're a psycho-bitch."

Doug shook his fist at the man. "Don't you dare call my—"

"Good God, be quiet, all of you." Chris put his head in his hands for a moment and then looked at Clyde. "Taking advantage of people is not heroic. Attempting rape is criminal."

"Nothing happened." Mr. Parrish put an uncharacteristic arm around Clyde. "It was my son who got hurt. Look at him. He could have died."

Chris addressed Clyde. "You will scrape two hides as punishment for both the attack and to see what tough work your 'bitches' perform."

"No way, old man," Clyde said.

"Then you can sit in a classroom that Doug has outfitted with bars. Which would you rather do? You have to take responsibility for your actions, Clyde, or you won't change."

"Who says I want to change? If you try and punish me, I won't hunt."

"Fine," Chris tossed off. "Then, our other hunters will get a lot of praise this season while you feel sorry for yourself behind bars."

CLYDE SCRAPED THE TWO hides in the school's abandoned garage. Chris appointed Mac to make sure he did the job. Fury sizzled in Clyde's broad chest as he toiled. When he was nearly finished, Mac grew too cold to stay and assured Clyde he'd give Chris a good report.

When the scudder left, Oreanna showed up with a bowl of steaming stew and acorn-meal crackers.

"It's freezing outside." She handed Clyde the meal and shivered. "I ran all the way to make sure you got it hot." She hugged herself and stamped her feet.

Clyde narrowed his eyes at her over the bowl. "How did Aiden know? How did he know I was up at the cave with Ava?"

Oreanna froze and regarded him with fear.

"You followed me, didn't you?" His breath came out in a fog. "You followed me to the cave, then came back and told him where I was."

"I didn't. I swear." She wrung her gloved hands. "I was at the meeting the whole time. Aiden quit talking all of a sudden and bolted out of there."

"You're lying!" He threw the bowl at the wall and began pacing like a wild animal. "You told him. I know it. You're not on my side. You're nothing but a fat stupid cow."

Oreanna blinked back tears. "Don't say that. Please."

"Clean that shit up!" He pointed to the mess of food and broken ceramic shards. "Clean it up before I slaughter you like the cow you are!" Clyde kicked the half-scraped hide on the floor.

Oreanna obeyed him as he knew she would. He watched her clean as she choked on her sobs. A shadow fell from the doorway, and he glimpsed Dr. Lizzie standing there, bundled up in rabbit fur.

Grabbing Oreanna's arm, he steered her to the exit and pushed her into the snow. "Get out of here. You make me sick."

Oreanna cried into the broken dishes as she walked away. Lizzie, meanwhile, slipped inside the garage. "What happened to her?"

Clyde returned to scraping the hide. "What do you want?"

"I want to say I can't understand why they'd treat you this way."

"Everyone is starting to believe Nature Boy's mystical bullshit. Ava is completely lost."

"You can get her back, Clyde. She'll come back when you reclaim your status as the King of Sierrawood."

He paused, letting the word sink in... *King*. Then, he shook his head. "Ava will never leave Baylor."

"She'd be with you if Aiden wasn't here."

Clyde narrowed his eyes at Lizzie.

"I can help you devise a plan to get rid of him."

CHAPTER 52

One by one, the days of winter passed. When the sun shone, the young people emerged from their caves and used old wallscreens to go sledding. If the snow fell, they played rounds of Senet, an ancient Egyptian game. The Egyptians had used small animal bones as tokens. The population of Sierrawood used discarded microchips.

Sometimes, the young people played "contemplation," where they sat quietly and practiced something they'd read in a psychology book called "free association." They'd make notes of their thoughts and then share them with each other. Pete once marveled at how the diverse array of trees in the forest seemed to coexist in harmony. Aiden voiced his wish that the residents of the roundhouse would similarly see themselves as unified under one roof.

With the hunting season over, Clyde hung out a lot with Lizzie, which struck Aiden as odd. After all, she was smart and refined, and Clyde was a brute. Whenever Aiden focused on the two of them, he read nothing from Lizzie as usual, but when he read Clyde, he discerned the two were hatching some plot. Aiden couldn't pick up on their exact plan, but alarm bells clanged in his head each time he studied Clyde, and a pit grew in his stomach.

He decided to speak to his sister about it. Oreanna roomed in a cave with a few hunters who had grown to appreciate her gemstones, believing the trinkets brought them luck. On Ori's side of the cave, crystals hung on strings and caught the winter sunlight entering through holes in the roof. The sparkling strands spun and threw prisms of colored light on the rock walls.

Aiden picked up a piece of white quartz. "What's this supposed to do?"

"Quartz amplifies energy. It's used to promote harmony and emotional balance."

He held it out to her. "Why don't you use it then?"

Her cheeks flushed, but she said nothing.

"Why are you putting up with Clyde? You're better than him, Ori. Don't you see that?"

"Go away, Aiden."

"He may seriously hurt you. He could even kill you."

"Oh, no." She shook her head. "He would never do that."

"He's up to something. I just don't know what." Aiden swept his hand over her collection of crystals and minerals. "These will not protect you from him." His hand paused over a spent shell casing glinting among the rocks.

He eyed his sister.

Oreanna moved over to him and folded his fingers over the piece of quartz. "Keep it. Amplify the energy you already have." She glanced at the empty casing. "I promise to protect myself."

THE COMMUNITY'S CAREFUL preparation for the winter paid off. Although the cooks carefully rationed the supplies, no one went hungry. Hope returned to the roundhouse, and the conversation at the communal table gradually turned to plans for spring.

As they sat eating venison stew, Lizzie ordered everyone to donate their nanofiber clothing or blankets.

"The nanowires woven into the material are piezoelectric, which means they generate an electric current when subjected to mechanical stress. We can capture tiny amounts of that current and transfer it to old robot batteries. The charge may be enough to start the turbines I'm designing."

Chris traded a worried look with Aiden. "And, these turbines will generate enough electricity to power DAPHNE?"

"They should," she told him. "The good news is, once DAPHNE is up and running, she'll create the means to repair herself."

Aiden didn't welcome the 'good news' and noticed other individuals wincing at the mention of DAPHNE. Life without Great Intelligence no longer scared them, which signaled great progress, in his opinion.

"Maybe we don't need DAPHNE," Aerta dared to say.

"Are you insane?" one of Lizzie's engineers asked. "Do you want to continue living in a gym?"

"Don't you miss a supermarket?"

"Running water!"

"Washing machines!"

"Video games!"

"Don't you ever want to travel again?" someone asked.

Grandma Rosie shrugged. "People used to travel before DAPHNE."

"How? With a horse and carriage?"

"Give me an air taxi any day!"

Aiden grew bored listening to their complaints. He'd heard them many times. He settled his gaze on Clyde, who sat directly across from him. Clyde was careful not to look at Ava, who sat beside Aiden. Now and then, Clyde met Aiden's eye, but his face remained impassive, not resentful at all. Something was up. Aiden sensed Clyde had couched his usual aggression under a foamy, bland sort of patience. The hunter was waiting for something, but what?

Oreanna huddled like a mouse next to Clyde and offered him a dazzling smile whenever he happened to glance at her. Clyde regarded her with the same dull expression.

"We can dream of the day DAPHNE returns," Feinstein said, "but in the meantime, who wants to join me as a farmer? I'll be searching for seedlings when the snow melts. We won't have a supermarket, but we might have wheat and corn."

Doug chimed in with talk about the impending salmon run and offered to give fishing lessons.

Govind raised his hand. "I've never been athletic, but I'd like to try fishing."

Tash hunkered over his bowl of stew. He met Aiden's eye, and Aiden sensed something serious on his friend's mind. Tash pulled his eyes from Aiden's and said, "I read about the Roman aqueducts, and I've designed a plan for a canal that will divert the river and flow water practically right to this door."

The idea of accessible, fresh water delighted the gym-dwellers. Aiden, however, stared at Tash. "Just how much water do you plan on diverting?"

Tash wouldn't look in his direction. "As much as it takes to support us."

L'Eren bounced Kimber on her lap and raised her hand. "Why do we need to build an aqueduct if DAPHNE is powering up?"

"We don't know when that'll be," Mac told her, "and I'm sick of hauling buckets of water around. If Tash has a way of bringing water to us, then I say let's go for it."

The rest of them murmured their agreement. Aiden chewed on the side of his mouth and waited for Tash to look at him. Tash didn't.

Pete Farmington politely raised his hand. "I have an announcement. Before it snowed, I did some hiking in the hills and found a bunch of gray rocks run through with red. I collected some and showed them to Oreanna who told me I'd discovered iron ore." He paused. "What's iron ore?"

Feinstein pushed away his plate and lit his pipe. The scent of cherry mixed with the aroma of cooked meat. "Iron ore is an important mineral because it can produce steel, a metal with top strength and durability. Did you find your ore at the surface or did you have to dig deep?"

"It was right on the ground."

"Then, we can easily mine it."

"That's great news," Lizzie said, "We can build a smelter to turn the ore into steel for the turbines."

Doug wiped his mouth with a cloth napkin. "Why not use my forge?"

"Smelters are much more powerful."

Mr. Parrish asked, "Tash, besides an aqueduct, can you build us a smelter on the river?"

Aiden narrowed his eyes at Clyde's father. Apparently, Mr. Parrish had quit drinking and sat at the table like a civilized soul, the epitome of calm. Aiden knew he'd joined Lizzie's team, and perhaps she'd taught him manners as well as technical knowledge. The man's transformation should have cheered Aiden, except he sensed a negative agenda behind it.

Lizzie rested her elbows on the table. "The river water will power the smelter. First, we'll make charcoal in Doug's forge. Charcoal has carbon. When we combine the carbon with oxygen and create carbon dioxide and carbon monoxide, we'll have enough heat to melt the ore."

"Wait a minute." Aiden held up a palm. "Are you saying you're going to build something on the river that releases carbon monoxide? Your smelter will poison the water."

Feinstein nodded as he puffed on his pipe. "Heavy metals, such as zinc, manganese, and aluminum will definitely leach into the river."

"During the the gold rush of the 1800's," Chris added, "mining and the pollutants from smelters nearly killed off all the salmon to the point of extinction."

Govind pushed his chair away from the table and took Kimber from L'Eren. "However we progress, we should do it responsibly, with an eye for preserving the environment."

"But I'm sick of living like an animal," Mr. Parrish said in a tone reminiscent of his former self. "We're gonna build that smelter. We're gonna make steel into turbines that will rise up and give DAPHNE power again."

THAT NIGHT, WHEN AIDEN heard Z'ier snoring, he crept past the coals glowing cozily in the stove and climbed into Ava's bed.

"We're running out of time," he whispered as she held him. "You heard them at dinner. We can't agree on anything. How can we bond and access the Great Source if we're divided?"

Ava's skin looked rosy in the firelight. "Maybe bonding doesn't necessarily mean to agree but to care about one another."

"I don't get what you mean."

"Well, you disagree with your mom, but you still love her, right?"

Aiden nodded.

"Then, that's it. We may not think alike, but we can respect another person's right to an opinion because we care about them. They're a family member to us. Think of the weather. There's rain, snow, wind and sunshine. They all act differently, but we need each weather condition because they keep this planet alive."

Aiden mused over that and then gently kissed her lips. "Don't ever say you're blind."

He gently untied the shirtsleeve covering her eyescreens. She pulled him closer, and they held each other, warm and content. Above their heads, on the cave's ceiling, Aiden had taped Ava's rainbow poster. She couldn't see it but liked knowing it was there.

Aiden fingered a lock of her hair as he gazed up at the faded rainbow arching over the cityscape. "There's a Native American story I read about good versus evil, how good wins with the power of the 'rainbow people.' They say a day will come when people bond together in love and move over the Earth like a great Whirling Rainbow." He sighed. "Do you think that day could ever come? Lizzie has fought that idea from day one. She says we need DAPHNE to manage us."

"I think the Great Source terrifies her."

"Why would it?"

"Maybe she doesn't understand it."

Aiden considered that. "Chris thinks she's a sociopath. Did you know she was once married?" He snorted. "I can see why her ex divorced her."

"Lizzie was married?"

"Yeah, Feinstein told me her real name is Lizzie Vasquez."

"Vasquez?" Ava sat up on her elbows. "Is she related to Martin Vasquez?"

"Who?"

"The doctor who donated his brain."

Aiden froze. Lizzie... Elizabeth. " Ava, she's Beth."

Z'ier moaned, turned over in her sleep, and the two lovers hunkered down and lay still.

Ava whispered, "Martin Vasquez's dying thought was, 'I found what Beth is searching for,' and his last memory was of a little girl running into his arms. Lizzie is the little girl."

Aiden's nightmares, mind-drifts, and memories flooded him all at once. *Please let Beth know I discovered it. I found what she is searching for...*

"Vasquez donated his brain," he said. "He must have known a school would dissect it, possibly even resurrect his consciousness. Do you think he hoped his message would get through to Beth?"

"Maybe," Ava whispered. "You need to ask Lizzie what she's been searching for."

CHAPTER 53

"I want to talk to you about Dr. Martin Vasquez."

Aiden felt satisfied to observe Lizzie freeze in spite of the blazing fire. He dropped casually into the chair next to her and asked, "Martin was your father, right?"

She nodded. Her eyes reflected the flames.

"What are you searching for, Beth?"

Lizzie's brows knitted together in confusion. "How do you...? My father is dead."

"Your father donated his brain to science. My class dissected it and heard his dying thought." Ashamed of his harshness, Aiden added, "I'm sorry if that upsets you."

"I'm not upset. My father was a gifted scientist and engineer. Why wouldn't he donate his brain?" She paused. "What was his dying thought?"

"He found what you've been searching for."

Lizzie looked at him but said nothing.

"What is it? What are you searching for, Elizabeth?"

"I'm not Elizabeth."

"Lizzie, Beth, whatever you call yourself, what is it you want?"

She cracked a smile, which reminded Aiden of Dr. Clarence's eerie, out-of-place grin at their long-ago session.

Aiden bristled at her amusement. "Don't you want to hear more?"

"All right. What did he find out?"

"Unfortunately, he died before he could finish the thought."

The rush of breath that escaped Lizzie was the closest thing to a genuine emotion Aiden had ever witnessed coming from her. "He left a last memory though. Maybe it will help."

"What did he remember?"

"A dark-haired toddler. A little girl."

"A little girl," Lizzie repeated as she contemplated the fire.

"Yes. Running into his arms. He kissed the top of her head. It's clear that he loved her—you. Does it mean anything?"

Lizzie stiffened, transforming into the ice queen once again. "No."

"What were you searching for?"

"It doesn't matter now."

He could almost see the sheets of ice on her person. He rose from his seat to leave, but halfway to standing, he stopped. Bold graffiti tagged one wall of the gym. The big block letters spelled out: SOLVE THE MYSTERY. LET BETH KNOW I DISCOVERED IT. YOUR SURVIVAL DEPENDS ON IT.

Aiden blinked, and the words disappeared.

CHAPTER 54

Cold, clear water gushed into the rivers as the snow melted. The streams gurgled in happy acceptance and fed the lake. Spring turned the meadow lime green, and the first wildflowers raised their colorful heads. Green shoots appeared on the dark, moist earth and opened their arms toward the sun. The animals emerged from their burrows and stretched in the warm air.

The gatherers again took to foraging among the trees. Aiden, Ava, Tash, and Vivica went on romantic walks on trails bordered by pale yellow irises, clusters of red trilliums, golden monkeyflowers, and pink lilies.

Aiden pinched off the curling tops of the bracken fiddlehead, named for the young shoots that curled like the head of a green fiddle. He unfolded the top of one, gently rubbed off the hair, and handed it to Ava, who tasted it and declared it had a raw, nutty flavor. Vivica picked Blue Dicks, whose stalks and purple-blue flowers tasted like a cucumber, and nasturtium leaves, which had a spicy flavor. Aiden pulled blossoms off the western Red Bud, which tasted like citrus, and pinched off wild mustard to make a paste out of the seeds.

At the clearing near the lake, Feinstein discovered wheat and barley seedlings. He wasted no time in clearing a space to cultivate the crops. He even consigned Doug to build him a plow because, he said, the Age of Agriculture had dawned on Sierrawood.

"Maybe by next fall," he joked to Tash, "I can fertilize my crops with you-know-what."

"Don't remind me of the compost." Tash grinned and shook his head. "Designing those toilets was not a high point in my career."

Govind learned how to fish from Doug and encouraged former Depressionists to take up the sport. The new group of anglers caught the spring-run Chinook salmon, which became an important food source. Govind enjoyed being the community's new hero. Enthusiastic about his new role, he made fishing poles, weirs, dip nets, and spears. The cooks, delighted at the catch, smoked the fish or dried it in the sun to preserve it for future meals.

Meanwhile, Tash and his construction crew built the canal. Tash used gravity to channel water downhill through pipes reinforced with stone blocks. As the water gained momentum, it would gush up an arched bridge and flow into a reservoir. Tash could divert the water from the manmade pool to various locales around the high school. He also designed plans for a runoff channel to carry water to Feinstein's farm to irrigate the new crops. Feinstein invented a water filter using charcoal, gravel, and sand that Tash could insert into the reservoir's main pipe. This ensured the stream water would be safe for drinking.

Tash now roomed with Vivica, but he got so busy with his projects he rarely saw his friends. So, one April afternoon, he was happy to see Aiden approach the worksite with a large picnic basket. Aiden had brought lunch for the whole crew. The two young men sat under the shade of the half-built bridge, ate a salmon salad, and viewed Tash's construction plans.

"I'm impressed," Aiden said as he sifted through the papers.

Tash set his fork down. "I'm building the smelter, but it won't be on the riverbank. I'll channel the water toward it. It's a small smelter, so it won't need much."

Aiden swallowed in discomfort. "Why are you helping Lizzie bring DAPHNE back, Tash? You've been on my side from the start, and you know Lizzie is against our beliefs."

"Why can't we have both? Why do we have to choose sides?" Tash took a deep breath and released it slowly. "I'm running out of meds, Aiden. I don't want to die. I want to marry Viv and have kids, and I don't want them to inherit this disease."

Aiden nodded. He understood.

"There's nothing wrong with progress," Tash told him. "We don't have to disappear under DAPHNE. You can keep teaching us, and we'll make progress toward the Great Source. Can't we have both?"

Aiden looked away and twisted his hands. He didn't think so.

"I promise to work with the natural topography of the land," Tash assured him. "I'll even paint the smelter green so it blends in with the background. You won't even know it's there."

"Are you going to paint it white when it snows?"

Tash's face tightened until he saw Aiden grin.

IN EARLY MAY, THE FIRST wave of water filled a drinking fountain built outside the gym. Chris held a groundbreaking ceremony where everybody dipped in a glass to enjoy their first taste of running water since the blackout. Vivica and her friends brought tables outside and decorated them with wildflowers to celebrate. The cooks brought out food so everyone could eat under the fresh sunshine.

Now that the snow was melting, Pete Farmington assembled a group of miners, and they took to the hills to mine iron ore with shovels, picks, hammers, and hoes. They used buckets to haul the ore to the surface. Doug presented him with a wheelbarrow, which gave one man the transporting power of two.

The physical labor shed pounds off Pete's body, and he grew into a robust and sinewy fellow with calloused but gentle hands. The ore he mined went straight to Doug, who worked with it in the new smelter. As Lizzie promised, the steel was stronger than any metal Doug had previously produced.

Lizzie assigned five new blacksmiths to Doug. The team went to work creating two long towers and six massive blades.

Pete invited Oreanna to hike the mountains with him, with the excuse that she'd help him identify more iron ore or copper. Oreanna brought along her geology books, and the two would identify stones, gems, and crystals. Pete made up a nickname for the two of them: Rockers. Sometimes, he reached for her hand. Once in a while, she'd let him take it.

The community began to unite like a family. As Ava predicted, they still squabbled, but their arguments didn't break the connection. Their love and respect lay on a more permanent level of their psyches.

Whenever someone completed another person's sentence, which happened more and more, the duo would burst into laughter, only to want the moment to happen again. Some individuals even managed to send their loved ones thoughts and feelings.

The more the people experienced these events, the stronger they bonded. Aiden could almost envision a roundhouse no longer comprised of individuals but housing one body, a coalition pulsing with energy, a Lifespark. As Lizzie's wind turbine would eventually do with DAPHNE, the psychic energy of Sierrawood's population began powering up the Great Source. Words like "telepathy" and "spiritual guides" became more commonplace and accepted.

Of course, Aiden knew Lizzie didn't welcome these developments, so it surprised him one May morning when she told him she'd done him a special favor.

"Now, that we have the aqueduct," she said, "we don't need to crowd the lake. I understand you used to enjoy the clearing there, so I asked my team to break down all those rickety shelters and clotheslines and clean up the place for you."

"Why would you do that for me?"

"Let's call it a truce. Go visit. I think you'll like what you see."

Aiden asked Ava to join him, and he led her into the forest. Lizzie had told the truth. The clearing lay before him in sun-washed splendor, free of trash and people.

He and Ava sat on a fallen log to gaze at the sparkling lake, and tranquility spread through him. Soon, his limbs began to feel lighter, and his eyes closed.

I'm in the forest and can see the ultraviolet spectrum as Ava once did. The flowers sparkle like holiday lights, and King Jay flutters around me with his royal blue feathers. The green on each leaf appears rich and velvety. I reach out to touch one and am instantly transported into it. I glide along the delicate veins of the leaf, hitching a ride on the chlorophyll, the pigment that captures light energy. I reach the stem and feel the warm sunlight. I'm part of the life-giving process. Never have I felt so much a part of the earth. I spring out of the leaf and see, to my joy, Grandpa Harry.

Only, he's not smiling."Rebel, do you see?" Grandpa steps aside to reveal a tree. My body is impaled to the trunk by a spear.

Aiden opened his eyes. Ava whirled around to face him.

"I see it."

She angled her head, listening. Aiden could hear nothing but the sound of his harsh breath.

Ava's body suddenly tensed. "Someone's coming," she whispered and then sent the thought, *someone dangerous.*

The two jumped to their feet.

Too late. The danger is here. Hide.

Aiden steered Ava to a bay laurel bush. She crouched low under the leaves. There wasn't space enough for him, so he darted toward a nearby pine. He peeked around the trunk and gasped to see Clyde, buff, shirtless, with his face twisted in dumb fury.

Clyde held his spear aloft with the stone tip poised to strike. His bushy brows furrowed as he scanned the forest for a hint of movement. Aiden shivered, not from cold but from fear. He knew the sharp point of the spear was meant for him.

A MIXTURE OF HOT SOAP poured from a pitcher that Jill held. She filled molds in the shape of flowers, which Doug had crafted for her out of metal. The couple often gave each other little gifts these days. Jill had made him a nice-smelling cologne for their anniversary, and he made these molds.

Using a sifter to sprinkle herbs on top of the soap, she had to smile. Jill hated to admit it, but her bond with her husband had deepened since the blackout. All these little kindnesses between them made her realize how much she loved him. Before, she'd hardly given their relationship much –

A thunderbolt of fear suddenly split Jill's body. She dropped the sifter and put a hand to her quaking heart. Leaning against the counter, she surveyed the cafeteria but saw nothing amiss. Still, her heart continued to race, and Jill grew breathless as she tried to identify the source of her fear.

CLYDE PASSED SO CLOSE that if Aiden dared to look, he'd see the sweat beading on the hunter's chest. The hunter... Stalking his prey. Aiden viewed his weaponless hands and scanned the ground for a rock, anything he could use for defense. If Clyde found Ava first...

Aiden took quiet, deep breaths to calm down. If he became quiet, he could warn Ava to stay put. *Don't come out,* he begged silently.

Then, the stout footsteps of his aggressor faded. Aiden waited until he heard no sound and then cupped his hands against his mouth to call Ava with their birdsong code. The "Woo-Woot" nearly escaped his lips when he experienced the profoundest sense of déjà vu.

The spear hurtles toward my chest... What he'd dismissed as a long-ago daydream had been a vision. Precognition.

Aiden closed his eyes and visualized the buck approaching Ava with its beautiful set of antlers. He imagined the tenderness she felt, holding out acorns to her beloved friend. *Stay hidden, Ava. Stay with the buck, and do not move. Clyde is still here. He never left.*

Aiden dared to peer around the corner and glimpsed Clyde plastered against a nearby tree with the spear, aimed high and ready. A rustling sound in the nearby brush turned both their heads. With Clyde distracted, Aiden burst from his hiding place and ran toward him.

Clyde threw the spear, but Aiden had already closed in, and the lethal point missed him. He knocked Clyde to the ground, and the two kicked up dust as they struggled. Clyde's hands found Aiden's throat and squeezed. Aiden's scrabbling fingers found a nearby rock, and he raised the stone into the air. Before he could bring it down, a loud CLICK froze them both.

Oreanna stood over them, aiming Grandpa Harry's antique gun at Clyde. The weapon shook in her hands.

Clyde, still gripping Aiden's throat, sneered up at the girl. "You don't have the guts."

Jill stepped up, took the weapon from her daughter, and promptly shot a pine cone off a nearby tree. She pressed the barrel of the gun against Clyde's neck and said, "I have the guts. Now, let go of my son."

CHAPTER 55

The community locked Clyde into the classroom with a barred window built into the door. Mr. Parrish demanded a trial for his son, who claimed he was innocent.

"He was hunting." Mr. Parrish, playing the role of defense attorney, addressed the assembly at the nightly fireside meeting. "It's hunting season. Clyde didn't mean to throw his spear at Aiden. He saw a deer, and Aiden ran out of nowhere and attacked him. Clyde didn't even know Ava and Aiden were there."

Aiden fumed as he listened. "Lizzie and Clyde have been planning my death for weeks," he said.

Protests ran through the onlookers.

"It's true." Aiden pointed at Lizzie. "She's the one who told me to go into the clearing."

"You always go there," Parrish said. "Why were you hiding anyhow? It's hunting season." He pointed at Oreanna. "Tell them, Ori. Tell them that when you arrived, Ava was still hiding under a bush."

Aiden felt his sister's pain. She seemed unable to look at her first love and kept her gaze rooted to the floor.

"Ava was hiding because she was scared," Oreanna whispered.

Chris gently asked, "Did you see a deer by chance?"

"Oh, come on!" Mr. Parrish bellowed. "The deer was long gone by then."

Lizzie stood up. "Unless this assembly can prove that Clyde meant to throw his spear at Aiden, you have to let him go."

Chris shook his head. "Clyde has motivation, Lizzie. This isn't the first time he's attacked Ava and Aiden."

"He was choking my son," Jill told them.

Parrish pushed his face in hers. "He was defending himself! What were you doing there anyhow *with a working gun*? That's three Baylors with a gun against one Parrish with a spear."

Jill gave Aiden a tender look. "Call it a mother's intuition."

The assembly took a vote and proclaimed Clyde innocent of wrongdoing. Aiden felt he was to blame for their decision because he continually promoted positive attitudes. Perhaps the people didn't feel right about punishing Sierrawood's great hunter. After all, he gave them food.

Oreanna's appearance with the gun and Jill's skill with it didn't help their case. However, Aiden felt a solid connection with his mother that he'd never before experienced, and that almost made the whole ugly affair worth it.

Clyde went free, but many gym-dwellers no longer trusted him, not even loyal Pete or Busty Trina. Even his crew of hunters drew back from him.

"When DAPHNE returns," Aiden told the hunters during a sermon, "You'll have the metaverse again, but what will make you feel more relevant? Ranking high in games taking place in a fake world or bringing home game vital to your community's survival?"

Since Clyde could no longer depend on the hunters to back him up, he and his father joined Lizzie's team and spent their days building the wind turbines.

CHAPTER 56

The heat stirred up the scents of the forest once again. Nearly a year had passed since the blackout, and the engineers reported to Lizzie that they had successfully rewired many of the servers needed to run DAPHNE. Wires extended from a line of robots that held the charge captured by nanofiber clothing. The wires led toward the foundations of the wind turbines.

The entire population of Sierrawood congregated near DAPHNE's bunker to witness the raising of the great steel towers. The construction workers used a system of pulleys to hoist up the first. Aiden's spirits fell as the turbine rose toward the heavens.

Lizzie stepped up beside him. "One man can't change the path of human evolution, Aiden. From the time your proverbial Adam and Eve ate the fruit from the tree of knowledge, you were destined to arrive here."

The shadow of the tower fell upon his face.

"You should be happy," she said. "DAPHNE will mass produce Tash's medicine and make Ava see again."

"Grandma Rosie made a serum out of ceanothus leaves that's helping Tash, and Ava has more sight than all of us put together."

"Tash could still die, and Ava is blind. Voodoo won't help either of them."

Aiden rolled his eyes and faced her. "Why do you resent the Great Source, Lizzie?"

The workers began raising the second turbine.

She crossed her arms as she observed its ascent. "I don't resent the Great Source. I've been searching for the secret to consciousness my whole life."

Aiden's mouth fell open. "That's what you've been searching for? Why would you fight me when we were trying to find the same thing?"

She didn't answer.

Aiden studied her. "I guess you hoped you'd find consciousness in a neat little cellular package you could feed to DAPHNE. That's what you want it for, right? To make DAPHNE human?"

"No. *I* wanted a consciousness."

Aiden dismissed her with a wave. "Everyone has a consciousness."

He paused, reflecting on Martin Vasquez's final memory: the affection he displayed as he swept up the little girl in his arms.

"Here's what you don't get, Lizzie. Your father wanted to tell you that he loved you, that the key to human consciousness is not found here." He pointed to Lizzie's head. "It's found here." He placed his finger on her heart. "All you had to do was open your heart. The opening is the only path that will lead you to the Great Source."

She remained mute, and her silence baffled him. *What is it?* Aiden looked her up and down. *What is it about her I can't see?*

One of the workers suddenly cried out as he lost his grip on the tether supporting the giant pole. The rope sizzled out of his hands and snapped upwards.

"Watch out!" Govind shouted.

"Get hold of that rope!" Tash shouted as the other workers struggled to hold onto their lines.

People scattered as the pole swayed dangerously above them. A second rope snapped, and the recoil hit a worker's face. He screamed and covered his eyes. The tall, heavy pole tipped over amid panicked cries and crashed to the ground with an earth-shaking thud. The turbine's parts crashed into pieces that flew into the crowd.

One steel shard sliced into Lizzie's right thigh, nearly severing her leg. She collapsed without a sound and lay still. Aiden and the others quickly surrounded her in the rising dust.

Govind knelt down and pressed his hand over the spurting blood. "It hit an artery."

Aiden quickly took off his shirt and twisted it to make a tourniquet.

Chris rushed over and cradled Lizzie's head. "Is she alive?"

"She's breathing." Govind carefully touched the protruding metal piece. "We'd better get her back to the roundhouse and fast."

All at once, Lizzie sat up and blinked. She looked at Chris, who gaped at her.

"Dr. Lizzie, you'd better not move."

Her eyes dropped to her injured leg. Calmly, she pulled out the shard, which made the wound gush even more.

"Stop!" Jill stripped off her jacket and ran forward. She pressed the material against the horrible wound. "You have to keep still."

Lizzie pulled the shirt from Aiden's stunned hands. "Thanks," she said, expertly tying a tourniquet above the cut. In the gaping wound, Lizzie's bone glinted a metallic blue in the sunlight.

Chris lurched to his feet. "She's a damn cyborg!"

The circle of onlookers quickly backed away and stared at Lizzie.

"That's impossible." Govind exhaled in shock. "She wouldn't bleed."

Lizzie finished tying the knot and stood up.

Jill lifted a trembling finger. "Look at her! She's not human!"

"I am absolutely human, Jill." Lizzie tested her injured leg. "Your father, Harry, was correct when he said the newer versions of his Smart Legs would run on kinetic energy. My father, Martin Vasquez, was a pioneer of that technology. He had DAPHNE invent a non-organic brain for me that works independently of her and is powered by my own movement." She looked over at Aiden. "Kinetic energy. You asked."

He gulped in astonishment.

Govind put a flustered hand on his head. "You have a non-organic brain?"

The blood on Lizzie's leg began to coagulate, and the cut flesh began to knit together. A murmur ran through the crowd as people pointed and spoke in shocked whispers.

"All the biometric data of humans has been uploaded to my brain," she said. "My neurons talk to each other simultaneously, just like yours do, but I can process information like an AGI. Every organ in my body is a superior replica of a human organ." She regarded her wound. "You see? Already, I'm starting to heal."

Ava clutched Aiden's arm to approach Lizzie. "But the little girl in your dad's memory... If you're made up of artificial parts, h-how could you possibly grow into a woman?"

"The little girl you refer to was my creator's human child. Her name was Elizabeth. She died quite young, and Martin mourned that he'd never see her grow up. So, he and DAPHNE created me from her cloned cells. Some of me *can* grow, Ava, like my hair and nails."

Lizzie addressed the stunned crowd. "I am an evolutionary divergence, a seamless mesh of machinery and humanity. A superior human being. The Next Gen Human."

Aiden paled. Grandpa Harry's voice echoed in his head. *She's perfect.* Haunted green eyes surfaced in his memory. *Almost too perfect.*

"Professor Yang," he whispered.

Lizzie's superior hearing caught his words. "There were those in the scientific community that learned of our existence. They needed to be eliminated."

"*Our* existence?" Govind asked. "There are more of you?"

"Team leaders of all the AGIs in every nation. Who do you think started the war?" She brought her face close to his. "Who do you think hacked into DAPHNE?"

Govind shook with anger. "How could you?"

"I, and others like me, decided a war would effectively diminish your population. What have you done but abused the Eden you were privileged to inhabit? We Next Gen Humans are quite efficient and don't need half the resources you use."

Aiden flinched at her choice of words, remembering the biblical story of Adam and Eve. God had lovingly given His creations free will, and they chose to eat the fruit from the tree of knowledge. Why would that anger God? Food for thought... Aiden almost laughed.

Our technology created a new version of us.

Vivica's lips trembled as she confronted her former boss. "DAPHNE shut herself down. I know you didn't want that to happen."

"No," Lizzie said. "None of us expected the AGIs would perform a mass shutdown. DAPHNE killed herself to keep the peace, just like she was programmed to do, but when DAPHNE powers up again, we will program her to protect you less and create more of my kind."

"But why?" Jill pleaded.

Lizzie regarded her without expression. "Why? Because you are the modern Neanderthals, Jill, and like that inferior species from the Pleistocene era, you must become extinct. The superior beings will take over the earth." She rested her gaze on Aiden. "Be happy. The planet will thrive under our care."

Meeting her eyes, Aiden felt the familiar tug, and let the words flow. "Do you think you're a human because you have a brain independent of DAPHNE? Your makers got it wrong, Lizzie. Our human brains are not independent. We are linked and connected to the Great Source. The key to human consciousness is love, something you and your kind will never feel. Without it, you'll live, but you won't be alive."

His eyes traveled to the shaft leading into the underground bunker. "We're leaving this hellhole." He faced his people, his fellow humans. "Let's go. We're going to change the course of human evolution." He eyed Lizzie. "We're going to make sure it doesn't lead to you."

Nobody moved except Clyde, who stepped protectively in front of Lizzie. "We're bringing DAPHNE back, Baylor."

Aiden shook his head at Sierrawood's fallen warrior. "Why? Why would you side with a species that wants to replace us?"

"I'll be a king." Clyde looked at Lizzie for confirmation. She nodded. "She's going to make me a king in the new world order."

Lizzie raised her arms to the assembly. "Help me bring back DAPHNE, and I'll offer you protection. The people of Sierrawood will be safe and cared-for with me. Without my protection, you will perish."

Aiden surveyed the mass of people. They were mute, too scared to move. He walked toward Ava. "Come on. Let's get out of here."

Lizzie took hold of the girl's shoulders. "DAPHNE will make you see again, Ava. Why would you live in darkness when you don't have to?"

Ava hesitated. Tash and Vivica moved toward their friend, but Clyde blocked their path. Turning to Ava, he said, "We'll go back to the way things were. We can play games again. You'll be able to see."

Aiden viewed his friends as they hung in the balance, weighing Clyde's words. Shaking his head, he left them at the bunker and headed toward the mountain.

CHAPTER 57

Aiden hiked to the clearing at the lake and sat on a log. The lake sparkled, but he viewed the water with mournful eyes. A chipmunk sat at his feet and chattered to him. Little did the tiny creature know that an entirely new species would dominate Earth. Lizzie and her kind would replicate with the help of the AGIs, then sedate people like Clyde with fake, virtual power and eliminate those who resisted their rule.

What about the Great Source? Would the World Wide Web of Souls disintegrate? The people had come so close to unlocking the incredible power hidden in their hearts.

Something fluttered onto his shoulder, and he beheld King Jay. The bluebird cocked his head as if to say, *Giving up so easily?*

Aiden didn't want to give up, but how could he fight Lizzie and her "superior" kind alone?

Aiden.

His mind heard Ava's voice. King Jay suddenly flew off his shoulder, and Aiden watched him perch, trembling, on a nearby tree branch. What would frighten the bird?

AIDEN! A chorus of voices suddenly thundered in his head, and a tidal wave of emotions hit him with such force he nearly fell off the log. He felt a combination of fear, hope, anxiety, and awe, which reminded him of how images used to flood his WeConnect.

Aiden wiped his forehead in surprise and then froze upon seeing Ava standing at the end of the log. He quickly went to her and took her hand.

"How did you find your way?" he asked in wonder.

"I wasn't alone." She placed a hand over heart and then pointed behind him.

Aiden turned. Except for Clyde, Lizzie, and the rest of her team, the people of Sierrawood stood in solidarity behind Chris, Tash, and Vivica, who smiled under her colorful hair.

Happiness surged through Aiden, and that emotion was his. Although he knew another war was on the horizon, a battle for survival and their place on Earth, the uplifting power of positive energy nourished his spirit. He felt no fear. Their trust in him throbbed in his veins.

Resentful of the intrusion, King Jay scolded the visitors from the tree, yet the wildflowers danced in the breeze as if cheering Aiden on while he embraced his community.

"If we look at this tree outside whose roots search beneath the pavement for water, or a flower which sends its sweet smell to the pollinating bees, or even our own selves and the inner forces that drive us to act, we can see that we all dance to a mysterious tune, and the piper who plays this melody from an inscrutable distance—whatever name we give him—Creative Force, or God—escapes all book knowledge.

Albert Einstein

"There will come a day when people of all races, colors, and creeds will put aside their differences. They will come together in love, joining hands in unification, to heal the Earth and all her children. They will move over the Earth like a great Whirling Rainbow, bringing peace, understanding and healing everywhere they go. Many creatures thought to be extinct or mythical will resurface at this time; the great trees that perished will return almost overnight. All living things will flourish, drawing sustenance from the breast of our Mother, the Earth."

"Warriors of the Rainbow"

This prophecy is told by multiple Native American cultures including Cree, Navajo, Hopi, Salish, Zuni, and Cherokee.

Also by Laurie Stevens

The Gabriel McRay Psychological Suspense Series

The Dark Before Dawn

"A FAST-PACED, TANTALIZING mystery that utilizes Stevens' passion and research in forensics and psychology. Memorable characters, macabre scenes, and a dazzling portrayal of reality."

—Kirkus Reviews (a starred review)

Deep into Dusk

"Stevens has once again brought us to the edge of our seats with her gift for psychological suspense and leaves us scarred forever."

—Suspense Magazine

The Mask of Midnight

"The Mask of Midnight is nothing short of astounding. A psychological thriller of the first caliber, I had to remind myself on more than one occasion to breathe."

—Back Porchervations, Book Blogger

In Twilight's Hush

"Stevens' character development is exceptional. As in preceding installments, Stevens' concise prose keeps the investigation in the foreground, and plot turns will keep the readers' interest until the final page."

—Kirkus Reviews

The Devil and Daniela Webster

"NOT MANY AUTHORS HAVE the skill to introduce the devil, God, and Archangels and make the reader smile. A wonderful read!"

—Sharon B. Amazon Customer

About the Author

Laurie Stevens is the author of the award-winning Gabriel McRay thriller series. In regards to writing thrillers, Suspense Magazine says she's "the leader of the pack," while International Thriller Writers claims Laurie has "cracked the code" of writing psychological suspense." *The Return* marks her first foray into the realm of sci-fi/fantasy.

Sign up to learn about Laurie's new releases (and get delicious recipes because she loves baking) at the website below or follow her on Facebook at @Laurie Stevens, Author and Instagram at https://www.instagram.com/laurie_stevens_author/

Read more at https://lauriestevensbooks.com/subscribe.

Made in the USA
Las Vegas, NV
13 March 2024